CW00523759

The Last Conflict

Copyright © 2006 Pieter Lawrence
All rights reserved.
ISBN: 1-4196-4797-0

To order additional copies, please contact us.
BookSurge, LLC
www.booksurge.com
1-866-308-6235
orders@booksurge.com

The Last Conflict

Pieter Lawrence

2006

The Last Conflict

Throughout the ages communities had been at war and were divided by civil strife. "The Last Conflict" is an example of how they thought, how they spoke and what they said. It is a dialogue for those times but it is also a story of change.

Across the planet populations came to face a great disaster that threatened annihilation. Mass campaigns demanded protection from the danger.

Fearing hysteria and panic, those in authority set out to control the people but they failed. Renewed conflict led to crisis and social breakdown. This took countries to the brink of civil war.

Then, out of chaos, deadlock and pessimism there came hope. People began to discover their strengths. The process was agonised but gradually, communities found unity. Through cooperation they saved themselves. In doing so they went on to create a new world of equality and freedom.

With special thanks to Katrina Frape, Kim O'Donoghue and
Phyllis Hart.

To Phyllis

I

The bright winter day did nothing to lift Blake's spirits. He felt weary and disillusioned. As a Minister he had entered the Coalition Government as a popular hero but the mood of his supporters had quickly changed; now he was called "traitor." He had always thought that given a position of power he would use it to do good things. With his appointment to the government the opportunity seemed to arrive. However, instead of success, he was presiding over failure. As he walked towards his appointment with the Home Secretary he thought back over the morning's events. It had been a nightmare. He felt he should resign.

The Coalition was seen as the best way to take the country forward in unity. Blake had been selected for his skills as a conciliator; his job was "trouble-shooter". It was a special appointment to prevent disputes becoming all-out conflict. As the Prime Minister had told him, "You'll be our fireman! It will be up to you to put out the flames."

In public the Prime Minister preached unity and compromise. He spoke of fairness for all at a time of great problems with the burdens shared by the whole community, but behind the rhetoric he believed the only route to economic salvation was a ruthless policy of spending cuts. He was driven by his favourite slogan, "It's costing us too much to do much too little."

One result was in the Health Services where all maintenance workers had gone on strike. The previous evening, the heating system had broken down in one London hospital, the Royal Western. The morning press showed sad photographs of patients being moved around in the middle of a freezing night. That morning, Blake had been quick to move. He met the strikers. The issue was money, but there was none. He promised them more, not now, but in the future. He told them they were first in line for more money. He promised them an enquiry. The meeting had lasted for hours with the strikers at last yielding to Blake's persuasions. They agreed a return to work. It had been a dialogue for the times with yet another round of tortured argument so well rehearsed during previous confrontations.

Behind Blake's back the Prime Minister's Office had encouraged volunteers to help with the maintenance. Friends of the Hospital could supply the skills for repairing its systems and were soon in the process of doing so. As the Prime Minister told Blake, "These hospital workers have struck against the sick. Do you imagine the public would want us to sympathise with that? There will be no more money. There will be no enquiry. They can stay on strike for as long as they like. We don't need them."

News of the volunteers spread and a wave of anger swept through the crowd of strikers gathered outside the hospital. As Blake returned to rescue the situation, he was surrounded by the hostile crowd. "Traitor" was spat into his face as police struggled to get him back to his car. As it sped off he felt shaken, not just by the violence, but by the treachery of the Prime Minister.

He tried to compose himself and began to wonder why Bill Charman, the Home Secretary had asked for an urgent meeting. When pressed for reasons, his colleague had been evasive. Blake guessed that he wanted to discuss the strike with a view to policing it. On arrival at the Home Office he made his way through to Bill Charman's office where he threw his coat over a desk. "You see what the PM has done? He's stabbed me in the back. He doesn't want to solve problems, he enjoys his power."

Bill Charman shrugged. "Yes, he is a bit worrying. I saw you were roughed up. You could do with a drink."

They were unlikely colleagues. Now part of the Coalition they came from opposite sides of the political divide. Blake had been a radical and although Bill Charman was conservative he was not against change. As a pragmatist he was able to adapt to events where this was no threat to the established order. Now put together by the realities of office, they met on the uneasy ground of mutual compromise.

Bill poured two glasses of whisky and handed one to Blake, who was still feeling angry. "They called me a traitor," he said. "They're supposed to be my friends."

The tall figure of Bill Charman took a seat behind his desk and struck a note of gentle sarcasm. "As the Prime Minister's hatchet man you should expect that sort of thing," he said.

"No one told me that was my job."

"Nothing personal. We all know you're the great conciliator." Bill tried to divert him. "I know you're feeling injured but there are other problems."

Blake appeared to agree. "Yes, this strike will spread. A lot of people would welcome strikes, chaos, breakdown. Who knows what the outcome would be?"

Bill Charman tried to reassure him. "I know the Prime Minister is obsessed with that scenario but I'm told there's no mood for confrontation, except for the usual fanatics of course, but they have no influence."

"You shouldn't believe everything your spies tell you," said Blake, "but I'll have to resign. I've lost credibility."

Bill Charman was unsympathetic. "You're suffering a temporary case of damaged pride, nothing more, and the idea that you should bale out is not very sensible. You've got to stay on and I'll tell you why." He paused as he thought how to continue.

Blake was reminded of Bill Charman's earlier evasions. "What is the reason for this meeting?" he asked.

"I couldn't say over the phone," said Bill. "I've been approached by our technical people, scientists working at one of our space installations. They also work with people at NASA. I don't understand all the technical data, but I don't need to. There seems to be consensus amongst a group of leading astronomers and astrophysicists. They're working with our most advanced technology."

Blake glanced at his watch. "Can you get to the point, Bill?"

"You must be aware of the work being done on potential near Earth objects," Bill continued. "Asteroids... that sort of thing... not many people realise, they pose a real danger."

"I'm vaguely aware," said Blake. "It's more earthly problems that bother me."

"And you must know that recently, the government spent a hundred million pounds on an early warning system to protect the world against natural disasters. These people are working under the government's chief scientist."

Ignoring Blake's apparent lack of interest, Bill recalled the pressure from the scientific community following the great tsunami that killed three hundred thousand people in the last days of 2004. The demand for a global alarm network also came from Space Guard UK, a safety awareness group. Bill continued, "A lot of the money was spent on the threat of space collisions. There are very good grounds for taking the work seriously. For example, in 2002 people in the Linear Observatory in New Mexico discovered a three mile wide asteroid that is in danger of colliding with the Earth on 1st February 2019. Even as we speak it's hurtling towards us at 150,000 miles an hour. It's regarded as the most threatening object in the history of asteroid detection. If it were to hit us, it would be at a speed of 16 miles a second, and would release energy of around a million tonnes of TNT." Bill glanced at some notes. "Its orbit is being recalculated every day in three different parts of the globe to determine whether it will hit Earth."

Blake refilled his glass and resumed his seat. "This is all very interesting, Bill...."

"I only mention it because to believe that we are somehow immune from any danger from space is to live in a fool's paradise. I don't need to remind you what happened to the dinosaurs..."

"But that was 65 million years ago." Again Blake glanced at his watch. "Look, Bill, I've got to get on."

"Well, alright, but don't imagine that nothing has happened since then. The moon and planets are scarred by collisions from asteroids and comets, but on Earth these are soon obliterated by natural forces... wind, rain, and vegetation." Bill Charman continued with a list of near Earth incidents including the passing of "Toutatis", a rock almost three miles across. In 2004 it came within a million miles, only four times the distance between Earth and the moon, travelling at 85,000 miles an hour. "It's been under observation since it was discovered in 1989. If it had hit the Earth, it would have gouged out a 30 mile wide crater and hurled enough dust into the atmosphere to blot out the sun's light. It would have killed millions," he said.

Quoting from a file of papers, he emphasised the major threat to humanity posed by thousands of asteroids with Earth crossing orbits. He cited the mile wide rock NY40 that passed at a distance of 329,000 miles in August 2002. "By astronomical standards that was a close shave." He gave the further example of a space object that hit Earth in 1908, devastating thousands of square miles of Siberian forest. "It was only luck that it didn't fall on a big city like London or Paris. It's not just destruction of cities. A severe strike from space could set off earthquakes, fires, a nuclear winter and tidal waves. Since we've refined our observation techniques, threats from space are being identified at more than one a day...."

Blake raised his hands in mock surrender to Bill Charman's relentless list of examples. "I appreciate the lecture," he said, "but you're still not getting to the point."

"The point is this", said Bill at last. "Our technical people have discovered a very large comet that will pass close to us. They're warning that released debris is likely to be attracted by Earth's own gravitational pull. The result could be a devastating missile bombardment."

Blake smiled in disbelief. "Really, and has this thing got a name?"

"It has a code," said Bill. "Normally, new comets are given the names of their finders. In this case, they were sensible enough to realise the implications of their discovery. So they've kept it secret."

"And what are the implications?"

"They're obvious: mass hysteria, panic, breakdown, disorder of the worst kind. You said it earlier, who knows what the outcome might be?"

Blake leaned back in his chair and stared through the window, trying to resist the thought that he was trapped in a surreal fantasy. The rush of the morning's events had begun with treachery and had now moved on to the amazing. "Are you really Bill Charman," he asked, "our usually sane Home Secretary, and are we really sitting in this office of yours with you telling me all this stuff about star wars?"

Bill Charman looked directly at Blake. "I'm afraid it's all too true," he said.

"So, why are you telling me?" Blake asked. "Why am I so privileged?"

"We've got to plan ahead. We've got to make sure we get the best information and we've got to prepare a programme of action. We've already done what we British do best. We've formed a committee: a Cabinet Committee. It's the reason for this meeting. I'm inviting you to join. Now that you know all about it, you can hardly refuse. You have a history of avoiding conflicts and as your troubleshooting skills will be invaluable, we are not giving you a choice. You've been drafted."

"Normally, the PM would ask me himself," said Blake. "At least he's had the tact to send you along. How many will be on this secret committee?"

"Just the three of us. With more you get a lot of arguments and anyway, we can't risk leaks."

"And where do we start?"

"That's what we've got to decide. The first thing is to meet with our head technical adviser, a brilliant young scientist, Dr Sandra Dale. She'll be here after lunch and will bring us up-to-date." Bill shuffled through a pile of papers. "She's hugely qualified and has done original work in astrophysics, much of it with a colleague, Dr. Stephen Jones. Unfortunately, he's had some dubious political connections. They live together."

"Is that relevant?" asked Blake.

"This is top secret stuff so we need to know these things." Bill Charman looked up and smiled. "It's no reflection on your own domestic arrangements."

2

Sandra Dale hurried through the corridors of the Home Office. She was late and looked forward to her meeting with the Home Secretary with mixed feelings. She knew little of the world of politics and regarded it with suspicion. It was likely, she thought, that politicians deserved their poor reputations. Whereas scientists worked objectively in the pursuit of truth, by the nature of their jobs, politicians pursued power. They seemed duplicitous, opportunistic and given to fine rhetoric that masked a contrived public image. This was the corruption of truth in an age of "spin" that concealed reality behind false appearance. Inevitably, it engendered distrust.

Nevertheless, she had also been impressed by Bill Charman's courtesy, his willingness to listen and his patience when she used technical language which he did not quite understand. He had also been responsive, providing her with every assistance that she and her team had asked for.

Having been a previous visitor, she went directly to the Home Secretary's office, knocked on his door and entered. She apologised for being late. She noted the presence of Blake, who sat at one end of the large desk that dominated the centre of the room. Bill Charman introduced him. "This is Blake Evans, who has joined our team. You may know him from his work as a Minister. He's going to be a great help."

Sandra Dale shook his hand. "Yes, of course," she said. "It's a pleasure to meet you." She pulled a thick file from her briefcase and spread papers across the front of the desk. She was a slight figure dressed neatly in a well tailored suit. She had an attractive round face with large glasses and seemed small and fragile, but this impression soon faded as she spoke with a confident voice.

She described the continuing work of the team of scientists which was observing the movement of the comet against its background of stars. The team was attempting to project the comet's orbit and speed of approach with greater precision. She then addressed the crucial questions. When would the comet pass Earth, how close would it be and what was its makeup? The answer to the last question would decide what material would be lost by the comet to become missiles attracted to Earth by its gravitational pull. From its distant appearance the comet was the usual "dirty snowball", a mixture of rocks and ice. It was the size of the rocks that would decide whether they would burn up in Earth's atmosphere or fall as a missile bombardment. She said it was too early to be precise on this last important point, but the closer the comet came, the better should be the quality of the information. She emphasised the precautionary principle. On the assumption of a worst case scenario, it would be up to all civil authorities to do everything they could to protect the population. Informal discussions by the scientific team had suggested the need for deep underground shelters.

Bill Charman and Blake listened in silence as Sandra Dale delivered her report. Finally she arrived at a point which she introduced as "some rather bad news". She went on, "I know we're all aware of the need for secrecy but it does appear that our comet has been discovered by an amateur. It's not surprising," she added. "Many comets are discovered by amateurs. Indeed, this is not the first one to be found by Edward Hurst."

Bill Charman and Blake gave no outward sign of their unease as she continued. "The usual procedure is to seek confirmation from other observers, and then the discovery is announced. You could say that Edward Hurst is something of a maverick and works with his own style. He likes to make any announcement in a more dramatic way in a public lecture. He's a prominent member of the Astronomical Society and he's giving a lecture in three days' time. That's when he will announce the approach of the comet. From that point on it will be public knowledge."

With increasing concern, Bill Charman questioned her gently. "You say that Mr. Hurst has worked on his own, but isn't it possible that he knows about your work and is simply using the same information? I believe the world of astronomy is a fairly close community."

Sandra Dale responded sharply. "No," she said, "that's out of the question. We have never published or revealed anything. Without doubt his discovery is completely independent. In any case it's not unusual for an amateur to discover a comet." She gave the example of Comet Hyukatake discovered in 1996 by an amateur working in Japan with nothing more than a pair of binoculars. "That came within 10 million miles of Earth," she added, "closer than any major space object except the moon."

Bill Charman apologised. "Please understand Dr. Dale, I never meant to question the security of your work." He paused as he tried to consider the implications of this new information. "At the same time it does seem unlikely that these discoveries are unconnected. In previous discussions you've stressed the enormous field of search and even the element of good luck. Is it possible that Mr. Hurst and your team were looking in the right place at more or less the same time, that is, in a completely independent way?"

Sandra Dale offered an explanation. "You're right, Mr. Charman, about astronomy being a small community. The number of people looking for comets and asteroids is fairly few. The same ideas can be taken up by different people and it doesn't mean that it's borrowing or stealing. All it means is that papers are published and discussions take place with the result that shared hypotheses can lead people to look at the same area of space. I am sure that is the answer."

"Yes, I can understand that," said Bill Charman, who remained unconvinced, and who was already thinking that the troublesome amateur should not be allowed to announce his discovery.

Sandra Dale continued. "Edward Hurst is a strong believer in the theory of Nemesis. This suggests that periodically, a companion star to our sun pulls comets out of their orbits in the comet cloud that surrounds our solar system. This can send them into new orbits, sometimes in our direction."

"And you think this may be the origin of our comet?" asked Blake.

"It's an interesting idea but it does have problems," she replied. "It's been linked with many of the catastrophic events in Earth's history. For this reason it's sometimes known as the Death Star. The theory has captured the imaginations of some people. Certainly, Edward Hurst is convinced it exists. That's why he's been working on the theory of a companion star to our sun for some years."

There was a long pause as the two Ministers tried to find their way forward in the conversation. At last Bill Charman broke the silence. "And you say that Mr. Hurst is about to announce his discovery of the comet?"

"Yes," she replied. "I have regular contact with Edward. He has told me his plans in confidence. However, in view of the circumstances, I thought it right to bring the information to you."

"And we are very grateful," said Bill. Again there was a long pause before he continued. "But what is your view of his impending announcement? Do you think it's a good thing? Do you think it's in the public interest?"

"He's a free agent," she replied. "I'm aware of the need to avoid public panic but I don't see how it's possible to suppress the information."

"No one is suggesting suppression. On the other hand, we all have to behave responsibly. As you say, we don't want any panic." Bill paused again. "Suppose we offered Mr. Hurst a job. Could he fit into your team?"

Sandra Dale's response was immediate. "He wouldn't be interested and nor would it work. Edward Hurst is a brilliant and dedicated amateur, but he is very much an individualist. He couldn't possibly fit into our team."

"Not even with all the resources we could provide?"

"He's a very wealthy man," she said. "He's paid enormous amounts to use the best facilities. That's how he's been able to make his discovery."

Bill Charman pressed her. "I understand that Mr. Hurst is the kind of maverick who couldn't fit into your team. We've all met them, but he wouldn't have to. He could work independently, without interference. He would surely be attracted by the government's immense facilities. We could let him choose his own programme of work and at the same time we'd pay him to do it."

"I can see what you are trying to do," said Sandra Dale. "He would have to accept the security conditions of government work. To speak frankly, he would have to keep his mouth shut."

"Yes," said Bill Charman, "but it would be a two-way arrangement. He would have access to our best facilities and we would buy some time to draw up plans before making the discovery public."

Sandra Dale remained sceptical. "You could try it, Mr. Charman, but I don't think he will accept. I happen to know him quite well. He's not the sort of man you can buy off."

The meeting continued with Bill Charman agreeing that the work of the scientific team should be expanded. Sandra Dale had brought a list of specialist people who required the Home Secretary's authorisation. As the names on her list had already been cleared by security, he had no hesitation in endorsing them. However, the more people involved, the more difficult it would be to keep the work secret, which meant a plausible cover had to be devised. Sandra Dale agreed to invent a new field of research close enough to the real work to be convincing.

The meeting ended with a tray of tea being served, and with Bill Charman emphasising that the Cabinet Committee was fully committed to the urgency of the work. He thanked Sandra Dale for explaining it so clearly. Her last words were to remind the two Ministers that the political side should work with equal urgency in drawing up plans for the safety of the population. She insisted that the best chance of surviving a missile bombardment would be to provide deep shelter protection.

"We couldn't agree more," Bill Charman assured her.

With the two Ministers at last alone, Blake could still hardly believe the course of the day's events but Bill Charman brought him back to reality. "It looks as though this Hurst character could be a nuisance," he said. "We need to know more about him."

"I was thinking further ahead," said Blake. "We can't afford to pay the hospital workers a bit more money, so how can we finance deep shelters for the whole population? I suppose the government will be safe, we've already got our boltholes."

"Are you suggesting the country can't afford to survive?" asked Bill. "That's absurd. It's unthinkable."

"You're a lawyer," said Blake, "I'm trained in economics and you're going to have to learn some of its lessons."

3

Blake returned to his office where Janet Barnett, his assistant, told him that TV stations were clamouring for an interview. The media were keen to get his response to the actions of volunteers who had taken over maintenance at the Royal Western Hospital. Blake said he would speak to them later. First, he would contact the Secretary of the Union. He would again try to build bridges. Janet mentioned some helpful news. Unemployment had again fallen and the monthly trade figures continued to be encouraging. Blake smiled. "You're writing my script, Janet. You're suggesting patience in an improving situation. I'll give you some news, patience is a lost cause."

It was a certainty that Bob Grantley, the Union Secretary, would be angry. The hospital workers had suffered the government's tight purse strings, but having struck against the sick they were an easy target for media attack. Blake was reluctant to join any critics but having few arguments he would do so if necessary. His phone rang and he was through.

"Hello, Bob."

"Hello, Minister."

Blake paused before sounding indignant. "Minister? That's a bit formal isn't it? We do know each other. My name is Blake Evans, and we come from the same side."

"Why are you phoning?" Grantley snapped.

"You know why I'm phoning. Have you and your members gone mad?"

The exchange quickly lapsed into a self repeating deadlock of irreconcilable positions.

"You've caused sick people to be shunted around in the middle of the night," continued Blake. "It's January, some of them could die. Do you call that responsible?"

"I agree it's January, but that's all. See it from our point of view. My members are desperate; they've run out of options. This is the first strike ever at that hospital. You can't say they're irresponsible. They don't need your lectures on morality, they need decent wages for their families. We'll take up the moral issues when they've got enough money to live on."

"What do you mean by a first strike? This is health care not war. You don't strike at the sick and the aged. How can you justify that?"

"You forget, your government has shut down more hospitals than my members. How do you justify that? We tried to keep them open."

"Bob. I'm asking you to recognise realities. Your members are camped out on my doorstep but let's see you come up here and do my job for a week. You can have the damned job. We'll see if you can pull any rabbits out of the hat because I'm not a magician. We're all in this difficult situation."

"Yes, some more than others. My members have come to the end. They're desperate. That's a bit of reality you've got to accept."

"You've got to get it into your head, there's no more money. It's not a negotiable issue at this time. If you think there's more money, you tell me where it can come from. Tell me that and I'll provide it."

"I don't believe it. You're spending massively on other things."

Blake decided on a more threatening tone. "You know as well as I do that we won't allow public health care to break down. You must know we've got contingency plans."

"You've already brought in scab labour."

"They're voluntary workers, Bob, decent people who want only to help the sick and we'll bring in more because problems are one thing but chaos and breakdown is something else. Some members of the Cabinet want all the striking workers sacked and if you want me to stop it you've got to give me a good reason for doing so." Blake then tempered his tone. "One good reason would be if you appeal for a return to work. You could call for patience while an enquiry takes place."

A further silence followed. Grantley was boxed in. He knew from long experience that the outcome of any dispute was decided less by arguments and more by the relative strength of the combatants, and his position was weak. He became evasive. "I don't see that another enquiry would get us anywhere. We've had them before."

Blake felt that he had gained the edge. He softened his tone. "Look, Bob, an enquiry can do two things. It would take the heat out of the situation and that would give us a breathing space. Second, it would bring all the facts into a clearer light and that's got to be useful."

"Will it try to find more money?"

Blake decided his position in the government was strong enough to include the possibility of more money. "Yes," he said, "there is some sympathy for your members but that will disappear if they stay on strike."

"Alright," said Grantley, "you set up an independent enquiry and I'll urge my members to go back to work."

"That's agreed then," said Blake, "but there's just one other thing. You've got your demonstrators outside my office. Could you arrange it so I can come to work without being called a traitor?"

"What makes you think I've got control? I'm not a magician either. Don't imagine I can deliver anything."

Blake put down the phone, put his head between his hands, stared at his desk and took stock of what had happened. At least he had set himself up for a positive sounding television appearance. For the hours ahead that was the important thing. He could speak of responsibility, an enquiry that would bring the facts to light with all parties cooperating and guarantees. What facts and what guarantees?

Any that could buy time and sound a note of hope in the deadlock of conflict.

He was interrupted by his head of Department who was due to report to him on the unemployment and trade figures. Jack Brightwell carried the standard issue civil service brief case which he opened at one end of Blake's desk.

"Good day, Minister."

"There's very little good about the day so far, Jack, so I hope you haven't come here to make it worse."

"On the contrary, the steady improvement continues," said Brightwell. "If we take the long term view, in that perspective, there are definite grounds for optimism."

"But that's the future, Jack, and no one is interested. We used to have a future and then it was a wonderful thing, it was a glorious sunrise on the horizon, well, yesterday's future has arrived," Blake indicated newspapers piled on his desk, "... and it's a mess."

Brightwell was undeterred. "I appreciate your immediate difficulties, Minister, but I'm sure you'll find the figures encouraging. Allowing for the season there would normally be an increase in the unemployed. After all, it's January."

Blake sighed. "I do realise it's January, Jack. That's one thing we have managed to clear up today."

4

In his television interview Blake was able to sound positive. He delivered a stream of platitudes that ignored the discontent simmering throughout the country. He spoke of the improved unemployment and trade figures as evidence that the government's policies were working and he praised the actions of Bob Grantley, who had urged the hospital workers to return to work. He sympathised with the genuine grievances of the strikers and assured them over the air that an independent enquiry would do everything it could to improve their conditions. He condemned what he called "irresponsible sections of the press" which had accused the strikers of using the plight of the sick for their personal gain. It was his usual competent performance, drawing together as best he could the strands of conciliation that would calm the situation, and hopefully, guide it towards a settlement.

In the meantime Bill Charman had asked him to go to Downing Street for a meeting with the Prime Minister. Blake arrived and was shown into a small office for what was his first meeting of the ad hoc Cabinet Committee on the approaching danger from space. The Prime Minister greeted him with congratulations on his television interview.

"I've promised Grantley an enquiry," said Blake, "and we're going to have to stick with it."

In spite of his earlier opposition, the Prime Minister waved the matter aside. "Yes, well, it can't do any harm," he said.

The remark was typical of the Prime Minister's ability to switch attitudes without regard for any self-contradiction. He was of short to medium build but burly, with a head that appeared to grow directly from his rounded shoulders. This gave him an air of pugnacity which he could use with great effect when intimidating colleagues. Those close to him knew of his talent for tuning in to the public mood by saying the right things at the right time and with the right emotional appeal. He was a master of adaptation that sprang from his unerring instinct for self-preservation. In private, he was unpredictable, often morose, and given to biting sarcasm.

They sat around a plain table. Bill Charman handed out a sheaf of notes and began to summarise the earlier meeting with Dr. Sandra Dale. He referred to the research on near Earth objects and the resources that were now allocated to identifying the most dangerous threats. He went over the work of the scientific team, which was to pinpoint with increasing accuracy the orbit of the comet and its speed of approach. He produced the list of extra people who were about to join the work and gave them full credit for recognising the need for security. Finally, he emphasised the urgency in planning how the country could defend itself.

As Bill Charman spoke, Blake sensed a growing attitude of scepticism in the Prime Minister, who, without showing any obvious interest, waited for the end of the report which was followed by an uneasy silence. At last the Prime Minister responded. "Yes. Thank you, Bill. It seems there's nothing very new." He turned to Blake. "But you are new to this apparent event. What do you make of it?"

Blake noted the phrase "apparent event" and decided to be emphatic in his support for Bill. "I'm convinced we're facing a very great danger," he said. "The evidence I've seen has certainly lifted me out of my complacency. At the very least we should take precautions. It's one reason why I've gone out of my way to rebuild bridges."

"You mean the promises you've made to Grantley?"

"Yes. Any action we may have to take will need cooperation from everyone. We won't get that if we stoke up conflict."

"I understand that," said the Prime Minister, "but there could be another view." Whether from disbelief, anxiety or caution, the PM set out to play the matter down. "You see, you often find that technical people... scientists and others... they can be carried away by their own theories. That's a common thing. They get an idea and naturally, they are very keen to prove it's true. They have an interest in advancing their careers and reputations. You admit yourself, Bill, that you're not able to fully understand the technical data. I note the very small number of individuals involved and I know the reason for it. Secrecy is paramount so you need to limit the numbers, but you see this has its dangers. By confining the work to a small number of people working in secret, it's not subject to the scrutiny and criticism of the wider scientific community. In these circumstances it would be very easy to get things out of proportion. I don't want to be misunderstood," the Prime Minister continued. "We should certainly look carefully at what these scientists are saying, but at the same time, we should not get caught up in what could be a miscalculation."

Suspecting a manoeuvre aimed at pushing the matter from the agenda, Bill Charman cut into the Prime Minister's remarks. "We cannot assume a miscalculation. That could be a fatal error," he snapped. He appeared to become angry and raised his voice. "Yes, the numbers of scientists on the investigating team are few but they are hugely qualified. They work with the best and most up-to-date technology and above all, they are totally responsible."

Like any shrewd autocrat, the Prime Minister knew when to retreat. He raised his own voice. "Alright, Bill. Calm down. You don't need to be the first to get hysterical. I've said we shouldn't dismiss it. Just tell us what you think we should do."

Bill lowered his voice. "As a matter of fact," he continued, "we were informed by Dr. Sandra Dale this morning that there is independent confirmation of this comet."

For the benefit of the Prime Minister he set out the work of the wealthy amateur, Edward Hurst, his discovery of the approach of the comet and his intention to announce it in a lecture to the Astronomical Society in three days' time. Again the Prime Minister sought to play the matter down. "Does it matter?" he asked. "Does anyone take any interest in lectures given to the Astronomical Society? I know I don't."

"The press will sniff it out," said Bill, "they would love to get their hands on this stuff. Imagine the dramatic headlines. There's no way we can allow Hurst to announce his discovery."

He looked through a further batch of papers. "I've had a report on this person." He studied his notes for a moment and continued. "Apparently, he's a bachelor aged 58 living on his own in a large house in Southsea. He inherited a fortune made in property and now devotes his time to astronomy. He is secretary of the local Astronomical Society and has his own small observatory. I imagine that's why he lives in Southsea... clearer skies."

"Southsea?" Blake asked in disbelief.

"He does his serious work from an observatory in Mexico, which he pays for." Bill Charman outlined the plan to offer Hurst time on government facilities, provided he first signed the Official Secrets Act and agreed not to make his work public. "I understand he is a great egotist," he said. "Well, we may be able to flatter him. We'll appreciate the brilliance of his achievements and promise him public recognition. He may find that hard to resist."

"Suppose he does resist," asked Blake. "What then?"

"Then it gets more difficult," said Bill. "We'll have to keep him quiet by some other means."

"You mean we'll have to arrest him?"

Bill thought for a moment. "I wouldn't put it quite like that. We'll keep him talking.... in a secure place."

"It takes two to talk. Suppose he doesn't want to. No violence, I hope?"

"I don't see it coming to that."

The Prime Minister became increasingly concerned. At first doubtful, he was now anxious about what could be the political fall-out from any arrest of Hurst. "I know you're a lawyer, Bill, but have you really thought this thing through? If we arrest Hurst and hold him in a secure place he is bound to be missed. He can't be a complete loner. It's clear that the Astronomical Society would miss him." The PM thought for a moment. "Suppose he does announce his discovery, could we not have him dismissed as a crank? I'm sure we've got ways of doing that. As an amateur he won't be speaking with any authority."

"On the contrary," said Bill, "his work is held in high regard. He is described as 'talented'. This isn't the first comet he's discovered." Bill Charman was also aware that Sandra Dale and her team would never accept any attack on Hurst as being a crank. The methods of expediency that came easily to politicians were very different to the outlook of scientists who placed a greater importance on the integrity of facts. "In any case," Bill continued, "by dismissing him as a mere sensationalist we would draw attention to what he is claiming and this could cause other parties to confirm his discovery. Our only option, one way or another, is to keep him quiet."

Blake asked him directly. "Bill, do you mean we should arrest him? Would it be legal?"

"We do have provisions under national security."

"But he's a private citizen, working on his own. He's had nothing to do with national security."

"We can't be sure of that. That's one thing we've got to find out. I think we could provide sufficient grounds for an arrest order. We wouldn't have to publish the reasons."

The three members of the Committee continued to discuss the various options open to them and the possible consequences of any action. The background fear that dominated their thoughts was the threat of mass panic and social breakdown. This seemed inevitable if the news of the approaching danger was made public. They had agreed that the best way to minimise the risk of panic would be to provide plans for the protection of communities, but this would take time. Before this happened, it would be necessary to prevent any release of information on the approaching comet.

The meeting dragged on with nothing resolved. At last, Bill Charman expressed a view. "We're coming to a crisis that is without precedent. For this reason our response to it cannot be decided by precedent." He paused. "Nor, for that matter, any legal niceties that were never designed for this situation and, therefore, could have no bearing on it."

For a moment there seemed to be a compelling logic in what Bill Charman had said, particularly as it pointed to a way out of their difficulty. "If it comes to it," he continued, "we should arrest Hurst and hold him in a secure place. We should do it in secret. I have absolutely no doubt it can be justified by the public interest. I'm happy that the public interest should be our guide to what we do."

Blake was reluctant to go along with the arrest, but in the circumstances, could see no other way forward. "So be it," he murmured.

"Just on a point of fact," the Prime Minister said. "You're wrong about one thing, Bill. There is precedent. This has been done before, more times than you could ever know, and for much less important reasons."

"We've got Hurst under surveillance," Bill Charman concluded. "As luck would have it he appears to be at his home and on his own. His house stands in its own grounds. There should be no problems arresting him, but we don't need to get ahead of ourselves. We've got a lot to offer him. We can offer him money, the status of government work, and eventually, all the glory he could wish for. We'll drown him in public gratitude and drape his chest with gongs. That should be enough for any egotist. Whatever we do, we now have a slot to work in and we should get on with it."

5

An unlit car coasted into Edward Hurst's drive and came to a stop inside the front gates. Its occupants were four Special Branch agents led by Senior Officer Border. For some hours this team had kept the house under surveillance and were satisfied that Hurst was on his own and working in a study at the front of the building. Border stepped from the vehicle, squeezed the door shut and made last minute adjustments to the receiver he kept hidden under his coat. Although the house and its grounds were surrounded by a high wall, for premises that included a small observatory, Border was surprised at the lack of security. Avoiding the gravel drive, he walked quietly over a lawn towards the large front door and rang its bell.

After some time, the door opened. Against the background of light, the figure of Hurst was framed in the doorway. Border noted a tall man, well over six feet, with an athletic build, and giving an impression of fitness. In spite of Hurst's age, it was clear to Border that if it came to an arrest, Hurst would be capable of strong resistance.

"Mr. Hurst?" Border asked.

"Yes."

"I hope you'll forgive the intrusion, sir, and my unexpected visit, but I was hoping we could have a chat."

"A chat," said Hurst, "what about?"

"About your work..."

"What work do you mean?"

"Your recent observations. I'm here to ask you for your help and I'm in a position to help you."

"Who are you? Are you a member of the Astronomical Society?"

"Not exactly. I represent a government agency. As I said, we're in a position to help you."

Hurst was suspicious. "I'm very busy. I haven't got time just now. Why don't you come to my lecture? I could speak to you there."

Border pressed him. "The agency I represent is interested in the same project as yourself. I'm sure we have information that you would find most important. What I've got to say to you is urgent. If I could come in I could explain."

For a moment Hurst was intrigued by the mention of work on the 'same project' which could only mean the approaching comet. He relented. "Well, I suppose you'd better come in but I can't give you much time."

Border moved into the large hallway as Hurst closed the door behind him and indicated a seat. The two sat each side of a small table.

"I had decided to contact the government," said Hurst, "after my lecture, that is..."

"Then it's just as well that we meet now," said Border.

Hurst remained distant. "Yes, but I still don't understand which agency you are from," he said. "I didn't know the government was aware of my research."

"Sir, you underestimate yourself. Your work is very well known."

At last Hurst appeared to respond to Border's well-mannered approach. "Oh, is it?" he said. "Yes, well, perhaps it is. I keep so busy I don't notice. But I shouldn't anticipate my lecture. I'll make everything public then. What you may not know is that my discovery means we could be facing the most appalling dangers, destruction never seen before." As if to emphasise the seriousness of his point, Hurst stared down at Border. "I'm convinced," he added, "that we're facing a great natural catastrophe."

Border had been fully briefed and his approach to Hurst was well prepared. He continued with a blend of respect, flattery and gentle persuasion. "That is what concerns the government, sir. Our scientists have been working along lines similar to yours and we're anxious to build up a clear picture of the dangers. Obviously, your work is well advanced and that is why I'm suggesting that you combine it with the work of our scientists. You would be a most welcome part of an official team."

Border explained that Hurst would have access to the government's most up-to-date facilities. He would be working alongside the country's leading astronomers, astrophysicists and other specialists. He would work independently with total control of his own work programme. He would be well paid and would be given full public recognition for his achievements.

Hurst thought for a moment as he appeared to find the offer tempting. "What you suggest is very generous, Mr. er.... In fact I'm very surprised. Would I be free to publish?"

"Certainly," Border assured him, "but appreciate that as a member of a government team, there would be appropriate security conditions. Then in due course, after consultation, you would be most free to publish."

Hurst looked disappointed. "That means I could publish only with the government's permission," he said. "Generous though it is, I'm not sure your offer would help me. You see, at this particular time, my research has come to a conclusion. Naturally," he added, as if wanting to respond positively, "I'll make the results of my work available to the government. That is the whole point of my lecture, to make it freely available to the government, the Astronomical Society and to the wider public."

Border tried a different tack. "Sir, what you say brings me to another matter of great concern. Have you considered the impact this information might have on the public?"

"Yes, I have thought of that," said Hurst. "It's bound to come as a shock, naturally, but people do have to face the facts. I can't say it's my problem. For me, you understand, it's an astronomical event and therefore a technical matter. I see my duty as making the facts known, but how the information is handled in public and what they do about it, that's really not my business."

Border persisted. "I understand that, sir, but you must know that such information can be sensationalised... distorted... written up in wrong perspectives. Think of what the press would do with this sort of material."

"But that wouldn't be my responsibility," Hurst replied emphatically. "Knowledge can always be distorted. That is not the fault of the scientist."

"But surely you realise, the immediate release of this information runs the risk of mass hysteria..."

Hurst's manner hardened. "You're asking me to remain silent. That's why you're here, isn't it?"

Even at this stage of the conversation, Border was determined to use every means of persuading Hurst to cooperate. "No, sir. Definitely not. We are asking you to join with the government in making the information public in a carefully prepared way. Our only object is to avoid panic."

"But you are asking me not to give my lecture."

"Not even that, sir, we are asking you to postpone it while the matter is discussed. If you give your lecture now there will be no control of the information. You may have to accept that, unintentionally, you will have caused great public anxiety... hysteria... circumstances in which a rational response becomes impossible. I don't think you want that... I'm sure you don't. I'm appealing to you from the highest level to cooperate with the government. We are asking for your help in the interests of the public and we hope you will see that as your duty."

Hurst's reply was disappointing. "But you should understand that a scientist has many duties, not only to the government and to the public, but duties to the science that he serves. What you are asking is impossible. There is a vital principle, we must not suppress knowledge. I understand the problem you've mentioned, but I don't see that being eased by my remaining silent."

At last Border ran out of patience. His voice took on a formal tone. "I must ask you finally and directly, will you postpone your lecture? Will you cooperate with the government?"

Hurst remained adamant. "I cannot do that, though I will cooperate in any other way."

"In that case, Mr. Hurst, you leave me with no alternative."

The words "no alternative" were a coded message that Border was about to arrest Hurst. Through his concealed microphone, the code was relayed to the three agents who had followed the conversation from a receiver in the car parked in the drive. Border stood up and opened the front door of the house as if to leave. Instead, he confronted Hurst. "I must advise you, this matter has other implications. Your work suggests a breach of national security. I am also enquiring into this. I must ask you to accompany me to a place where these enquiries may be continued. We won't detain you for long. You will be returned in an hour."

Hurst was startled. "You're accusing me of illegal access to government work. That's outrageous."

"We shall only know that from our further enquiries. You must now leave with me."

"But I can prove my independent work. I have all my notes. You'll see the record of my observations."

"Then you have nothing to worry about. But I must ask you to leave with me now."

Hurst became desperate. "Who are you anyway? You're not from the police. What government agency are you from?"

Three suited figures entered the hallway. With silent and practised efficiency they surrounded Hurst and slipped him quickly into handcuffs. Border was relieved that Hurst offered no resistance as he was led out to the waiting vehicle and driven into the night. Border was left with one other agent. They moved into Hurst's study to examine his papers.

The conversation between Border and Hurst had been relayed to the car outside and then on to the Home Office, where it had been recorded and printed out. As the transcripts came off the printer, Bill Charman read them and passed them on to Blake. Disappointment set in as they realised that Border's mission had failed.

"What happens to Hurst now?" Blake asked.

For Bill Charman disappointment had become anger. "No problem," he said. "We'll put him in a sack and dump him in the Atlantic."

"I could think you're serious."

"Border did his best. That was a good offer we put to Hurst. A reasonable man would have accepted it."

"Hurst is a man of principle," said Blake. "That was our mistake. We forgot they exist."

"I don't believe it. It's about vanity. He wants to be the first to announce the dangers. That's all he cares about."

Bill Charman got through to Border and was assured that Hurst seemed calm and was being held in a safe but comfortable location, attended by Special Branch agents who were now his guards. "At the moment he seems very compliant," Border reported.

"Yes, but we can't trust him now," replied Bill. "I don't think any agreement would be genuine. He could easily go back on any promise if we were to release him. Stress the gravity of his situation. That he's in possession of secret government information, that he could be facing a long term in prison. That should concentrate his mind. Did you get his papers?"

"Several boxes."

"You may find something in them." Bill put down his phone and explained to Blake. "I'm not normally so hands-on when it comes to operations, but in the circumstances I thought it best to take charge."

Blake nodded. "It's all very educational," he said. The hour was late, he was tired and his mind was still reeling from the day's events. He got out of his chair and looked for his coat. "If there's nothing else, I'm going home."

Bill Charman arranged for a car and they said good night. Blake was driven from Whitehall to Islington, to the Georgian terraced house he shared with his partner, Dr. Rachel Hollis. It was a typical winter night; the fine day had become cold and wet with the lights of the city glistening through his car windows. Outside, people hurried along the busy streets with heads down, pursuing their own reasons for being out in such an unpleasant night. Preoccupied with their private worlds they could not know that above the city, in regions of space, beyond distances that could only be imagined, a lethal object had detached itself from its normally benign orbit and was speeding towards Earth.

Blake arrived home. Rachel was in bed but still awake, reading. He poured himself a drink and took it up to the bedroom. She looked up. "You're very late," she said, "you usually ring."

"Yes," he explained, "I've been caught up in this hospital dispute. What's happening at your place?"

Rachel was a doctor at their local hospital. "I'm surprised you ask," she said, "you're supposed to know. Some of our people are joining the strike. I believe it's called 'in sympathy,' but there's not much sympathy for our patients. Volunteers are taking over the maintenance. There's a lot of anger with the name of Blake Evans being mentioned quite a lot and not in any friendly way. Apparently you're the cause of the problem." She smiled. "Carry on as you are and I'll be one of the few friends you've got left."

He moved to the window, took aside the curtain and stared into the dark. "Voluntary workers," he murmured. "They may sound good but one person's volunteer is someone else's strike breaker."

Realising his downcast mood she tried to cheer him up. "I did catch your television interview. It was your usual very good performance. But it doesn't seem to have done much good."

"Performance is right," he said. "Is it real life or live theatre? If it's theatre it's farce and if it's farce, it's a bloody awful script."

"Does it have an ending?"

"No, it goes on and on. Same old issues, same old deadlock and now it's on television, the longest running show in town. Only the actors change."

"I don't know if you're aware of it," she said, "but it seems you no longer believe in what you're doing. You're becoming a cynic..."

He thought of the illusions of power and his inability to control events. "A cynic?" he asked. "Maybe. Perhaps it comes with the job."

"You could get another job."

"Really? I don't think so. The banalities of politics, that's all I'm trained for."

Again she smiled. "I should make notes of all your private remarks and sell them to the papers. Imagine the headlines, 'mistress reveals all.' I'd make a fortune."

At last he returned her smile. "Would we share it?"

"We'd spend it on a world trip." She paused for a moment. "But short of that and seriously, you need a break and so do I. Let's take a holiday."

It was impossible for him to get away. He wished he could give her a full account of the day's events. It wasn't that he didn't trust her. He was of course bound by secrecy and he knew that she would place less importance on the need to suppress information, especially when it affected the lives of so many people. He also felt a sense of guilt at the arrest of Hurst and knew that Rachel would be horrified to hear that he had been part of it. "A holiday," he said. "It would be good to get away but I have a feeling that things are coming to a head. I need to be in London. It's nothing definite. Just a politician's instinct. Where you can't control things you get tuned into signs, portents and subtle indicators. Things could tip in any number of directions and none of them is good."

"You're not making sense," she said, "I don't understand any of that."

"How could you? You've got a sane job. You diagnose what's wrong and you cure it. Nothing like that ever happens in my work."

"I do know one thing," she said. "If you're managing a permanent crisis you should take a break now and again. And if you worry about something you can't do anything about, that's useless stress."

"Is that medical advice?" he asked

"It could be," she replied, "but I'm your lover not your doctor. Are you coming to bed?"

6

Blake's fears that events were heading towards a new crisis were confirmed by the hostile crowd that had gathered outside his office next morning. Bob Grantley's appeal for a return to work had been ignored. It was also clear that it was not only hospital workers who were demonstrating. The dispute had become a focus for widespread discontent.

After some years of prosperity the economy had take a sharp downturn. Unemployment had gone back to being in the millions. The government's income had been slashed with the inevitable result that its spending was cut. Many hopes had been placed in the formation of the Coalition Government which was to be a Government of National Unity, but as it wallowed in failure, the hopes that brought it into being had dwindled into disillusion. In turn this was fast becoming a festering anger.

From long experience Blake knew that bringing in volunteer workers to break a strike would only inflame an already bitter confrontation. He also suspected the Prime Minister of deliberately provoking the dispute and of picking on the hospital workers because they were weak. He could depict them as taking action against the sick. In public this would enable him to command the moral high ground. The hospital workers were being subjected to political manipulation, for it was the view of the Prime Minister that only cuts in labour costs could move the economy out of deep recession. His aim was to impose an ignominious defeat on the hospital workers with the result that other, perhaps more important, sectors of the labour force, would hesitate before taking similar action. Whilst the Prime Minister, by steering events from the background, could preserve his benign public image, the problem for Blake was that he was being blamed for the worsening situation. This left him with the feeling that he was also being manipulated.

As he arrived, police surrounded Blake's car and formed a cordon that pushed its way towards the front door of his Department. Once inside, one of the police apologised. "Sorry about that, sir. We're shorthanded and we didn't expect the numbers."

"You'll see a lot more," Blake snapped.

Back in his office the news got worse. His constituency agent, Clive Poole, wanted Blake to phone him. His local party was about to hold a meeting to discuss the hospital dispute and, as Blake was being blamed, it had been proposed that it should formally dissociate from his actions and possibly de-select him as their candidate.

"I've warned you, Blake," said Clive over the telephone. "It's been simmering for some time. Now you've brought in voluntary workers to break the strike. Things have come to a head."

"Clive, I had nothing to do with it. You've got to believe me."

"Who cares if I believe you, nobody else will. You'd better get up here and try to explain things. It's not going to be easy."

"We've fought a lot of battles, Clive. None of them was easy."

"No, and we didn't always win."

As Blake put down the phone, Bill Charman came on the line. He sounded annoyed. "I've been trying to get hold of you."

The previous day's events that ended with the arrest of Edward Hurst flooded back into Blake's mind. "I've got my own problems," he replied. "What's happening?" "Complications."

"Serious?"

"I'm not sure. We're meeting in an hour's time, at Downing Street."

Preoccupied with his own difficulties Blake protested. "Look, Bill. I'm hard pressed....."

"This is top priority and we've got to work to the Prime Minister's schedule."

Blake sighed and glanced at his watch. "Alright. I'll see you in an hour."

He glanced through the morning papers that were piled on his desk, looking for any mention that he was in trouble with his constituency party. Finding nothing he scanned the editorial comments on the hospital dispute and noted their patronising tone.

"The expedient use of voluntary work must not be allowed to relieve pressure on the government to create a stronger economic base from which it could then draw funds for restoring public spending to higher levels."

Blake cast the papers aside. There was no shortage of high minded preaching but it would be a rare day when the press printed some practical solutions. The truth was that the government spent most of its time reacting to events, not controlling them. He heard the clamour of conflict as outside, police moved against the demonstrators. Looking down from his window he saw that the police had brought in extra numbers equipped with batons and riot shields. When protecting government buildings the police were likely to be aggressive. Above the noise of barking police dogs he thought he heard the chant of "traitor". If so, it was being echoed all the way back to his constituency.

It was vital that he should keep on good terms with his local party. He got back to Clive Poole and they discussed the best means of doing so, identifying the local members who mattered most and the tactics that would succeed. Satisfied that he could now see his way forward he left his building by a rear exit that took him into a neighbouring building. From there he walked the short distance to Downing Street.

On arrival, Blake went through to a small office for a further meeting of the secret Cabinet Committee. He found the Home Secretary reading through a file of papers.

"How is Hurst?" Blake asked him.

Bill Charman looked despondent. "He's saying nothing. He's totally withdrawn."

"Not responding to threats?" Blake asked. "You must have told him that he could be in possession of secret government information. Isn't he worried?"

"Not at all," said Bill. "He knows that charge would never stick. His papers confirm his independent work. He can prove that so he's not in the least worried. As Sandra Dale said, his observations and conclusions have been entirely his own."

"That adds credibility to the approaching dangers..."

"So it would seem."

"And that's even more worrying..."

Bill Charman shrugged. "Have you told the Prime Minister?" Blake asked him.

"Not yet."

"So, this is the complication you mentioned."

"No. There's something else."

The Prime Minister came into the room. His manner was brusque. He drew up a seat, sat down and glanced at his watch. "I've got very little time so let's get on with it."

Bill Charman explained the events of the previous evening; the failure to secure the cooperation of Hurst and his eventual arrest.

He emphasised that Hurst's papers reinforced the evidence for the approach of a massive, destructive comet. The Prime Minister listened with a sour expression as Bill stressed the gravity of the threat.

"And we've got another problem," Bill continued. "Amongst Hurst's papers we found his working diary." He took the diary from his brief case. "It's a record of his activities. It shows he's been in contact with a reporter from his local newspaper. I've checked on this young journalist. She was obviously keen to get a good story about Hurst's work. No doubt Hurst was flattered by the attention...."

"Get to the point, Bill," the Prime Minister snapped.

"The point is that she's been interviewing Hurst and preparing a profile article. It's clear from his diary that she will also publish his material on the approaching comet to coincide with his lecture. Prime Minister, I've got a list of the relevant diary entries, if you wish to see them..."

"No. I'll take your word for it."

Blake took up the diary and scanned through pages of Hurst's tidy writing, reading some of the entries on his contact with the local reporter. The PM frowned with irritation. "And you say all this is about to be published, the full details of his discovery?"

"Yes," Bill confirmed.

The PM became impatient and glanced again at his watch. "You know, I really don't have time for all this. What is our objective here? We want to stop this dangerous nonsense from becoming public, don't we?"

"That is what we want, Prime Minister."

"Well, aren't you getting anywhere with Hurst? The Prime Minister stood up and began pacing the room. "He's the one who could put a stop to all this. He could have this article postponed. He could say he's had second thoughts, the story no longer reflects his findings... anything of that sort."

"He won't talk to us," Bill said. "He thinks he's being framed on a false security charge so he's remaining silent."

"He thinks he's being framed on a security charge? Who does he think would frame him?" The Prime Minister paused. "I suppose he thinks we would."

"Yes. That is what he thinks."

"In that case put a security ban on this material."

"On what grounds?" Bill asked.

The Prime Minister exploded. "Find some. If it's against national security it doesn't matter where the rubbish comes from and we don't have to give any reasons for banning it."

Bill Charman stayed calm. "There's no way we could ban it discreetly," he said. "It's gone too far. I imagine the story is already set up for printing. That means a lot of people would know about the clampdown. It involves too many risks and I don't think we should take them."

The Prime Minister continued to press Bill. "In that case approach the editor... informally. Get his cooperation. He could withdraw the story. How could that arouse suspicions?"

"We could only do that if we knew in advance that he would cooperate and that's impossible. If he refused to go along with us we'd be in a worse position. He'd go ahead, knowing we've got special reasons for stopping it. In any case, he's not the only one involved. There's this reporter, she's got a good story and she'll want to make the most of it."

Blake thought ahead. "She might link the ban with Hurst's disappearance. She'll have an even better story if she thinks Hurst has been arrested."

The Prime Minister sat down, exasperated. He looked at Blake. "So, what do you think?" he asked.

Blake passed Hurst's diary back to Bill Charman. "You get these problems when you start out on this sort of thing. It builds up. You start and then you have to keep going. Every new step justifies the next, but where does it lead? Eventually the whole thing is out of control...."

The Prime Minister stopped him. "Yes, alright, we're not looking for lectures."

"I'm trying to be practical, Prime Minister. I'm saying we can't stop this publication. We should think about limiting any damage. What are we talking about? It's a local paper. I mean... they're full of house sales and car adverts. We aren't talking about serious national news."
"So you're saying do nothing, just let it appear?"

"I'm saying that of all our options, that's the one with the least risks for us," said Blake. "Let it appear and hope it goes unnoticed."

Bill Charman looked again through Hurst's diary. "On balance I agree with Blake," he said. "It's a very small paper. It's likely that it won't be taken seriously... just another sensational story. There's an element of risk but then every option has its risks. Reluctantly, I would say do nothing."

The Prime Minister resigned himself to the situation. "Alright, if that's what you two think I'll go along with it but at the same time we need some means of discrediting Hurst. We should put it out that he's a crank... some kind of lunatic."

"I'm afraid his reputation is too good for that," said Bill. He thought for a moment. "Fortunately there were no witnesses to his arrest. What we could do is say he was arrested for trespassing on a government space installation. We don't have to say which one. We could say that he broke in pursuing his theory. That would suggest that he's mentally unstable or having some sort of breakdown. It would also be a good reason for releasing him. It should leave us completely in the clear whilst casting doubt on anything that Hurst says."

Bill Charman's suggestion appeared to be an elegant solution to the difficulties being faced by the secret Cabinet Committee. The Prime Minister seized on it. "Good," he said, "that's excellent." Giving the impression that he already believed it to be true he repeated, "Yes...yes... it's obvious... Hurst is a sick man; a neurotic suffering from delusions." He stood up. "Deal with it that way." He was anxious to leave. "Is there anything else?"

"We're just about to see the head of our scientific team," Bill informed him. "In view of the supporting evidence provided by Hurst... it is in fact a confirmation... I'm sure you will agree, Prime Minister, that more intense research is most urgent?"

"I'm not convinced of anything. We've already put millions into this ..."

The meeting continued with the Prime Minister reluctantly giving his consent to the allocation of more money to the scientific team. On completing the brief agenda he turned to Blake. "I hear that you've got troubles in your constituency."

"It appears that bad news travels fast," Blake replied.

"Yes... well... you shouldn't make so many enemies... but I'm sure you'll handle it. You didn't survive this long without being competent in these matters."

Blake replied with an ironic smile. "It's good to have your confidence."

"Don't worry, we won't let these lunatics win. If it comes to it we'll find you a more congenial seat."

"That's most reassuring."

"And I'm sure we're all pleased to see the hospitals back to normal working."

"Naturally," Blake agreed, "but the demonstrations seem to be spreading."

"They'll soon get tired of it. They've got nowhere to go except back to work. You might remind them of that."

"I might let them come to their own conclusions."

"Well, I don't care if they do or not. We can run the hospitals without them. Frankly, I'd be glad to see the back of all those damned troublemakers."

The Prime Minister left as abruptly as he had arrived. Blake looked towards Bill Charman. "He gets nastier by the day."

Bill thought about the Prime Minister's increasing ill-tempered behaviour. "Yes, but only in private…"

"You didn't tell me we were meeting Sandra Dale," said Blake.

"No, I couldn't mention it on the phone. She's keen to update us." Bill paused. "By the way," he said, "she might refer to Hurst. For the time being I suggest we know nothing of his whereabouts. She wouldn't like what's happened." He looked at his watch. "It's time to go."

7

The two Ministers were driven to the Home Office where Sandra Dale was waiting in Bill Charman's office. Surrounded by papers, she gave a further account of the more intense observations now being carried out by the scientific team. She spoke dispassionately, maintaining a cool objective tone without evading the dangers that now threatened people across the world. Whilst there was nothing very new in her report she was now able to say that the approaching comet was larger than it appeared from their first calculations. Whilst it was still not possible to know its exact make up, the team continued to assume it was an immense agglomeration of various sized rocks encased in a mixture of planetary dust and ice. She repeated her prediction that near to the sun, with the melting of its ice, part of the comet's cargo of rocks would be released. Attracted by Earth's gravitational pull, the larger rocks would fall as missiles.

As Sandra Dale came to the end of her report, again, a feeling of gloom began to settle on the two Ministers. Bill Charman asked if she could be more specific on the dangers but her reply remained unhelpful. "I'm afraid, even up to the last minute, the severity of the missile bombardment will be impossible to predict."

"It's a question of what defences we should plan for," he explained.

"As we've emphasised all along," she said, "the only conceivable defence is the construction of deep shelters; a safe underground environment in which people could survive. This has surely been agreed?"

"Yes, of course," Bill assured her and then paused, "but it will mean a nationwide programme of work and the details will take some time."

"That's exactly why we've emphasised the urgency," she said. "It's vital that the government should begin planning the defences immediately."

As Blake listened to the exchange he compared the work of the scientists with the scene in which he and Bill Charman operated as politicians. No doubt the work of the scientific team was complex but in building up a picture of the dangers it did make progress. In response to the dangers, he and Bill Charman faced all the difficulties of mobilising the country for its defence. It would be a massive project carried out within the economic limitations of what was possible. The costs would be enormous. In this view, the way forward was, to say the least, hazy.

With the meeting over, Bill Charman showed Sandra Dale from his office, came back to his desk and took up a document. "We already have some plans," he said, "plans for a war emergency. There's a useful quote here." He read from the document. "There is much common ground between war planning and all the preparations required for the organisation of a major peace time or natural emergency." He passed it across his desk. "There you are," he continued, "that's what we're planning for, a major natural emergency."

Blake picked it up. "And where does this come from?" he asked.

"It's a Home Office document; part of a civil defence review. It covers every threat of chaos, the breakdown of power supplies, food supplies, health services, communications, law and order and government. It's just what we need."

As Blake glanced through the document Bill Charman continued. "In extreme circumstances, government would be carried out by a subcommittee of the Cabinet, a civil contingencies unit. It would consist of ministers, police and the Services. It would direct action through thirteen regional areas."

"I know about those plans," said Blake, "and so do a lot of people. They're highly suspect. They're also plans for dealing with widespread industrial strife. They provide for control of the population by a government with unlimited powers. Under that regime the police and armed forces would be given lethal powers; powers to shoot to kill."

Bill Charman looked weary. "We don't anticipate having to shoot people," he said, "and if you can forget for a moment your leftist paranoia you might see the practicality of these plans. Given a worst case scenario we will need this organisation."

"Then why only the government, the police and the armed forces?" asked Blake. "Why not people from all parties, the trade unions and perhaps some voluntary organisations? A great project to construct deep shelters will need the cooperation of everyone and the best way to get that is to include them in decision making and organisation."

Bill appeared to agree. "Well, alright, I didn't say these plans were complete. You draw up a list of people who you think could be included but don't make it too big. Then it will be your job to get them involved."

8

Blake spent the rest of the day in his office where, against the noise of the demonstration outside, he prepared for his meeting with his local party. Whilst Bill Charman seemed unwilling to confront the problem of scarce financial resources, he became more focussed on how a national programme of deep shelter construction could go ahead. Although the voluntary workers who had taken over some hospital work were being vilified as strike breakers, he felt that their example might be a key to how people could be mobilised for the work of building shelters. He was mindful that throughout the country there was an abundance of labour resources. If these reserves of energy and skill could be used without the need for finance, it might avoid a problem that had every prospect of tearing the country apart.

Towards evening he travelled north where he met his agent, Clive Poole. Over a drink Clive was surprised to find Blake cheerful and more inclined to reminisce over past battles than talk about the meeting in front of them. When the meeting began, Blake sat silent as he faced wave after wave of personal attack. As Chairman, Clive Poole had urged restraint but this did nothing to stem the tide of hostility.

Blake thought back to the campaign that had taken him into office. Its optimism had now been replaced by disappointment. Where could he find fresh words to re-kindle the enthusiasm of his erstwhile supporters? Suppose he found them, would it only prolong the sequence of raised hopes followed by failure? He was tired of it. What good reason could there be for leading them further into disillusion?

Perhaps Rachel was right. All the guilt and anger was futile; nothing more than useless stress. If this were true how could he tell it to his local party? How could he convey the message that their demands on him were impossible? He could not lead them to a better world. He had made a decision. He would placate no one, nor would he defend himself. He had no powers and he had nothing to defend. His was only one weak voice in the endless war of words that kept them trapped in a deadlock of conflict. If their disappointment required a sacrifice, they must get rid of him. If that was their wish, so be it, he would not dissuade them.

The attacks were unrelenting. "... We didn't want this Coalition. We've made a pact with our enemies but at least they are the enemies we know. Now we've got an enemy we didn't suspect, our own member. He's betrayed our campaign; betrayed everything we stand for..."

Clive Poole intervened. "We should have a constructive discussion. Let's not call each other enemies. We can be frank without being abusive."

"I am being frank. He was elected to represent us but he hasn't got time for that because he's too busy attacking our own people. I am being frank; that is a betrayal."

"All we've got is our member asking us to make compromises. What about a few compromises from the government. We've compromised on jobs, our housing programme, health services, welfare schemes, and our community care projects. We've compromised on everything but what do we get from the government? Cuts, cuts and more financial cuts!"

"We've had to take those cuts when we need more money not less...."

Though engulfed by the hostility, Blake remained silent. He was a veteran of a thousand stormy meetings. He looked down at his papers, unperturbed, as each speaker kept up the tirade.

"He should walk around our City for a change. Look at our housing estates with thousands of unemployed. Our young people are turning to drugs, crime and vandalism because they see no hope. If they are cynical it's because the government is cynical.....”

“Why is he using voluntary workers to smash the hospital workers' strike? That's another betrayal of the people we represent. We cannot be associated with it.”

Blake resigned himself to the verbal blood-letting. It was a ritual. The victimised had found a victim. All their disappointments were now thrust on him as their traitor. But where would they be without their traitors? They would stand alone with nothing but a responsibility they could not face. Their anger was an elaborate evasion of their own part in shared failure and Blake had served out his time as the object of blame. They were now in the process of selecting another traitor.

Even now, from his reserves of experience, he might find the means to renew their faith in him. As the Prime Minister had cynically observed, he hadn't survived this long without such skills. With their rage exhausted, perhaps he could set aside their disillusion with carefully chosen words that might set out a new term of hope. He had decided against it. His part in the deceit was over.

At last the attacks came to an end. With its energy spent, the local committee looked to him to respond. He spoke calmly. “We did fight a good campaign and I said that with victory we would solve the City's problems. I believed it and I was wrong. You believed it and you were wrong. We were all wrong because it's time we learned that governments don't have the powers we think they have. But if you really believe all the things that have been said then I must tell you now I will not stay. I'm ahead of you. My resignation is on the table. I think you should accept it.”

The committee was surprised; they had expected a fight. After a silence one of them spoke. “Is that it then? Not a word of explanation?

"No," said Blake firmly. "I will not serve without the support of my local party. As I don't have it I will resign from the government and resign from this seat."

Sitting next to Blake, Clive Poole became nervous. He was anxious to see Blake stay. "You all realise," he said, "that if Blake Evans resigns, especially in these circumstances, it will mean a by-election and we could lose it."

There was hesitation as committee members thought about the implications of an immediate by-election. Clive Poole continued. "While we're thinking about it, I'll ask Blake to give some further reasons for his sudden decision."

"All I would add," said Blake, "is that even if you select someone else, and even if that person is elected, whoever it is will be in exactly the same position as I am. It won't change anything. We've got to forget about the government; we've got to forget about Whitehall. It's a useless structure. The more we look to the Treasury the less we see the advantages that are under our noses. And this is where I am going to upset you a lot more. You hate seeing volunteers working in the hospitals, but useful lessons can be learned from it."

"You've got your facts wrong when you said I was behind it," he continued, "I tried to stop it but I'm not concerned about that now because we should see the best side of what's happened. These volunteers don't see themselves as strike breakers even if that's what they are being used for. They're just everyday people who want to take care of the sick. They've put themselves forward to do a useful job and we should just think for a moment about all the willing people in our City who could be doing useful things."

Blake was interrupted. "This voluntary work undermines real jobs; it's a threat to proper employment. It's an excuse for the government to do nothing. People on the dole doing voluntary work means they'll be working for dole level wages. It's a strategy for forcing down living standards, that's the motive behind all this..."

Blake cut across his critic. "I hear that dated rubbish every day, it's the same old message of despair. Sit around and wait for money from the government like manna from heaven. I'm telling you from the inside, there will never be enough money and while you do nothing but wait for it, thousands of voluntary workers could be doing useful things. We've got to think of ways of using our real assets, not money from the government but the many people who could be cooperating to improve life in the City."

"I haven't come with a detailed plan but I know some of you control the City's councils so it's up to you to work it out. You've got equipment and transport standing idle so make it available for voluntary schemes. Voluntary work can improve housing, the environment, care of the elderly; it can service the health centres. These are just some ideas and you could think of more. Organise it and you'll get a good response. Voluntary projects could be started in other cities. I could get things moving in the House of Commons with other Members who are in the same position. We'll swap ideas and develop projects as we go along."

As Blake spoke, the anger of the Committee began to subside. He had placed them in a dilemma. They had not expected his resignation. A lost by-election could weaken their control of the City. Perhaps fearing this, they gradually warmed to the idea of organising voluntary schemes.

A young councillor, who had not been part of the attacks on Blake, spoke in support. "Community projects run on voluntary lines have great possibilities," he said. "People don't like being idle; they want to be involved with useful activity. It will improve morale and restore a sense of civic pride. We should definitely go ahead with this."

Blake noted this first positive voice. "Who is that?" he whispered to Clive Poole.

"Chris Lawson," he replied. "If you were up here more often you'd know." Clive Poole judged the moment right to move the meeting forward. After more argument about the threat to "real jobs" and a proviso that it should not interfere with existing employment, the

Committee decided to organise voluntary work. Chris Lawson and Clive Poole were amongst those given the job of preparing plans.

As the meeting broke up, Blake went out of his way to approach those who had been so hostile. They were still reserved, feeling that he had skilfully out-manoeuvred them by exploiting the fact that no one wanted a by-election. Even so, Blake felt that he had created a more constructive outlook.

Throughout the evening he had also been mindful of the approaching dangers. As Bill Charman had earlier pointed out, the thought that the country couldn't afford to survive was absurd. With this echoing in his mind he looked ahead; perhaps voluntary work could play a part in the construction of deep shelters. If so, the initiatives now being taken in his local party could be the beginning of a nationwide effort that would not depend on government money.

Blake left the Town Hall with Clive Poole and was surprised to be confronted by a crowd of newsmen. The event had been arranged as a private meeting but had obviously been leaked to the press. The reporters pressed close.

"Have you lost support?" they shouted. "Was there a vote to drop you?"

"No one proposed it."

"Then what was the meeting for?"

"Routine business."

"What is your position now?"

"I'm standing upright. I'm tired and you're blocking my way."

They pushed past the reporters, walked to the car park at the rear of the Town Hall and drove to Blake's hotel. They ordered drinks and relaxed in the lounge.

Clive was surprised at the outcome of the meeting. "Offering your resignation was risky," he said. "I thought you'd gone mad. Still, it came off. You kept your nerve."

"Clive, it wasn't a manoeuvre," said Blake.

"Really?"

"I want you to believe that. I was ready to walk away. I've been too boxed in... by my job, by the lack of money and never ending arguments with the Treasury. Boxed in by the unions, the Cabinet and now my own local Party; boxed in by the whole damned impossible situation. I don't need it. I can do without it."

Clive persisted. "Even so, I'm relieved. It's a very good result."

"You still think the idea of voluntary work is a ploy, don't you? A tactic...?

"I'm not saying that."

"But that's what you're thinking."

"It's what others will think. Everyone has got so cynical. They'll think it's a diversion from the real problems."

"Well they're wrong. I'll tell you the real problem. People are so used to depending on useless governments, they've forgotten what they can do for themselves."

9

After returning next morning from his constituency, Blake was late arriving at his office where he was followed in by Janet. He explained the outcome of the previous night's meeting. "... So you'll have to put up with me for a while," he said.

She smiled. "I won't complain."

He smiled back, "You'll be the only who doesn't."

She said that Bill Charman had been trying to contact him and drew his attention to a confidential package that had arrived by messenger from the Home Office. He sat down at his desk and opened the large envelope. It was a copy of the local Hampshire newspaper which was expected to carry the story on Hurst. Scanning through the paper he was relieved to find the story buried amongst the inside pages. It showed a photograph of Hurst. He read it through.

"Southsea may be the home of a most important discovery. If his observations are confirmed, Mr. Edward Hurst, a local astronomer, will be credited with spotting a new comet that will pass close to Earth.

For some years he has been researching a theory that our sun has a companion star named Nemesis. He took up this theory from the work of astronomers in America which suggests that the companion star can disturb the many millions of comets that are slowly circling our solar system. He says it has the power to dislodge comets from their orbits and send them into new orbits, sometimes towards the sun and the inner planets. Mr. Hurst is convinced that Nemesis is at an advanced stage in its return to our region of space and that the comet now approaching is a result of its disruptive influence.

He has also issued a warning that the comet now speeding towards us is likely to bring a bombardment of large rock missiles which could be released from their frozen state by the heat of the sun ...”

The story went on to give details of Hurst's lecture and Blake noticed the name of Janice Fearn, its author. This was the name he had first seen in Hurst's diary and which had alerted Bill Charman to the intended publication. He read it again. The story was brief. He was relieved that it was understated and his hope that it would go unnoticed seemed justified.

The photograph of Hurst stared at him from the page. For the first time Blake could associate a face with the events which had led to the arrest of the astronomer. Its expression seemed accusative, appearing to anticipate the powers that had removed him from his home.

Blake put the paper in his briefcase and rang Bill Charman, who sounded desperate. “You've been out of contact all morning.”

“I've only just got back from my constituency. Remember?”

“Yes, I heard it went well. Did you get the package?”

“I've read it. It doesn't look too bad. It's technical and restrained.”

“It's a lot worse than it looks. You'll have to get over here.”

Blake sighed. “Bill, I'm spending more time in the Home Office than in my own Department.”

“Just get over here. I can't say anymore.”

Bill Charman hung up. Anticipating a new crisis Blake put on his coat. Janet was surprised to see him going out so soon. She reminded him of the pile of documents in his in-tray. He looked at them. The importance of routine work was fading fast. “Line them up and I'll sign the lot later,” he said.

Avoiding the demonstrations outside his office, he used a connecting door that took him through a neighbouring department and walked the short distance to the Home Office. As he arrived Bill Charman passed him a different newspaper. It was the mid-day edition of a London daily. "You obviously haven't seen this," he said. "Take a look at page five."

Blake turned to the page and saw a very different piece on Hurst but by the same reporter, Janice Fearn.

"Now it's in the nationals," said Bill. "I said she had a good story."

"I must admit," said Blake, "this is more sensational."

The story was spread over two pages with illustrations of cities obliterated by missile bombardments and hordes of panic-stricken people. The same photograph of Hurst stared out from the chaos. Blake glanced through the text.

"A sinister death star has sent a comet hurtling at cosmic speed towards Earth bringing catastrophe and a reign of terror. According to a prominent astronomer we face a period of destruction far worse than anything in our history..."

Blake tossed the paper back on to Bill's desk. "We didn't anticipate this..."

"This story is going to spread like wildfire. It's unstoppable."

"Even Hurst wouldn't approve of it," said Blake.

A note of anger came into Bill Charman's voice. "He just couldn't resist the publicity," he said, "and anyway, like all of us, he's lost control".

"What's happening with Hurst?" Blake asked.

"He's gone to pieces. First he went quiet and then he became withdrawn. Then, suddenly this morning he went berserk, smashing things."

"Your secure house? Perhaps we should charge him with damaging government property."

Bill Charman grimaced. "This isn't funny, Blake. He threw chairs through the windows whilst demanding to leave. He's a big man, difficult to restrain. We had to sedate him."

"So, now you've got him drugged up?"

"We had to calm him down."

Bill went on to explain that with the failure of Hurst to appear at his lecture, people were now looking for him, including Janice Fearn, who was asking for a national search. At his deserted house the telephone had not stopped ringing. Reporters were now prowling his garden, knocking on neighbours' doors and asking questions. With Hurst becoming a figure of national interest, Janice Fearn had been to the local police to report his disappearance.

"Do they know anything?" Blake asked.

"No, but the idiots started looking for him. We had to warn them off. Now we've got them wondering what's going on."

"You trust your own police, don't you?"

Bill Charnan sank back into his chair, resigned to a situation that was now beyond any control. "Who can you trust?" he said. "I'll tell you, you can't trust anyone."

Again the two Ministers looked through the press coverage of Hurst's claims and the mystery of his disappearance. "What about the Prime Minister?" Blake asked. "Is he in the picture?"

"He's seething. He blames it all on us. He says we've bungled the whole thing from the start." He paused. "We've got to release

Hurst and then we'll have to limit the damage. We need a cover for his release, something that questions his behaviour. There's a Radio Astronomy Observatory not far from his home which also happens to be a secret listening station. We could say he was arrested breaking into it, pursuing his crank theory. We'll discredit him as some kind of lunatic. After all, he has gone berserk."

"Yes, but so would any sane person," said Blake.

"Maybe so, but we can use it." Bill referred to the newspaper reports. "You must admit, these pictures of missiles destroying cities, they look fantastic and that could help us. We can suggest these papers have used an eccentric to get a sensational story. People know they're less interested in the truth than in selling their damned papers so we can play on that and calm things down. We'll say we have no reason to hold Hurst... he's just a harmless crank."

As coffee was brought into the Home Secretary's office he at last began to relax. "Yes," he said, "that should work but only if we keep our own information secret... if that leaks out..."

"But we don't anticipate that," said Blake.

"I've already said, the rule in this job is that you don't trust anyone. We've got a bigger team of scientists now and that means bigger risks. It includes people like Stephen Jones, brilliant in their work but also with a history of dubious political connections. You run security checks, you hear what people say, you make a judgment but you can never really know what's going on in their heads. If people were reliable we wouldn't need all this surveillance."

"But at some time we're going to have to make our information public. It will confirm that Hurst was right all along. If we're also saying he's a lunatic, it won't add up."

"We can't worry about that now," said Bill. With an air of superiority he continued. "In any case, popular opinion is a momentary thing, it doesn't make connections; it's fickle. You should never assume that in the minds of the public one thing has got anything to do with another."

"I never knew that," said Blake.

As they considered the situation, the two Ministers at last accepted that because of the pressure of events, the growing risks of security leaks and the work of Hurst now in the open, it was necessary for the government to announce the approach of the comet. They went on to discuss how it should be done. One way, they agreed, was for the Prime Minister to make a special broadcast. For all his private faults, he would be the one to strike an appropriate note of calm; he would emphasise that any action would be simply precautionary. If anyone could soothe people's fears, it was the Prime Minister.

In the meantime they agreed that Bill Charman would update the government plans for dealing with a possible national emergency. Concerned that so far the Home Secretary had only mentioned the police and the armed forces, Blake again warned that the plans would have to be more inclusive, involving a wide cross-section of the public. It would be a dangerous expression of the arrogance of power to assume that the great mass of the population would be content to be the passive tools of a central governing authority. He pointed out that if the exercise of power was such an easy option why were they acting so secretly behind a screen of deception?

At the same time Blake would work with his Department to produce a clear picture of labour resources. There was little doubt that millions of people could be available for the work of constructing deep shelters. As in wartime, industry, manufacture and construction could be adapted. Agriculture could be organised to produce a reserve of basic foods. The one great problem was finance. Where would the money come from? The lack of any answer to this question gave urgency to his plans for working with other MPs on voluntary projects. Perhaps the voluntary workers now maintaining the hospitals had set an example which was more important than he realised. The promotion of voluntary schemes could play a critical part in future action.

As Blake prepared to leave the Home Office, Bill Charman asked where he would be if anything should come up. "You'll know where I am," said Blake. "I'm sure your agents follow me about. You seemed to know the results of my meeting last night before I did. It was supposed to be private."

Bill responded with surprise. "Follow you around?" he said. "Do they? Well, I daresay they follow me about and I'm supposed to be their boss."

10

Blake returned to his office and began sifting through figures on national labour resources. His Department head had arranged them on a regional basis but Blake had not disclosed the reason for the work. He told Brightwell it was merely to bring a civil defence review up-to-date. As he worked on, he realised the enormity of the task that lay ahead and the difficulty of keeping it secret before the approaching dangers were announced. If plans for the construction of deep shelters were to make progress, secrecy would be impossible. Planning would require the skills of a wide range of specialist people who would all have to know the object of the plans. With the numbers involved, it was likely that some would make their own judgments on whether secrecy was in the public interest. A few would say "no" and would speak out. Despite loyalty to the government, Blake was increasingly embarrassed by his situation. Feeling a sense of guilt he was tempted to make his own public statement on the matter and knew that others would be much less reluctant to do so.

After working late he returned home to find Rachel slumped on a couch waiting for the news on television. He poured himself a drink and noticed a newspaper with the Hurst story at her feet. She asked him about his meeting with his local party and he explained the outcome. She was surprised at the plans to use voluntary workers. "I thought they were hostile to all that," she said.

"Yes, well, they are," he replied, "but how can you tell what motivates people? My resignation from the seat would have caused them difficulties. They didn't want that. Whatever the reasons, I'm a bit more hopeful now."

"You don't seem all that happy," she said.

"No, well, there are other problems."

He asked about her hospital. "It's working," she said, "but the demonstrations are a lot worse. There's been fighting with the police. We're now treating the casualties of our own dispute. That's not what hospitals are for."

Blake shrugged. "There's nothing I can do. We've got the same crowds outside the Department. I can't use my own front door."

He switched on the television news and they listened as it reported on the build-up of demonstrations. It then came to an item on Hurst.

"Following the apparent disappearance of the astronomer, Edward Hurst, the Home Office this afternoon issued a statement. It said that he has been held for questioning in connection with an alleged offence against a government observation and listening station. As a result of further enquiries, he will be released tomorrow. According to the Home Office, the offence, at first thought to be serious, does not justify the further holding of Mr. Hurst who is described as an over-enthusiastic amateur whose activities have brought him in breach of the law."

Rachel picked up the newspaper. "This is the man who claims we're being approached by a deadly comet," she said.

Blake took the paper and looked again at the photograph of Hurst with its accusing stare. "Yes," he said, "the same person." He switched off the television and replenished his drink.

"Did you know that item was being broadcast?" she asked.

He felt unable to lie. "Yes," he said.

"You arranged it?"

"More or less."

"You've been involved with this man Hurst?"

"In a way."

"Why are you so monosyllabic?"

"It's awkward."

Rachel took up the newspaper. "According to this story we're going to be bombarded with huge rock missiles from a comet."

"That's what he claims."

"And according to the Home Office he is some kind of lunatic?"

"They do suggest that."

"Well, is he a lunatic?"

"I've never met the man."

"But you did arrange the news item?"

"I had a hand in it."

"Blake," she protested, "why are you being evasive? Lately, you've become so remote."

At last he decided to be more forthcoming. "If you really want to know, he's not that crazy."

"But has he broken the law?"

"I shouldn't think so."

"Then why was he arrested?"

"He's an embarrassment."

"You can't arrest someone for being an embarrassment."

"Who says we can't?"

They reached an impasse and for a moment fell silent. Eventually, Blake continued. "You're asking about sensitive, secret information but Hurst is not a criminal and neither is he a lunatic. He is a totally sane, law abiding person and that's the problem."

He went on to reveal that a group within the government knew about the approaching comet and had mounted a large scale operation to plot its movement; that Hurst had made the discovery on his own; that best efforts were made to persuade him not to make his discovery public and when he refused, he was arrested. "Unfortunately, it was too late to stop these newspaper reports," he said.

He tried to explain that it was all done for the best of motives which were to prevent mass hysteria and panic, and that by implying that Hurst was mentally unbalanced the newspaper reports would be ignored. It was designed to buy some time to allow plans for the protection of the population to be prepared. "The arrest of Hurst was the last thing we wanted," he continued. "We wanted his cooperation. We explained the difficulties and offered him all sorts of inducements but he refused everything. I think it's fair to say that he had an equal part in creating an impossible situation."

Rachel softened her tone. "You don't have to apologise to me. I'm only a sideline critic."

"All we wanted was some time."

Seeing his depleted state she smiled in sympathy. "Try to understand," she said, "I'm not blaming you. I wouldn't know who to blame; perhaps we are all to blame." She refilled his glass. "So, all this stuff in the paper could be true and we really are facing great dangers from space?"

"They've made the story sensational but basically, yes, it's true."

"Suddenly, life seems different," she said. "There may not be much of it left."

As once again they fell silent he wondered whether the entire episode was a focus of anxiety not on any threat from space but on an earthly inability to decide the future, even one day ahead, without anguish and conflict. Whatever the case, he was relieved that he had told Rachel as much as he knew.

The Home Office statement on the arrest of Hurst broadcast on TV was also heard by Sandra Dale and her partner Stephen Jones. Together in their home they listened to the news with amazement as it was suggested that Hurst had broken into a government listening station in pursuit of his theories. For them, the report had no credibility. As members of the Astronomical Society they were both acquainted with Hurst and, whilst knowing him as a maverick personality, the suggestion that he could break into a listening station to advance his work was impossible to believe. It could only be the action of an irrational person and for all his faults, they knew Hurst to be a person of reason and intelligence. They had both attended the meeting at which Hurst was to have given his lecture and, with others, were puzzled by his non-appearance. There had been no explanation or apology from Hurst for his absence and every attempt to reach him by telephone had failed.

Sandra Dale recalled her close questioning by the Home Secretary on the wisdom of allowing Hurst to give his lecture. She had accepted that public knowledge of the approaching comet could be dangerous but she had also insisted that Hurst was a free man with a right to express his ideas. Inevitably, she began to wonder if the absence of Hurst was connected with the two politicians who were her colleagues. She found it difficult to believe that Bill Charman and Blake Evans, whilst conducting themselves so positively with charm and courtesy, could be the same people responsible for Hurst's disappearance. After speaking with Stephen she decided to contact Hurst as soon as possible.

II

Back in Downing Street, Blake and Bill Charman sat reading press reports whilst waiting for the Prime Minister. With little information to go by the reports asked questions. What was the offence alleged to have been committed by Edward Hurst? At which government plant was Hurst arrested? Where was Hurst held and who exactly was holding him?

The Prime Minister joined them. He was more than just morose; his eyes glowered with anger; his shoulders seemed more hunched than usual. "When are we releasing this lunatic?" he demanded. "He's more trouble than he's worth."

Bill glanced at his watch. "In about an hour. We've returned his papers." He went over the plans to release Hurst at his home and read drafts of further statements that could be made in response to press questioning.

The Prime Minister ignored them. "I just hope they don't get us into deeper trouble," he said as he began pacing the room. "Is it possible to hope that? Everything we've done so far has made things worse." As he spoke, his anger increased. "You see what we've done? We've given Hurst all this publicity. We've got this press interest. All over the country people are asking questions. Hurst hasn't done it, we've done it for him. We've built him up as a national figure."

Bill Charman was exhausted by the affair and knew that unless the Prime Minister was checked he would launch into a tirade, blaming everyone but himself. "Everything we've done has been the result of our collective decisions," he insisted. "Prime Minister, you were the first to say that Hurst should be kept quiet by any means."

"Oh, was I indeed?"

"The interest in Hurst would have happened anyway."

"Would it?"

"His claims were bound to be sensationalised."

"I see."

"We've now got to make the best of a difficult situation," said Bill Charman. "In the circumstances, the line we are taking is right."

The Prime Minister turned his back on his colleagues and stared through a window. "What I'm most concerned about are these demonstrations. We've got them outside the hospitals getting bigger every day. Outside government offices..." He turned to Blake "You've got them outside your Department. That doesn't want to go away, does it?"

"You were too optimistic when you said they would tire of it," Blake replied, "but I don't see them as threatening. We've seen it all before."

"That sounds like complacency to me," the Prime Minister snapped. "We shouldn't tolerate it in Whitehall." He turned to Bill Charman. "Why are you so reluctant to move on it, Bill?"

Bill Charman had been advised by Blake that any response to the crowds of protestors should not be heavy-handed. In the growing crisis they would soon have to enlist the cooperation of the trade unions and every section of the community. Against a background of confrontation this would be more difficult. Bill answered the Prime Minister. "At the moment we don't want to be too provocative."

"It's a bit more than provocative for them to demonstrate in Whitehall, don't you think?"

"I take your point, Prime Minister. It is close to Westminster."

"And they're not just hospital workers, are they?"

"That's true."

"They're a lot of political activists, with their own agendas."

"You always get them in these demonstrations."

"Political activists? A lot of extremists, close to Westminster? I don't like it."

"None of us do."

"You know they welcome this kind of chaos, they thrive on it. And you know what they're aiming at. A political takeover."

"I suggest we keep things in proportion," said Bill Charman, "We should distinguish between the rhetoric and any real threat. We know the main activists and we have full knowledge of what they are doing. I can assure you, they are divided amongst themselves and hopelessly incompetent. They have no credible plan, which means they are incapable of going beyond negative protest and mostly that is spontaneous."

"Yes," the Prime Minister insisted, "but don't you see, spontaneous movements are the most dangerous of all. They could catch us unawares, build up and rapidly get out of hand. By tolerating these demonstrations in Whitehall we could be encouraging a threat to Westminster itself."

Bill Charman sagged as he replied. "As I said, Prime Minister, that view is out of proportion. In any case, we have abundant reserves of force which we can move at a moment's notice. In my judgment, our interests are best served by not being heavy-handed at this time... even if it does mean that Blake has to use the back door of his office."

The Prime Minister appeared to calm down. "Just so long as we've got control.."

"We're monitoring the situation very closely," Bill assured him. "You need have no worries." He tried to bring the Prime Minister back to the most urgent problem facing the secret Cabinet committee. "What does concern us is the need to put more detail into our Civil Defence Review. Assuming that we now face a great natural disaster, it's most urgent that we draw up a detailed plan for the protection of the population."

A further look of annoyance spread across the face of the Prime Minister as he looked at his watch. "Yes, well, I've no time to discuss that now. There's no harm in you two thinking about it but I've got to get on. Thanks to your bungling I've got questions to answer in the House." He again turned to Blake. "It might be an opportunity for you to show your face; members have forgotten what it looks like." Turning his back he walked abruptly from the room.

The remaining two Ministers could only smile in disbelief as the door closed behind the retreating Prime Minister. "He's never going to face up to the dangers," observed Blake.

"He's paranoid but it proves one thing, you don't have to be sane to be Prime Minister." Bill Charman took out a bundle of papers. "These are plans for a deep shelter," he said. "They give us an idea of what we may have to do. We should also think about an emergency budget."

Blake stuffed the papers into his brief case. "I'll get back and look at them."

He left Downing Street and took what he thought was a discreet route back to his office. On his way he was waylaid by reporters. He quickened his pace, determined not to stop as they crowded around him shouting questions.

"Minister, what is your comment on the approaching comet?"

"Why ask me? All I know is what I read in the press."

"Is the government taking it seriously?"

"We always take the press seriously."

"Is Hurst a crank?"

"You decide. I've never met the man."

He disappeared into the building that led to his Department, annoyed that his back door route had been discovered. In his office he took out the plans for deep shelters and looked at a drawing for a standard shelter for 20,000 people. Designed in the 1950s to give protection from a nuclear bomb, it had been passed on by the scientific team who were researching its ability to withstand impacts from variously sized rock missiles. Dug to a depth of 150 metres, access to its floors were by lifts or emergency stairs. Each floor was set out with rows of bunk beds. The original cost had been updated to a new figure of £100 million.

Additional costs would cover fresh water, food and canteen facilities, lighting, heating and medical care. A further list included power generators, air filtration, sanitation and waste disposal systems. These doubled the costs of basic construction.

The plans also included the conversion of the London underground railway system, unused coal mines and other underground facilities as a network of deep shelters. Further spending would be for the production and storage of fuel, medical supplies and food. Blake made rough calculations applying the costs of a single shelter to the needs of the total population, but then stopped. It was futile to experiment with fantastic figures that went far beyond economic realities. Bill Charman would have to accept the plain and stark truth: it would be impossible to provide an emergency budget to cover the costs of deep shelter protection for the whole population.

He was interrupted by Janet who brought in a large envelope sent by the Home Office. Inside was a transcript of Hurst's statements to the press when he was released at his home. Blake scanned the document. It was clear that Hurst was no longer withdrawn but was angry, bitter and determined to make public every detail of his arrest which, for him, had obviously been traumatic.

"I was kidnapped, abducted, taken from my home because they wanted to stop my work. They've taken my papers, destroyed them, but they won't stop me. The government will never destroy the truth. I don't know where I was held. I was intimidated, threatened, blackmailed, mentally tortured and forcibly given drugs. The government are the criminals, inventing lies and concealing the truth. Minute by minute the dangers increase. We must act now to defend ourselves. Join with me. That is the message you must tell the country. We must act now before it is too late."

The typescript came to an abrupt end with a footnote saying that Hurst was taken into his home by the young reporter, Janice Fearn and two other persons, ".. assumed to be members of the Astronomical Society."

Blake read the report several times. Hurst did seem to be hysterical; the tone of his outpourings would tend to confirm the government's statement that he was an eccentric. It was unfortunate that Hurst had mentioned his papers; these could become a new focus of media interest. Worrying too, was the possible response of Sandra Dale and the scientific team. They were the first to know that what Hurst was claiming was true. They had also pressed the urgency of preparing civil defence plans but no progress had been made. How could Sandra Dale and her team be reassured on all these questions? At first Blake had been encouraged by his reading of the report. It seemed that Hurst had played into the hands of the government by behaving as a crank, but with other questions crowding into Blake's mind his feelings of unease returned. Much would depend on how the Prime Minister dealt with questions in the House.

Resuming his work he gave up on costing deep shelters and returned to his notes on the use of voluntary workers. These now took on a greater importance as being the only realistic way forward. He decided to go to the House to canvass other inner city MPs whilst seeing how the Prime Minister might smooth over the problem of Hurst.

He hurried to the House, took his seat beside Bill Charman and found the Prime Minister addressing every side in his most reassuring manner. Again Blake marvelled at the Prime Minister's ability to adapt his public persona to the needs of the moment. Gone was the morose paranoia that had gripped him earlier in the day. In its place the Prime Minister caressed the House with irony and humour.

"No. As we are succeeding in bringing the country out of deep recession the government has not found it necessary to go into the kidnapping business as a means of raising funds. I have been advised that Mr. Hurst was arrested for questioning following a breach of security regulations. As a result, it appears that this was a harmless intrusion in pursuit of various cosmic theories and as the House is aware, Mr. Hurst has now been released. So far as the Security Forces are concerned the matter is now closed.

I cannot comment on matters of national security but I can give an assurance that, for what they are worth, the views of Mr. Hurst are entirely his own and in no way do they involve any breach of government information.

I cannot comment on any speculation concerning the questioning of Mr. Hurst, but I can draw the attention of the House to his vivid imagination, not only about what may be happening in space, but also about what may have happened here on Earth over the past few days.

As I understand it, the theory in question has been taken up by reputable scientists, purely as a speculative idea. It is not new and I am informed that any evidence is far from conclusive. Even as speculation, the theory concerns space events that may occur at intervals of many millions of years. In other words, Mr. Speaker, this is not a matter that need concern us during this particular parliamentary session."

Blake was relieved to see that on all sides, members broke into laughter. At least so far as the House of Commons was concerned, the Prime Minister had succeeded in removing any serious interest in the Hurst affair.

12

Following his release, it was expected that Hurst would deliver his lecture but events caused him to change his mind. A small group that included Janice Fearn and members of the Astronomical Society persuaded him to hold a public meeting to discuss the threat from space. The meeting was to be held in his local library hall which could hold only a few hundred people. In the event it was full to capacity with hundreds more gathered outside.

As the main organisers, Hurst and Janice Fearn faced the audience from a platform at one end of the hall. When the last person to find space had squeezed in, it was Janice Fearn who introduced the meeting and spoke of her work when preparing a profile of Hurst for the local press. She also mentioned the esteem in which he was held both internationally and in academic circles. She was tall, slim, and spoke with confidence. In addition to being a reporter she had now become Hurst's assistant.

Following her introduction, Hurst spoke for some thirty minutes. By now he had recovered his composure. The hysteria that was evident at the time of his release had been replaced by a calm and measured delivery. He did not mention the background theory of a companion star to the sun which could disturb the normal movements of bodies in the outer solar system. Instead, he explained in simple language his discovery of the approaching comet and how, over a period of weeks, he had been able to plot its orbit which was bringing it towards Earth. As the comet passed close to Earth gravitation would attract any released rocks. It was then that Earth would go through a period of meteoric bombardment. Though its severity was unpredictable it was possible that other threats, such as a nuclear winter, would follow. He emphasised that all his papers were freely available to any authority able to confirm his observations.

He also spoke of the night visit from an unidentified person who claimed to represent the government. This person was on a mission to prevent the public from knowing about the dangers. It was confirmation that despite its public denials the government was aware of the lethal comet. It was when he refused to be silent that he was taken by force from his home and held in a secret location. Still speaking calmly, he emphasised that in view of the approaching dangers it was vital that action should be taken to protect the public.

Hurst urged that a campaign be formed to discover the truth behind his abduction; to compel the government to release its own information and to prepare deep shelter protection for the whole population; it should also publicise the threat throughout the world.

Hasty arrangements had been made, through a public address system, to relay the talk to the hundreds gathered outside. As he stopped speaking his listeners burst into prolonged applause. Janice Fearn called for volunteers to act as an organising committee and with Hurst elected chairman, within a short time, a Campaign had been formed.

Present at the meeting was an officer from Special Branch who, posing as a member of the public, had volunteered to serve on the organising committee. His name was Chivers and it was his report that Blake and Bill Charman were studying at the Home Office. Blake read carefully through the final security assessment.

"The Campaign has been formed against a background flood of enquiries. If this level of support continues and is repeated throughout the country, the Campaign will develop as a significant national organisation.

At present, the Campaign indicates no strong leaning toward any political outlook. In the majority, the present activists appear to be politically neutral, motivated partly by their loyalty to Hurst as members of the Astronomical Society and partly by their genuine concern for the threat of catastrophe. Only two individuals on the organising committee are known politically and these have been active in the Ecology Movement. However, any growth of the Campaign will become attractive to a wide range of political activists. Experience shows that more extreme elements will be able to move into the Campaign and influence its policy and campaign methods.

It should be noted that Miss Janice Fearn is on close terms with Edward Hurst and is now his personal assistant. It appears that she will be the main source of information to the public on Campaign policy and tactics. In particular it should be noted that she is investigating all the circumstances relating to the recent arrest of Hurst.

The finances of the Campaign seem assured. Edward Hurst can call on extensive funds and, in addition, cash donations have been promised. These cash resources will enable the Campaign to promote its activities through every media outlet and will give it a strong voice wherever public issues are discussed."

The report included a profile of Hurst, identifying him as "a determined character with a record of success in a wide range of life projects."

Blake leafed through the report. "It seems we picked on the wrong man," he said.

By now, Bill Charman was resigned to the tide of events. "I don't remember choosing him," he replied.

"What about Janice Fearn? What can she find out about Hurst's arrest?"

"Only what she gets from him and we can deny that.... unless someone opens his mouth."

"Is that likely?"

Bill Charman shrugged. "I'm more worried about Sandra Dale," he said. "She's been trying to get through to Hurst."

"What's her object?"

"I don't know. There's been no conversation. His phone is in constant use with people offering money and wanting to join his campaign. She can't get through but she keeps trying. I suppose she wants to hear his version of events on the night he was arrested." Bill Charman paused. "When she finds out it could put a strain on her loyalty to the government."

With a note of sarcasm Blake asked "Is there any way we can arrest her?"

Bill Charman took him seriously. "No. That's out of the question."

In a silent admission of defeat the two Ministers realised they had at last run out of options. They lapsed into thought as they considered the best way forward. Bill Charman slumped in his seat and stared into space. Blake looked again through the Special Branch Report on the formation of the Campaign and the prediction of its rapid growth. With Hurst identifying the area of space in which he had made his discovery, it would only be a matter of days before observers across the world would be focussed on the approaching comet. There was no alternative but to reveal the work of the government. For this, they would have to convince the Prime Minister that he should broadcast to the country.

With this agreed, Blake went on to the costs of deep shelters and the work he had so far done on what he called "fantasy figures." It was impossible for the government to provide sufficient funds. The only way that work could begin would be with voluntary workers. With the example already being set in the hospitals, the population would have to be persuaded to give their skills and energies without financial reward. Their efforts would be for the safety of volunteers, their families and also for their communities.

However, Blake also anticipated that voluntary work could be resisted. Some people would see it as undermining the value of "real paying jobs." Having already seen the hostility to voluntary work in his local party, he was aware of the need to approach the subject with caution.

By now, Blake was convinced that existing power structures would be incapable of dealing with the impending crisis. The people who would matter most would be those doing the work of construction and those able to coordinate such a great community project. In view of the need to include the entire labour force the name of Frank Bell came irresistibly to mind. This was the Secretary of the Trades Union Congress who was able to wield wide powers of influence.

Chastened by their recent blunders, the two Ministers were ready to consider any option that might take them out of their difficulties. "Have you spoken to Frank Bell lately?" Blake asked.

"No!" Bill replied. "I avoid speaking to Frank Bell. In fact, I avoid even thinking about him."

Knowing Frank Bell's hostility to the Home Secretary, Blake could only smile. "Yes, but unfortunately he does exist and we will have to deal with him."

"Well, rather you than me." Bill Charman paused. "I should warn you it was Frank Bell who instigated the nasty little plot to have you de-selected by your local party. It appears you're number one on his list of traitors to be purged. In my case his hostility is understandable, after all, I'm the traditional enemy, but you're supposed to be his colleague."

Blake thought for a moment about the fragility of political labels and the loyalties of people when tested under the pressure of events. Frank Bell was known as a tough warrior but having never held a position of responsibility his reputation was based mainly on his talent for striking postures. To maintain his position as a side-lines critic he had refused a job in the Coalition Government and being Secretary of the Trades Union Congress gave him a loud megaphone. It was interesting that Bill Charman should know about Frank Bell's part in the plot to get rid of Blake but it did not come as news. Clive Poole, Blake's agent, had already informed him. However, he felt the incident should be set aside. It would be a weakness to allow personal feelings to stand in the way of an opportunity to make progress.

"No doubt Frank felt he was doing the right thing," Blake said with an ironic smile. "He may even have been sincere. Whatever the case, I should try to get his support for voluntary work because it's the only way we're going to get anything done. If we succeed in convincing Frank Bell, we'll convince everyone. I'll go back to my office and make contact. No doubt, with your excellent sources of information you'll know the result before I do."

Bill Charman ignored Blake's last remark but agreed that Frank Bell would be a key person to win over to the need for voluntary work. He also agreed to persuade the Prime Minister to broadcast.

Blake returned to his office where he guessed that Frank Bell would be at TUC Headquarters. Eventually he got through. "Hello Frank, its Blake Evans here. I hope I'm not interrupting..."

The response was terse. "What can I do for you?"

"It's been a long time since we spoke..."

"Or not long enough. It depends on your view."

"I would say it's been too long."

"You haven't telephoned to tell me that."

"No. I think we should have a meeting. I thought I'd ring before you made arrangements for the next few days."

"I've already made them. You keep us very busy."

"We're all busy. I'm working myself."

"I'm sorry to hear that. It would help us if you did a bit bloody less."

"I regret the way things have gone. It's why we should meet. Something informal, outside normal working hours."

Frank Bell remained hostile. "I'm not at liberty to hold secret meetings with the government. I don't work that way."

"I said informal, Frank; not secret. Even so, it's best if we avoid attention."

"What about?"

"Nothing in particular. The general situation. Matters of concern for both of us. Important matters that merit a meeting between you and me."

After a long pause Frank Bell relented. "Alright, I don't mind a meeting. I've got a few things to say to you."

"As I said, we should meet soon."

"As it's informal I could spare some time on my way home tonight. You know the hotel opposite the TUC? I could meet you in the lounge bar at 9 o'clock. Is that informal enough for you?"

"That suits me fine, Frank."

13

Blake arrived at the hotel in good time for his meeting with Frank Bell. He ordered a drink and found a seat. Frank Bell arrived late, collected his own drink and brought his large frame over to where Blake was sitting. "Is this quiet enough for you?" he asked.

Blake tried to smile. "It'll do."

"What's on your mind?"

"A great deal." Blake set out to be friendly. "Before we say anything, I want you to know ... I realise how you feel and what you think."

"You do? That's a good start, but it's not just me. It's how millions of our members feel and they're very angry. Everyone at the TUC is angry. We don't like what's happening, we don't like it one bit. Still, if you want to put your cards on the table and be a little more honest ... it could be helpful."

The words 'a little more honest' struck home. It was part of the language of attack, the only posture that Frank Bell ever adopted. In spite of having asked for the meeting, Blake decided he wouldn't be the object of the big man's gratuitous insults. He remained calm. "We're all very worried, Frank. The TUC doesn't hold a monopoly on concern. None of us likes the way things are heading and we've got to look at it from everyone's point of view. Things are bad and we don't want them to get worse. We can at least agree on that?"

Frank Bell remained distant. He sat in his overcoat, slightly away from the table and sipped his drink. "Where do you think things are heading? You tell me, then I'll tell you what I think."

Blake was not yet in a position to be open about the approaching dangers. "What I can tell you is that we're heading for a very difficult time. If we don't listen to each other it will only get worse. On its own, the government can do very little and that's why we have a need to get together now. I might remind you, we did share a common outlook once and it all looked simple then. We thought we could solve all our problems if we got the right people in the right positions of power but we should now admit it's not as simple as that..."

"You mean people like you got the power then you turned your backs on those who gave it to you."

"No. I simply mean that we made a lot of mistakes about what could be done with power."

"What is this? Have you got me here to justify what you've done?"

Blake was disappointed. Frank seemed determined to maintain his hostility. "What do you think I've done, Frank?"

"You said you knew what I thought. You obviously don't, so I'll tell you. You've used your power to stab the people who gave it to you in the back. That's what you've done."

"I could get very angry at that but I won't. I didn't come here for a row. I'm not interested. We've got to get away from sterile arguments. I'm worried about the dangers of more conflict, that's why I wanted to see you."

"What do you want the TUC to do? Surrender to the government ... do nothing ... sit back and take anything you dish out?"

"Look Frank, I know you've got a job to do and interests to represent but we both know the limits of what can be gained. We've got to recognise that and be realistic. If people don't accept those limitations ... continue to make impossible demands ... take more and more disruptive action ... it can only go in one direction, towards more and more chaos. Well, that gets to be dangerous, doesn't it? Politically dangerous. Eventually, control has got to come from somewhere and there's no shortage of people who would like to take advantage of chaos. You've got a few people on your side who would like to take control. If this Coalition fails, these people could battle it out, and what would be the outcome? Who would take over? Whoever it is won't be very pleasant and there'll be no place for me or you."

"I've got a feeling you're trying to threaten me, Blake."

"Not at all. I'm trying to assess the dangers of more and more conflict and I'm being honest about so called government power. I'm telling you from the inside, we don't have total control and we didn't choose the present state of things. I'll tell you what we do. We spend all our time reacting to things we can't control. That's the truth of it. That's the reality of power and if people don't accept it ... instead, go on creating more and more chaos ... then we can't prevent the consequences of that either."

Frank finished his drink and stood up. He went back to the bar then returned with his refilled glass. Blake waited for his response. "It all sounds like blackmail to me. Get to the point, Blake... What do you expect the TUC to do?"

"I understand why it's happening. I know people are angry and frustrated, but I've got special reasons for telling you. Just at the moment, things are on a knife-edge. I want you to understand that it's a particularly bad time for all these demonstrations to be increasing; and it's a particularly bad time to move against the voluntary schemes being organised in the cities."

"You've only got yourself to blame for the demonstrations. The hospital dispute was unofficial until you moved in with the voluntary workers. You went back on your deal with Bob Grantley. You thought that was a clever move but now you're seeing the consequences ... demonstrations with many others joining in. Don't come here complaining to me. You've brought the whole thing on yourself."

"I was opposed to it ... I told Grantley that."

"What else would you tell him? You were going through the motions of doing a deal and at the same time you were bringing in the voluntary people to smash the strike. Now you've got the gall to say that people shouldn't demonstrate against strike breakers. Have you actually got me here to tell me that?"

Frank Bell was becoming angry and Blake realised that the meeting had been a mistake. He and Frank now moved in two different worlds and it seemed that communication between the two was impossible.

"What about the needs of the sick, Frank? At least they're being cared for. Are you opposed to that as well?"

"You said it was a local response in one hospital. That was another one of your lies. Voluntary workers have taken over the maintenance of every hospital in the Southern Region. That's an all-out attack on the trade unions and you organised it."

"That's not true. You believe it because you want to. The voluntary people have always done work in the hospitals and when things broke down it was natural for them to offer their help."

"And it was natural for you to accept it. It was part of your plan to break the strike."

"I can't stop you from believing it ..."

"You won't negotiate ... you'll make no concessions ... you move straight in with the army, the police, voluntary workers or anyone else you can use to attack the unions."

"Don't you think you've got things a bit out of proportion? I was hoping that we could talk about some of the good things that voluntary work could do."

"Yes, I know you're taking it all much further. I know what's going on. You're not the only one with information. I know about your schemes in the cities and your All Party Group of MPs. People are going to work for dole level wages, that's why your group has gone for it. It's part of your plan to reduce standards throughout the country and make it difficult for unions to resist."

"Those schemes won't interfere with normal jobs ..."

"That's what you've told people and some of them may have believed it but they'll soon realise that it's another manoeuvre to undermine living standards. Don't think you've won a lasting victory in your local party because it's early days yet."

Blake abandoned any attempt to find common ground with the Secretary of the TUC. "That's where you're wrong. It's not early days. It's already too late. We've had years and years of this argument. It's never got anywhere in the past and it's not going to get anywhere now. There's nothing secret about the facts. This government is constrained by lack of funds and that's not new either. Your own research departments should tell you that. They're stuffed full of intellectual fugitives from the real world. How is it they've never told us where to find a bottomless well of ready cash?"

"It's not our responsibility to stimulate the economy and generate more cash. That's down to the government."

"You just keep blaming the government, Frank. That way you can always evade responsibility."

"Responsibility? Unlike yours, my hands are clean."

"I'll keep my own conscience on that."

By now their meeting had degenerated into a useless row. Frank was unyielding; a tough veteran of such arguments, he was now determined to antagonise Blake.

"Don't think we're going to stand by and watch our members' jobs being undermined by unpaid work. You'll see demonstrations and much more. You might think you're in a strong position now but people like you come and go; the TUC is here to stay. Governments like yours come and go but no one can do without our members. Remember, nothing can happen in this country without them."

"It all sounds heroic, Frank, but all these struggles are from a dead era. You sound like an old record with your voice stuck in a groove but there's no point in going round in the same circle."

"And what have you said that's so original? You're just another part of another government attacking the unions. There's nothing original in that. It's all governments have ever done, so don't preach to me about living in the past."

"At least I'm trying to get away from it. There should be more to life than struggle. I'm trying to look forward but you can't see beyond your next wage claim and all you ever hear is your last round of applause at the TUC Conference. All that cheap rhetoric comes by the yard but where does it get us? Surely we've got to expand our vision? There could be a different future but we'll never see it while we fight the same useless battles over and over again. Don't you ever think about that, Frank? I thought we both did once."

"It's not me who is looking backwards. Your use of voluntary workers to break a strike, that's all been done before and we haven't forgotten it. I'm not surprised your local party wanted to get rid of you ..."

"You're not surprised because you organised it."

"Yes ... well ..." Frank stood up and swallowed his drink. "I've said what I came here to say." He glanced at his watch. "It was no great inconvenience. I often call in here for a drink though usually with better company."

"Then you know your way out."

The meeting had been a disaster. Frank Bell had taken some verbal revenge and this had been his sole intention. Blake caught a last glimpse of the big man as he disappeared through the door and for a moment saw him as a tragic figure. Frank was a life long fighter.

His job was to make demands and press them on those who were seen as having the power to grant them. He depended on those he attacked and though he didn't always win he knew how to survive and fight again another day. He never questioned the struggle, nor did he ever ask how it could be ended. Defeat or victory made little difference. Either way, these only set the scene of further battles. Nothing was ever resolved. It was a commitment to struggle without end by a popular hero. Frank Bell could never be an agent of change; he was a permanent fixture of the status quo.

There was tragedy about Blake as well. He sat by himself, feeling isolated and depressed, staring into an empty glass. Now estranged from his background his work had lost its meaning. His role had become ambiguous. He occupied an undefined space distant from past loyalties but without a cause to replace them. Disillusion was not enough; it could point to no useful way forward. He sat for some time, struggling to find a new purpose and then abandoned his thoughts. Now the servant of events, he would go home and wait to see what happened next.

He left the hotel, buttoned his coat against the cold night air and walked some distance looking for a taxi, but none appeared. Further on, he found the entrance to an underground railway station and disappeared down its steps.

14

With the rapid growth of the Campaign, the MI5 agent on its National Committee sent a stream of reports to the Home Office. As it was an open organisation, Blake questioned the need to keep an undercover agent. Its meetings were held in public and the minutes of its business were published. There was nothing in the agent's reports that could not be read in the press or freely observed by anyone attending its crowded meetings. Each day saw more support for the Campaign. The first response of hundreds was soon swelled by tens of thousands; even the organisers were uncertain of the true numbers.

Each new attempt to deal with the flood of enquiries which came by mail, e-mail and telephone was overwhelmed. The Campaign moved its headquarters into an empty warehouse where bags of mail stood unopened. As new helpers attempted to process the letters their inability to cope required yet more helpers, who soon arrived. Every helper asked the same question; when would the increasing support begin to lose its momentum? As the build-up of membership continued, the work was diverted to regional centres. This relieved pressure on the national headquarters. Cash donations poured in with some individuals wishing to contribute substantial sums.

The National Committee met every evening making hurried decisions, trying to convert disorder into a well-organised movement. At last, order began to emerge through a network of local branches. Between these and its national headquarters, regional committees were set up to coordinate the branches in their areas. Efficient communications were established with leaflets being dispatched from headquarter to the regions and then to local branches where they were reproduced for distribution in towns and cities. Through this structure the Campaign communicated with millions of people throughout the country. Swept up by the movement, supporters threw themselves into the work, giving their time and energy for any required task. The massive response cut across differences of age and background as more and more people joined in with enthusiasm.

With Hurst's papers returned to him, leading figures in the Astronomical Society supported his claim that the planet could be facing disaster. This reinforced the demand that civil defences should be prepared. Pressure on the government to protect the population mounted rapidly. Existing demonstrations were a ready-made focus of popular action and the demands of the Campaign soon appeared amongst the crowds outside government departments and hospitals.

Demonstrations were planned in cities throughout the country. These included plans for a great march to begin at London assembly points and then to end at Trafalgar Square and Hyde Park. The groundswell of popular protest was irresistible and as Blake arrived at Whitehall each morning, he surveyed the scene. A great crowd occupied the pavements outside his department. Each morning, the police inspector on duty appeared desperate, advising Blake that it was impossible to guarantee order and that the army would have to be brought in to clear the crowds. With demonstrations building up in other places, the pressures on the police were becoming intolerable. Knowing that the situation was volatile, Blake could only urge restraint.

Back in his office he read hurriedly through news reports. Prompted by Janice Fearn, the press insisted on knowing more about the Hurst affair. He glanced through a typical comment.

"What is the truth about the arrest of Edward Hurst? Was it really because he breached national security or was it to silence him? Why was he suddenly released? Was it because the interest in his disappearance was an embarrassment to the government? Is it possible that the appeal to government security has been used to cover up an illegal act? It is clear that the government has a great deal more information than it has so far revealed. The public must know what it is."

It was a morning when Blake and Bill Charman were due to have a further meeting with Sandra Dale. Bill Charman insisted that

Blake should arrive early. " ... It's important that we first have a talk. Something has turned up."

Blake wasn't surprised. There were now any number of ways that the two Ministers could be embarrassed by events. "Is it something you can tell me?" he asked.

"No, get over here," said Bill. "You'll see for yourself."

Blake put down the phone as Janet brought in coffee and stared at the crowd from a window.

"You're beginning to see what it's like to be under siege," he said.

"We've had demonstrations, but nothing like this."

"What do think of this Campaign?" he asked.

"If there is any truth in what Edward Hurst is saying, then obviously, the government should do something."

"So you think this Campaign is a good thing?"

She thought for a moment before giving a guarded reply. "It's not for me to say."

Blake pressed her. "But you must have an opinion. I'm not asking if you'd join it. Do you think it's a good thing?"

"I admit ... I did put some money in their collection box."

"That's a kind of support."

She looked slightly alarmed. "Was there anything wrong in that?"

"Of course not," he said. "We're told it's a free country."

Her remark underlined the potential strength of the Campaign. Usually, Janet maintained a professional detachment from public issues. If she had donated to the Campaign's funds then so would the whole country. He glanced at his watch, swallowed his coffee and left.

At the Home Office Bill Charman went straight to the point of their early meeting. "You were wrong about the use of our man on the Campaign's National Committee," he said. "He's come up with something."

"I just think it's risky," said Blake. "With the coverage of the Campaign his picture could appear in the press or on television. Someone could recognise him as a security agent."

"Don't worry about his cover. He's told us that Sandra Dale has met up with Hurst."

"So what? We knew she was trying to make contact."

"The reason for their meeting is that she supports the Campaign, and she's actually joined it."

"Really?" From his earliest meeting with Sandra Dale, Blake had recognised that she was sympathetic to Hurst but he was surprised that she had actually joined his campaign. "Has she told him anything about the work of the scientific team?"

"We don't know that but even in joining she's broken the terms of her contract and probably the law."

The news was final confirmation that the two Ministers had been defeated. They were in no position to do anything but wait on events and then do their best to smooth over any embarrassment. "It's unfortunate," said Blake. "Even so, except by quiet counsel, there's nothing we can do to stop her. Do you intend to bring it up at this meeting?"

"It's a routine meeting," said Bill, "another progress report on the work of the team."

"Then we should sound her out – cautiously. Never mind what your agent says, we should hear what she has to say."

"She's joined the Campaign, Blake. That's a fact."

"Yes. My assistant has given them money but we're not going to arrest her, are we?"

"It's not the same. We're talking about the head of our research team. Sandra Dale is a mine of secret information."

"And that's the reason why we can't do anything."

Bill Charman re-arranged the papers on his desk as his assistant announced the arrival of Sandra Dale. He looked at Blake. "We've got to anticipate the response of the Prime Minister. You realise, he gets these MI5 Reports before me." He got up, brought a chair to his desk and ushered in Sandra Dale. She sat down and took some files from her briefcase.

"Home Secretary, you've asked for a further progress report. There isn't a great deal to add."

"You've got everything you need?"

"So far, yes. We've used the new people and the better facilities to check our work up to date. This has confirmed what we previously thought."

"What about Mr. Hurst's papers? Have they been a help?"

"Not really. We found nothing new, though for an amateur he has been very thorough and much of his data corresponds with our own."

"Having seen it, is there any possibility that his work could have come from yours?"

"No. It's clear that his results have come from his work with facilities in Mexico."

"So, what's the position now?"

"Our immediate problem is to interpret our observations more accurately. As you know, this concerns the size of the space body, its make-up, its position, speed and its precise orbit. We're hoping for early results from our work with the American agencies. The most important news is that they have agreed to launch a space probe. We're discussing the technical details and as soon as we know anything more we'll let you know."

"We don't like to press you but as you can see we're coming under mounting pressure to take action on civil defence."

"Can I ask about the progress of the work on deep shelters?" she said.

Bill Charman looked down at his papers, giving an unfortunate impression of being evasive. Blake took up the reply. "Dr. Dale, we hope you appreciate the complications on our side. The political and economic problems could be just as difficult as those on the scientific side."

"But we're working on those problems day and night. Surely you are planning for civil defence? It should have equal urgency. People have a right to expect it."

Blake continued. "So, you would support the aims of the Campaign that has sprung up?"

With disarming frankness she replied. "Of course. We must plan for the worst and take urgent steps to protect the population. That's been our advice from the beginning. Surely this Campaign could help with the work of civil defence. That's why I've joined it."

Blake became nervous as Bill Charman looked at Sandra Dale directly. "So, you're saying you've actually joined this Campaign?"

Her voice took on a sharper note "Mr. Charman, I've just told you that."

"But this Campaign is in effect a political movement in opposition to the government."

"I disagree," she said. "It's a movement of ordinary people whose only concern is the protection of the population. It's not a political party. I'm not interested in politics."

"I should be frank with you," said Bill. "A person in your position, an important government employee in charge of highly secret information, information that carries the most serious implications; you must surely see that you cannot be a member of this Campaign – even granted your good intentions?"

"I'm afraid I don't see it that way, Home Secretary," she said firmly. "In fact I've been very disturbed at the treatment of Mr. Hurst. It was outrageous that he was arrested, and then to see it justified by the feeble lies put out by the government."

"But you gave us to believe you recognised the importance of security," he said, "that it's in the interests of the public. We hope that's still your view. Have you disclosed any information to the Campaign?"

"I've been considering the question of what is government information and the answer is not clear. What we know about this danger comes from a broad background of public material. I prefer to think that we're public employees. Our ultimate responsibility is to the public and therefore, in this case, the public has a right to the information."

"What does that mean, precisely?"

"I've thought about it carefully. It means that I will make everything I know available to the public."

Bill Charman was startled but managed to keep his composure. Seeing his discomfort, Blake intervened. "Dr. Dale, we're doing what we can to plan for civil defence. We've been working day and night as well. There has never been any intention to conceal information from the public. We've been working towards a full and frank disclosure of all the material on the approaching comet and the fact that we have not yet done so is only a matter of timing. We want to complete our plans for civil defence before releasing it and you do know the reasons for this. We have to avoid mass hysteria and you, in fact, have agreed with this. It was you who organised the secret cover for the work of the expanded team. You've been working with copies of Mr. Hurst's notes. What we need is more time. You see, at the moment all the talk about a threat is unofficial, it comes from Mr. Hurst. But if it carries the stamp of your authority as a leading government scientist, well, it becomes a very different matter; it's no longer just the opinion of an amateur astronomer. If the government work is revealed with no plan for protecting the population, obviously, we'll risk the most appalling chaos. You've seen the support for this Campaign. Have you considered the consequences of what you intend? We would ask you not to be responsible for creating panic."

Sandra Dale turned to Blake. "That's a strong argument," she said, "and I accept that both you and the Home Secretary have always taken the matter seriously. You've given us all the help we asked for. You arranged for our joint work with American colleagues and that has been most useful. However, I asked you specifically what progress you have made in your plans to protect the public and you have said nothing. In my view, this is not a matter that can be left to a small group of politicians or indeed, to a small group of scientists. It affects all our people and they have a right to be informed. One reason why I joined the Campaign is that they impress me as being responsible. I haven't seen any sign of the panic you keep talking about. Moreover, the Campaign can help with the work of civil defence and that's another reason why it should be brought in."

Blake winced at the hard edge to Bill Charman's voice as he answered Sandra Dale. "You do realise that what you intend is against the law, and that you are bound by the law?"

Sandra Dale was not intimidated. "I am also bound by my conscience, Home Secretary. In this case, I place that higher."

"Above the law?"

"But not above the public interest. If the law doesn't serve the public, it's nonsense."

Bill Charman responded with gentle sarcasm. "You seem to be an authority on everything, Dr. Dale."

Blake tried to rescue the situation. "Dr. Dale, you're basing your intention on the fact that we have no ready-made plan for civil defence, is that right?"

"That's one part of it."

"So, if we were able to produce a plan, would that make a difference?"

"You'll arrive at those plans sooner if you involve the public."

"But in the end, we all want the same thing, I'm sure we agree on that?"

"I presume so."

"Good. You see we're politicians, we're not scientists. We're not in a position to make technical judgments on your work. We wouldn't presume to have an opinion in your field. We trust what you have told us and because of that trust, we have given you every assistance. Well, when it comes to our side of things, don't you think you should trust our judgment and give us your assistance? Trust what we tell you that on our side the problems are much more difficult than you might imagine. All we want is a little more time."

Sandra Dale wavered. "How much time do you want?"

"You want to set us a deadline? Do you realise what civil defences would cost? I shouldn't joke but your training could be an advantage because the figures are astronomical. You're trying to identify the size, speed and orbit of a lethal space body but do you think it's less difficult to find hundreds of billions of pounds?"

"If finance is the problem it's a compelling reason for informing the public. It's everyone's responsibility."

"I'm afraid that's not how the public sees it. If it's your final decision not to help us, that's going to be very disappointing..."

She relented. "What happened to Mr. Hurst was very wrong, but at the same time I know that you're trying to deal with the problem in a responsible way and despite what you may think, I do appreciate the difficulties. You've said enough to make me think again. I'll go away and think about it afresh."

Blake was relieved. "Good. We'll leave it at that then," he said. "A final word; we've brought the Americans in on the strict understanding they'd keep the work secret for the time being. It's going to look damned funny to them if our own people betray that confidence."

At last Sandra Dale smiled. "If there's nothing else I should get back."

She put away her files and Blake showed her from the office. He returned to Bill Charman who was looking depressed. "You nearly blew that, Bill. You can't threaten people like that... not with the law or anything else."

"I told you, we can't trust anyone."

"No. She's not into treachery; you see how open she is. With her it's a different case. She's another person of principle. I told you, we're so caught up in the machinations of government we've forgotten that principles exist but, anyway, we moved her towards us."

"And what does that mean?" replied Bill. "It means nothing. We've got our own government scientists in the enemy camp. That's what it means."

"No," said Blake. "You can't think of her as the enemy. If we're not on the same side as decent people like that then I suggest we take a look at what we're doing wrong."

"Don't start your preaching, Blake. We can do without that sentiment. Sandra Dale is just shrewd enough to know that our acting against her would land us in a worse mess." Bill Charman looked at his watch. "You realise that we're due to meet the Prime Minister. If Sandra Dale tells what she knows it means he lied to the House."

"He did lie to the House."

"Yes, but everyone will know he did."

15

Back at Downing Street they returned to the small room where the secret Cabinet Committee held its meetings. The Prime Minister joined them and the two Ministers knew at once that events had done nothing to lighten his mood. He threw a pile of security reports onto the table and began to scan through them. "Where have you two been?" he snarled. "I've been waiting."

Bill Charman apologised. "Our last meeting with Dr. Dale couldn't be rushed."

"I'll come to her in good time." The Prime Minister paused over one document. "I'm concerned about this young reporter, Janice Fearn. I see she's still prying into Hurst's arrest. I've asked you before, Bill, how far can she get? You've seen the press. They're suggesting I lied to the House."

"Yes. They do suggest that."

"There are going to be more questions."

"That's inevitable," said Bill.

Blake and Bill Charman sagged wearily in their seats as the Prime Minister launched into yet another tirade. "We've got Hurst still capturing the headlines. He's now got a campaign around him. My integrity is being questioned and now I see that one of our leading scientists has joined this campaign." He turned to Bill Charman. "Have you confronted her with this?"

"I'm afraid it's even worse," said Bill, "She's not only joined the campaign, she's threatening to reveal details of the government's work."

The Prime Minister's hands trembled with anger as he clenched the MI5 report. "Just say that once more, Bill. I'm hoping I didn't hear you right."

"She's threatened to reveal details of the government's work. That was her intention but we persuaded her to think again."

"Is that all?" the Prime Minister demanded.

"In the circumstances it was quite a lot."

"So, you've persuaded her to think again?"

"It's given us time to consider our options," said Bill. "What more would you expect?"

The Prime Minister dropped the report on the table, got up and began pacing the room. "Well, let's see what more I would expect. You two have been appointed to an ad hoc Cabinet Committee on National Security. It's a body with not a little responsibility and a great deal of authority. Having that authority I would expect you to secure an immediate repudiation of her action and in failing to get it I would expect you to arrest the damned woman on the spot. That is what I would expect, Home Secretary."

Bill Charman glanced at Blake and shrugged. "That's all very well but in the first place she hasn't actually done anything; there's no conspiracy to do anything and thinking about a crime is not in itself a crime."

"What about joining this campaign? Isn't that a criminal breach of her terms of employment?"

"We would have to prove it in court. I feel as strongly as you, Prime Minister, but arguably this campaign is a non-political pressure group and even if she went as far as revealing information, I remind you, in recent similar cases we haven't been too successful in getting convictions. It could be another case where a jury decides that her duty to the public is greater than her duty to this particular government."

"We arrested Hurst, didn't we? We didn't get a list of your legal niceties when we did that."

"Yes. And now we're seeing the consequences."

"Are you seriously telling me we're being threatened by our own employees that they're going to release high security information and there's nothing we can do about it?"

"Not at all. We could dismiss her. We have every ground."

"Well do it then. Get rid of her today."

"It would be easy enough, but it needs a bit more thought." Bill Charman was now convinced that no immediate action should be taken against Sandra Dale. If he had a mind to, the Home Secretary had many ways of removing her from the scene. He turned to Blake. "What do you think, Blake?"

Blake supported him. "I can't think of a single good reason for even sacking her."

The Prime Minister exploded. "Am I surrounded by madmen? First you allow this whole business to get out of hand, then you place me in difficulties in the House and now you're about to give encouragement to enemies of the government. You might just as well invite Hurst to join the Cabinet." The two Ministers sat silent as the Prime Minister stormed up and down the office. "Can you not see that if we fail to sack this person the government will have no authority, no control of any kind? Is that what you are proposing, Blake?"

"No," said Blake. "I wasn't proposing that. I was considering the consequences of sacking her, if I may say so, in a calm manner." Convinced now that the Prime Minister had lost contact with the realities of the situation, he continued. "It's impossible to stop Sandra

Dale from telling what she knows. Now that Hurst has released his papers it will be only a matter of days, if not hours, before his observations are confirmed. In a situation where the approach of a lethal comet is accepted by authorities throughout the world, the government would look extremely foolish if it tried to deny it, and in any case, it should be obvious that we depend entirely on the work of our team of scientists. If we did anything to impede their work we could never justify it to the public."

For the first time Blake began to assert himself on the beleaguered Cabinet Committee. "We've put ourselves more and more on the defensive, we're in a position of siege and we've got to break out. We've got to regain some initiative. We've got to win people over to the government's side and for that we should reveal the work of our team. That would immediately remove the problem of Sandra Dale. Being entirely open about the approach of the comet could be a first step towards regaining the authority of the government."

As Blake spoke the Prime Minister sat down and stared disconsolately at the bundle of Special Branch reports. Blake added a final tempting point. "And, incidentally, you would regain your own authority, Prime Minister."

The Prime Minister looked up and glared at Blake. "I wasn't aware that my authority was being questioned."

Blake's proposals meant a complete change of direction. Nevertheless, he continued to press them on his colleagues. "Coming out into the open is the best of a set of bad options but if we don't do it we'll either become paralysed by inaction or forced into desperate measures that could become dangerously counter-productive. We can reveal our information in ways that play it down. Whatever we do, we've got to be open with the public."

A silence fell on the Committee which was eventually broken by Bill Charman. "We don't need to be completely open," he said. "We can be open in a way that is selective. For example, it wouldn't be a good idea to admit that we have no credible plan for civil defence. We could release our own information on the dangers and say that we are considering emergency powers for dealing with them. This could be announced as a contingency plan for the protection of the population. At the same time we would be organising powers for dealing with any panic and for maintaining law and order." Bill Charman sensed that he had found a way forward that would appeal to the Prime Minister. He looked towards him. "What would you say to that, Prime Minister?"

"It's the first sensible thing I've heard all day," he said. "Law and order, that's our priority."

Bill Charman proposed that the plans for emergency powers should be brought up-to-date and that if they became necessary, they should be operated by just six members of a Civil Contingencies Unit. These would be the Prime Minister, the Home Secretary, the Defence Minister, a Minister in charge of Public Liaison and two senior officers from the police and the Services. It would represent every part of the coercive powers of government.

Bill Charman as Home Secretary would be assisted by a Security and Policy Methods Committee and would direct the actions of the Police, MI5 and all Intelligence Services. The Defence Minister, John Dudney, assisted by an Armed Services Co-ordinating Committee would direct every branch of the Services. Acting as a Minister for Public Liaison, it would be the work of Blake Evans to bring public bodies, civil services and local government into a single, national organisation. The Prime Minister would act as overall controller applying the authority of the Civil Contingencies Unit throughout thirteen regional areas.

Bill Charman again emphasised that although the plans had been made in anticipation of a war situation, in practice they were no different from those required for the organisation of a major peacetime or natural emergency. In view of this, they were appropriate for the dangers that arose from the approaching comet. They covered every threat of chaos and social breakdown.

They continued to study the secret plans with a view to adapting them for a peace-time emergency. Under the emergency powers all law providing for civil rights could be suspended. As Bill Charman had outlined, state action would result from the decisions of a small group of Ministers working with police commissioners and senior members of the armed forces. From its underground headquarters in London this Civil Contingencies Unit would direct the actions of the thirteen regional seats of government.

Central to the organisation would be the power to impose curfews with extreme consequences for those who broke them. All public communications, including the national telephone system, would be shut down. In place of press, radio and televisions services a National Information Unit would be the sole source of news and would direct a civil defence corps. A system of national control would have its own communications designed to be adaptable. Any damage to a single part would be by-passed without affecting the efficiency of the whole. Similarly, in the unlikely event of the central government unit having been put out of action, a group of regional commissioners would assume its powers.

Blake noted the list of 13 underground bunkers marked for use as regional seats of government which would be served by 30 communications centres. In turn these would be supported by 116 facilities providing for a nationwide distribution of police, armed forces and civil defence units. Typical of these was the once secret nuclear bunker with its many floors descending deep below ground level near Brentwood in Essex. Built in the early 1950s its levels were divided by massive concrete walls into rooms providing for generators, communications equipment, dormitories, canteen facilities and control rooms.

Despite Blake's insistence that the wider community would have to be involved, Bill Charman continued to emphasise the role of the police, the Services and the few individuals who would act as a government. He referred to the Command and Control centre buried deep underground in High Wycombe, Buckinghamshire, which had been used as the country's primary defence headquarters during several wars.

This brought him to the war bunker which he suggested would be the obvious place from which a Civil Contingencies Unit could operate. The high technology command centre had been built during the early 1990s under the code name "Pindar" and was buried 140 feet below the Ministry of Defence building in Whitehall. It was designed as a Services nerve centre for any national crisis. From this concrete refuge, the Civil Contingencies Unit would direct the police and armed forces. It was equipped with the most sophisticated communications technology and was linked through a network of tunnels to Downing Street and important ministry buildings. At first constructed in secret, its existence had come to light after an argument over its spiralling costs when the Treasury had confronted the Ministry of Defence because of massive overspending. It had cost £66 million, which was £23 million more than its original estimate.

"You do realise," Blake said, "that we're heading for a big fight with the Treasury over money. If the government's bolthole under Whitehall cost £66 million, how much would it cost now? And how much would deep shelters for the whole population cost?"

As if to avoid the question Bill Charman shrugged. "I suppose we'll deal with the Treasury when we have to," he said vaguely.

The Prime Minister intervened. He was still unwilling to accept the need for deep shelters and the costs of construction. "At this point we are only concerned with national security. Law and order is the main question in front of us," he said.

As Blake read through the plans, which had been retained by all governments but kept secret, he became increasingly sceptical. Still plagued by doubts as to whether he had been living through a surreal fantasy he began to have the strongest fears that events were becoming a totalitarian nightmare. But trying to keep a sense of reality he realised that whoever had drawn up the plans had conjured a neat scenario on paper that could never be applied in practice. What was missing was the vital element of public consent. Even in the desperate circumstances that were envisaged, total control of the population by the police and the Services was impossible. The plans were about the arrogance of power and the illusion that greater force equalled greater control.

What was needed was a new approach in which all people would be able to act as responsible members of their communities. For this the voluntary actions of all citizens would need to be informed. It was free access to information that should guide their decisions and actions. The idea that just six individuals at the head of a power structure could take the country through the impending crisis sprang from outdated modes of thought that could no longer serve any useful purpose.

The outlook of the Prime Minister had first developed and was by now, deeply frozen, in the practice of manipulation, control and force. Even the more liberal minded Bill Charman, who appeared to accept the need for change, regarded adaptability only as a means of retaining power. It was for these reasons that Blake realised that he would have to speak and act cautiously. His best chances of influencing events would arise from staying at the centre of power. He had little doubt that if he argued too strongly for more open ways of conducting government he would be removed from his position. Though the authoritarian attitudes of his colleagues belonged to the past and were in every practical sense redundant, they still survived as the dominant means of imposing the status quo.

With the formation of a Civil Contingencies Unit agreed, the Prime Minister was confident that it would be endorsed by Cabinet in which case even Parliament would have to work under the superior powers of the emergency arrangements. With one appointment outstanding it was logical that John Dudney, the Defence Minister should be included. "Dudney is very sound," said the Prime Minister.

Bill Charman nodded and Blake also agreed. If the proposals meant revealing the government's work and removing any threat to Sandra Dale, he was less concerned with the contingency plans. As the Prime Minister contemplated the use of Emergency Powers he became more relaxed. "I'll think about the police and army appointments later," he said. "Yes, the outlook is better, things seem more secure."

"There's the question of the campaign demonstration in Hyde Park and Trafalgar Square this Sunday," Bill Charman reminded them.

Blake cut in before the Prime Minister could suggest that it be banned. "Let it go ahead," he said, "It's soaking up a lot of frustration and anger. We'll know what we're dealing with."

To his surprise the Prime Minister agreed. "You're right, Blake. We'll know exactly what we're up against and with the mobilisation of the forces under emergency powers, we'll have every means of dealing with them. Of course," he added, "we're not just concerned with confrontation, there is also conciliation." He turned to Blake. "That's supposed to be your department. I was very sorry to hear of your row with Frank Bell. He'll be a key person and yet you seem to be pursuing a vendetta against him."

"It was never my vendetta, Prime Minister."

"No? By the time you two have finished bungling things there'll be no one in the country we haven't antagonised."

The Prime Minister had glimpsed the prospect of a new popularity. Behind the scenes he would be organising every power of emergency control. Publicly, he would project the image of a caring leader responding to the concerns of the population. Suddenly, his ebullience had returned.

16

The three members of the Cabinet Committee left their small office and moved on to a full meeting of the Cabinet. With all its members in place, Blake sat back, content to be a silent witness to the Prime Minister's skills in manipulating its decisions. Now full of confidence, the Prime Minister launched into an extended summary of developments beginning with the work of the scientific team and the formation of the ad hoc Cabinet Committee on National Security. He spoke at length on the public's response to Hurst's claims and the sudden growth of the Campaign. He said that the new movement had been provoked by sensational press reports. Hurst had become a cult figure and was exploiting the mood of frustration in the country. The Campaign had latched on to existing demonstrations and had become a danger to good order.

Blake noticed that he made no mention of Sandra Dale, or to the decision that morning not to arrest her. Instead, he said the government would announce the research being carried on by its own team of scientists. The work was academic and had been pursued over a long period with no special significance. It was true that it had now resulted in the sighting of an approaching comet but this was a normal solar event. The sensational claims being made that it would bring destruction were unsupported by any evidence.

The Prime Minister said he was confident that things would soon calm down. Once the facts were known the public would take a more sober view. Until then it had to be accepted that, urged on by fanatics such as Edward Hurst and activists who wanted to destroy the government, a mood of hysteria was threatening the good order of the country. Seen in this light the threats were not from space but from extremist elements within the country and in these circumstances, the security forces must be in a position to move decisively against them.

The Prime Minister spoke without interruption until Ministers became bored and restive. Blake recognised the technique, intended to prepare the Cabinet for a sudden, dramatic proposal. At last it came when he announced the need for full emergency powers. Under the terms of the Civil Defence Review, which he said had been endorsed by Parliament, special powers would be granted to a select group of Ministers who would operate as a Civil Contingencies Unit. This body would also include senior personnel from the police and the army. Its powers would be operated in the regions through emergency committees or regional seats of government and this would displace much of the work of local government. It was therefore a matter of the utmost urgency that the Cabinet should endorse these proposals.

As the Prime Minister stopped he glared menacingly round the table. Only John Dudney responded and his question was tentative. "Conciliation should also be an option," he said. "The demonstrations sprang from the hospital dispute so what happened to the public enquiry that Blake proposed? I thought the unions supported it."

"That's where you're wrong," the Prime Minister replied. "You've seen the response of the unions; they've stepped up the demonstrations. Blake will tell you himself. He had a meeting with Frank Bell and met with nothing but hostility. That enquiry is not on our agenda. The issue in front of us is the growing threat to law and order. We don't need to have a wide ranging discussion."

Dudney persisted. "But if we can calm people's fears about this threat of destruction, surely that's the best way to deal with this Campaign. On the other hand bringing in full emergency powers may aggravate anxieties."

The Prime Minister raised his voice. "I haven't mentioned any threat of destruction. That sort of talk is irresponsible. We are dealing with a Campaign that is cynically exploiting the false fears it has itself created. That's all there is to it. I've said, there is only one threat, the growing threat to law and order which is coming to a head this weekend with demonstrations by people who could turn to violence. We must have these emergency powers. We must be able to move swiftly and decisively…" He looked directly at Dudney. "Being in charge of Defence you are an obvious candidate for this Civil Contingencies Unit. I trust you will accept that responsibility?"

This was a clear warning to Dudney. If he did not agree he would be sacked from his post. Dudney remained silent as the Prime Minister turned to other members of the Cabinet who he trusted would support the emergency powers. The support soon came. "In past disruptions," the Prime Minister continued, "we only succeeded by taking a tough line. Any weakness now would make us hostage to chaos which cannot be in anyone's interests, not even the misguided, well-meaning people who are supporting this Campaign."

Having the support of Bill Charman and by combining verbosity, threats and an overbearing manner, the Prime Minister moved relentlessly towards the setting up of emergency powers. "It makes sense that the present Cabinet Committee should form the core of the Civil Contingencies Unit." He looked again at John Dudney, "and I take it that you are willing to serve?"

Dudney agreed and the Prime Minister concluded the meeting. "The only outstanding matter is the service appointments and on that I'll take the advice of the police and Services."

Blake looked round the resigned faces of the Cabinet. The Prime Minister had easily got his way. With scant knowledge of the background details they had acquiesced in setting up the widest powers of force to be operated by a few individuals. The new government unit would be the hand of absolute rule.

Blake returned to his Department with the Cabinet's decision still weighing on his mind. It was a negative response reflecting little more than the Prime Minister's retreat from reality. If the threat of destruction was real what could be the object of total government control? If its intention was to take the population into oblivion in an orderly manner the idea was not only absurd; it could never work. Long before the point of catastrophe was reached the community would break up in disarray. As scattered fugitives from their own lack of control a hopeless mass of people would react desperately.

Even those who stood to control them would have already joined the panic.

He took out his file on the community projects to be run by voluntary workers but was interrupted by Janet who again pressed him to clear his routine work. He lifted a pile of correspondence from his in-tray and began signing it. "I know what you're thinking," he said. "You think that I should read all this stuff."

"Some of those documents involve important legal commitments," she warned.

For a moment he wondered if this would continue to be true. He carried on signing. "We might find they are not as important as we imagine," he said.

After clearing his in-tray he took up the policy document on voluntary work which he had prepared for the All Party Group of MPs and put it in his briefcase. It was the best hope for any constructive action and indicated a shift of responsibility away from the government to the House of Commons. Blake now accepted that the Prime Minister's reliance on total force would solve nothing and if he took the Cabinet further along that futile course, the role of Parliament could yet be decisive.

Unobserved, Blake left his Department and walked hurriedly to Westminster where his All Party Group had assembled in a private office. They confronted him with the contradictory statements being issued by the government; first the denial of the approaching comet and then the admission that it was speeding towards Earth. "No one knows for certain that there will be a catastrophe," Blake insisted. "We do know that it will pass very close and that we may be bombarded by some of its released missiles. What is certain is that we must develop our community projects. They may be vital to our survival."

Blake said as much as he dared about the developing dangers and the problems caused by lack of finance. After more persuasion, the MPs agreed to become more formally organised with the appointment of a secretary and chairman. Perhaps their action was a response to the sinister atmosphere of uncertainty, distrust and apprehension that had spread throughout the country. The fact that the government had kept its work on the comet secret and had been forced to be more open only after Edward Hurst had made his claims public, inevitably, raised questions as to why it had acted in a contradictory manner. This in turn seemed to justify the widespread fears of a missile bombardment. In these circumstances, the MPs forming the All Party Group felt they should have an organisation that was based in Parliament, was independent of the government and entirely under their own control.

Eventually, Blake left the House, satisfied that the All Party Group was now established with a solid base. He took a taxi home trying to think through the possible ways the situation might yet develop. As he joined Rachel in the lounge he found her weary of his constant preoccupations.

"I hope you're not going to work tonight," she said.

He poured himself his usual drink. "It seems a lot of people would like me to do less."

"I see you've admitted the government's work on the approaching comet. What brought on that rush of honesty?"

He smiled. "Sometimes people act out of character."

"I suspect there's something more sinister behind it."

"That's more like the truth."

"I've also seen your Sandra Dale on television. That doesn't add up, either."

Blake was surprised. "Really?" he said. "That is news. What did she say?"

"She seemed embarrassed. Reporters had caught up with her in the street. She said the comet was a fact and that communities should take precautions by taking cover in deep shelters. She said the Campaign was a good thing and that people should support it."

"Did she say that a missile bombardment was inevitable?

"No. She said it was possible, hence the need for precautions. I'm surprised she was allowed to speak at all."

"It's public knowledge," he said.

Rachel persisted. "It still seems curious. You talk about the risk of panic. You commit the most outrageous acts in secret, then you blandly announce the information and allow your own people to speak freely."

Blake opened another bottle and refilled both their glasses. "It didn't happen like that," he said. "We were forced into it."

"You mean with all your powers, you were forced into it."

"Let's say we had no choice. The only way to keep her quiet was to arrest her. That wasn't practical so we got the best result we could. She's now the voice of moderation within the Campaign."

"So, you did a deal."

"No. She doesn't do deals. She does what she thinks is right."

"How inconvenient for you."

Blake could only guess at how reporters came to know of Sandra Dale's government work. "Janice Fearn would have got it from Hurst," he said, "and then she tipped off the press. She will also have told them about Hurst's arrest."

"And I suppose you thought about arresting her?"

"I believe we did."

"You've probably thought about arresting everyone at one time or another?"

"That's why it's impractical. It gets out of hand."

"So, it's inexpedient?"

"What else?"

Seeing Blake's discomfort, she was amused to continue the exchange. "Let's see what other reasons there might be for not arresting everyone," she said. "It could be respect for freedom."

"Freedom hasn't been on the agenda lately." He changed the subject. "What's the latest from your hospital?"

"As well as the casualties from the demonstrations there's something new. Today I saw an elderly patient who's withdrawn into a state of extreme anxiety, a catatonic stupor. She's a very frightened lady. You should warn the media about the language they use. Their talk of a death star is dangerous and you're in a position to remind them."

Usually, Rachel treated politics with disdain. For her, its conflicts and shifting manoeuvres were incomprehensible, understood only by those who were involved. For all the energy and emotion that sustained the life of politics, nothing useful ever seemed to emerge. "If you don't do something to calm people's fears we'll get a lot more patients going into a shell," she continued. "They'll retreat into their own mental bunkers."

"She's not alone," he said, "the government is retreating into its own bunker."

"What does that mean exactly?"

"It means that today, whilst there's no protection from a missile bombardment the government has set up powers to control the entire population. It's set up what it calls a Civil Contingencies Unit which might sound benign but it's just six individuals with absolute powers of force"

"And are you one of these people?" she asked.

"For the moment, yes."

"Even with all your liberal pretensions?"

"There's no way I could stop it, and it's best if I stay at the centre of things. It's based on an illusion. The idea that six people can control the country is impossible. Even so, finding an alternative is difficult."

17

Amidst batteries of television screens Blake sat with Bill Charman in an anteroom adjoining the Home Secretary's office. From helicopters, buildings, bridges and other strategic points, cameras relayed pictures of scenes throughout the Capital. London was alive with the ferment of protest. Never before had so many people travelled to the city to demonstrate their feelings and their determination to bring pressure on the government.

The Campaign organisers had decided that Trafalgar Square should be the main meeting place and had prepared platforms decked out with banners and slogans. It had been arranged that demonstrators arriving at the Square would immediately disperse to allow others to follow behind, but the organisers had not anticipated the numbers. The exits from the Square were soon filled with people unable to move on but these were only a fraction of those who had set out to attend. Throughout the city, roads were jammed with cars. Public transport was unable to cope. Streams of people filled the pavements all heading in one direction. The police had blocked off Whitehall and Downing Street but these soon became surrounded by demonstrators. The only way in or out of Westminster was by helicopter. At the Home Office, Blake and Bill Charman felt besieged.

More distantly, trying to avoid chaos, police had stopped coachloads of demonstrators on motorways and other main roads leading to the city. Suspecting the police of trying to stop the demonstrations campaigners gathered in confused crowds. Angry at the police, tempers flared and fighting broke out. Overwhelmed by the numbers the police abandoned their attempts at control and retreated. As a result, miles of traffic built up. On every major route campaigners stood by vehicles, unable to get through. The same scenes were being repeated in every other city.

From their commanding view at the Home Office, Blake and Bill Charman observed the crowds with little comment and growing dismay; the numbers were much greater than those predicted by the security forces. It was well after the scheduled time that figures appeared on the granite plinth at the base of Nelson's Column. At last, one person stood holding a microphone as a deafening roar of cheers went up from the crowd.

"That's Patrick Laurie," said Bill Charman. "He's been on its National Committee from the start. One of the brains behind the organisation. He never expected to see this."

Laurie held up his arms as he waited for quiet. After some minutes his voice echoed from the many loudspeakers round the Square and was relayed to the room at the Home Office.

"I want to welcome you here today. I can tell you that many thousands have been unable to arrive. Trafalgar Square isn't big enough for a meeting of our Campaign. No place could be big enough because we now speak with the voice of the whole country, and today meetings are being held in towns and cities in many other countries. That is what we now represent; we are speaking with the voices of people throughout the world."

He was stopped by the noise of the crowd which drowned out the loudspeakers. Determined to make its own voice heard the demonstration cheered, clapped and shouted slogans. Again, Laurie raised his arms, appealing for quiet.

".. I want you to know that thousands are still joining our Campaign and donations are pouring in. I want to tell you what you can do in your own areas. I want to invite some of you to speak from this platform. This is not a movement of leaders. Whoever speaks for this movement sends the same message and the message is clear. It is a message to the government. We will not stand by whilst nothing is done. Action must be taken and action must be taken now."

Blake was unable to resist an ironic comment. He turned to Bill Charman. "Your Special Branch man on the National Committee, does he have a name?"

"You really don't need to know," replied Bill, "but for what it's worth, it's Chivers."

"And will your Chivers be speaking for the Campaign?"

"Very amusing," said Bill. "I believe not."

Amidst continued roars of support, Laurie continued.

"......Our Campaign is increasing so fast we cannot say how many have joined. I can't tell you how much money has been donated because we can't count it fast enough. What began with hundreds became thousands, then tens of thousands and then hundreds of thousands. What began with a trickle of funds has become a flood of millions of pounds. Through our National Committee, through all our local branches we now have a nationwide organisation. Through our links with campaigns in other countries we now have a worldwide organisation. We are now dedicated to putting our demands to our National Government and to every level of local government down to the district and the parish."

"If they aim to be organised at every level of government," said Blake, "they'll be well placed to take it over."

"Yes," agreed Bill, "don't mention that to the Prime Minister."

Laurie's voice continued to boom through the loudspeakers.

"... I want you all to express your support for our National Committee. I want to hear your support for our demand to see the government. Even at this moment the government is watching and listening to this demonstration, so let them hear your support loud and clear..."

Laurie stopped speaking to hear the roar of support from the crowd. He waited as it continued then again held his arms up for quiet.

"...You have just spoken with the voice of the whole people. That voice is demanding that the government must now see our Committee...."

Blake glanced at Bill Charman. "He's just booked you an interview with Hurst," he said.
"Really?" Bill replied, "I might leave that to you."

Laurie again appealed for quiet.

"... Listen everyone, please listen. I want to invite a speaker to the platform: a person who has acted with great courage; who has taken risks and who has come here today to give her support to our Campaign. I want to introduce Dr. Sandra Dale, a government scientist. I want you to express your appreciation for the brave way she has put herself forward..."

Blake leaned forward in concentration as amidst more cheering the slight figure of Sandra Dale walked to the centre of the platform. She composed herself, glanced at some notes and began speaking.

"Ladies and gentlemen," she said, then, apparently conscious of the formality of her address, added, "... and fellow campaigners. I hope that whatever we do in the time ahead we shall all act with good order and dignity. We all agree that this Campaign should go ahead with urgency but at the same time we must face the coming months with calm. If we stay calm and work together I am certain that we shall overcome any dangers that might exist."

Blake noticed that she struck a note of restraint. She spoke about the work of the government team, emphasising the absence of any final proof for an impending missile bombardment. She explained that the work indicated the need for defensive measures and this was why she had joined the Campaign; it was right that the public should be fully informed. She spoke of her contacts with the government.

"... I agree with all those who have condemned the arrest of Mr. Hurst but I also want to say this: as soon as the government was informed of a possible missile bombardment it acted swiftly. Our team of government scientists was given all the assistance it requested. With every help from Ministers, the team was expanded and we are now working in full cooperation with American space agencies. I also want to say that no one has prevented me from speaking at this great gathering. The government has given me every encouragement and has acted with great urgency. So, when we are being critical, I would ask you to remember what I have said because in every important way, the government has acted in a responsible manner."

The crowd fell silent. Her message was not what they wanted to hear. There was nothing in her remarks to excite the groundswell of hostility to those in authority. In this atmosphere of quiet disappointment she continued.

"... I would like to say that we are here not only to make demands of the government. We all share a responsibility to stay calm and work together constructively. Each of us must help in every possible way. Thank you all for listening."

Sandra Dale walked from the platform amidst some polite clapping. She had brought the crowd back to a more sober mood but the demonstration was unreceptive to her message of restraint. She was finally heard out with a respect that fell short of enthusiasm.

The two Ministers felt some relief. "That was just what we wanted," said Blake, "If we'd written her speech ourselves it couldn't have been better."

Bill agreed. "Let's hope it carries on that way."
Laurie returned to the microphone.

"... Since our meeting began we have discovered that a member of our National Committee, Alan Chivers, is in fact an MI5 Special Branch agent. The government has placed a spy in our Campaign..."

Bill Charman stared grimly at the television screen as Laurie continued.

"... But we all know we have nothing to hide. Unlike the government we have no secrets. If they want to place agents in our Campaign, and if they are doing useful work, then they are welcome."

Bill Charman was embarrassed. "I don't understand it," he said. "There must be another story behind that announcement."

Against a background of ironic cheers Laurie made nothing more of the news. Instead, he turned to the figure of Hurst who had appeared on the platform.

"... I want to introduce someone you all want to hear. We all owe a great debt to the work and the courage of Edward Hurst.... "

Hurst stood tall and erect before the microphone. Events had taken him from obscurity to the centre of national attention. His voice rang throughout the crowd.

"... I speak to you now because I made a promise that I would be honest with the people. I come here today to tell you that we all face the threat of destruction. With our great campaign I am at last able to warn the country that we must prepare to face the dangers now upon us. Even as we speak the dangers are closer. The longer we do nothing our destruction is more certain. And I come here to warn of another danger. We are also under threat from the government. The government is the enemy of this Campaign and as it tried to stop me speaking so it will try to smash our movement."

Again the crowd fell silent as it listened to Hurst.

"I was kidnapped by the government. They took me from my home and held me in secret and when the Prime Minister denies it, the Prime Minister is a liar. Their object was to stop the people being warned. But they did not stop me and they will not stop this great Campaign. The government told lies that I was a spy but they are the spies. They are spying on this Campaign which means they are spying on every one of you. That is why they dragged me from my home, to stop people knowing the truth. So I come here to warn you of great dangers but I also warn you against the government. They are both threats and if we do nothing, together, they will destroy us..."

As Hurst spoke the mood of the crowd changed. There was no applause and no cheering as many thousands of silent faces looked anxiously towards the platform, eager to catch every word that came from the tall figure now commanding the demonstration.

"For an astronomer, he makes a very good demagogue," said Blake, quietly, "... and they've already forgotten Sandra Dale." A new look of concern came to the face of Bill Charman. "Yes, Hurst is the one who speaks for this crowd."

Hurst continued his hostile theme. As his voice rose he became repetitive; his words became disconnected but with an increasing power to grip the feelings of his mass audience.

"This government will answer to our Campaign. Every wasted moment means the dangers are nearer and we must ask, when will be the time? When will be the time of destruction? Now is the time to prepare... prepare now before it is too late and before we are all destroyed. Before then we will deal with this government. They will answer to our demands... they will answer to this great gathering now and before the time of annihilation. That is my message to all of you. This day has shown that the truth has found its strength in our great movement and nothing will stop it from going forward.... and nothing will stop us dealing with this government which is our first enemy."

Hurst suddenly stopped speaking. The crowd was tense. The speech had been disorganised. Despite this, it had conveyed a brief and compelling message which had captured the great mass of demonstrators. For a few moments, as his words echoed in their minds they stayed silent. Then, as one, they applauded. Their cheering swelled to a roar. A forest of placards was held high demanding, "The Death Star – Prepare." The Square was filled with the voice of an uncountable mass of people who were now determined to deal with the government.

Laurie returned to the microphone and waited for the noise to subside. Swept up by the fervour of the demonstration his own voice was raised to a shout.

"What Edward Hurst has said to you confirms our message to the government. We will be seeing them tomorrow."

Blake turned to Bill Charman. "Did you know about any meeting?" he asked.

"No," replied Bill, "but I do now."

A telephone rang and Bill Charman took the receiver. It was the Prime Minister demanding that a security cordon be erected around the entire area of Whitehall and Westminster. He had also given instructions to the army to move armed troops into the cordon and to use every means of excluding demonstrators. Blake made no comment as Bill repeated the Prime Minister's instructions. "He also wants us in Downing Street. It'll be the first meeting of our Civil Contingencies Unit. He's made the service appointments and we're to see him in half an hour."

Blake noted the time and returned to the screens. In Trafalgar Square a churchman was addressing the crowd.

"The Bible has given us the prophecy that the Earth shall quake and the heavens shall tremble. Matthew has told us that with the tribulations of our days the sun shall be darkened, the moon will not give her light, the stars shall fall from the sky and the powers of the heavens shall be shaken. But in this prophecy we find not the promise of death but the challenge of life. In our tribulations we shall find our salvation in Christian brotherhood. In our coming together we shall find our strength as one mankind in one universe which has a purpose. In our troubled days we shall find God's destiny for mankind and we shall find peace in His purpose. Yes, the sun will be darkened, we shall see stars fall from the heavens, and this will be the message that we have lived in the sin of divided purpose, and we have lived in our denial of the one mankind that was ordained for our being; but now we shall come together as our movement has come together...."

"Who is that?" Blake asked.

"A radical minister," said Bill. "He gets into every campaign looking for the Promised Land."

"Strong in faith but weak in economics," said Blake. "It's a pity the prophets didn't do the cost calculations. They'd have known we can't afford the New Jerusalem."

"I never knew that," Bill said as he took his coat. "We'd better get to Downing Street."

They set out for Downing Street amidst the hurried work of police and troops who were setting up a security zone. With the river as a boundary on one side, steel barriers were being erected to block off every bridge and street leading to Westminster and Whitehall. Overhead the sound of helicopters added to the frenzy. It was a race to complete the work whilst the crowds around Trafalgar Square were attending their meeting.

On their arrival they went through to the Cabinet Room where they found John Dudney, the Defence Minister, with the two uniformed figures from the police and army who were the Prime Minister's appointees to the Civil Contingencies Unit. Dudney introduced them as Police Commissioner Anderson and Brigadier Sir John Culverton. They seemed ill at ease and unsure of their roles as Bill Charman invited them to sit at one end of the table where the group waited for the Prime Minister.

After some embarrassed conversation the Prime Minister entered, looking strained. He took his seat, ignored the two uniformed men and stared directly at Bill Charman. "What about this man you've got in the Campaign?" he demanded.

Having expected the Prime Minister to launch into the more important events that were raging on around them Bill was taken aback. "You mean Chivers?" he said, lamely.

"Whatever his name is, what's happened?"

"I'm not quite sure," said Bill, "I've had very little time to check. It appears that his position in the Campaign has been exposed, and he's disappeared."

"Disappeared? Well, what are you doing about it?"

"Obviously, we're trying to find him, Prime Minister."

"He's your responsibility, Home Secretary. You'd better find him quickly. We can't have him on the loose."

"Quite so."

Again, the Prime Minister set out to reassure himself. "As I have said, there is no real crisis. There's a lot of hysteria, that's all we're seeing. People have become the victims of rumour and alarm." As his colleagues looked on he again spoke at length about politically motivated activists who were inflating the issues for their own ends. "They have only got one thing in mind, instability. That's what it's about, a lot of troublemakers who have got their own agendas and who are using this maniac Hurst." The Prime Minister seemed tired and his remarks were unconvincing. Sensing this he altered course. "However, the hysteria is real enough, we can't deny that and whatever has caused it we're seeing an unprecedented threat to law and order." He turned to Bill Charman. "How do you see things, Home Secretary?"

Bill Charman set out to report on events in a detached manner. He referred to the difficulty of knowing how many people were now supporting the Campaign and its rapid accumulation of funds, though he confirmed that its support numbered millions. He also denied that it was organised around any particular political view. "Prime Minister, you've mentioned hysteria and that is certainly one factor involved but it is also true that behind this Campaign there are some shrewd minds at work."

"Exactly," said the Prime Minister. "Political extremists. For example, what do we know about this Laurie?"

"We know a great deal about him and he's not the sort of fanatic that you've got in mind. Calculating, yes, but his background is reasonably moderate. He's the architect of the Campaign's organisation and it is now capable of bringing pressure on every level of administration from local councils right up to government itself."

"So, it's poised for a political takeover. Isn't that what you're saying?"

"Not necessarily," said Bill Charman, "So far, there's been no talk of a takeover. However, with the organisation they're building they could eventually see that as an option. We're monitoring that closely."

The prospect did nothing to ease the Prime Minister's anxieties. "What about this demonstration? How do you assess that?"

Again, Bill Charman gave a sober account of the event so far. "It's been orderly. In view of the numbers, that is remarkable. The provisional figure for those attending is well over a million in London alone with no violent incidents reported. The police were instructed to be good-humoured and tolerant and perhaps that was conducive to good order."

"But there was violence in other places," the Prime Minister insisted. "Your tolerance didn't get you far there, did it?"

Bill Charman accepted that on main roads leading to the city there had been misunderstandings. Traffic had come to a stop and the police had tried to sort things out but some campaigners thought they were being obstructive and in some places fighting had broken out. Faced by the numbers the police had lost control and retreated. "I'm afraid some of them were injured," he said.

"So, the police lost control?"

"Just in a few places, Prime Minister."

"What you've just said is very depressing, Home Secretary."

"I'm giving you the facts. I'm not trying to depress anyone."

"So," said the Prime Minister. "We've sealed off Whitehall and Westminster so that is secure." Still ignoring the service chiefs he turned to John Dudney. "I hope we can at least rely on the army to protect Westminster? Is the army going to retreat and lose control?"

"There's no reason to think that," replied Dudney. "I'm sure the Brigadier will confirm that."

"Absolutely," said Culverton. "No problems whatsoever. We've more than enough men in position."

Sullen and introspective, the Prime Minister glanced through a pile of reports. "One thing we can agree on," he said. "We've got a full-scale national emergency on our hands."

From what he had seen of the demonstration, Blake was convinced that the government would have to swallow some pride and meet its representatives. "Prime Minister," he said, "in my view, it's not enough to think solely in terms of a national emergency. We've got to make some conciliatory moves. We've at least got to talk to the Campaign."

"Are you suggesting that we respond to blackmail by a mob?" the Prime Minister demanded.

Blake was insistent. "I don't see that millions of our fellow citizens constitute a mob."

"Don't you, indeed? Well, I say they are a mob and I won't be intimidated. Nor do I think that weakness will placate the mob. All experience shows that weakness will only encourage it."

"What I do concede, Prime Minister, is the danger of converting the Campaign into a mob through the brutal use of emergency powers."

The Prime Minister stared icily at Blake. He spoke quietly but with a grim determination. "I would have thought we've made too many concessions already. Let me remind you, we've allowed the media the freedom to spread their poisonous filth. We've given this maniac Hurst every freedom. We've allowed our own scientists to betray us. We've allowed this demonstration to go ahead, and where has it all led? It has led to a full scale national emergency with a protective cordon around Westminster. Now you want us to sit round a table with them? Is this a serious proposal, Blake?"

Blake continued to press his point. "Well," he said, "if we refuse to talk with them we should at least consider the likely consequences."

"I have considered them," said the Prime Minister. "We have every reserve of force capable of maintaining public order. That is the only consequence that interests me."

Dudney supported Blake. "Prime Minister, we all accept that law and order is paramount: there is no argument about that. It's simply a question, in present circumstances, of how best to preserve it. The Home Secretary has told us bluntly that we face a campaign of millions so obviously, we've got to be careful. As I understand these movements they tend to be unstable. They can suddenly appear but they can also disappear just as quickly, so we need time. I don't see any harm in gaining time by talking with this Campaign. In the meantime of course, we'll hold all our powers of control in reserve."

Bill Charman was quick to reinforce this view. "It may come to the point where we have to take the firmest line but we always have that option. Experience also shows that compromise can take the heat out of situations without necessarily giving anything away. At present, the Campaign is a pressure group. It's very strong, but it at least has no political identity. Its political elements run across the spectrum and tend to cancel each other out. That's what our reports tell us, and that's to our advantage. We've got to be damned careful not to force this campaign into a political mould. The way it's organised, that could be very dangerous indeed."

"I don't yet see Mr. Hurst as being able to lead the country," the Prime Minister snapped.

"No, well, perhaps not, but there are others, the shrewder minds that I've referred to. It should be obvious to Parliament that our emergency powers are justified but we've go to be careful how we present them to the country. Above all, we've got to be seen to be acting positively. The solution, in my view, is to talk to the Campaign and assure them that our emergency powers are a response to the threat of destruction; that we've brought them in for the protection of the population. Who could possibly object to that?"

"No one could object to it," added Blake, "but they will object in their millions to a reckless use of force."

The Prime Minister wavered. The two service chiefs had been silent. Unused to the artful methods of political manoeuvre they found it difficult to contribute. Moreover, their position was ambiguous. Whether their role was to help make decisions or merely to take instructions had not been made clear and they were intimidated by the Prime Minister, who had ignored their presence.

As the arguments of Blake, Bill Charman and Dudney began to congeal in firm opposition to his own the Prime Minister shifted his ground. Although disturbed by events and obsessed by fears his cunning and instinct for survival moved him towards them. "So," he said, "you're saying we should present our emergency powers as a precautionary move for the protection of the population?"

"In that way we could win public support for them," added Bill Charman, who then began to flatter the Prime Minister's vanity. "Prime Minister, you are the one to explain our actions to the country. You are the one to explain that we are responding positively to public anxiety. You could do this with a television broadcast. You're the one to rally the country round to the constructive use of emergency powers."

The Prime Minister yielded. "Yes," he said, "well, Home Secretary, if you think a broadcast from me would be useful, I suppose that's something I could do."

"And what about talking to the Campaign," Blake insisted. " They're demanding a meeting and we should go ahead with it. We could put the same arguments to them, that we're mobilising the forces for civil defence. It's the best means of countering their attack on us."

"And it would give us the breathing space we need," added Dudney.

With a pained expression, at last the Prime Minister conceded. "Yes," he said, "I suppose there's a certain logic in what you suggest."

The meeting continued until at last the Prime Minister was satisfied. He now saw his way clear to answering anything difficult from the House of Commons. He now had a plausible response to the Campaign, whilst behind his assurances, every reserve of force would be prepared to ensure the government's authority. He summarised their decisions. "I'll broadcast to the country. We'll meet a delegation from the Campaign and in the meantime," he said, speaking directly at the service chiefs, "I want every available unit of the army and the police fully mobilised. We don't want any more reports saying that the services or police have lost control and had to retreat. That's as far as we can go for the time being."

He collected his papers and beckoned to Blake and Bill Charman who joined him in close conversation. "About this meeting with the Campaign," he said, "you realise it's not for me. You're the ones to speak with these lunatics. Dudney is right, we need more time to deploy our forces so you can tell them what you like. Just make sure they go away from the meeting feeling happy."

"We'll see them tomorrow," said Bill Charman.

At last the Prime Minister appeared to relax. "I'll broadcast tomorrow night," he said. "Give me something I can use."

As the Prime Minister stalked from the Cabinet Room, Blake turned to Bill Charman. "They're bound to send Hurst."

"And Laurie," Bill replied. "I'll talk to Laurie and leave Hurst to you."

"He doesn't seem to be a man who listens."

"You're the great conciliator," Bill reminded him, "you'll think of something. It's an exercise in buying time."

"How much time?"

Bill Charman shrugged. "Who knows?"

Bill Charman left for the Home Office and Blake set out to return home. His official car came to a stop at the barriers which now surrounded the security zone. Trafalgar Square was shrouded in the evening gloom. Most of the demonstrators had dispersed or moved on to Hyde Park where a further rally had been organised. A few campaigners still stood in groups outside the defensive cordon. Some had intended to march into Whitehall but had been outmanoeuvred by the speedy actions of the security forces who now confronted them with the barriers and a solid show of force. A barrier was moved aside and Blake's car attracted little attention as it sped through the gap and took him home.

He found Rachel watching scenes from the demonstration on television. "It's your Mr. Hurst," she said. "It seems he has quite a talent for whipping up a crowd. You should see it."

He poured himself a drink. "I saw it the first time."

"What are you doing about it?"

"We're meeting with them."

"Saying what?"

"I've no idea," he said. "I imagine they'll do most of the talking."

"Ironic, don't you think?" she said. "First you lock Hurst away and now he's dictating terms."

Rachel was amused by the apparent fragility of power and by now Blake was used to her gentle teasing.

"It's not the only irony," he said.

"By the way, your agent phoned. He sounded quite worried."

"Clive Poole is always worried."

"Apparently, your local party has decided to support the Campaign. He says if you act against it you'll be in fresh conflict with them."

Blake sagged and took a seat on the couch. "That's all I need," he muttered.

18

The Campaign members had asked for the meeting to be held at a place of their choosing but Bill Charman took this to be an attempt to humiliate the government. He insisted that if they wanted serious talks their delegation would have to come to the Home Office. He had a further reason. By meeting in Whitehall the party from the Campaign would have to pass through the security zone where they would see the strength of the army and police defences.

Blake and Bill Charman waited in a conference room where eventually Hurst, Laurie and Betty Stevens were ushered in by an official. They seemed ill at ease and tense. Introductions were made and for the first time Blake confronted Hurst, face to face. For a fleeting moment he recalled the night of Hurst's arrest when events had been set in motion. He dismissed the thought and welcomed the tall figure who stood before him. "Hello, Mr. Hurst. It's a pleasure to meet you. We apologise for the absence of the Prime Minister. He wanted to be here but he's been advised to take some rest. Naturally, our concern for the problems you raise is keeping us all very busy."

Hurst ignored him and moved stiffly to a seat at the table. Laurie and Betty Stevens took their seats whilst the two Ministers sat opposite. Bill Charman took up Blake's friendly approach. "I'm sure we're in for a long discussion so make yourselves comfortable. We're having refreshments sent in; no doubt we'd like some coffee. We don't have an agenda so ...."

With a hard edge to his voice, Hurst cut him off. "We have a very definite agenda," he snapped.

Bill hesitated, taken aback by Hurst's hostility. "Yes, of course," he said. "All I'm suggesting is that we're free to raise any matters and we're here to be as helpful as possible."

"In that case," said Laurie, "Mr. Hurst wants to raise some personal questions."

Hurst sat erect in his seat. "I want to know who arrested me," he demanded. "It wasn't the police, so who was it? I want to know why I was arrested and who gave the order? I want to know why the Prime Minister lied when he said I was a spy."

Blake responded immediately. "Unfortunately, Mr. Hurst, the Prime Minister was badly advised and your arrest was an error of judgment which we all regret. You're right to say it wasn't the work of the police, it was the work of the security forces. I'm sure you agree, we do need them. They do a vital job but they're not perfect. Like all of us they can make mistakes. In your case, they were over-zealous and acted on false information. What they did was wrong but as soon as your arrest was known you were released and we apologise for any distress or inconvenience."

Hurst was unmoved and looked directly at Bill Charman. "Why isn't the Home Secretary answering? It's for him to reply."

Bill Charman took up Blake's conciliatory tone. "I can only endorse what my colleague has said. We apologise, unreservedly, for a serious error of judgment. What more can we say? Surely, we're here to be constructive about the future."

Hurst persisted. "Then why did you put a government agent into our organisation? We know a lot about this individual. We know his real name isn't Chivers."

This surprised Blake. The knowledge that "Chivers" was not the real name of the agent could only have come from the agent himself. For Blake, this confirmed the fear that "Chivers" had defected to the Campaign. In which case, it was certain that the delegation knew a great deal about the arrest of Hurst. For a moment both Blake and Bill Charman were embarrassed.

Blake tried to smooth over the situation. "Mr. Hurst, we both assure you, there is no intention in the government to interfere in the affairs of the Campaign. The proof of this is Dr. Sandra Dale. She is an important government scientist in a high security post yet she has complete freedom to work with you. She has spoken at your demonstration, which went ahead with no interference. We all want to work with your Campaign but please accept that where security is concerned people have a job to do and sometimes they make mistakes. We should get down to the real problems. Isn't that what we're here to talk about?"

Hurst glared at Blake. "Of course it is."

"Well then, can we get on? It's you who insist that we don't have much time."

"Even so," said Laurie, "we want the Home Secretary's assurance that there will be no more interference in our Campaign. We won't particularly trust what he says, but for what it's worth we want that assurance now and we want it on record."

Bill Charman could barely hide his discomfort. "There's no question," he said. "I need hardly say, I don't hesitate in giving that assurance. But may I repeat what my colleague has said; we should get down to our real problems."

Betty Stevens intervened. "Home Secretary, obviously you are recording this meeting but you will notice that I am taking notes which we intend to publish. We shall put out a statement that the government has apologised for the arrest of Mr. Hurst and for placing an agent on our Committee. We shall also publish your assurance of no more interference in our Campaign."

"That's entirely up to you," said Bill. "I would say, let's get on."

"Will you put out a similar statement?" she asked.

Lamely, Bill agreed. "If that's what you want, we'll certainly consider it."

Blake could only smile. Knowing that they commanded the support of millions, the delegation had drawn its first blood. It was also likely that with the defection of "Chivers" they were in possession of a vast amount of government information. The Prime Minister had been right to say that the meeting would be a humiliation.

Laurie continued, "I agree we should get on." He went on to insist that the meeting would be the first of a series which would enable the Campaign to monitor the government's response to its demands. He said they wanted a statement of intent from the government which would be a commitment to carry out the Campaign's plans for the protection of the population; these would be plans for the construction of deep shelters throughout the country. Also, they were seeking a guarantee that the government would begin work on the plans as soon as they were presented.

Bill Charman replied that the forces were already being mobilised and this would provide a range of skills and equipment that could quickly be applied to the construction of shelters. Laurie found this unacceptable. "We are not interested in token work by the forces using spare army equipment," he said. "We want your guarantee that you will carry out our plans for a massive programme of deep shelter construction, and that you will do it in full consultation with us."

Bill Charman insisted that he and Blake were not empowered to commit the government to such a programme of work but that they could put the proposal forward with their recommendation that it be accepted. In the meantime they recognised the urgency and he again emphasised that they had taken steps to mobilise the forces for the work of civil defence.

At this, Laurie became angry. "Home Secretary," he said firmly, "we haven't come here to waste our time, or to be insulted by your evasions. In fact we have no need to depend on this particular government. Do you want us to walk out now and tell millions of people that you are not interested? We'll do that, it's up to you, but if we do walk out you will have to bear the consequences."

This was a threat to replace the government. For the two Ministers, the object of the meeting was to buy time and ensure that the delegation left the meeting feeling reasonably happy. It looked impossible. As Bill Charman's restraint was being tested by the stream of aggressive questions and demands, his patience seemed to be running out.

Blake intervened. "From your side it may look simple but it's more than a question of drawing up plans. Such a programme of work would cost billions of pounds. As well as plans, are your people working on the costings?" He looked directly at Laurie. "You do agree it will all have to be paid for?"

For the first time Laurie hesitated. "Yes," he said, "of course."

"So, you are working on the costings?" Blake repeated.

Laurie turned to Betty Stevens. "Are we looking at that side?" he asked.

She looked uncertain. "I imagine they are taking costs into account."

Blake pressed her. "But you're not sure?"

"We were more concerned with the actual plans and the number of deep shelters required," she said, "after all, the government would have to pay for them."

Blake pressed her further. "But we already have those plans, Mrs. Stevens. You're not offering us anything new. They have existed for years, and deep shelters have been built, but carrying out the plans will require a vast amount of money. Surely you agree?"

"I suppose so."

"Good, and you must also be aware of the government's lack of funds. You've seen what's happened in the hospitals. The Home Secretary has explained that we are mobilising the services because that can be done at little cost. The Prime Minister will broadcast tonight and he will announce the government's programme of action. However, if you walk out of this meeting it could only be because you are turning your backs on the positive steps the government is taking. I'm sure that's not what your supporters would want. On the other hand you may agree that we are taking action which has been more carefully worked out. So, how do you react to this? Do you accept that we are ahead of you and proceeding in a more practical way?"

The delegation was now in a difficulty. They were inexperienced bargainers and they had no answer to the question of costs. Their main strength had been in their threat to walk out but Blake had forestalled this, warning that if they did so, he would use it against them amongst their supporters. Momentarily uncertain, Laurie turned to Hurst and Betty Stevens. "What do you think?" he asked.

"I think we should discuss it on our own," replied Betty Stevens.

Laurie faced Bill Charman. "We need to talk in private," he said.

Bill Charman stood up. "By all means," he said. "Please do. Just say when you'd like us back."

The two Ministers left an official outside the room and went through to Bill Charman's office. "I thought all their business was open," said Bill. "They say they have no secrets, but they're talking in private now."

"But they know the room is bugged," said Blake.

"Yes, but it still makes them hypocrites."

"Hurst let it slip that they know Chivers' real name."

"I heard that," said Bill. "We believe he's taken up with Janice Fearn and defected to the Campaign. That's why he's disappeared." He thought for a moment and then added grimly, "but we'll find him."

"This Campaign could test the loyalty of a lot of people," said Blake. "They could develop a whole network of informers within the government. We'll be leaking like a sieve."

A depressed look crossed Bill's face. "It's nothing new. I've said all along, we can't trust anyone."

They discussed the meeting so far and noted that when Hurst was not ranting on about the impending catastrophe he had very little to say. Bill Charman had always known that Laurie would be more difficult, but the weakness of the delegation arose from the question of costs. It was evident that the Campaign had been so demanding of a massive programme of deep shelter construction that the crucial matter of finance had eluded them. "Like all such movements," said Bill, "they don't live in the real world." They agreed to continue pressing the Campaigners to produce costings.

The official knocked on their door and said the meeting could now continue. The two Ministers rejoined the delegation and Laurie resumed. "We've got some questions."

Bill Charman maintained his friendly response. "Of course," he said, "ask us anything you like."

It became evident that Laurie was aware of the emergency measures the government was putting in place. He knew they came from a Civil Defence Review and provided for 13 regional areas controlled by the army and the police. He also knew that the entire country would be under the control of just six individuals acting under the euphemistic title, "Civil Contingencies Unit."

Laurie put it frankly to Bill Charman. "Sole power will be with a tiny section of the government." He was getting dangerously close to the real intentions of the government in setting up its emergency powers.

Bill Charman was anxious to divert him. "You shouldn't see it that way," he said. "We're talking about national cooperation not central control. The work of local people will have to be coordinated.

That will be the job of the government unit. We're talking about coordination not central direction."

"We've anticipated your reply," said Laurie, "and it is unacceptable. We will not trust a structure of power controlled by a handful of Ministers. However, your Civil Contingencies Unit could be accepted if it includes members of our Campaign Committee and if its meetings were open to the public."

This demand was impossible and whilst Blake could only smile, Bill Charman looked uncomfortable. "Well," he said, "I do remind you that Ministers are answerable to Parliament whose members have been elected by the country." He was unable to resist a note of sarcasm. "But your honourable members have not been elected by anybody."

Laurie was unmoved. "If you press that point, Home Secretary, you could be replaced by a government that does represent our millions of supporters."

"But your suggestion would be unconstitutional," Bill insisted, "it wouldn't be legal."

"On the contrary, it will be the real test of whether you are serious about cooperating with our Campaign. If you don't want to cooperate just say so now and we'll all know where we stand."

To avoid a stalemate Blake intervened. "I'm sure you've given us something to think about," he said to Laurie. "You want Campaign members on the Civil Contingencies Unit and you want its meetings open to the public. Well, as the Home Secretary says, it raises complex constitutional issues that are far beyond our powers of decision. You don't want meaningless assurances, do you, so you'll have to give us time."

"We'll give you forty-eight hours," said Laurie. "We'll meet again in two days' time and you can give us your answer then."

"Alright," replied Blake. "We'll consider it and let you know." He then decided to put Laurie back on the defensive. "From our side we are saying that we have made a practical start in response to the approaching dangers, do you accept that?"

"For the time being we'll reserve our judgment."

Blake pointed to Betty Steven's notes, "Are you placing on record that you don't accept the government's emergency action?"

"I didn't say that," Laurie protested. "I said it wouldn't be enough."

"So, you won't even accept it as a useful start? Do you want action or not?"

"Of course we want action."

"Then why are you being evasive?"

Laurie was no match for an experienced verbal campaigner like Blake, who was now determined to take something from the meeting that the Prime Minister could use in his broadcast. "Say now whether or not you approve the government's emergency action," he continued. "That is a test of whether you are being sincere."

"We haven't come here to be harassed."

"Perhaps not," said Blake, "but we're beginning to wonder why you have come here."

Betty Stevens tried to reply. "Our only object is immediate action," she said.

Blake turned to her. "With respect, Mrs. Stevens, I'm beginning to doubt it. I have asked you a straightforward question. Do you approve of the government's action to protect the population?"

She hesitated. "Well, of course."

"Good, your approval is on record."

"But we insist it won't be enough," added Laurie.

Blake softened his tone. "That's a fair point. We can agree on that."

Hurst had been silent. As a lone scientist amidst the tortured argument he was at a loss, and as it continued, he was unable to contain his frustration. He interrupted in a loud voice. "All this talk is getting us nowhere. Don't you realise, even as we sit here the dangers are approaching. This is a life or death matter and all we're doing is playing with words. I'll tell you about costs; the costs in human life if we do nothing."

Precisely," said Blake. "That is why the government has taken urgent action and we are glad to see that you approve. So, when we meet in two days' time we expect to see your plans together with detailed and viable costs for a nationwide programme of deep shelter construction."

Laurie was uncertain. "I don't see the costs as the work of our Campaign."

"Why not?" Blake asked. "You've got as much information as we have. The details of government finance are freely published, so we expect to see from you a fully costed programme."

"There could be other means," said Laurie. "Perhaps not everything would have to be paid for. There could be voluntary work. You're using it in the hospitals and we know about the community schemes in the cities. If the government cooperates with our Campaign, we're in a position to organise the voluntary work of millions of people."

This took Blake by surprise. It was clear that the Campaign was in close touch with every development. He wanted to take up Laurie's suggestion but he wasn't free to get ahead of Bill Charman or his position in the government. Nevertheless, he encouraged Laurie's line of thought. "Then perhaps in two days' time you will also present us with plans for the use of voluntary workers?"

"That would depend on Campaign members being part of your Civil Contingencies Unit," insisted Laurie.

Blake knew this was a demand too far. The Prime Minister would never agree to it but there might be other ways of including the Campaign. "Yes, well," he said, "we've agreed to consider it. We've pointed out the problems. That would seem to be as far as we can go at the moment. We hope you think it's been useful."

Laurie remained impassive. "We'll see," he said.

Bill Charman proposed that the two sides should issue a joint statement saying they were working together but after a brief exchange amongst themselves the delegation refused. Laurie insisted there was no basis for a joint statement as clearly they were not yet working together. Bill Charman also suggested that the Campaign could show some goodwill by calling off its demonstrations. He pointed out that the need to provide security reduced the availability of the army and police for the work of civil defence. Laurie remained adamant. "We'll stop our actions when we've got your cooperation," he said. "So far we've got nothing."

The delegation prepared to leave with Laurie still hostile. "There is one other thing, Home Secretary," he said. "Under the emergency you'll have wide powers of arrest, the use of lethal force, internment, special courts, control of communications and all movement. What is the true reason behind the Civil Contingencies Unit? Is it repression? Is it simply a means of controlling the population?"

"If that was our aim we wouldn't be talking to you now," replied Bill. "We've explained its purpose and you've given it your approval."

"That's if you're telling the truth. If not, you should know that many in the army and police support our Campaign. Their families have written to us sending money. If you attempt to use the army to put down our movement, that will be the end of you." Laurie moved out with Hurst and Betty Stevens. "I thought it right to mention that," he said, finally.

As the delegation was escorted from the room a large tray was brought in and placed on the table. Blake smiled. "I think Laurie has the measure of us," he said. "We're not going to fool them." He contemplated the tray of refreshments. "Not a very friendly lot, are they? They didn't even stay for a free cup of government coffee."

"With the huge support they have they don't need to be friendly," said Bill. "If we had that kind of support we certainly wouldn't be talking with them. Even so, we got something out of the meeting; in fact, more than I hoped for.

Blake reached for his coffee. "Yes, all of two days' respite."

"We've got their approval of what we're doing on record. I'll get a transcript to the Prime Minister and he can use it in his broadcast. That's one thing he's good at."

"It's all just words, Bill. We use them, but what do they mean? We speak from minds in which everything is distorted and no one listens. We never get through to each other. By the way, when the Prime Minister knows they want their people on the Civil Contingencies Unit, he'll explode."

"And all its meetings open to the public," said Bill. "It's democracy gone mad."

Blake reminded him, "I thought you were in favour of the open society."

"Of course I am, but not that bloody open."

19

On being driven to his Department from the Home Office, Blake was now accompanied by a bodyguard. As the short journey was within the security zone he thought the protection absurd and he looked at the tight lipped individual sitting next to him. "What's happening outside the zone?" he asked.

"A big build-up of demonstrators, sir."

"And you think they're a threat to me?"

"It's my job to assume that."

"Yes, but what do you think… personally?"

"I just do my job."

"Are you carrying a firearm?"

"It's routine, sir."

Within minutes they arrived at the Department where Blake went to his office. Amongst the items that Janet mentioned was the news that Frank Bell had phoned wanting a meeting between the TUC and the government. Janet was aware that the Secretary of the TUC and Blake had become enemies and it was with an ironic smile that she added, "he sounded quite friendly."

Blake guessed that Frank Bell was feeling pushed aside by the Campaign. "It's his job to be hostile to the government," he said. "He doesn't approve of usurpers."

The ever anxious Clive Poole had also phoned. Blake phoned him back. It seemed that his local party had been joined by a radical activist of great popularity named Erica Field. She was now fully involved with the Campaign and it appeared that she had joined for a particular purpose. Her intention was that the local party should lead a move to occupy a security bunker that had been built in the City against the threat of nuclear attack in the 1950s. The bunker was situated in the main car park beside the Town Hall and the object of the Campaign was to use it as a deep shelter and also as one of its own control centres.

The bunker was now an important link in the government's communications system operating under the Civil Contingencies Unit and Blake was reminded of Laurie's threat to step up the Campaign's pressure. He also realised that any move against the bunker would mean violent confrontation with the security forces. "You say they are only talking about it?" he asked.

"I'm not sure how far it's gone," Clive replied. "The Campaign is well organised here and if they made a decision they could move fast. If you want to prevent Erica Field from getting our Party involved you'd better get up here and bring a definite programme for public protection. It's the only way to head things off. Otherwise we've got a battle on our hands. I don't mean arguments, I mean blood on the streets." Clive paused then added, "the meeting is tomorrow morning."

Blake put down the phone. Events were heading inevitably towards violence. He considered the forces that were now summoning their strengths. First, the government with its massive powers of force; then the Campaign, issuing threats and ultimatums, ready to move against the security forces with the support of millions. If the dangers from the comet were real it was approaching with a deadly ability to cause disarray amongst its victims. They should be united. Instead, their strengths were dissipating in renewed conflict.

Janet brought in an evening paper and pointed to its main headline. "Government Snubs Campaign." Blake read on.

"At today's meeting between Ministers and a delegation from the Campaign, the government refused to give any assurance that it would cooperate with its National Committee. Speaking to demonstrators just outside the security zone, Mr Hurst later described the meeting as a 'waste of time.' 'This is clear proof to the people that the government refuses to prepare the country against the threat of annihilation,' he said. There will be a further meeting in two days' time when the Campaign will again attempt to secure the cooperation of the government. In the meantime, the government has said it is allocating every available resource from the services to the work of protecting the public. For this to be possible it has appealed for an end to all demonstrations. It has been announced from Downing Street that the Prime Minister will broadcast to the country tonight."

Blake felt that the report was reasonably balanced and was relieved to see that there was no mention of the Campaign demand to have its members on the Civil Contingencies Unit. He was, however, annoyed when Janet informed him that he was no longer free to move about the country at will.

"Whose idea is this?" he asked.

"It comes from the Home Office," Janet replied. "You are now subject to close security cover."

"Then get me Bill Charman."

Janet made the connection. "Bill," he demanded, "what's this about my travel? First you dump an armed goon on me and now I have to clear all my movements with you."

"You've got it all wrong," Bill assured him. "You can go where you like but you are subject to the security cover assigned to all members of the Civil Contingencies Unit."

"I don't need your bodyguards."

"Don't be difficult, Blake. It's policy." Bill Charman changed the subject. "You realise your local party is about to assist the Campaign in taking over our security bunker in your City? They're being led by

Erica Field and she's a bundle of trouble. We've got enough files on her to fill a library."

"That's why I'm going up there."

"Good. Now you're more popular you might get them to see some sense."

"You're wrong on two counts. First, I'm not popular and second, they don't see sense. What about my travel?"

"You'll go by helicopter," Bill replied. "Noisy, perhaps, but a lot more direct. You'll go straight to the bunker. We can't have you roaming the country without security cover."

"And you should realise, Bill, we can't govern the country by remote control...."

"I would never suggest it."

"The day we can't show our faces in public we're finished."

"Really, Blake. You do dramatise."

Blake slammed down the phone, walked to the window and stared down. The crowds and normal traffic had disappeared from Whitehall, leaving only the movement of police and troops. He thought back over the morning meeting with the Campaign and the sticking points that might make further discussions difficult. Their demand to have a place on the Civil Contingencies Unit was naïve, or, knowing that it was impossible, a shrewd means of showing that the government was being uncooperative. If it was merely a ploy, how could it be outmanoeuvred?

He turned to the bookcases that lined his office and looked for references to the work of a previous coalition, the Second World War National Government. Though circumstances had been different, that coalition had dealt with a similar problem of how best to secure national cooperation at a time of great threat. As one means of achieving this it had set up a National Consultative Council. The council had provided a forum in which every problem of the wartime crisis had been discussed and though it had few powers of decision, it had brought together a number of important bodies. To Blake it seemed an ideal solution and he began to draft a plan for a new National Consultative Council that could include the Campaign, the TUC, the Confederation of Industries and the government. Though it would be an advisory body only, Blake guessed that Frank Bell would grasp any opportunity to be involved at the centre of events. Demanding powers of decision-making, the Campaign would be more suspicious, but their refusal to participate would place the government in a good position to say they were evading responsibility. In failing to join, but with the TUC present, the Campaign would risk isolation.

The main problem returned again and again to his thoughts. What would be the use of national consultation if the finance for deep shelter protection was lacking? For the moment he set these worries aside and continued to work on his plans, drawing on more references from wartime crises of the past. As the evening drew on he was mindful of the time. It was important to return home to join Rachel in hearing the Prime Minister's broadcast; much would depend on it. He put his papers together and left the office.

In the deserted street outside his office his car was waiting with its driver and now, two bodyguards. He felt embarrassed as he got into the back seat. The car moved off and soon came to a stop behind the ranks of police and troops at the boundary of the security zone. In Trafalgar Square stood groups of campaigners. The atmosphere was sinister; quiet but threatening. Barriers were opened up and his car passed through with his bodyguards watchful, observing the crowds for any sign of a suspicious or sudden movement. Beyond the square the car sped on.

Blake insisted that the vehicle should stop a distance from his home. After some protest from his protectors the car came to a stop. He got out and walked the last hundred yards, relieved to be free of the trappings of state security. He let himself in and joined Rachel in the lounge where she poured him his usual drink.

"Thanks," he said. "There's something you should know. We've got bodyguards camped out on our doorstep. Sorry about that."

"Literally on the doorstep?" she asked.

"Well, somewhere out there."

"That is charming."

"There's nothing I can do. I'm told they'll be discreet."

"So, now you need bodyguards?"

"That's what they tell me."

Rachel had observed Blake's steady acceptance of things he had always opposed. "So now you need protection? Who from? Is this supposed to be the politics of national accord?"

Caught between the pressures of political reality and the need to uphold his principles, Blake was naturally disappointed to give an impression of compromise, especially to Rachel whom he knew to be a person of integrity. Even so, he had at least an intuitive sense that what he was doing was right. He was also becoming unwilling to explain the complexities of his situation. In answer to Rachel's question about the politics of national accord he could only say, "I'm not sure what happened to that."

He relaxed on the couch as Rachel passed him a piece of paper. It was a Campaign leaflet with an account of the meeting that day with the government at the Home Office. "They're giving them away by the thousand," she said. "It's freedom of information, you understand."

He glanced at the leaflet, impressed by the ability of the Campaign to communicate so speedily with the entire population. "It's freedom of their information," he said.

"So, the meeting didn't go well? Rachel asked.

"It could have been worse."

"You mean you could have strangled each other? You might get a second opportunity. I see you're meeting them again."

"Yes, but they're not really talking, except between themselves. In fact they're getting nasty. They're moving in on government installations, hoping to take them over. I've got to go north tomorrow. That's where part of the action is being planned. They'll never succeed. All it means is violent confrontation."

"So, there'll be more self-inflicted injuries with the medical services picking up the pieces," she said.

He shrugged and looked at his watch. "I don't want to bore you but I'd like to catch the Prime Minister's broadcast."

She switched on the television and sat beside him. The broadcast came from Downing Street and showed the Prime Minister sitting behind a large desk. Blake noticed that he looked fresh with no trace of anxiety as he smiled into the camera. He was always at his best when performing in public. His smile faded as he contrived a more earnest look.

"I want to talk to you tonight about recent events which some people are describing as a crisis. I want to speak frankly about the truth of these events and I want to tell you what the government is doing.

Like most of you I have become aware of various claims that suggest we're heading for a time of danger. But I suggest to you that the more immediate danger is that we may be taken over by fear, panic and hysteria. We should all remember that there is nothing new about such predictions. In the past, if all the so-called sightings of space objects had been true we would now be taken over by all sorts of alien creatures. We would have been attacked by all sorts of destructive forces. The fact is, it has never happened, and those of us who kept our normal senses never believed it would. It is up to all of us now to keep things in a proper balance.

This is certainly no time for complacency but it is a time for separating fact from fiction. What we know is that our home in space, Earth, is being approached by a large comet, but the passage of a comet is a normal space event so there is nothing about it that should cause us alarm.

What is also a fact is that our comet will pass relatively close to Earth and it is because of this that we have been drawn into sinister speculation. It's being suggested that because of the heat of the sun, combined with Earth's gravitational force, much of the comet's cargo of rocks will become detached and will be pulled towards us as missiles. But we should remind ourselves of yet another important fact. Around 50,000 fragments of space debris fall to Earth every year and most of us are unaware of these because they are harmless. I have to say to you that there is no reliable evidence that any rock debris will be large enough to survive a passage through our atmosphere. Any suggestion that we will suffer a space bombardment is theoretical speculation, and I want to say a word about that.

It is right that science should be held in high esteem but it is part of science that it involves assumptions which are yet to be proven. Science is a human activity carried on by people with all the frailties of being human. This can mean that scientists can have certain ideas and they become, quite naturally, anxious to show that they are true. This can take them into claims that cannot, upon close examination, be justified. The idea that we are heading inevitably towards a bombardment from space should be treated with a great deal of caution. I repeat, there is no firm evidence for it.

But I have also said that we will not be complacent. It is right that the government should respond to the concern that is being expressed. As a precaution, we have taken steps to make our combined Services available for the work of civil defence. This work is being directed by a special government team, a Civil Contingencies Unit.

We have also begun talks with the popular movement that has gained so much support and today its representatives endorsed the government's actions. This constructive attitude is very much to be welcomed.

But I want to say one other thing. It is possible at a time like this that past misunderstandings and past disappointments could be used to create fresh conflicts. Unfortunately, there are some who will seek to exploit these feelings for their own ends. They won't be so concerned with any possible dangers to our community. They'll seize any opportunity to create chaos in pursuit of their political objectives. But I am sure we can rely on the common sense of our people to resist any attempt to cause disruption. I know you will all give your full support to any steps which may have to be taken to ensure safety and public order.

So, we shall keep matters in their proper balance. We won't be complacent but nor will we be prone to rumour and alarm. We shall carry on with our normal working lives and all our plans for normal living. At the same time we shall take every necessary step in protecting our community.

When I look forward I can tell you that my family is planning another holiday in the West Country. We love that part of our island and have arranged to spend some time there again. We plan to relax and enjoy ourselves. We're taking our grandchildren and we hope this member of the family enjoys it too... "

The Prime Minister took up his pipe and stooped to stroke a golden retriever that padded up to him. The image was then faded from the screen, leaving an impression of calm domesticity and continuity towards a safe future.

Once again Blake marvelled at the wide gulf between the Prime Minister's public and private personalities. It had been a soothing performance. However, from what he had seen of the work of Sandra Dale and her team of scientists, work that was being confirmed daily by other authorities around the world, it was clear that the Prime Minister had glossed over the very real dangers. For all his instinct and talent for survival, this may have been an error of judgment that would come back to haunt him.

Ever sceptical, Rachel was also amused. "He strokes the public the same way he strokes his pet," she said. "Who arranged the walk-on part for the dog?"

"The dog isn't a prop," said Blake. "It really is his. He prefers it to his colleagues."

"And who wrote the script? Was it you?" she asked.

"No," he replied. "It was all his own work."

"So, what did he say?"

"He said you can't trust scientists and there's a lot of frustration that troublemakers have blown up for their own ends. He said that things could get out of hand so the army is being deployed to control the population and in the meantime there will be no concession to anyone's demands."

"That's your translation."

He shrugged. "I know the language. It's part of my job to invent it."

"And who invented the Civil Contingencies Unit?" she asked. "You should call it the Civil Control Unit."

"Yes, well. That might well be true, but we can't call it that."

"And now you're going north to be involved in violence?"

"I'm hoping to avoid it," he said.

"You've got to admit, Blake, in spite of everything you've tried to do, things have got worse."

Reluctantly he agreed. "Yes," he said. "That's right."

Rachel pressed him. "I know you're trying to avoid the worst but you know damned well you've got no control." Her voice became more serious. "So don't be too compromised. All I ask is that you don't come back with a lot of blood on your hands. May I ask that?"

It was a prospect that he had never envisaged. He felt embarrassed and his response was weak. "Of course," he said.

"When the world goes mad," she continued, "there has to come a time when you decide to have nothing to do with it. And it's better to make that decision sooner than later."

For a moment he stared into his glass. "I am aware of that option," he murmured.

20

Before going on to Downing Street for a meeting of the Civil Contingencies Unit, Blake sat in his office noting the press comment on the Prime Minister's broadcast. He was disappointed to see that it was reserved.

"Although the Prime Minister set out to be reassuring, his broadcast raised more questions than it answered. He appeared to recognise the need for civil defence but made no mention of what work would be done or how it could be financed. Public anxiety will not be eased until these matters are explained."

He took up a second editorial.

"The Prime Minister has warned against panic but we must warn the government against any abuse that could arise from its use of emergency powers. The sole object is to free the Services for the speedy work of civil defence. This commitment must be honoured. The government has been given no licence to act against our democratic institutions and, in particular, the freedom of the press must be upheld."

These were clear warnings that any attempt by the government to abuse its new powers would be resisted. The Campaign had established its own network of communications capable of reaching every person in the country. If the press also became hostile, it would leave the government isolated. It was a danger.

He chatted with Janet to get her impressions of the broadcast. She thought the Prime Minister had spoken well. "Everyone I have spoken to is glad that things are moving," she said.

Blake was relieved to hear that the Prime Minister had gained some goodwill amongst his listeners. For them he had said the right things and perhaps it was not so important that he had failed to convince the press.

He swallowed his coffee and again took the short but guarded route through the security zone to Downing Street. He took his seat next to Bill Charman, who pushed a file in front of him. "You asked about Erica Field," he said, "that's her file. She's a troublemaker if ever there was one. And I've had more information," he added. "The Campaign is definitely moving in on the control centre in your City. They plan to take it over. You'll see from her file that Erica Field has got a strong position both in the Campaign and in your local party. She's the one you'll have to deal with."

The Prime Minister arrived late. Blake had expected him to be encouraged by the results of his broadcast but instead he looked tired and grim-faced. He sat down, set out some papers and at last looked up. "I've been delayed," he said. "I've heard from our American colleagues. They confirm our own scientists' observations of the comet except for its size. They now feel it's a lot bigger than our own people had originally supposed."

The members of the unit observed the Prime Minister's depressed mood as he continued quietly. "They're launching a space probe that should ensure more precise details. They're working as fast as they can and of course, I've promised them all the help we can give."

"Are they making the information public?" asked Bill Charman.

"They don't need to," the Prime Minister snarled as he glared round the table. "The whole damned business is out in the open. We can't keep a single word confidential. The point of their message was to inform us first and it's going to make things a lot more difficult. People are going to seize on it... blow it all up again. I thought last night that we'd managed to calm things down but this new information will give these Campaign lunatics fresh justification... and I see they're stepping up their actions."

The Unit remained silent as the Prime Minister shuffled through his papers. "We've got to face the fact," he continued, "that in the recent demonstrations we lost control. In some places the police abandoned their positions. They were forced to retreat. It appears they were taken by surprise so perhaps we shouldn't blame them. I'm not blaming anyone but we can't use that excuse again. We now know what we're up against. It's more serious than a threat to public order. It's a threat to the government; a challenge to its authority. In view of this I want to make it clear; from now on we place no limitations on the use of force." Once more he looked round at every member of the Civil Contingencies Unit. "I want to repeat that," he emphasised, "from now on, wherever we have to maintain the authority of the government, we place no limitation on the use of force. There will be no more reports about losing control."

He paused to allow his remarks to sink into the minds of everyone present, then continued. "I want to list three priorities. First, we have to maintain all essential services. These include transport, communications, power supplies, food supplies and medical services. These are all listed in detail in the Civil Defence Review and, from now on, army personnel must be in a state of readiness to ensure that they continue to operate. Second, we must be in a position to control all movement and keep all public places clear of demonstrators. Third, we must safeguard the security of every administrative centre and every government installation."

The Prime Minister looked towards Brigadier Culverton. "It will be up to you, Brigadier," he said, "to communicate these priorities to every army commander in all areas. You will work with the Police Commissioner and all the facilities of the Home Office. Any questions?" he asked.

Culverton was quick to respond. "I foresee no difficulties, Prime Minister. We do have some logistical problems arising from the movement and disposition of troops but I'm sure these will be quickly overcome."

"You realise that you are now acting under powers to requisition any building in any location," the Prime Minister said.

"I do understand that."

"Anything else?"

Culverton was satisfied. "Not for the moment. We can iron out any details as we get into the operation."

The Prime Minister turned to the Police Commissioner. "What about you Anderson? Do you see any problems?"

"No, I don't think so," Anderson replied. "The contingency plans are comprehensive. Most things seem to have been anticipated but there is one grey area. In the past, and this has also arisen from our computer models, where the police and the army have worked together some confusion has arisen over command and responsibility. On the scale we now envisage, where there is joint action by the police and the army, what precisely will be the chain of command? If we are to act decisively, this should be clarified."

"That is a most important question," said the Prime Minister, "and I hope you won't resent the answer. All the combined forces must take their orders, ultimately, from the army commander on the spot. What I am saying here is that the police chiefs must work within a chain of command under the Services. Is that clear enough for you."

Anderson persisted. "If I may say so, Prime Minister, the police do have more experience of crowd and riot control. We are trained for it and I'm not sure the army has that training. We've got the organisation, the National Reporting Centre and the Police Support Groups. These have been most effective in controlling the disruptions of the past. The army hasn't got this experience. They haven't got ..."

The Prime Minister suddenly brought his fist down on the table and shouted at Anderson. "Stop now Commissioner. I don't want to hear your arguments. We're not just dealing with strikes. We're dealing with a threat to the government and haven't I just reminded you that the police lost control. From now on you will operate under the Army. You will pass that direction to every police rank. If you're unhappy about it then say so now and I will relieve you."

In the face of the Prime Minister's formidable anger Anderson backed down. "No.. of course," he said. "I quite see the point."

The Prime Minister continued his tirade. "I began by asking you not to resent it. There is no grey area. There will be no confusion. If any difficulties arise I will hold you personally responsible. Is it clear to you now?"

"Yes," said Anderson. "I do understand that, Prime Minister."

The Prime Minister softened his tone. "Naturally," he said, "the police will have a lot to do on their own. In these cases you will carry on as normal. Is there anything else?"

Anderson was now reluctant to raise any further matter. "No," he said. "I've already mentioned... arrangements are well covered by the contingency plans."

Blake could only smile at the contrast between the homely style of the Prime Minister's broadcast and his tough, uncompromising manner in the government unit. Then he had talked about family holidays, now he was grim-faced and resolute. Perhaps it was inherent in the body politic that it should distrust the apparatus of state power. Whether or not the Prime Minister was conscious of this, his exchange with Anderson had been a further opportunity to stamp his authority on the service chiefs. The incident left no doubt that he was their overlord.

The political members of the unit went on to discuss the need for a government information service designed to reassure the public. Blake knew that with no credible plan for the protection of communities, any public relations exercise would be seen as propaganda, masking the government's real intention to control the population.

It was also becoming clear that there were great dangers in the extraordinary powers commanded by the Prime Minister. He was a shrewd, self-confident politician but he was also flawed by vanity and obsessive fears and these could lead to a faltering of his tactical skills. Acting too much alone, with these weaknesses, he could lead the government into great difficulties. The meeting had convinced Blake that the Prime Minister's sole reliance on force was in danger of ignoring the wider realities in which the government unit had to operate and which in the long run would be decisive in determining the outcome of events.

To offset these dangers, Blake realised that a broader-based forum for public discussion was necessary. He took out his plans for a National Consultative Council and explained how such a body had been so useful in a previous crisis. "We could invite the Campaign to participate," he said. "In that way they would be directly involved with the problems of civil defence."

The suggestion immediately roused the suspicions of the Prime Minister. "I'm not sure what you mean by civil defence," he said. "In any case it can only be a government matter. I've no idea what you mean by involving the Campaign."

Blake persisted. "If we bring the Campaign into consultation they would see the difficulties at first hand and this would encourage them to be more realistic. In that case, they would moderate their demands."

"But they're not interested," the Prime Minister insisted. "You know what they want. They want a place on this government Unit. They've told you that."

"That's precisely why I'm suggesting a National Consultative Council, Prime Minister. It would be separate from our own machinery but it would give them a voice on an official national body. We could promote the offer as a constructive move and if they refused to participate we could use it against them. It would prove their irresponsibility and that would help us to isolate them."

The Prime Minister was much more cautious with his political colleagues than with the service chiefs but he was still a long way from accommodating the Campaign. "Yes, Blake," he said, "I can see your objective but I'm damned if I'm going to sit down with anyone like Hurst even if it is on a useless body like a consultative council. We might consider bringing in the TUC, they're asking for a meeting. You could patch up your quarrel with Frank Bell and put it to him. See how he reacts, but there's no question of bringing in this Campaign. You know perfectly well what they're doing in your own area. They're moving to take over our control centre. By breaking the law in that way they've disqualified themselves from being part of any official body. I understand you are going up there tomorrow?"

"Yes."

"Well, I've given instructions to establish a security zone around that bunker and I want you to see that it's enforced. You'll go directly to work with the local army commander." The Prime Minister shuffled through his papers. "I've got his name here..."

Culverton reminded him. "His name is Champney, Prime Minister. Lieutenant Colonel Champney."

"Yes," said the Prime Minister, "and remember, Blake, this gives us an opportunity to establish our absolute authority. When we've done that we can think about a few concessions; things like a National Consultative Council. If we do it, we'll do it from a position of strength."

For a moment their eyes met. The Prime Minister's stare was that of a man anxious to soothe his fears by relying on force. Blake was concerned to avoid violent confrontation. He replied to the Prime Minister quietly. "I hear what you say, Prime Minister, and I would ask you to remember my own words. We will never, I emphasise, never, enforce these emergency powers without some support from the majority of the public. National consultation is vital."

Blake's reply had carried an edge of threat. The Prime Minister frowned but resisted a hostile response. "Dammit, Blake, I've said we'll make some concessions but only from a position of strength. That will be when we're certain there is no threat to the government. If that mob takes over our control centre where do you think it will leave us? We cannot contemplate that. We don't contemplate any weakness of any kind and it will be your job to liaise between the army commander and Whitehall." The Prime Minister at last left some room for compromise. "We'll monitor what happens and then review the situation. That's as far as we can go for now. We've all got a lot to do so let's get on with it."

Abruptly, the Prime Minister adjourned the meeting and left the room. Blake turned to Bill Charman. "Suddenly, I can see the streets running with blood."

Bill shrugged. "If you've no taste for it you'd better say so but before you do, remember that others would do the job. I think it's better for you to be up there than some I can think of."

"It might be better to let the Campaign take over," said Blake. "We'll see how they deal with the problems."

"There'd be no point," replied Bill. "They'd replace us and find themselves in exactly our position. They'd spawn another Campaign and we would all be back to where we are now."

"We could at least offer them a place on a consultative council. It wouldn't get in our way. It would only be a talking shop."

"Then offer it to them," said Bill.

"Behind the Prime Minister's back?"

"Yes. Do it. I'll support it and I'm sure Dudney will agree."

Blake thought about how the Prime Minister would respond. "He'd throw the three of us out of this Unit," he said.

"No way," said Bill. "If he got rid of us he'd be stranded with a gang of sycophants, leaving us free to criticise. He'd risk his position and he's too crafty to let that happen."

"Alright, I'll take some soundings."

"Approach Erica Field. She's big in the Campaign and she's also in your Party. If you can't talk to her no one can."

"I thought you said she was difficult."

"I didn't say she was difficult," replied Bill. "She's bloody impossible. You've got your problems."

21

Early next morning, after being driven to the Westminster security zone, Blake climbed into a waiting helicopter. His first stop was to be the government bunker at the centre of his City. The vehicle lifted, turned and flew north. Bill Charman had promised him comfortable transport but he found it difficult to relax in his upright metal seat. He took out the Campaign's latest leaflet and strained to read it in the poor light of the compartment. It gave information on the make-up of the Civil Contingencies Unit, its political members together with Brigadier Culverton and Police Commissioner Anderson. It outlined the special powers of the Unit, including arbitrary arrest, the use of deadly force, powers to set up special courts, internment areas, control of all movements and communications, and the takeover of all services by the army. He read it several times and noted its final sentence. "... Under cover of providing civil defence the sole object of this so-called Civil Contingencies Unit is to control the population and to smash our Campaign..."

Blake put the leaflet back in his briefcase. It was further evidence that the Campaign had up-to-the- minute information on every government action. It knew this from its network of supporters throughout the state system and was able to pass information speedily to the public. The Campaign had reversed the government's system of surveillance; it now had the government under close observation. Through its informants, some obviously working at a high level, the official system of secrecy no longer existed. Blake found it disconcerting to think that even his journey north was being followed by the Campaign. For the first time he felt vulnerable.

He took out the file on Erica Field. She had been an activist in many protest campaigns and was clearly a person of immense drive and organising ability. Trying to think ahead, he was conscious of Rachel's remark that so far every action by the government had made things worse. It was a true and depressing sign that suggested violence at the end of his journey north. At a loss to know how it might be averted, he gave up on any anticipation of events.

The gloom of early morning had settled into the grey of an overcast day. The helicopter approached its destination and circled the Town Hall. The car park and the control centre were lit by floodlights from its perimeter fence which was a cordon of high razor wire. He strained to see if any demonstrators had assembled outside the cordon but in the glare of the lights he saw nothing. The helicopter hovered before landing neatly in the compound of the bunker. His bodyguards opened the door and he stepped down onto the tarmac. Stooping beneath the whirling rotor blades he approached the steel doors, which stood above ground level in a low profile. The doors opened and he moved into an entrance area where he waited for a lift to take him underground.

He was met by a senior police officer who introduced himself as Commissioner Gavin Fraser. "A good journey?" he asked.

Blake shook his hand. "I've no complaints so far. It's what happens from now on that concerns me." The lift began its descent. "Is this lift the only access?" he asked.

"We've got emergency stairs. Hundreds I'm afraid. You have to be fit to use them."
"That counts me out," said Blake. "You could be trapped in a place like this."

"We don't envisage that, Minister."

The lift reached the bottom level and Fraser led the way out. "I suggest you first meet the army commander", he said.

"Your senior, I presume", said Blake, before realising that he may have touched a raw spot.

"Yes, I suppose so. The Colonel is in his office".

They crossed the floor of the main chamber and entered a room of about four metres square. Its walls were covered by maps and at a desk sat an army officer who rose as Blake entered. Fraser introduced them. "This is Lieutenant Colonel Champney."

Blake shook his hand. "Hugh Champney," said the Colonel warmly. "I won't say it's good to see you, Minister, the circumstances are not what we would like. It's all very unfortunate. However, let's show you what we've got."

The Colonel took Blake on a tour of the bunker, explaining that it provided for three main functions; communications, intelligence and the direction of security operations."

"It's supposed to be for civil defence", said Blake.

"Yes, but we interpret that very broadly," said the Colonel. "It's versatile, adaptable, similar to war planning."

"We're not starting a war, Colonel."

"No, of course not. What I mean is that we can deal with threats from any quarter". He waved his hand at batteries of screens. "As you can see, our command of the local area and our links with the national network give us a complete overview. These days it's very easy for hostile elements to cause chaos. For example, shut down power supplies and you bring the whole country to a halt. We couldn't allow that to happen."

He stopped to point out the work of signals personnel who were testing systems for cutting out all public communications whilst leaving the links between the security forces intact. This was an independent national network connecting all regional control centres. "It's part of what we politely call the Telephone Preference System", Champney explained. "The name is an ingenious bureaucratic invention. It means we prefer other people not to talk to each other." He smiled at his joke. "And of course it operates mainly from your Command Bunker in Whitehall", he added.

The Colonel took Blake to the opposite side of the chamber. A similar set of television screens stood flickering from a long bench. "This is surveillance", the Colonel continued. "These screens connect with cameras throughout the city and at strategic points on routes leading to it. We also have mobile units which operate from helicopters so we don't have to move from the bunker to know what's going on. This section also gives us direct radio contact with personnel on the ground at every key point, roads, junctions, railways, the airport, telephone exchanges and radio stations. All part of our local overview which again links up with the national network."

The group moved into an anteroom which adjoined the surveillance unit. "What we've got here", explained the Colonel, "are all our local intelligence records. This enables us, among other things, to target hostile subjects in preparation for any programme of search and arrest".

"Search and arrest?" Blake asked.

"Yes. The bulk of the records are membership lists of potentially hostile organisations."

"Including the Campaign?"

"Well, I must admit, we're in a bit of a mess with them. It's grown so rapidly that even their local branch records are confused so I don't see how we can do better. It's where our own lists come from. The names include key undesirables, individuals who are known to be hostile to security and public order. Using this information we can search them out and detain them."

"The use of snatch squads?"

"As I said, it's a prepared programme of search and arrest."

Blake was surprised to find that Champney did not in the least fit the stereotypical idea of what a colonel might be like. He was tall, lean, and with a manner that suggested a quick mind and good-humour.

Champney took him into a further anteroom, which was furnished with a large table and chairs. This was where a Regional Council would meet if the system of central control broke down. As well as politicians of ministerial rank, the Council would include police, an army commander and local government officers. "But they would have to be reliable", Champney explained. "Their local knowledge would be vital but they would have to be cleared on security grounds. At the moment we're processing Special Branch files, sorting out which local officers we can depend on."

"I'm afraid, Colonel", Blake said with a smile, "you may not find many in this City."

The group then entered the main chamber where Champney continued in his cool, detached manner to list more facilities. These included rooms for accommodation, toilet facilities, a dining area with kitchens and food stocks and also an armoury with a wide range of small arms, gas canisters, masks and other riot control equipment.

For Blake there was very little that was new in Champney's tour of the bunker's facilities. He had noted all this information in the various plans he had examined with Bill Charman and John Dudney, but what surprised him was the intention of the army commander to extend an exclusion zone beyond the cordon of razor wire that surrounded the bunker. This would be an area extending about 200 metres from the perimeter fence from which all unauthorized persons would be excluded. Only residents would be permitted and would be issued with passes. Blake foresaw that the exclusion of campaigners from the network of streets surrounding the bunker would be very difficult to maintain and would inevitably give rise to violent confrontation.

"Do we need that exclusion zone?" Blake asked. "That could cause more problems than it might solve."

"It's not my idea", said the Colonel. "It's an instruction from Whitehall."

Blake was unaware of this and assumed it came from the Prime Minister. He pressed the Colonel. "So, you could do without it?"

"It's not for me to say" said the Colonel. "It's already in place. We've got street barriers preventing access."

Champney went on to list the deployment of army personnel set up in barracks within five miles from the City centre. These included signals, transport, infantry, a detachment of paratroops, medical and catering services. "It's been a large scale operation", he said, "and then, of course, we've got the backup of combined air force and army helicopters. In addition we've got Fraser with his police and support groups. Taking everything into account, I think you'll find we can escalate our response to any required degree."

Blake looked at the Colonel. "Yes," he said, "it looks very impressive. However, there are some questions. I believe you mentioned a canteen, Colonel."

Champney smiled. "If we go back to my office, I'll have coffee brought in."

They returned to Champney's office where they were rejoined by Fraser. Blake took off his coat and sat down at one end of the desk. "There's no doubt", he said, "the systems are all very sophisticated."

Champney detected a note of scepticism in Blake's voice. "I've no illusions, Minister," he said. It takes more than technology and force to win this sort of battle. It's not for me to comment on the political side but I must tell you frankly, I'd be a lot happier if we had some strong arguments to justify what we are doing."

Blake winced. The Colonel had identified the reason why the entire structure of force was likely to be useless. The government had no credible arguments. He looked at Fraser. "What about internal security? No worries there?"

"No special worries", said Fraser, "but we're not complacent..."

Blake felt it was a certainty that the Campaign had supporters inside the bunker. He took out the Campaign's leaflet which gave details of the Civil Contingencies Unit and the special powers of the security forces. He passed it to Fraser. "Have you seen this?"

"Yes, we've seen it. Thousands are being distributed."

"They could only get this information from the inside."

"It's obvious, Minister, they're very well informed. Unfortunately they've won a lot of misplaced sympathy."

"And they've got millions of supporters?"

"It's why we're here."

"What exactly are you driving at, Minister?" asked Champney.
"Well, you say that you're prepared for anything, but have you considered whether there could come a point where the sheer weight of the Campaign's numbers could make control impossible?"

Fraser was emphatic. "I don't see that possibility. I for one have got every confidence in our resources and our organisation."

Blake pressed him. "Even to the point, across the country, of having to deal with millions, where the Campaign's resolve is being strengthened by daily confirmations of a threat to our communities; where the government system is full of its supporters; where there could even be support for the Campaign amongst the security forces? In those circumstances, do you still have every confidence?"

Champney intervened. "Minister, I appreciate it's your job to press this sort of point. It's our job to carry out the instructions of Whitehall and we've done everything we can to implement the contingency plans. If you are asking how far our actions should go, then that is not a matter for us. It's a political decision."

Blake persisted. "You've answered very properly, Colonel, but you must have an opinion on whether the security forces, even with all their powers, could control millions of disaffected people. You must have an opinion on whether the army could control a hostile population?"

"I'm not sure what you mean by control," Champney replied. "The army can prevent an unlawful seizure of power. There's no doubt about that."

"That's assuming a completely loyal army."

"Have you any reason for doubt?"

"No, but would the army fire on the civilian population? Would they fire to kill and would you give that order?"

As Champney hesitated, Blake continued. "It's nothing personal, you understand. I'm trying to think through the purpose of this bunker and the organisation of force it represents. We can all admire technical systems but the logic leads ultimately to killing people in the streets. Are we prepared to do it?"

As Champney hesitated, Fraser replied, "Surely it won't come to that."

Blake turned to him. "I'm a politician, Commissioner, we invented evasions so don't feed them to me. Just what is our resolve? If necessary are we resolved to kill our fellow citizens? We do think of them as our fellow citizens, don't we?"

"In a manner of speaking, I suppose so."

Blake persisted, "Then we will kill them in the streets?"

Fraser stumbled into a reply. "If the country's vital interests are threatened, and we are instructed to do so.. yes."

Champney took a different view. "Surely, Minister", he said, "the point is to maintain the law whilst avoiding that extreme measure. I'm sure it can be done. Everyone here is instructed to act with restraint and with the use of minimum force and I would add this; these days it's not enough just to give orders, the ordinary soldier has to be convinced that what he's doing is right."

Blake helped him. "I think I know what you're trying to say Colonel. Don't ask the troops to go too far. We may find them reluctant."

"If they feel justified, they'll go anywhere with you," Champney added. "You can trust them but trust must go both ways. For our part, we trust that the political side will do everything it can to avoid your projected scenario. You see, we're more used to the idea of defending our population, not attacking it."

Blake was relieved to hear Champney's reply. "Yes, of course," he said. "Colonel, I've got a feeling that you and I can work together."

Fraser seemed anxious to take some initiative and suggested that in line with the search-and-arrest programme, Erica Field should be detained. He pointed out that she was at the centre of the Campaign's plans to take over the government bunker, and should be removed immediately.

Blake glanced at his watch. "She's one of my local party," he said. "I'm due to meet her in an hour or so. She has a lot of influence. I'm hoping she'll see some sense."

Champney took the point. "It's not a good idea to move in now and remove their leadership. It would leave a vacuum. It could create anger and confusion. We need to be able to talk to someone with authority in their camp."

"If it leaves them confused, surely that's to our advantage", said Fraser. "We're instructed to assert our authority. What better way than to arrest her now?"

Champney was unmoved. "I'm aware of our instructions."

Fraser looked angry. "Colonel, I'm bound to say, this is getting off on the wrong foot. We should take her out of circulation."

Champney's demeanour suddenly altered. He stared icily at his police colleague. "I've heard your view, and I've made a decision."

Blake was now anxious to attend the meeting of his local party. "Look, I've got to get on," he said whilst putting on his coat. "Thanks for the tour. I'll let you know about Erica Field after I've spoken with her. She may not be as bad as her reputation suggests. I want to see what's happening outside. I need to judge the mood of things. I can't do that in this bunker."

Fraser objected. "Have you consulted your security people?"

"If I took their advice, I'd never go anywhere. I also want to check into my hotel."

"You mean you're not staying here?"

Blake was determined to keep some distance from a place that could soon become a symbol of oppressive state power. "No offence," he said, "but there's a risk of a bunker mentality down here that could be contagious. In any case, it's not exactly five-star accommodation."

"But at least it's secure."

Champney smiled. "Just be careful, Minister. We'll be in radio contact with your security people and naturally, I'd like to know the result of your meeting with Erica Field."

Blake took up his briefcase and was joined by his bodyguards as he took the lift up to the bunker compound. The area was quiet with police and dog handlers patrolling the perimeter fence. The party climbed into a waiting car which moved through the barbed wire gates of the compound. It then drove the short distance to the barriers of the security zone and then on to his usual hotel. He checked in and took his two guards into the lounge bar where he bought them drinks. "You know my plans for today", he said, "I'm attending a meeting. You won't need to accompany me."

"We've got our instructions, sir," one insisted.

Blake raised his voice. "Look, there's no security risk. I'm meeting colleagues I've known for years. It's impossible for you to be present. You'll be an embarrassment."

"We'll stay in the background, sir. We won't be noticed. There's no problem."

Blake wondered how it was possible for two burly men with short hair and suits to be discreet. "I don't know how you put up with your jobs," he said, "hanging about at all hours. Why don't you take the day off?"

"We've got our instructions, sir."

Seeing that, in their impassive way, they were resolved, Blake gave up on the argument. "I'm not sure whether you're here to protect me or to spy on me," he said.

22

As Blake walked through the corridors of the Town Hall, he anticipated another hostile reception from his local party. Because of his position on the Civil Contingencies Unit there was no doubt that some of its members would regard him as an alien presence. He had delayed his arrival until the meeting had begun. The hall was crowded and as he entered he found Erica Field already on her feet and in confrontation with Clive Poole, the chairman. She was of stocky build with broad athletic shoulders, full of confidence, speaking loudly and surrounded by a devoted entourage.

"We know what we're here for," she said. "We're here to help organise the occupation of the car park and the security bunker. We want that bunker for a deep shelter. We want it for our own communications. We should get on with it. There isn't much time."

Clive Poole was adamant. "That's what you say we're here for, but I understand the meeting was called to help organise the voluntary work."

"Yes, but the immediate issue is securing the site for a deep shelter."

"This isn't a meeting of the Campaign," Clive reminded her. "You only ever come down here when you want support for an outside organisation. This is still our local party."

Erica pointed at Blake who could only find standing room at the back of the hall. "What about the individual who's just dropped in?" she asked. "Does he belong here? I'll tell you where he belongs. He's a part of the new political junta; the gang of six who have set themselves up as dictators."

"Blake Evans has a perfect right to be here," Clive insisted. "You know that."

"He should stay in the bunker where he belongs. I object to sitting down with traitors."

"Unfortunately, you're not sitting down and we shouldn't be calling each other traitors. You should withdraw that."

Clive Poole was ignored and, to loud cheers, one of Erica Field's supporters intervened. "I want to hear what Erica has to say. Campaign or not, we should all be concerned with the safety of the country."

Erica renewed her appeal to the meeting. "We can't sit around here wasting time. This so-called government is doing nothing. It's not even a government. It's six people controlling the country and one of them is sitting down here, spying on this meeting, ready to report back to the army commander." Her voice rang with contempt. "This squalid junta, this self-appointed gang of six has sealed off the car park site. They are mustering the police and the army at points throughout the City and what do you imagine is the point of all this? I'll tell you. It is not just to smash our Campaign. It is to destroy every freedom that the people of this country have fought for. These are the issues now at stake. What we are fighting for now is a lot more than the safety of our communities. Thanks to the traitorous actions of Blake Evans and his kind we are back to fighting for our basic rights. Some of you might think you've got an inalienable right to move freely about the City. Let me correct you. Thanks to the dictates of the gang of six, as represented by the individual who has just crept into our meeting, from midnight tonight, if you set foot in the exclusion zone around the bunker, you could be shot on sight. That will be an act of legalised murder for which no one will be held to account."

"I can tell you now what they're doing in that bunker," she continued. "The army commander, a certain Lieutenant Colonel Hugh Champney and his cohort, Police Commissioner Gavin Fraser, are going through Special Branch files sorting out all you troublemakers, who in the past might have been active against the government in some way. You are being blacklisted with a view to being searched out and arrested. You will be detained by the agents of MI5 without trial and without any kind of legal representation, and there are no prizes for guessing who is first on that list. That doesn't worry me. I've been there before."

Blake was reminded of Bill Charman's remark that Erica Field was impossible and seeing her in full flow and dominating the meeting, he knew that she would never modify her views. She was driven more by her reputation and the expectations of her supporters than by the practical needs of the moment. In the face of this, reason would stand little chance. Her attack on the Civil Contingencies Unit was relentless and her constant use of the world "junta" reduced the government Unit to a gang of despots in a banana republic. She was very good both at invoking the imagery of dictatorship and implanting it in the minds of her listeners. Blake sensed a build-up of anger in the hall and with it a rare moment of inadequacy.

She spoke on, "We must occupy that bunker. It will be a message to the junta that it must be for the benefit of people not for their oppression. Campaigners are already on the move. Are we going to sit here like a lot of cowards and refuse to help? No, we've got to put out the word and mobilise our members to do the same. If we all act together we'll win. There can be no doubt about it, we will win. So let's join the campaigners; let's go out and do it."

At last Clive Poole was able to intervene. "It's not that simple," he said.

"Yes, it is!" Erica shouted.

"Well, why don't we hear what Blake Evans has got to say," Clive shouted back. "He's been our respected member for years and I'm sure he's able to propose something constructive."

Erica smiled sarcastically. "That's fine by us. Let him say what the junta is doing. Let him tell us about its plans to begin work on civil defence immediately. We're all listening."

She sat down as Blake made his way forward to a more open space and began to reply.

"Despite what Erica Field says, I have been in discussions with representatives of the Campaign. I've met with Edward Hurst and others, and I am going to meet them again. We haven't met in a hostile way and there is no need for it now. Violence will only end in tears and that won't get us anywhere. What we want is a solution to our problems; that is what we've got to work for."

Blake tried to ease the tension in the hall. "Now you can call me a traitor or anything else you like, I've been around for a long time and it doesn't bother me. Nor am I impressed by demagoguery even though I admit, Erica is very good at it. What we need to do is take a calm look at the facts. The basic problem is that we do not have the money to finance a nationwide programme of deep shelter protection. Look at it another way. Suppose, after a lot of violence, you take over the exclusion zone and the bunker, what are you going to do then? We'll have a lot of broken heads. We might even have worse, and all you will have done is become an unnecessary burden on our medical services. We will be back to where we are now with the problem of how to finance the construction of shelters. It's not just the government's problem, it's everybody's problem. All we'll have is a lot of blood on our hands. Nothing could be more futile."

"That's a lie," shouted Erica. "What we will have is our first deep shelter and that will save many lives."

Blake pressed her. "But you don't face up to the question, Erica. So you take over the bunker, what then?"

"I don't have to answer your questions," she said. "I don't even want to talk to you. We're going to take it over and you won't stop us. That's my answer to you."

A more neutral member of the audience interrupted. "Is Blake saying there's nothing we can do about civil defence? How can that make sense?"

"I'm saying two things", Blake replied. "I'm saying there's no point in useless violence and I'm saying that no one can find hundreds of billions of pounds that don't exist. But that doesn't mean we're helpless. Let's see how we can adapt the community projects. Let's see if all the millions of people who say they support the Campaign will work voluntarily for civil defence. Let's combine all these efforts with the work of the All Party Group of MPs. This way we can get the whole country working together. Even at this moment I'm setting up a National Consultative Council to include every section of the community. I put it to Erica now, would the Campaign accept a place on this Council?"

Erica glared at Blake. There was no way she was going to fall into the trap he had set. "We're not going to be sidetracked by your squalid manoeuvres," she said. "We don't want your phoney consultation which leaves power in the hands of your gang of six. When we asked for a part in decision-making you refused. Now you come here with your hypocritical mouthings about consultation and cooperation. Why haven't you told this meeting the truth about what you've really done? You know why. It's because you're a bloody liar and you can't be trusted. Consultation? Look what you did with the arrest of Edward Hurst. We know all about your part in that. We know about the Cabinet Committee which put spies in our Campaign. It was you who made those decisions. We know everything about how you operate. We know where you were before you came here. You were in the control bunker, conspiring with the army to smash our Campaign. I don't know where you get the gall to show your face in this meeting..."

Under Erica's verbal onslaught Blake felt a moment of embarrassment. Much of what she said was true. With the help of Chivers and its network of informants the Campaign was aware of everything he had done. "I'm the first to admit," he said lamely, "we made mistakes, but there's no point in dwelling on that. We've got to put them aside and go forward, constructively."

Erica responded with more sarcasm. "Alright, I can be constructive. You revoke the exclusion zone around the car park and the bunker. Make them available for the protection of the public now. Do that and we'll abandon our action. We'll even consult with the government. That's being constructive, isn't it?"

"You know very well I can't make that instant decision," Blake replied. "This is theatrics, not sensible discussion. You may think I'm a dictator but I don't have that sort of power."

Erica turned to engage the whole meeting. "We've just heard another pathetic evasion," she said. "Behind the scenes he engages in vile, secret acts. Then he comes hawking his conscience around meetings like this. Is this a person you can trust? Are we going to sit back, do nothing and leave the action to others? Well, I don't know about all of you but I know where I'm going. I'm going to leave this hall now and I'm going right down to that bunker. I'm going to join with others and together we are going to take it over. Are you with me...?"

With this she walked past Blake without giving him a glance, made her way to the door at the back of the hall and disappeared. As she did so, most of those present stood up and followed her out leaving a few members of the constituency party. Blake looked towards Clive Poole who shrugged as if to confirm that the outcome of the meeting had always been inevitable. The shrewder members of the local party who now remained had realised the futility of any violent struggle with the security forces. Some of them were veterans of many confrontations and knew that in this case, regardless of any human cost, the government would never concede its control centre to the Campaign.

The few who were left gathered in a group around the chairman's table. The best they could do was to consider how the resources of the country could be released for the work of shelter construction in view of the limitations imposed by costs. Chris Lawson, who had been so helpful to Blake at a previous meeting, reported on the progress being made on the community projects using voluntary labour. He posed the question of how these could be adapted for the work of civil defence. He also mentioned a difficulty. Any work on deep shelters would need a vast amount of machinery, equipment and materials and it would be impossible to supply these without financial resources.

"However," said Chris Lawson, "there is one thing we could take up. The idea of a credit scheme. Things wouldn't have to be paid for immediately. Local authorities could be empowered to issue credit notes in exchange for labour, machinery and materials. We'd use these credit notes to enable the construction of deep shelters, then, when the crisis has passed and the government's cash position improves, it could pay out on the credit notes over a much longer period. This would be a way of getting the work started, especially if it's combined with the community projects."

Blake was reminded of his own work researching the problems the country faced during World War II. He had picked up on the example of a National Consultative Council but had paid little attention to the post war credit scheme that had been successful in raising many millions of pounds.

For a while the rump of the meeting discussed and developed a plan for linking a credit scheme with voluntary work. It was agreed that Blake should put the proposal to the government, to the All Party Group of MPs and to the proposed National Consultative Council. He was also determined to put the plan before the Campaign. Surely it included people who were more reasonable than Erica Field. He made notes of the discussion, becoming more convinced that the idea was a practical means of getting work started.

Eventually the meeting adjourned. Some important ideas had emerged, giving grounds for optimism. However, these hopeful moves were overshadowed by the conflicting forces that were gathering strength in the centre of the City.

23

Blake was met by his bodyguards on the steps of the Town Hall. He was now anxious to return to the Bunker. Streams of campaigners were heading for the City centre. With the roads to the bunker now sealed, the only access to it was by helicopter. Though his destination was only a few hundred metres away they began the journey by first driving out to an airfield.

As he waited at the airfield one of his bodyguards passed him a copy of the Campaign's latest leaflet. It was directed at police and army personnel, urging them not to act against the Campaign. He read it through. Its message was simple.

"Our Campaign is working for your safety and for the safety of your wives, children and parents.

You are being used to smash our attempts to care for your families. Your place is with us.

Our object is to occupy the government bunker. It should be used as a deep shelter for the protection of all of us.

Our Campaign is your Campaign. Do not act against us.

Join our Campaign now."

Blake turned to his bodyguards. "This is addressed to you," he said. "What do you think of it?"

One replied. "I don't think of it, sir."

The landing space in the bunker's compound limited the ferrying-in of men and equipment to single journeys, which meant that Blake had to share the flight with some troops. Eventually, he walked to a waiting helicopter and made his way to the front where he had all-round vision from the forward compartment. The helicopter took off and within minutes it was back over the City centre, where it edged its way down and landed. Its doors slid open, the troops spilled out and joined the riot police in the compound. Blake climbed down, ducked beneath the rotor blades and entered the doors of the Bunker, where he took the lift down and headed for Champney's office. He found the Colonel studying a wall map with Fraser.

Champney welcomed him. "Ah, Minister, you got here alright?"

"In a roundabout way."

"I believe there was not much joy from your meeting?"

Blake shrugged. "I was never hopeful."

Champney pointed to the map. "We're discussing our options," he said. "Crowds are assembling just outside the exclusion zone, so we're reinforcing our barbed wire defences. I don't think they can get in, but if they do, the narrow streets will present a problem. They'll quickly become congested. We could appeal to the crowd to disperse but of course they'll take no notice. We could reinforce that by threatening the use of CS gas but they'll ignore that as well. In a worst case scenario that brings us to the use of actual force. Normally, we'd gain ground with baton charges and the use of plastic bullets but as we can see, there's nowhere for them to run. Similarly with CS gas. They would stand choking with no means of escape and that wouldn't help us, either. In any case, I'm disinclined to use those methods at this stage...."

Suddenly, the lights went out, leaving the office in total darkness. Taken by surprise, Champney, Fraser and Blake stood momentarily silent until Fraser groped his way to the door. In the main chamber every monitor had flickered out, the telephones were dead and personnel sat in front of their useless batteries of screens.

Fraser shouted orders. "Get those generators going. Start those generators."

Shafts of torchlight flashed through the open office door. Blake and Champney made no move. They waited, aware of the frantic efforts to activate the bunker's own power supply.

"Not a very good start," said Blake.

"No, but predictable." Champney then sat at his desk, took out his pipe and began to light it. "It's a good time for a quiet smoke, Minister. Do you mind?"

Blake noted the nonchalant manner of the Colonel. "Go ahead," he said, "but I don't smoke."

"Nor should I, really. Not with my bronchitis." Unperturbed, Champney sat lighting his pipe. "I'll say this for the Campaign," he said, "their intelligence is brilliant and they are very resourceful."

"I've noticed that," said Blake.

"You know, Minister, this bunker isn't as good as it looks. I'm here because of my orders but I wouldn't have chosen it."

"You mean it's vulnerable?"

"It would only take a canister of CS gas to be released in the main operations room and we'd be out of action. I'm sure they've got a supporter amongst our personnel and whoever it is wouldn't have to be very bright to do it."

"And that wouldn't help your bronchitis," said Blake.

"Exactly," said Champney. He paused for a moment as if he were reluctant to raise the matter. "What worries me," he continued, "is that the Campaign has got the numbers but not only that, it's got the best arguments as well. I have mentioned this, but it's not for me to get involved in politics. "He paused again. "May I speak freely?"

"Of course," said Blake. "I welcome your view. Say what you like."

"Well, you've seen the Campaign's seditious leaflet aimed at the morale of the troops. It's a powerful message and it's backing it up with a constant stream of argument from megaphones saying that action against the Campaign is against the families of the Services. It's going to make sense to the ordinary soldier and it leaves the question, what arguments have we got?"

"I've already admitted," said Blake, "we are very weak on that side."

"You see, Minister," Champney continued, "you never go into counter-insurgency without a good argument and this conflict is more or less the same thing. We've assembled all this force, we can escalate our response in any required degree, but when is the political side going to get some good arguments together? You realise that in the long run the arguments could be the deciding factor."

Before Blake had a chance to reply, the sound of generators began to throb throughout the bunker. The lights came on and Fraser returned to the office, his face flushed with anger. "Those bastards," he said, "they cut off our power supply."

"Do we know where?" asked the Colonel.

"We're connected to the national grid in the basement of the Town Hall," replied Fraser. "It's the obvious place to cut us off. I've sent a party of men in from the outside. They'll sort it out."

The Colonel faced Fraser. "I again want to emphasise," he said, "that where your men are involved they've got to be firm but good-humoured. We want no vindictiveness. If the situation turns nasty, we'll have to respond with greater force, and then we'll have a mess on our hands. We don't want that."

"Yes, but I know these people," Fraser replied. "They can be damned provocative."

"Deliberately so," said the Colonel, "but we won't let them upset us, will we? We'll be patient even if it takes us days. We've got as much time as they have."

Blake joined the Colonel as he left his office and moved into the main chamber where he observed the outside scenes on the monitors. At all strategic points, motorway exits, crossroads and junctions, police and troops were in full control. Campaigners trying to reach the City centre by car and coach were stopped and shepherded to assembly points from where they were told to depart the City.

Blake watched the reactions of the campaigners who made no moves to interfere or resist. Some put leaflets into the hands of the troops and, when pressed, the troops took them with a smile. Despite these good-natured exchanges Blake knew it would take a miracle to control the crowds in a congenial manner.

After watching for some time, he went to the canteen, collected a mug of coffee and returned to the monitors. From all around the chamber he heard the ringing of telephones and the noise of radio contact as Champney gave out a constant stream of orders and checked the progress of the army and police action. One monitor switched to the city's main football ground, which was alive with the movement of army vehicles and groups of campaigners who were being assembled. Champney explained that troublemakers were being brought to the sports-ground then dumped miles away from where they would find it difficult to return past road blocks.

He switched back to the streets immediately outside the exclusion zone where the Campaign's loudspeakers were broadcasting their messages to the troops and police behind the barriers of razor wire. "Yes, they are very resourceful," said Champney with a note of admiration. "They cut off our power supply and they never stop undermining the morale of the troops. Earlier, they said that the bunker's water supply had been contaminated."

As Blake heard this he spat out a mouthful of coffee. "Christ, Colonel, I thought it was the taste of your army coffee. Don't tell me they've poisoned the water."

Champney smiled. "I think you'll find they're bluffing, Minister," he said.

"But you won't mind if I don't take the risk. Your coffee isn't worth it."

"Sorry about that," said the Colonel. "The coffee has been a problem for years. We've never solved it."

A signals clerk shouted across to Champney. "A serious incident reported, sir. You're wanted."

Champney hurried over to the clerk. "What's the problem?"

"A man has been shot, sir, in the basement of the Town Hall."

"Shot? How badly? Is he dead?"

"They're not sure, sir."

Champney grabbed the receiver and shouted into it. "Say no more over the air. Stay where you are and do what you can." He returned to the monitors where he switched to the scene in front of the Town Hall. Troops and police were in full control. He strode back to the signals clerk. "Get an ambulance to the Town Hall. Get that person to hospital, fast." He waited as the clerk sent out instructions and then asked, "Was that report picked up by the Campaign?"

"It's very likely, sir. They are in tune with all our frequencies."

"Dammit," said the Colonel. "How do they do it? Where's Fraser?"

As Fraser joined him, Champney looked grim. "You see what's happened, Fraser. Those men you sent to the Town Hall basement. They've shot a campaigner."

Fraser looked embarrassed. "I heard the message," he said. "No doubt my men were under threat."

"When this gets out amongst the crowd they'll become an angry mob. I ordered restraint. What the hell are your men doing?"

"But we don't know what's happened," insisted Fraser. "They've done one good thing. They've restored our power supplies."

"We didn't want it at this cost."

"Let's wait for the facts. I'm sure we'll find that my men were under threat."

For a moment Champney stared at Fraser. "I know one thing," he said. "You've failed to carry out my orders."

At this, Fraser became angry. "Look, Champney. My men are allowed to defend themselves. If you say different then put it in writing, then we'll all know where we stand."

Champney switched back to the scenes at the boundary of the exclusion zone, where it soon became clear that the campaigners were aware of the incident. As a message came quickly from its loudspeakers it was picked up inside the bunker. Blake and the two service chiefs listened intently.

"We speak to all members of the security forces. You have murdered one of our members. We are here for the benefit of you and your families. We offer no violence but we must be protected. Commissioner Gavin Fraser is now a marked man. He will find no place to hide. He will be dealt with."

"Can't we stop that filth?" demanded Fraser. "They're saying the man is dead. How can they possibly know?"

"They know," replied Champney, "and they've named you as being responsible."

"I'm not intimidated by those bastards," said Fraser. "They've already put pressure on my family. I don't know why we're pussyfooting around. We'll be here for weeks at this rate. We should put a few dozen rounds of plastic bullets into them from the compound. That would shift them. Why don't we show them we mean business?"

For all its bravado Fraser's outburst was unconvincing. Champney stopped him. "Shut up, man!" he said. "Get a grip on yourself."

He observed the movement at the edge of the exclusion zone. Campaigners were now pressed close to the barriers and suddenly, behind the barbed wire, police and troops began to scatter as a shower of missiles, stones, bricks, broken paving and bottles began to rain down on them. Taken by surprise in the confined area, some fell down whilst others ran back, desperately trying to shield themselves. In more than one section the barriers which had sealed off the exclusion zone were dragged aside and hundreds of campaigners began pouring through the gaps. The police and troops were overwhelmed. More and more campaigners streamed in from the outside area until they occupied the exclusion zone and were brought to a halt by the more difficult razor wire that had been erected high and wide at the perimeter of the bunker compound.

Champney moved quickly. He strode to a microphone that was linked with an outside public address system. His voice boomed out across the bunker compound.

"This is Lieutenant Colonel Champney speaking. I am the officer commanding the security zone. In two minutes I will give the order to fire plastic bullets and riot control gas into the crowd. You have two minutes to cease your action. You have two minutes from now."

He checked the monitor. Just inside the tangled mass of razor wire, riot police now stood in solid ranks behind a screen of shields. Behind them, others stood at the ready, aiming their weapons directly into the crowd which was now only a few feet away. He spoke again into the microphone.

"You have one minute to cease your action. I repeat, in one minute I will give the order to fire gas and bullets into the crowd. Cease your action now."

He looked again at the monitor showing the macabre phalanx of riot police standing amidst the debris of missiles. Those campaigners just outside the razor wire stared directly into the barrels of the weapons. Suddenly, the missiles ceased. Champney waited for a few tense moments and then spoke again.

"You have ceased your action. Stand where you are and stay calm. I repeat, stay calm. If your actions recommence the police will fire without warning. I repeat, the police will fire without warning. Stand where you are and stay calm."

As he spoke an orderly file of more riot police marched from the steel doors of the bunker and took up position, again aiming their weapons into the crowd. As the campaigners closest to the razor wire fence tried to back away, Champney repeated his message.

"Stay calm. If your action recommences the police will fire without warning. Stay calm and you will not be injured or killed. This is Lieutenant Colonel Champney speaking. You are safe if you stay calm."

For Blake, the tension seemed unbearable as Champney stared for minutes at the monitors. The crowd stood still in an eerie silence until eventually it appeared to relax. What had been the exclusion zone was now filled with campaigners. The barriers which had sealed it off were no longer in place. Only the smaller area inside the bunker compound was secure.

Even so, Fraser was encouraged by the Colonel's ultimatums. "You see my point, Champney," he said. "Tough action, it's the only thing that works. We've go to keep it up."

Champney said nothing but kept his eyes fixed to the screen, studying the crowd. At last he seemed satisfied that the critical point had passed. He gave orders that the riot police in the compound should lower their weapons and stand at ease. Satisfied that the situation had at least achieved stalemate, he turned to Blake. "Minister, I think we should talk things over," he said.

Blake nodded and followed him into his office where they were again joined by Fraser. The Colonel took his seat. "You realise," he said, "that what we've just seen is only a dress rehearsal for the real battle which is yet to come. What the Campaign has done here today is test our reactions. They now know how far we'll go so in future, in any more decisive conflict they will adapt their tactics."

He paused as the voice of the Campaign was relayed into his office. He tuned his receiver and listened.

"... we give the names of six police who have betrayed their families and now stand guilty of aiming lethal weapons at our Campaign. We name Clark, Lock, Brady, Davis, Simms and Rodgers. These individuals will be dealt with. They will find no place to hide."

As Champney switched off the receiver, Fraser exploded with rage. "Who are they to threaten me and the ranks?" he demanded. "That's a criminal act. We know the names of their activists so let's get out there. We should search them out and put them away. What's stopping us? We've already seen that tough action is the only way to deal with these people. We've go to stop these threats, Champney."

The Colonel seemed unconcerned. "We have to admit," he said, "their information is first class."

"It's only because of traitors in our own camp," said Fraser. "We've got to root them out as well."

"Their informants are a measure of their support and we'd be foolish to ignore it," replied the Colonel.
"We've got to stop these threats, Champney."

"I'm afraid we'll see a lot more. It's one of their weapons: intimidation." He looked wearily at Fraser. "And it works."

Blake was anxious to know the next step. "Colonel, what are our options now?"

"I was coming to that, Minister. My orders are to prevent a takeover of this bunker and to maintain an exclusion zone between the bunker and the City. Well, you see what's happened. We've lost control of the exclusion zone." He paused for a moment and relit his pipe. "As I've said, it's not for me to interfere with political decisions but I would like to understand the strategic objective. That's never been made clear."

Blake could only tell Champney what the Prime Minister had said that morning, "The object is to secure the bunker and maintain the authority of the government."

Champney persisted. "Of course, I understand that but can I ask you, is there a political plan for dealing with the Campaign? Does the government have a strategy for meeting its demands or does it intend to ignore them and rely solely on force?"

Blake was embarrassed. The truth was that the use of force had been the only matter discussed. He evaded the question. "I don't see what you're driving at," he said. "Can you get to the point?"

"Well," replied Champney, "given our situation, dispersing this crowd is now a massive task and it will involve a large area of the City. Now that we've killed a campaigner I don't think we'll see passive resistance. We can achieve our object but violence is inevitable; it is certain that the Campaign has firearms. The City could become a battleground and, even if we win, in the longer term our success could work against us. We've got to be realistic. The Campaign has got massive public support. As a result they've got the numbers. They've also got the best arguments and their blend of persuasion and intimidation could succeed in undermining the morale of the troops. If that goes, we're in real trouble." Champney looked towards Fraser. "And you've already seen one example."

"The point is this," Champney continued. "If a plan for supplying deep shelter protection does emerge it will inevitably involve the Campaign. So, why can't we agree on a compromise now? Provided they cease their action and provided the crowds throughout the City disperse, we could allow them to occupy the exclusion zone.

What harm could it do? We'll still keep control of the bunker. In the meantime we could use the truce to discuss how we can all get out of this mess."

Fraser leapt at the idea. "With the main crowd dispersed and just a few of them left, we could easily deal with them."

Champney glared at him. "Fraser," he said, "I want you out of here on the next transport. For one man you've done too much damage."

Fraser went pale. "But Champney," he protested, "you don't even know the facts. You'll see that my men were justified. You were on the point of using firearms yourself."

Champney replied with icy calm. "I'm not arguing. I want you out of here!"

Blake realised at once that Champney had proposed the right course of action but he also foresaw a giant obstacle; the recalcitrance of Erica Field. He took her file from his brief case and tossed it on to Champney's desk. "Read that," he said.

Champney glanced at it. "We all know about Erica," he said. "There's no doubt, she can be a very difficult lady."

"Some say, impossible," said Blake.

"Yes," agreed Champney, "but they also say they don't have leaders. Others could be more reasonable. It's worth a try. There's a lot to gain and nothing to lose."

"I'll have to clear it with Whitehall," said Blake.

Fraser had sat grim faced and silent. He suddenly got up. "I won't be a party to any of this," he said, as he left the office. "It's a surrender."

Champney watched him go and then turned to Blake. "I wish you'd contact Whitehall now," he said. "And while you are at it, I want a replacement for Fraser."

Blake left the office to contact Bill Charman at the Command Bunker in Whitehall. On his way he stopped to check the scene in the security zone. It was still quiet with the crowd more relaxed after having been taken to the brink of all-out violence. Some riot police who had been casualties of the sudden rain of bricks and bottles were being attended by medics. The Campaign's loudspeakers were continuing to maintain their pressure, naming Gavin Fraser and six other police who were marked for retribution and warning them not to return to their homes. In some places police and troops were in open conversation with the campaigners.

Blake was soon through to Bill Charman at Whitehall. "Things are not going too well, I understand."

"It's stalemate at the moment."

"We've also had our problems," said Bill and went on to explain that some groups in Trafalgar Square had tried without success to break into the Westminster zone. "That madman Hurst was involved so he's been rearrested," he said. "We're releasing him yet again at his home in Southsea. But you've killed a campaigner. Was that necessary?"

Blake said he would explain the full story later, together with an account of the events at his City centre. "In the meantime," he said, "we want to negotiate a compromise." He went on to spell out Champney's proposal that the Campaign should be allowed to occupy the exclusion zone in exchange for stopping their actions in the City. In the meantime, discussions would take place. "The bunker will remain secure," he concluded.

"Alright," said Bill. "Do it."

Blake was surprised at Bill Charman's immediate response. "What about the Prime Minister?" he asked. "We need his agreement."

"I don't think so. If you think it's right, do it."

"Bill," Blake insisted, "we can't decide this without the Prime Minister."

"Don't worry about it. I'll put him in the picture. I'll take full responsibility. You go ahead, Blake."

"Alright, I will. There's one other thing," Blake added, "our police chief, Fraser, Champney wants him replaced."

"Fraser? Sacked?"

"Call it what you like but Champney wants him out of here."

"I hope he knows what he's doing," said Bill.

"I think he does."

Blake put down the receiver, concerned that the Prime Minister had not been consulted. Both he and Bill Charman would need some very good reasons for making the decision on their own. He rejoined the Colonel and told him the result. Champney explained that without direct telephone contact it would be necessary to get a man with a radio into the Campaign's headquarters. "If you need to bring pressure," he said, "you could emphasise our determination to clear the area regardless, and if it helps, you could also mention that Fraser has been sacked. That will give them something."

"Is he your sacrificial lamb?" Blake asked. "So, what are we left with? The usual blend of intimidation and persuasion?"

"I'm sure you don't need my advice, Minister."

Blake waited as contact was made with the Campaign's headquarters and was disappointed to find that he was again speaking with Erica Field.

"You're lucky to get me," she said. "I'm just back from the Town Hall. You're not just a traitor, Blake Evans, you're a marked man."

"I don't give a damn for your threats," he said. "I want to propose a compromise."

"We don't compromise with bastards like you."

"I'll tell you anyway. You occupy the security zone but you cease your threat to the bunker and the main crowds disperse. At the same time, we'll begin discussions about the Campaign joining a National Consultative Council."

"You call that a compromise? With our main people dispersed you'd have no problem clearing the exclusion zone. It's an obvious trick."

"If that crowd is cleared by the army you'll be left with nothing."

"If you could do it you wouldn't be talking to me now."

"It will be cleared, at any cost."

"Go ahead. We're ready."

"You don't care about the casualties?"

"They won't be our fault and they'll be on both sides. In time we'll deal with all the guilty people."
"Fraser has been sacked."

"He's got a lot worse than that coming to him."

Blake was exasperated. Dealing with Erica was like arguing with a brick wall. He would have preferred to speak with someone else but despite its denial of any leadership it was clear that she had established herself as the undisputed leader of the Campaign locally. He decided to take a more aggressive approach.

"If you turn this down the blood of the casualties will be on your hands and I'll make sure the whole country knows it. I'll use every means of making it clear that your only object is useless violence.

I regard you as a very grave danger to public safety and I'll use every resource of the security forces to have you removed. That's a promise and you'll find it is one I'll keep. On the other hand, you could use your talents constructively. You could join with us in the serious work of consultation and civil defence. That begins with the agreement I've set out."

Erica was shrewd enough to know that her attitude may have gone beyond what her local and national membership would endorse. In view of its possible consequences, any decision not to agree could leave her subject to criticism or even leave her stranded. At last she wavered. "You say we'll occupy the exclusion zone?" she asked.

"Yes," said Blake.

"And you say Fraser has been sacked?"

"Yes. You can claim that as a victory as well."

"Alright," she said, "we'll ask most of our people to go home. But it's only a truce. If you don't honour your commitments we can be back in our thousands at a moment's notice."

He tried to be conciliatory. "Erica, I think we've just prevented a lot of casualties."

"Don't imagine it had anything to do with your threats, which only reveal your true intentions. I've agreed for other reasons. All you've done is make a fool of yourself."

Erica put down her receiver and as the line went dead Blake felt chastened. He could barely resist a feeling of respect for this resolute lady. He asked the signals clerk to get back to Whitehall. Bill Charman was soon on the line and Blake told him the outcome of his exchange with Erica. "That's very good work," said Bill. "Can you leave now? You need to get down here as soon as possible."

"When do I get some sleep?" Blake asked.

"We need you here. There are new problems I can't mention over the air."

"Yes, but when do I get some sleep?"

"Blake, just get down here."

Blake looked for Champney and found him issuing provisional orders to his reserve units. "Don't bother, Colonel," said Blake. "I've just got our agreement with Erica Field."

"Can we rely on it?"

"There seems to be no doubt about her authority. At least, she has no doubts."

"But we won't suspend our action," said the Colonel. "Let's get some drinks and see what happens."

Blake reminded him. "What about the contaminated water?"

"I told you, Minister. They were bluffing. You feel alright, don't you?"

"I don't feel good about anything."

They went through to the canteen with Blake still concerned that the Prime Minister had not been consulted over the terms of the truce. It seemed strange and out of character that Bill Charman should have taken it into his head to ignore the proper procedures. With the Prime Minister so unpredictable, it was a risk, but there could be no going back on what had been agreed.

He expressed his thoughts to the Colonel. "You will have noticed," he said, "that my credibility with the Campaign is very thin. What's left of it depends on our honouring the agreement, and you won't mind if I remind you, it was your idea in the first place."

Champney reassured him. "You can rely on it, Minister."

"Erica Field has emphasised that this is only a truce," Blake continued. " She left no doubt that they could all be back at a moment's notice and even you have said that it's been only a dress rehearsal for the main conflict which is yet to come. It's all very fragile."

Now at ease with Blake, Champney felt he could relax. "Can I mention again," he said, "there's got to be a political solution."

Blake was tired. "Yes, I'm not short of that advice," he said. "Lots of advice, threats, ultimatums and pressure, but no practical ideas: no solutions."

They returned to the monitors. True to the agreement, campaigners had begun to move from the City centre, leaving some groups in what had been the exclusion zone. Even on screen it was clear they were in a buoyant mood, satisfied they had won a victory. Champney ordered the police and troops in the bunker compound to break ranks but to remain prepared. Blake asked him for transport back to Whitehall. "It seems to be over here," he said. "For the time being."

"If we meet again," said Champney, "let's hope it will be in happier circumstances." Blake smiled. He had been impressed by the army commander.

After a short wait, Blake moved into the lift with his bodyguards and re-emerged at the surface into the early morning air. Beyond the compound the ground was littered with stones and bottles: the debris of conflict. Campaign organisers were cheerfully handing out hot drinks to those who had been delegated to remain. Again, he climbed into a helicopter. As its engine roared and it took off, he caught a last glimpse of leaflets being handed out to some troops. The helicopter then circled and headed south.

24

As the helicopter flew on, Blake struggled against the torment of noise and movement, finding sleep impossible. He was also preoccupied, thinking back over the events in his City, and from this he took some encouragement. It was true that one campaigner was dead whilst others, together with troops and police, had been injured. It was bad enough but at least they had avoided all-out violence. Also, against the background of stalemate and truce, some hopeful ideas had emerged.

The helicopter landed and he was thankful to leave it. He walked with his bodyguards towards the entrance to the Command Bunker, past a security check with its armed guards and into a lift area where he was taken underground to be confronted again by batteries of telephones, computers and monitor screens.

Alerted to Blake's arrival, Bill Charman greeted him. "We've got an early meeting in the Conference Room. Did you have a good journey?"

Blake was exhausted. "No I didn't. You promised me comfort, there's none in that bloody helicopter.

They went through to the canteen. "I've just had the latest report from your area," Bill said. "You did a good job."

"We didn't start a civil war, if that's what you mean. For that you can thank Champney. I still don't understand why we didn't consult the Prime Minister."

Bill Charman was unconcerned. "I had my reasons and I didn't have time to argue. Don't worry, he'll go along with it."

"You'd better be right. There's no way we can go back on that deal." Blake swallowed some tea. "Bill, you didn't explain your reasons for acting on your own."

Bill looked at the time. "We should get into the meeting. I'll tell you in there. There's no point in going over it twice."

They moved into the Conference Room where they joined Dudney, Culverton and Anderson. As Blake sat down, Culverton greeted him across the table.

"How did you get on, Minister, working with Champney?"

"Very well, Brigadier. He's very competent..."

"He should be. He's an expert in counter-insurgency."

"That's interesting."

The Prime Minister entered, looking drawn. Without acknowledging anyone present, he sat down and opened the meeting. "Yes... well, to carry on where we left off yesterday. We seem to have had some success. We've got a tight security zone around Whitehall and Westminster. We've dealt with the threat in Blake's area and in the rest of the country things seem fairly quiet ... that's my reading of it. I'm not saying it's going to last." He shuffled his papers and carried on in a subdued voice. "We've brought forward our contingency plans. The eleven areas of control are secure and are now in operation. For a more detailed report we'll turn first to the Home Secretary... "

"You said a more detailed report, Prime Minister," began Bill Charman, "I should begin with the agreement we reached with the Campaign in Blake's area..."

The Prime Minister looked up sharply. "Agreement? What agreement? I'm not aware of any agreement."

Bill Charman kept a firm voice. "When I say agreement, it doesn't mean that we've weakened our position. On the contrary, we've established the security zone around the control bunker but we have allowed the Campaign a presence in what was planned as an exclusion zone."

"What are you telling me, Home Secretary?" the Prime Minister demanded. "I didn't agree to this."

"It was very late Prime Minister you were resting and I didn't want to bother you with minor details."

"You call it a minor detail? That exclusion zone was to provide a buffer between our control centre and the City and now you say it's gone."

"It's just a few people who are not going to bother us," Bill Charman insisted. "The agreement was put to me and I endorsed it."

"Who put it to you?"

"Blake put it to me on the advice of the army commander, but I endorsed it and I want to tell you why. This brings me to another part of my report. We face a rapidly deteriorating situation throughout the country. Public morale is disintegrating. The problem we face now is more serious than any threat from the Campaign. I'm talking about absenteeism from work, hoarding, looting and crime. If these continue at their present rate we'll see a complete breakdown. It will include the collapse of some vital services on which our security forces depend."

Undeterred, the Prime Minister confronted Bill Charman. "That doesn't entitle you to make decisions without first consulting this Unit, and above all, without first consulting me."

Bill Charman faced him squarely. "There had to be a quick decision to prevent all-out conflict. I took that decision and I also take full responsibility."

"But you had no responsibility. Your decision was unauthorized and is therefore invalid." The Prime Minister turned to Blake. "So, this unauthorised action was your idea, Blake?"

In spite of being tired, Blake roused himself to the argument. The usual way to deal with the Prime Minister was to flatter his vanity or play on his fears but now it was a time to stand up to him. "I didn't know about the collapse of public morale," he said. "Had I known, I wouldn't have consulted anyone. I would have made the decision myself. Due to an unfortunate incident, a campaigner was shot dead."

Anderson had been waiting for an opportunity to complain. He interrupted Blake. "Prime Minister, I want to protest at the way my colleague was removed and is being held responsible for the death of a saboteur. Fraser is a sound police officer with many years experience..."

The Prime Minister stopped him. "Yes, alright Anderson, we'll come to that later." He turned back to Blake. "I repeat: your action was unauthorised. I'll revoke it."

Blake continued. "Before you do, Prime Minister, you should consider all the facts. To begin with, things were going well until a campaigner was killed, and that created a very different mood. From that point on any dispersal of the crowd would have meant all-out violence raging through the City. In the opinion of the army commander..."

"Since when did any army commander give us political advice?" the Prime Minister shouted.

Blake shouted back. "Well, whatever it was, I agreed with it and I acted on it. Like the Home Secretary, I take full responsibility."

"You've got no responsibility. I'm the one with the responsibility. What do you mean? Are you both telling me that if I revoke this so-called agreement, you'll resign?"

"No one has mentioned that, Prime Minister," said Bill Charman.

"But you've both implied it..."

Bill Charman also raised his voice. "No, Prime Minister, nothing would please the Campaign more than splits in this government." He lowered his voice and continued. "The collapse of public morale is now our most serious problem." He reviewed the information which had been flooding into the Home Office, beginning with mass absenteeism from work. If this continued, production would break down and services would come to a halt.

Seeing no government action, people were staying at home to construct their own makeshift shelters. There had been a wave of panic buying. People were hoarding food and other essentials causing shortages and price increases. With living more expensive there would be renewed discontent. More industrial action was inevitable. Where people were unable to buy stocks, they were stealing. In some areas, because of overstretched police resources and with little fear of arrest, crime was rampant.

Bill Charman looked through a file of leaflets issued by the Campaign and described its systematic attack on the morale of the security forces. He reminded the meeting that individual members of the security forces were subject to the same fears as the rest of the population. Some of them saw no sense in putting down a movement which appeared to be acting in their interests and those of their families. Some even felt they should be cooperating with the Campaign. He gave examples of members of the security forces who had been won over to the Campaign's cause.

There had also been a collapse of business confidence, with panic selling causing share prices to fall steeply. The loss of share values amounted to many billions of pounds.

In his long report he came to the problems of internal security, describing how the government's administration was now full of informers who were actively working for the Campaign. Every decision of the government was being made public, except for those made informally at the highest level.

He eventually concluded. "These reports, coming to us hour by hour, reveal a disintegration of morale on a scale that threatens national breakdown. So, coming finally to the events of last night, I was advised by Blake that extreme violence was about to break out. I could only see this as aggravating widespread economic and social collapse. That is why I endorsed the compromise which had been proposed. It was a decision which took account of the very serious national situation..."

As the Home Secretary spoke, the Prime Minister became more withdrawn. As the sombre report was completed there was a lengthy pause before he was able to respond. "Home Secretary, you say this difficult situation in Blake's area was caused by the death of a campaigner?"

"That is what the report of the army commander states, Prime Minister. Whether the police lost their nerve, it's difficult to say, but it does appear that they acted against his instructions. It seems they went straight in with firearms. In other words, they didn't use them as a last resort."

"And you confirm that, Blake?"

"I haven't seen Champney's report," Blake replied. "All I know is that things were going well up to that point."

The Prime Minister turned on the Police Commissioner. Unable to vent further anger on his political colleagues, he glared at the one member of the Committee who was immediately dispensable.

"Anderson, do I understand that you were complaining about the removal of your colleague?"

Anderson saw the danger in his position and reacted nervously. "I'm only surprised, Prime Minister. As I said, Fraser is an officer of many years' experience..."

The Prime Minister pressed him. "You don't think he defied the army commander's orders?"

"I'm sure it was an over-hasty response by his men."

"But you do endorse the removal of this officer?"

"In the circumstances, of course, Prime Minister. Yes, I do."

With Anderson having backed down, the Prime Minister seemed even more at a loss. In view of Bill Charman's pessimistic report, it was clear that force alone could not prevent the national breakdown that he feared. He put his head between his hands and stared down at his papers. "Where does all this leave us?" he murmured.

Blake replied. "Prime Minister, we've got to find a political solution. We need action based on national agreement and for that we need national consultation."

The Prime Minister looked up. "Suppose we provide it, what are we going to talk about? You know the demands of the Campaign. They're impossible."

"I'm not so sure," Blake replied. "A lot of people have been thinking about the problem. I don't mean the Campaign, I mean serious people who recognise the government's difficulties. I've looked at one proposal which I think is very useful."

Blake went on to explain the credit scheme which would allow the millions of unemployed people to work on the deep shelters. Their monetary benefits would be made up to the average wage with the issue of credit notes which could be exchanged for cash once the dangers had passed. He reminded the Unit that as a result of the recent recession, there were stockpiles of building materials around the country that could not be sold. Companies would welcome the opportunity to contribute these for credit notes which, again, in due time, could be exchanged for cash. Local authorities, as well as the Services could make transport, equipment and machinery available.

The example of the voluntary workers in the hospitals had shown that many people would be willing to give their time and energies free for the safety of their communities. The self-help schemes in the cities could also be adapted for the work, which could be organised by local production boards. The work of cooperation would go ahead under a National Consultative Council which could include the Trades Union Congress and the Campaign.

"We've got immense resources which are not being used," Blake concluded. "This system of post-crisis credits could release everything we need. With this scheme, I can't think of a single reason why the work on deep shelters shouldn't begin immediately."

The Prime Minster was sceptical. "I'm still not convinced there's any real crisis. There's still no conclusive evidence."

Blake pressed him. "But we've all heard the Home Secretary. The danger of national collapse is very real and so is the threat of chaos and political upheaval."

Blake's reference to political upheaval reminded the Prime Minister of a possible threat to the government. "I don't want to be misunderstood," he said. "We should look at your idea." He turned back to the meeting. "You've all heard what Blake has said, does anyone want to comment? How about you, Dudney?"

Like other members of the Committee, the Secretary for Defence was exhausted. He had spent many hours in contact with army commanders, coordinating troop movements throughout the regions. He roused himself to reply. "On the face of it, the idea seems practical. In our position we've got to look at any proposal. I suggest we take some wider advice. We should consult the Treasury."

Bill Charman also agreed. "I trust Blake's judgment, but we ought to get the views of the Treasury which would have to draft any detail."

"Alright," said the Prime Minister. "We'll take a look at it. I suggest a break. I'll consult with the Chancellor and the Treasury."

He glanced at his watch. "We'll meet again in an hour's time." He took up Blake's file on the credit scheme and without a further word, left the Conference Room.

Blake and Bill Charman went through to the communications centre where they flashed up reports from around the country. They came to Blake's area. "Your agreement is still holding," said Bill. "Things look quiet."

"Don't imagine that Erica Field is being quiet," replied Blake. "She'll be organising the Campaign's next move. The truce is conditional upon work on shelters being started. If nothing happens, they'll be back. Champney warned me that next time they'll be better prepared, so you've got to support this credit scheme."

Bill Charman flashed up more reports. "It sounds useful," he said, "but I'm not an economist. You told me that yourself."

"To hell with economics. You told me it's absurd to think we can't afford to survive. This scheme gets round it, the credits will defer payments to the future, and this way, we'll have a future."

"I'm sure we'd all prefer that," said Bill. "Lindsay and the Treasury will find all sorts of problems but I'll support it. If you're ignorant enough you can support anything. The Prime Minister will support it. He'll do it for reasons which will have nothing to do with economics. It might be useful if we get him to give another broadcast."

Blake decided to consult Dudney but found him asleep in a rest room and felt like joining him. Instead, he returned to the Conference Room, where he made notes on the new work of his Department should the credit scheme be introduced. After an hour, the Committee began to reassemble. Blake was joined by Culverton and Anderson, then Bill Charman returned, followed by a bleary-eyed Dudney.

They waited for the Prime Minister, who eventually swept into the room accompanied by Lindsay the Chancellor. The Prime Minister resumed the meeting. "Yes, well, to carry on, we've had a look at this credit scheme. It's sketchy but it's interesting. The essentials are there. However, there are some Treasury objections. I'll let Lindsay put them."

The Chancellor was noted for his cautious book-keeping and a lack of imagination that many blamed for the sluggish economy. "As I understand it," he began, "local authorities would be empowered to issue credit notes in exchange for labour, machinery and materials. Work would go ahead on the construction of deep shelters and in due course, the government would pay out on the credits. The idea isn't new, it's happened before, but the problem will be this. Without constraints on the issue of credit notes, we'd run up a huge debt that no future government could honour. It would never find the cash."

Blake had no doubt that the Treasury could find a dozen objections to the scheme, but he was also relieved when the Prime Minister overruled Lindsay. "Personally," he said, "I don't find that argument insurmountable. We can't be irresponsible. We can't lumber any future government with an impossible debt, but these are grounds for caution, not grounds for abandoning this scheme."

"But there is another point," said Lindsay. "It must be voluntary. The decision of any business to provide materials or equipment must be left to their commercial judgment. There must be no pressure which might threaten their business viability. I don't have to spell out the problems that would arise from that."

"It's not proposed as a compulsory scheme," said Blake. "Surely, firms will welcome the opportunity to exchange their unsaleable stocks for credit notes."

"Yes," agreed Lindsay. "So long as we don't run up an impossible government debt."

"We've agreed to keep an eye on that," said the Prime Minister. "We'll control the whole thing from Whitehall." He paused and looked round the table. "So what have we got here? We've got a voluntary scheme based on national cooperation. That's how we'll present it. I'm certain the country will respond. We've had this splendid example of voluntary work in the hospitals. Volunteers came forward. They didn't hesitate. They've maintained the hospitals and it hasn't cost the government a penny."

Blake pressed the need for a National Consultative Council, but still found the Prime Minister unwilling to sit down with the Campaign.

Bill Charman intervened. "It's distasteful, I know, Prime Minister," he said, "but we've all got to swallow some pride. After Frank Bell's conspiracies, it won't be easy for Blake to confer with him but we expect him to do it. To get this scheme off the ground you should broadcast to the country. You are the one to secure national cooperation but we can't ignore the Campaign. We've got to rebuild public morale and the only way is through the Campaign's millions of supporters. Your broadcast would carry more weight if we made that gesture, so I would urge you to agree."

Dudney reinforced the pressure on the Prime Minister. "Now that we've got a practical plan for civil defence, we can invite the Campaign for talks on condition that they bring the demonstrations to an end. That would release more of the security forces to deal with law and order."

The Prime Minister was wary of the combined influence of his senior colleagues, but was also attracted to the idea of a further broadcast to the country. He saw once more the possibility of being a leader, gathering together the strands of national unity at a time of crisis. "Yes, well, perhaps you're right," he conceded, "perhaps I should make another broadcast. Consulting with the Campaign is against my better judgment. However, I did say that with our authority not in question we could make some concessions. Perhaps this could be one of them."

He contrived a long pause in his remarks then looked earnestly round the meeting before continuing. "You know, I'll be perfectly frank with all of you. There was a moment early this morning when I felt I should resign. It was a long night for all of us and this was during the early hours. It's a good time for reflection. I could hardly believe what was happening in the country, and for a moment I felt that it could best be served by a change at the top."

Culverton and Anderson listened intently, impressed by the drama of the Prime Minister's remarks. The political members sat with patient forbearance. It was another self-indulgent performance and they had heard it all before. "That's what I thought," he continued, "I honestly thought it needed someone fresh. But now with a new day, new circumstances and new ideas, I'm convinced we've got a team that can see this thing through. I'll do what you suggest. I'll broadcast to the country tonight. I'm satisfied that with persuasion we can get the nation to unite. We've got the means which are radical I know, but they'll enable us to deal with the problem whilst preserving stability. I suggest we all get to our stations. Let's get back to our Departments and get this plan organised."

So saying, the Prime Minister adjourned the meeting, stood up, and approached Blake. "Look Blake, this young man who suggested the credit scheme, who is he?"

"He's from my local party," Blake replied. "He's one of our young councillors. His name is Chris Lawson."

"I want him in Whitehall. We need his fresh thinking."

"It won't stay fresh in Whitehall, Prime Minister."

"You can take him into your Department."

"I don't think Jack Brightwell would welcome that."

"We won't let him interfere," said the Prime Minister. "You realise, I overruled the Treasury on this credit scheme?"

"I appreciate that."

"So, bring him in. In our situation we've got to be adaptable. Don't you see? Our ability to adapt ensures stability in the long term."

"I do see the point."

"Good," said the Prime Minister, "and by the way, try not to have another row with Frank Bell. I know he's difficult but we need him now to offset this Campaign. Remember, they're a flash in the pan but the TUC is always with us."

"That's what he says."

"Like it or not he's right, so set up the machinery for consultation. Anything will do so long as it doesn't interfere with us."

25

Blake returned to his office where his plans were pre-empted by a telephone call from Frank Bell.

"Hello, Blake," he said, "I've been trying to get you for days."

Blake noticed his more friendly tone. "Yes. I've been diverted."

"Look, about our last meeting..."

Blake stopped him. "Forget it, Frank. As I said at the time, there's no point in looking backwards."

"We want a summit meeting. Prices are going mad so we want price controls, and there are other issues."

Blake stayed his hand. "That's very difficult."

Frank persisted. "If you can't give wage increases you could at least give us price controls."

"Yes, but the government has its own agenda."

"So, what do you want?"

"We want the TUC to get behind our plan for starting work on deep shelters."

Frank Bell was wary. "What do we get out of it?"

"Nothing, if you keep on thinking like that," said Blake. "We're trying to deal with the worst crisis in our history and all you want to know is what you're going to get out of it."

"Yes, but I'm not too caught up in all this hysteria."

"You can call it what you like, but everyone else is taking it seriously, and we're taking steps to deal with it. We've set up a National Consultative Council. Do you want a place on it?"

"What's it going to do?"

"It's going to work with local production boards for the construction of deep shelters using voluntary workers and the unemployed."

"You mean you're creating real jobs?"

"The work is real enough but there'll be no money. We'll issue credit notes and we'll pay out on those when the crisis has passed. If you support this credit scheme we'll get the work started. Also, you'll get your statutory price controls."

The ever suspicious Frank Bell was now even more wary. "It means trusting a future government to pay out on the credits," he said.

"That's right, Frank. It means trust and voluntary cooperation. It means not asking what you can get out of it except the survival of the country, and it means something else, millions of your members are now represented by the Campaign, so if you don't join in, where will it leave you?"

"Blake Evans, you're a ruthless bastard. This is blackmail."

"Not at all," said Blake. "You asked for a summit meeting: I'm giving you more. I'm giving you a part in local and national decision-making. You asked for price controls; I'm giving you those as well. In exchange, we want you to help organise the work on deep shelters under the credit scheme."

Frank Bell hesitated. He was trapped. If he refused to participate the TUC would risk total isolation. Blake continued to press him.

"The Prime Minister is broadcasting tonight. Can he say that you're behind our plans?"

"I'll have to take it up with the General Council."

"Don't give me that, Frank. We all know who's boss of the TUC. Alright, then what's your personal view? If the Prime Minister can say that you support our action, that's good enough for me, but I want it now." Blake took a gamble. "We've finalised our plans; after today there'll be no place for you."

"I thought you said it was voluntary? This is a lot of bloody pressure."

"The urgency is the pressure," said Blake. "We've got to get the country working together. Are you joining in, or not?"

"All right, you can say I support it and I daresay that goes for the TUC. We'll join in on condition we get price controls."

"You've got my word on it, Frank."

"Your word on it? Thanks for nothing."

Blake put down the phone and after more difficulties eventually got through to Patrick Laurie at Campaign Headquarters. "Mr. Laurie?" he began, "it's Blake Evans here. You'll remember, we met recently at the Home Office."

"I'd rather forget it," said Laurie. "What can I do for you?"

"I want to apologise for the death of the campaigner last night, and I want you to know we sacked the officer who was responsible."

"We know that but it doesn't help our member, he's dead."

"Sadly, there were casualties on both sides."

Inevitably, Laurie was suspicious. "Minister, what do you really want?" he asked.

"I want to make sure there are no more tragedies," Blake replied, "and I want to tell you what the government is doing. At our last meeting you asked for a part in decision-making. Well, we've set up the National Consultative Council. I'm inviting you now to join and help organise the work on deep shelters. The Prime Minister is broadcasting tonight. Will he be able to say that you have accepted?"

"It's a pity it comes so late," said Laurie, "but yes, of course. Of course we'll join in."

"Good, but we want you to stop the demonstrations. We need a different demonstration now, one which shows that we are all working together. That's not possible if your people are on the streets, acting against the government."

"No, Minister," said Laurie. "We'll help organise the work on deep shelters, but we'll also keep a presence on the streets. Don't worry, if the work goes ahead, they'll be orderly."

"That's unacceptable," replied Blake. "I should tell you now that the TUC has agreed to cooperate with the government and they've got millions of members as well. We'll work with you but only if you clear the streets, otherwise we'll work solely with the TUC and you'll be excluded. We'll make it obvious to the whole country that your only object is to cause disruption."

"I'll have to discuss it with our National Committee."

"No," said Blake, "there isn't time." Again he took a gamble. "You are the ones who have always stressed the urgency, so we've finalised our plans. If you don't agree now you'll be excluded. Do you want to join or not?"

There was a long pause as Laurie hesitated. "The most I can say is this, Minister. Whilst the work goes ahead we'll agree to what you ask."

"And you'll stop the demonstrations from now?"

"Yes."

Blake was relieved. "Good, then you're officially invited to join the National Consultative Council. The Prime Minister will announce your acceptance tonight. Oh, and there's one other thing," he added. "Are you sabotaging the telephone lines into Whitehall?"

Again Laurie hesitated. "Why? Are you having problems?"

"You know very well we are," said Blake. "It doesn't make sense even for you. How can you listen in on government conversations if we can't get through?"

"Minister, we've had a useful talk."

Laurie hung up, but Blake was satisfied. There was now a practical plan for beginning the work on deep shelters. Both the TUC and the Campaign had agreed to participate, and Laurie had agreed to remove the demonstrators. In combination, these steps should help to restore public morale.

After more difficulties with the telephone, he informed Bill Charman of the results of his contacts with Frank Bell and Laurie. He suggested that news of the National Consultative Council could be included in the Prime Minister's broadcast. With this done, he took out his notes on the new work of the Department and continued his planning. He called in Jack Brightwell and together they drafted a long memorandum to the Treasury on the problems of administering the credit scheme. Whitehall would maintain an overview of the work of local production boards. This would be the central check on local authorities; it would also assist with coordinating the national effort. They went on to assess the new demands on the Department's communication systems and its facilities for processing information.

As they worked on, Blake was conscious of the time. He should get to the House of Commons. It was important to keep the All Party Group fully informed but as the evening closed in and Janet left the office he abandoned any idea of getting to the House. Eventually he called a halt. "All right, Jack," he said, "we're not going to settle all the problems at once."

Brightwell's enthusiasm was undiminished. "Yes, there's always another day," he said. "Minister, I believe you were up all night, so why don't you go home and get some rest. I'll carry on."

Blake looked at him. "Jack, I sometimes think you live in this Department."

"I'll continue to clarify the problems. Once we've done that, things should go smoothly."

"I don't believe it," said Blake. "Nothing ever goes smoothly."
He stood up and put on his coat, leaving Brightwell surrounded by paper. It was clear that his senior bureaucrat was intent on keeping a close grip on every new development. As he left, Blake was suddenly aware of being engaged in useful work. There was a great deal to do and the frustrating barriers which normally prevented action seemed to be falling away.

Accompanied by bodyguards, his car took him to the edge of the security zone where groups of demonstrators still remained in Trafalgar Square. He was disappointed. It had been some time since Laurie had agreed to disperse the crowds. He found a police inspector. "What's happening?" he asked. "I'm expecting these people to leave."

"They're gradually going, sir. The square was packed after the violence of last night. They seem reluctant but they are moving off."

"You're sure?"

"Definitely. Our men are amongst them so we know what's going on. They're a bit surprised at being told to go home and, let's face it, some of them like it here."

"So they'd soon return?"

"Very quickly, I'm sure."

Blake got back into his car, satisfied that Laurie was keeping to his side of their bargain. He felt relieved, and slumped into the back seat as the car picked up speed. With his relief came exhaustion.

26

Blake let himself into the house. He had kept in contact with Rachel and she was expecting him. On hearing him return, she met him in the hallway, where they embraced. For a moment they stood locked in each other's arms. He was glad to be back, desperately tired but also satisfied with the outcome of events. She had followed the news, and had no doubt that he had played an important part in creating a more hopeful outlook.

She stood back and smiled. "You do look ghastly," she said.

"And I feel it."

"You look definitely haggard."

He dumped his briefcase, took off his coat and jacket, went upstairs and threw himself on their bed. She followed him up. "If I had a drink this could be paradise," he said.

"I'll join you." She closed the curtains. "We'll just shut out your bodyguards."

"They're hard to shake off."

"So long as they don't join us in bed."

As Rachel went downstairs he thought back over the events of the past two days. A crowd of images tumbled through his mind. Characters appeared and reappeared. Parts of what they had said echoed from a mix of confused situations. It was only in his clearer moments that he knew they had pulled back from the brink of violence.

Rachel returned with a bottle and two glasses. "If people are buying everything in sight we should stock up on drinks," she said.

"We're trying to stop the hoarding."

For all that she was pleased to see him, Rachel was unable to resist her teasing manner. "Are you now beginning to practice what you preach?" she asked.

"It depends on the state of our cellar."

He propped himself up, sipped his drink and looked at her as she sat on the bed. "It seems an age since I saw you," he said. "So much has happened. How are things at the hospital?"

"We've got some peace at last," she replied. "Suddenly, this evening the demonstrators melted away. It seemed like a miracle."

"It was no miracle," he said. "I've been twisting arms all day. Last night things were on a knife edge."

"Were you in danger?" she asked.

"No. I was safe in the bunker with the army commander."

"Delightful company," she said.

"He's not what you might think. I was surprised." He thought of the part played by Champney. "He did a good job. He knows that in the end people need each other. The problem is getting them to realise it and to motivate them into action."

"And what are your motives?" she asked.

For a moment he thought about his own part in conflict and the tortured arguments that propelled them from one crisis to the next. "Who can tell?" he said. "In my best self-image I mediate between warring factions, trying to reconcile opposites, striving for the impossible, trying to break an eternal deadlock." He looked at her and smiled. "But you may not think so."

She smiled back. "I think you're as power-crazed as the rest of them."

He looked at the time. "Speaking of power, big brother is about to broadcast."

Rachel switched on the bedroom television. Again, the broadcast came from Downing Street, but instead of showing the Prime Minister in cosy, domestic surroundings, the camera brought him into closer focus. His head and shoulders filled the screen and his face looked determined. This was the Prime Minister in the role of strong leader.

"You will all understand why I speak to you again. We all have to accept that now is a time of grave crisis. I also have to tell you that the crisis has been made worse by our own actions. False rumours have spread alarm and have made our situation worse. At a time like this, our greatest enemy can be ourselves.

However, it is undeniable that as a national community, we do face some possible dangers, but the truth remains as I have put it to you; no responsible body is saying that it is certain we face the threat of destruction. We can and we will protect ourselves. We face a great challenge and we will win.

For this we must not be complacent. As your government, we have deployed all branches of the Services for the protection of our people. Despite this, as we have seen, tens of thousands took to the streets, making it impossible to carry on with the work of civil defence. This has caused a tragic delay. We've seen the needless death of a protestor. Our police and troops have been attacked and injured. They have been diverted from their vital work. Surely, if there is any threat to our community, we should not declare war on each other. We should stand together, in unity.

Despite this setback, the government has been getting on with its job. We have set up the necessary organisation for a great national project but it can only be brought to success through cooperation. We must now put all our differences behind us. Any individual or group who attempts to frustrate our efforts will be guilty of the worst kind of sabotage. We must give our full support to the police and security forces. Without cooperation, without law and order, we will degenerate into chaos. We will destroy our communities by our own hands. Particularly at this time, disruption and crime must be seen as deeply repugnant, and a danger to us all. It will not be tolerated.

A National Consultative Council will bring together every section of the community. Every local authority will establish production boards. You will see the details of a credit scheme in the government's information. These measures will release the labour, the materials, machinery and equipment for the work in hand. Contact your local councils, listen to your local radio stations. They will direct your efforts to where they are most needed."

Throughout the talk the cameras kept the Prime Minister's face in close focus. His eyes penetrated the homes of millions as he warned against panic buying, hoarding and the wave of absenteeism which had swept the country. He spoke earnestly, urging the population to stay at their jobs and to work harder.

"We now have the means to go forward. The government is acting with speed and urgency but on its own it can do nothing. None of us can evade our responsibilities. It is up to all of you to respond to the initiatives we have taken. Our success depends upon the willing efforts of every member of the community. Having secured the means, it is up to all of us to achieve the ends. I know I can rely on you."

Having spoken as both a strong leader and, more intimately, as a candid neighbour, the image of the Prime Minister was faded from the screen. Blake considered the impact of the broadcast. The impression had been one of total honesty. In truth, there was a wide difference between the Prime Minister's account of events and the reality behind the scenes.

He got up and switched off the television. "What do you think?" he asked Rachel.

She had been impressed. "He spoke well and I'm sure everyone will respond," she said.

"Things didn't happen quite the way he said."

"Don't tell me, Blake. If there were lies, I don't want to know. I want to believe that everything is just as he said."

Blake understood. In choosing between the truth and the needs of the hour, it seemed wrong to recall the facts.

27

Under the direction of the Civil Contingencies Unit, the Whitehall machine moved into action. In each of the eleven emergency areas local production boards were established and began to co-ordinate the work of civil defence. When Blake saw the make-up of the board in his own area, he could barely resist a smile. A more unlikely group of individuals sitting round the same table was difficult to imagine. Even less predictable were the alliances which soon took shape. To Blake's surprise, Erica Field and Champney found themselves working easily together. With his experience of military organisation linked with her enthusiasm, they formed an energetic partnership. These were not the only former enemies who began to share common ground. At the same time Ron Jackson, the trade unionist, often found himself in agreement with Michael Buckfast from the City trades council, who represented business.

The board established its headquarters in the Town Hall. Some of its meetings were brief, whilst others continued for hours as its members hammered out the details of local organisation. The self-help projects were adapted. More voluntary workers came forward and thousands of the City's unemployed also became available. To keep the public informed, the Campaign's network of communications was combined with a stream of information put out by the local radio station. Buckfast presented a list of local firms who were able to supply equipment and materials whilst from the Services, Champney organised a supply of specialist skills, transport and heavy equipment. Clive Poole and Chris Lawson contributed every available resource from the City's councils.

With Blake in Whitehall, Chris Lawson kept him fully informed. Erica Field and Champney shared the same method of work, making swift decisions followed by immediate action. It was clear that Champney admired Erica's boundless energy and her influence throughout the Campaign. Against this, Ron Jackson remained cautious about the use of voluntary workers, insisting that the work on civil defence was an opportunity to create what he called "real jobs". Buckfast was anxious to safeguard the interests of local firms. Time and again he joined with Jackson in arguing that the work should not interfere with normal economic arrangements. Despite some tension, work went ahead with massive excavations for deep shelters at convenient points in the City and surrounding areas.

Following his broadcast, the Prime Minister basked in renewed popularity. Throughout the country he was enjoying the prestige of having created the new spirit of cooperation. He presided over the meetings of the National Consultative Council, which were held in rooms set aside at the Home Office. In deciding the make-up of the Council, Blake had urged the Campaign not to send Hurst, whose volatile presence could only be disruptive. As a result, the Campaign appointed Patrick Laurie and Betty Stevens.

With some misgivings, the TUC sent Frank Bell and Ken Adams, another leading trade unionist, whilst the Confederation of Industry appointed Sir Gordon Rowan. The make-up of the National Consultative Council was completed with the addition of every member of the Civil Contingencies Unit. Whilst the Council gave the impression of being a decisive national body, the Prime Minister was careful to ensure that its work was confined to a consultative role. Confidentially, he saw the work of the Council as a means of monitoring the mood of the country. He used the Council to guide the real power of decision- making, which remained with the Civil Contingencies Unit and which continued to meet in secret.

Reporting to the Civil Contingencies Unit, Bill Charman confirmed an immediate improvement in public morale. Absenteeism from work was reduced. Transport and other services were back to normal. Food and other goods were no longer being hoarded and the government's price controls had resulted in less industrial unrest. Crime was down and the police were enjoying their best relations with the public. There was a mood of confidence in the country. The visible evidence of the work on the deep shelters, and the responses of people to what needed to be done, had lessened anxiety and had begun to create a strong and healthy sense of community.

Bill Charman reminded the Civil Contingencies Unit of the crucial question that had been put to him. Following the Campaign's demonstrations throughout the country, he had been asked whether the security forces could maintain law and order in all circumstances. He was not then in a position to give that guarantee. At the time he had no doubt that the government could prevent any threatened seizure of power but the recent collapse of public morale had confirmed that, without the goodwill and support of the majority of the population, not even the massive powers of the security forces could ensure good order. Now he could report that the government had reclaimed the public's goodwill. It had never enjoyed so much support. He also confirmed that the Prime Minister had never been so popular.

In the mind of the Prime Minister, these reports confirmed him as a great leader. More arrogant than ever, he intervened directly in the affairs of all government departments. Manipulating the National Consultative Council with skill, he kept it under his firm control. Exploiting the fact that both the Campaign and the TUC had agreed to join it on the government's terms, because they feared being isolated from the national initiative, he was able to set one against the other. With veiled hints at his power to exclude either of them, he compelled each to act with restraint.

Behind the scenes he also prepared a wide range of further options. He instructed Dudney and the Army Chiefs to keep specially trained army units isolated from the civil defence work. There was no need, he argued, for every army unit to become involved, and the less contact they had with civilian projects, the more they could be relied upon to deal with further civil strife.

Each day, Blake spent long hours in his office working with Jack Brightwell, who was now reconciled to the part-time presence of Chris Lawson. Together they adapted the Department to the task of coordinating the work of civil defence. This required a constant flow of information from the local production boards. As each board assessed its requirements of labour, machinery, equipment, transport and materials, these were communicated to Whitehall to be processed by the Department. To cope with the flood of information, new analysts were brought in. In this way, the Department operated as a central pool of statistics which collated the requirements of labour, equipment and materials in each locality. As a result, Blake and his colleagues commanded an overview of the entire national picture.

It was only as the Department's systems were expanded and the mass of detailed information began to pour in that Blake began to pick up some worrying indications. The supply of labour was abundant. Some local production boards were unable to use all the people who had put themselves forward. However, there were early doubts about the supply of materials and equipment. Blake had at first relied upon the availability of unsold stocks, but it now appeared that these would be insufficient. Perhaps his optimism had clouded his judgment but as more accurate summaries of total demand were collated it became clear that there would be shortages.

The first surge of work was applied to excavating the sites of deep shelters. For this, local authorities, private firms and the Services had supplied cranes, bulldozers, excavators and heavy transport. The work had gone ahead, but beyond this there would be a need for millions of bricks and building blocks, tonnes of cement, sand and quantities of steel reinforcing. Thousands of air filtration plants and heating installations would be required, and in addition, there would be a need for water supply systems and sanitary units. As Blake studied the summaries of everything required for a national programme of deep shelter construction, his optimism ebbed away. The figures were undeniable. To complete the work, vast quantities of materials and equipment would have to be newly produced.

Blake threw his pen at the paperwork that covered his desk and summoned Chris Lawson. They noted the demand for materials and equipment and compared it with the amounts that would be available under the credit scheme. They would never be enough. The young councillor, who had first proposed the scheme, looked dejected. "It was never worked out," he said. "Everyone seized on the idea without thinking it through."

Blake recalled the decision to take up the credit scheme. For its own reasons the Treasury had opposed it but they had been overruled by the Prime Minister. The decision to go ahead had been taken hurriedly in response to compelling political pressures and with little thought for the practicalities of the idea. Blake looked at the depleted figure of Chris Lawson. "Don't be depressed," he said. "Look on the positive side. Your plan got people working together."

"We've only postponed the crisis."

Partly to cheer up his young colleague, Blake disagreed. "We've done more than that," he said. "We've got a clear picture. We know we've got the labour resources and we've got the production capacity. We've also set up a national organisation."

Chris was not encouraged. "But the lack of materials will soon show up. What happens then? Inevitably, the work will come to a halt. We need a compulsory scheme. Local production boards should be given powers to requisition production facilities."

Blake knew that the proposal was impossible. The Prime Minister would never accept it, and in any case local production boards would face the same problems as would private companies. To continue production, they would still need a surplus of income over expenditure, and public finance could never pay the bills. He put the arguments to Chris.

"In that case," said Chris, "we should at least make all our information public."

Blake leaned back in his chair and thought for a moment. "There is another option," he said. "We could keep quiet. We could say nothing and let people find out for themselves. As you said, it won't take long."

"But what would be the point, and what about Mr. Brightwell? Would he agree?"

"There's no problem there," said Blake. "Jack is always in favour of restricting information. He's a bureaucrat, he does it by instinct."

Chris persisted. "I still don't see the point. Everyone accepted the first idea, so why should there be any problem with compulsory powers of requisition? It's the logical way forward."

Blake smiled patiently. "You think that's why people do things, because it's the next logical step?"

"Well if they don't, they should."

"Think back," said Blake. "The Treasury objected to the credit scheme but the Prime Minister overruled them. Why do you think he did that?"
"I haven't got the faintest idea what goes on in his head."

"Yes, well I have. He took up your idea because it got him out of trouble. It gave him a new hold on power and he's thriving on it now. The TUC agreed because they were scared of being isolated by the Campaign. The Campaign agreed because they didn't want the TUC taking over their role. The business people agreed because it was voluntary and because it averted upheaval. From their point of view it was a safe way of preserving the existing state of things. In other words, they were all thinking of their short-term interests and none of them considered the practicalities."

"It seems a hell of a messy way to get things done," said Chris.

"It's the only way we know," said Blake. "People react to pressure not logic."

Chris persisted. "We can't just sit here and do nothing."

"I'm saying we should say nothing and let people find out the facts for themselves. In the meantime, we should work out what powers of requisition are needed and then pick our own time to bring them forward."

Having been reminded of the complexities that surrounded their situation, Chris Lawson looked defeated. "I never imagined that things could be so difficult," he said.

"Of course you didn't," said Blake. "Why should you? You still believe that people think and act reasonably."

28

In less than two weeks there was a shortage of materials at the sites of deep shelters. Chris Lawson kept Blake in touch with the reactions of the production board in his area and reported on its problems. At first there were no difficulties. At each site, day and night, excavations went ahead reaching deep into the earth. A fleet of lorries took away the debris. With this work well under way, local suppliers delivered materials. Sand, cement, bricks, building blocks and reinforcing steel began to pile up, but soon the supplies slowed down, became infrequent and then stopped. Firms had supplied all the materials possible under the credit scheme. Cooperation gave way to impasse and dispute. Enthusiasm was replaced by a new mood of frustration and anger.

Blake had been expecting it and flew north to attend a crisis meeting of the local production board. It was the first time he had been back since the night when the Campaign had threatened to take over the control centre. As he landed in the compound he recalled Champney's grim comment that the night of violence had been only a dress rehearsal for the main event which was yet to come. He could only hope that the army commander had been wrong.

Now able to move around without bodyguards, he walked through the gates of the perimeter fence which were still guarded by police and armed troops. He then headed for the Town Hall, where he found the production board already beginning its meeting. He took a seat beside Clive Poole who, as chairman, was opening the business with his usual appeal for calm.

"We all know about the slow-down in the work," he said. "It's frustrating for all of us, but there's no reason for anyone to get angry. It won't help. The work has gone ahead but, let's face it, there were always going to be some problems. We're not getting the materials we need, and that's disappointing, but it's not the end of the road. We're here to work out a solution."

As Blake expected, Erica Field was the first to speak. He was reminded of her final words to him the last time they spoke. The Campaign had agreed to a working truce only while the work went ahead. Her anger was ominous. "One thing you haven't mentioned, Mr. Chairman," she began, "is that the people who matter are not here. We expected some of the main suppliers of materials. There's no point in this meeting without them."

Clive Poole tried to reassure her. "Mr. Buckfast is here. He's representing all the local firms."

"Yes, but can he make decisions on their behalf? Can he assure us that more materials will be delivered?"

Clive Poole looked towards Buckfast. "Are you able to commit the local suppliers?"

Buckfast was uneasy and shuffled his papers before answering. "I've consulted with all our people. I've gone into the matter at great length. I can explain their problems."

"Good," said Clive Poole. "Obviously, we'd all like to know."
Buckfast continued to rearrange his papers. "If you'll all be a little patient I've got a mass of figures that give us the full picture. We've got to understand the limits on the materials that can be released for credit notes. Firms have got to remain viable. They've got to maintain a cash flow. They can't operate with the promise of future cash, and it's not in anyone's interest for them to go bankrupt. If they're forced to close down, that won't help anyone. It's one thing for them to make voluntary contributions, but you can't expect them to commit business suicide. If you want the figures, I could explain things in greater detail."

Blake brought some gentle pressure on Buckfast. "Your Confederation has been very helpful in supplying my Department with statistics. I've looked at them closely. They reveal a considerable stockpile of unsold materials. For example, there are still millions of bricks piled up around this City. Mr. Buckfast, I would have thought it was in the interests of your people to exchange these for credit notes. I agree, you won't get the cash now, but you will get it in time. Surely deferred payment is better than not selling them at all?"

"That's a fair point, Minister," Buckfast replied, "and I'm glad to hear we've been helpful. You've got to appreciate that firms have their capital tied up in those stockpiles. This means they've run short of cash. They've had to run down production and lay off workers. To stay in business, they must sell their stocks for cash so as to buy in what they need from their own suppliers. If not, they'll go bankrupt, and as I said, that won't help anyone. They'll have to close down."

Gently, Blake pressed him. "Are you certain they've done as much as possible?"

"Naturally, they want to do as much as they can and as you know, quite a lot of materials have been delivered. As you're here, Minister, I'd put the same question to you. Are you certain the government has done all it can to find more cash for this urgent work?"

This brought the argument back to its old stalemate, and, although Blake had answered it a hundred times before, he still felt bound to reply. "You've got to realise the cost of this civil defence work. It runs to hundreds of billions of pounds. The government can't provide even a fraction of it."

"In that case, Minister," replied Buckfast, "you seem to be expecting private firms to lend hundreds of billions to the government. That, in effect, is what the credit scheme amounts to. Well, even with the best will in the world, private firms haven't got that sort of money, and I do assure you, they want to do everything possible."

In line with his newly found alliance with the Confederation, the trade unionist, Ron Jackson, supported Buckfast. "The trade unions also think the government should provide more cash. We've got an opportunity here to create real jobs. Instead, people are working for the dole and getting these useless bits of paper called credit notes. It's labour on the cheap, that's what this scheme amounts to."

Blake stared impassively at Jackson as he replied. "I don't think that represents the trade union view. The TUC is cooperating with the government." He decided to push the meeting into further impasse. "The Confederation has got its figures. I'll give you some of mine. Just take the one example on our doorstep, a deep shelter designed for 20,000 people: 250 metres deep with 64 tiers. The basic cost is £200 million. Add to that the cost of facilities and equipment. These are lifts, power supplies, air filtration, sanitation and waste disposal, fresh water, food and fuel, cooking, lighting, heating, medical care and all the rest of it, which would cost an extra £100 million. It gives you an estimate of over £300 million for just 20,000 people. Increase that figure for the entire population and then tell me where the government is going to find the money?"

Seeing the futility of the same old argument, Erica Field cut across the meeting. "I'm not interested in any of these figures," she snapped. "I don't care what they are or where they come from; I'm only concerned with getting the materials delivered on site. We've got willing people waiting to use them and they're not going to wait any longer. Our Campaign has done its own check and we know exactly where these materials are. It's simply a matter of shifting them to the various sites, and if there's no agreement to release them voluntarily, we'll take the transport and collect them ourselves."

Clive Poole tried to restrain her. "Yes, all right, Erica, let's not be too hasty."

She glared back at him. "And I don't want to be treated to stupid remarks about not being too hasty. We've wasted too much time already." She looked around the meeting. "There is no problem. It's simply a matter of shifting the materials from one place to another, so that's what we'll do." She turned to Champney. "We'll use some of the Colonel's transport. That won't cost anything. Not even one of your stupid credit notes."

Champney smiled at her. "Of course, Erica, we'll supply anything, so long as it's within the law." Behind his smile he was anxious not to return to any confrontation with the Campaign and, in particular, with Erica. He turned to Clive Poole. "May I say something, Mr. Chairman?"

"Feel free, Colonel."

"You understand, I don't want to get into any arguments which are not my business. I'm here to provide assistance from the Services. That's what I've been doing and I think we've all worked well together, but now there are fresh difficulties, and if I'm allowed to put in some ideas...?"

"Just get on with it, Colonel," said Clive Poole.

"Well, because of being in the army, I suppose, I tend to think of what we're doing as a kind of military operation. That's how I'm trained to see things. I've taken an interest in how war economies have been organised in the past when there were similar problems of production and supply, and so on. As you may know, in previous war situations, both the government and local authorities had the power to requisition certain things that were needed. They could take over land and buildings. We've got some of these powers now under the emergency, but then it was possible to take over materials, various production units, factories and so on, and even to direct labour. Well, as we've now got this problem of supplies, it might be useful to reconsider bringing in powers of requisition. Everyone was perfectly happy about it in the past and it got the job done, so why not do the same thing now?"

Blake and Chris Lawson exchanged glances. What Champney had said was precisely in line with their own plan. Buckfast had listened to the Colonel with increasing alarm and was quick to point out an bjection. "That's all very well, Colonel, but those powers of requisition were carried out within a definite war budget. This meant it was fair because there was financial compensation wherever the powers of requisition were used. All the work of production and supply was paid for, but now there is no budget for the construction of deep shelters. The Minister has told us that himself so, without compensation, how could any system of compulsory requisition work?"

"Well, I don't know much about economics," said Champney quietly. "I only pointed out how useful those powers have been in the past. It would be a pity if some fine point of economics were to prevent the country from protecting itself, that's all I'm saying. It seems to me that no one else has suggested a way forward."

Again, Erica intervened. "I agree with the Colonel but with one difference. We've already got the powers of requisition. We've got more than enough people to shift those materials to the sites. Is this a production board or are we powerless to act? Are we going to move this stuff or not?"

"It's obvious," Buckfast insisted, "we can't act against the law."

Erica turned on him. "It is within the law. It's the law of what must be done."

Buckfast raised his own voice. "And who decides what has to be done?"

"It's bloody obvious what has to be done," Erica shouted. "What sort of law are you talking about?"

"You can't put yourself above the law."

The meeting sat helpless as Erica Field and Buckfast continued their shouting match. By now Erica was completely enraged. She stood up and turned on the meeting. "This so-called production board is useless. Our Campaign will shift the materials, not just here, but everywhere."

As she stormed out Blake looked across the table towards Champney. They both realised that renewed confrontation between the security forces and the Campaign would result from Erica having left the meeting in a rage.

Buckfast grabbed his papers and stuffed them into his briefcase. His face was flushed. He stood up and turned to Blake. "Minister, we're all aware of your position on the Civil Contingencies Unit. I trust that you will do everything necessary to protect my members."

Blake said nothing as Buckfast left the room. After an embarrassed silence, Clive Poole asked if the meeting should continue. "I said at the beginning we shouldn't get angry. I knew it could come to this. I don't know if it's worth carrying on. All that's come up is the idea of compulsory requisitions. Do we want to pursue it?"

"I'm totally against any direction of labour," Ron Jackson snapped.

Clive Poole reassured him. "That won't come into it. We've got masses of volunteers for the work."

"The Colonel mentioned direction of labour. Who is going to direct it, the army?"

Even Clive Poole was running out of patience. "For Christ's sake, Ron," he said, "be reasonable. You've got to support requisitions. You know bloody well there's no alternative."

Blake looked around the depleted meeting, knowing that the views of the production board would mean nothing to the Prime Minister. He turned to Clive Poole. "As a matter of fact, Clive," he said, "Chris and I have been thinking about ideas similar to those of Colonel Champney. The best thing now is for me to get back to Whitehall and try to get the government to agree. I think I should get a move on. The last thing we want to see is a return to violence."

The meeting adjourned, and Blake left the Town Hall with Colonel Champney, who could barely conceal his disappointment. They walked towards the bunker. "I thought you expected that something like this would happen," said Blake. "It was you who said that the last confrontation was only a dress rehearsal."

"But a lot of good things have happened since then," said Champney. "I honestly thought we were past the violence. Now I'm back in that damned bunker preparing for another riot. I know that people like Erica can be difficult but, with respect, Minister, I think there's been a political failure."

"Yes, I know, Colonel. It's all the fault of a few politicians. I've been told that so often I almost believe it myself."

29

Having returned to Whitehall, Blake went on to Downing Street to the room where on previous occasions he had met with the Prime Minister and Bill Charman. He found them sitting around a table surrounded by reports.

As Blake entered, Bill Charman looked up. "We're back to where we started," he said. "So much for your credit scheme."

"I've known for some time it would run into trouble," Blake replied.

"Then why the hell didn't you say so?"

"What difference would it have made?"

The Prime Minister intervened. "All right, it's no use getting into that argument. We were all committed and that includes you, Bill. The point is we've got to measure the reaction." He turned to Blake. "What happened on your local production board?"

Blake took off his coat and threw it over a chair. "The same as everywhere else, I imagine. With the blockage of supplies the work has broken down. That meant fresh arguments, another stalemate. It was all predictable. The member from the Campaign stormed out. She was followed by Buckfast from the local firms. It left the production board in tatters."

The Prime Minister frowned. "I would expect local business to act more responsibly."

"Buckfast was provoked," Blake continued. "Provoked by the Campaign's threat to seize materials. He was also embarrassed. The board felt that suppliers could have done more and this put him on the defensive. I think it suited him to walk out."

"And have they done as much as they can?" the Prime Minister asked.

"It's difficult to say. Buckfast had a lot of figures to show they have, but we can all produce figures. That's easy, but no one is interested."

"Yes, it's very disappointing," said the Prime Minister. "I appreciate how everyone must feel. Clearly we've got to take some action. We need a new initiative."

For Blake, this sounded hopeful. "Have you got something in mind, Prime Minister?" he asked.

"Yes. I think it's a job for our National Consultative Council. We can bring pressure on the suppliers to do more. I know we're operating a voluntary scheme but if it isn't working, if people aren't pulling their weight, we could look into it. If the complaints are justified, the Council can bring pressure on them to do more. Yes, a bit more pressure. That should be our next step."

Blake knew this would be useless. It was the Prime Minister's way of evading the problem. He looked at Bill Charman and picked up the Home Secretary's obvious misgivings. There was a pause before Bill indicated the paperwork that littered the table. "You've seen these reports, Prime Minister," he said. "They tell us the Campaign is organising a seizure of supplies."

The Prime Minister seemed unconcerned. "Yes, I've taken note of those reports."

Bill continued. "The Campaign isn't giving us much time. Even if your suggestion could produce results it would be too little and, I'm afraid, much too late."

"We're not going to be rushed into anything, Home Secretary. I hope you're not suggesting that we respond to blackmail?"

Bill Charman persisted. "Prime Minister, the whole country expects us to take some positive action. We can't ignore that demand without again destroying public morale and neither can we ignore the Campaign. Its National Committee is meeting now and we know what's on its agenda. They're planning a nationwide seizure of materials. We'll have to sort out the blockage of supplies sooner or later, so let's deal with it now."

The Prime Minister became annoyed. "Home Secretary, I have already put forward a constructive proposal. We'll ensure the delivery of supplies by working through the National Consultative Council. We'll treat that as urgent but if it takes a little time, then so be it."

"Well I'm sorry, Prime Minister, I don't think it will be accepted as being good enough."

"Don't you indeed?"

"No, I don't."

"You mean you don't accept it?"

"I'm speaking for the country."

"Don't you think I speak for the country?"

"Prime Minister, I'm going by these reports."

Blake cut across their argument. Seeing that Bill was anxious to get a solution, it was likely that he would support compulsory powers of requisition, and, with both of them pressing the Prime Minister, it was possible that he would also agree. "Prime Minister," he said, "we know the emergency legislation gives us wide powers of requisition. These could be extended. It's been suggested that local authorities should have powers to requisition supplies and, where necessary, to take over production facilities."

The Prime Minister's eyes narrowed with suspicion. "Is this your idea, Blake?"

"There is nothing new about it. These powers were used in the war years."

"I don't recall any system of legalised theft where people had their property and production facilities seized, not by local authorities nor anyone else."

"But they were taken over..."
"Yes, but with full compensation, and that makes the difference," said the Prime Minister. "You know we're not in a position to pay out compensation."

"We could cover it with the issue of credit notes."

"You know that's impractical as well. We've already been warned by the Treasury. We'd create an impossible burden of debt. In any case, we're fully committed to a voluntary scheme."

"But it isn't working, Prime Minister," said Bill Charman.

The Prime Minister raised his voice. "Then it's our job to make it work. Clearly we haven't done enough to ensure cooperation. That's what we've got to do now through the National Consultative Council." He remained adamant before coming to the real reason for his objection. "Can't either of you see where these powers of requisition would lead? You'd have local production boards or even worse, local authorities, running the country. Where would be the control? Where would it leave the government?"

"I don't see the difficulty," said Bill Charman. "We could arrange for ultimate control to stay with us."

"I'm not interested in ultimate control. I don't even know what it means. I want continuous, direct control. If Blake's proposal can include our direct control, then maybe we can look at it."

Blake took up the argument. "If you're suggesting that a government department could run the work, then I'm afraid it would be impossible. Whitehall could never cope with the thousands of decisions that would have to be made every day. You've got to leave it to local people who understand what needs to be done in their own areas, people who can best organise local resources and who can keep on top of things as the work proceeds."

"There you are," said the Prime Minister, "you've said it yourself. There would be no government control. We wouldn't even know what's going on. I'm not prepared to abdicate responsibility. I'm damned if I'm going to preside over the destruction of our system of government." He stood up and began pacing the room. "Nor do I want to hear any more about what the Campaign is plotting. If their Committee is organising a seizure of property, it's an illegal conspiracy."

"It's a very public conspiracy," said Bill Charman. "Everyone knows about it."

"That makes no difference, it's still a conspiracy to commit illegal acts. We've got powers to arrest the whole damned lot. Why aren't we using them?"

"It's not very practical, Prime Minister," said the weary Bill Charman. "Arrest the National Committee and others would simply fill their places. We can't arrest the whole Campaign."

"I don't accept this over-dramatic nonsense," said the Prime Minister. "I don't know what's got into you two. You both seem to be influenced by the Campaign. Our priority is to uphold the authority of the government. That's first on our agenda, and we don't compromise on that. If it's true that we're facing a new threat, I want all our security forces alerted and placed on immediate standby."

The Prime Minister appeared to calm himself. He sat down. Aware of having rejected the views of his two closest colleagues, he was anxious to avoid a break with them. At last he spoke quietly. "You both know very well that I supported the civil defence work under the present scheme. I overruled the Treasury. I broadcast to the country. All I'm saying now is that we should persist with this initiative. I'm reminded that any day now, we'll get firmer information from the American space probe. I'm convinced that it will settle people's fears. So all we need is a bit more patience until we know exactly what we're dealing with. In the meantime, tomorrow morning, we've got a meeting of the National Consultative Council, so, working through that, we can step up the pressure on suppliers to release more materials."

"Yes, well I for one can't see that it will achieve anything," said Bill Charman. "I want to make that clear, Prime Minister."

"All right, Bill. You've made your point but try to understand that I'm not shutting the door on anything. If both of you are right and I'm wrong, we'll take a closer look at the idea of requisitions. It would have to be carefully worked out, keeping the government in full control. Then it would be something we could keep in reserve. Surely that goes a long way towards meeting you?" He turned to Blake. "I'm not rejecting your views," he said, "I'm trying to create a little more time during which we'll keep our options open."

"I don't think we have that time," said Blake.

"We'll see. I take it we close the meeting still feeling amicable, and still committed to working together?"

For a moment, the Prime Minister seemed a lonely figure, but Blake knew from experience that this was merely a ploy, part of his repertoire of manipulative skills which could just as quickly switch to ruthlessness. Despite knowing this, Blake gave the Prime Minister the assurance he sought. "Of course," he said.

Yet even as he did so, he also decided that his next step must be to go to the House of Commons to seek out Dave Reed. Reed was now secretary of the All Party Group of MPs which was organising voluntary work in the constituencies. Working confidentially with Chris Lawson, Blake had drafted a set of amendments to the Emergency Acts which would give local authorities all the necessary powers of requisition. There might come a time when the House of Commons would have to assert its authority, but Blake knew that any approach to MPs at this time would be seen by the Prime Minister as a betrayal and would therefore be risky. However, without giving them sight of any actual texts, it was nevertheless, important to put the question of requisitions into the minds of the All Party Group.

The informal discussion was adjourned and it was agreed that a full meeting of the Civil Contingencies Unit would take place at 8 o'clock the next morning. This would be ahead of the National Consultative Council, when the plans of the Campaign would be known in more detail.

"I could tell you what their plans are now," said Bill Charman as he gathered his papers.

Anxious to get away, Blake left the Prime Minister and Bill Charman having final words. He left Downing Street, hoping that Dave Reed would be in the House. As he walked along Whitehall, fresh movements of troops and police were reinforcing the security zone. Army transports were again moving into position.

On reaching the House he found an atmosphere of tension. Members were present in large numbers, anxious to know what was happening. He found Dave Reed discussing rumours with a group in a bar. Blake moved in close to him. "Look, Dave. I want a word in private. Can you get away for a moment?"

"Surely."

They found a quiet table and sat down. "You look very worried," said Dave. "That's unusual for you."

"We should all be worried. We're into a new round of violence but far worse than before."

"Yes, we've noticed the troop movements around Westminster."

"And all over the country," said Blake. "We're on the brink of violence in every town and city. Even at this moment the battle lines are being prepared." He explained the stoppage of supplies to the deep shelter sites, and the plans of the Campaign for seizing materials. "But there's another problem. We've got a one-man government. The Prime Minister now has powers that would be the envy of the worst dictator."

"That's inherent in the emergency," agreed Dave, "and of course, it's a risk. Does this explain your worried look?"

"In a way, yes." Blake paused as he thought how to continue. "Can you remember when the House last took charge of events?"

"I think I need notice of that question," replied Dave. "No, I can't remember. Why do you ask?"

"One solution would be to give local authorities powers of requisition. The Prime Minister is against it but we can't allow one man to block our progress. It means the House will have to assert its powers. The All Party Group is already involved in voluntary work, so it is well placed to carry this forward."

Dave Read was reluctant. "I don't know," he said. "Why don't you introduce the amendments yourself? You're the one who created the All Party Group."

"You know I can't do that, Dave. You know I can't act in the House against the Prime Minister, and this is no time for a split in the government. I've built up an efficient organisation in my Department for coordinating the work throughout the country. I can't risk being booted out."

"So, you want to take a back seat and conceal your moves?"

"I don't think you should put it like that, Dave. I'm trying to keep the ship afloat. We've got to have these powers but we can't have a crisis in the government. There's enough chaos already."

"What about the other members of the government? What's their attitude?"

"What government? There's only Bill Charman, Dudney and myself with two Service chiefs who don't count at all. It's the Prime Minister who makes all the decisions." Blake pressed his colleague. "Look Dave, you've got to make up your mind. We're on the brink of civil war. Either you spend your life complaining about the House being impotent or you take back control. If it's necessary I'll resign from the government and do it myself. Is that what you want?"

Although Blake was unaware of it, word had spread through the House that he was doing a good job. Dave thought for a moment. "No, it's best if you don't resign. This is what I'll do. Leave the idea with me and I'll take it up with other members of the All Party Group, but I have to warn you, they might not be reliable. They joined the Group because it made them popular in their constituencies, but supporting wide powers of requisition will be a different kettle of fish. Even so, I'll do my best, so on that understanding, leave it with me."

Satisfied with Dave Reed's response, Blake left the House and walked quickly amongst the hurried movements of the security forces which were once again reinforcing Westminster. On reaching the Home Office he went through to Bill Charman's office where he found the Home Secretary besieged by a mass of further reports. Bill was surprised to see him. "What are you doing here?" he asked, "I thought you went back to your Department."

Blake had decided to put Bill Charman fully in the picture. "I've just come from the House. I'm not happy with what we're doing. We're too much in the hands of the Prime Minister. It's dangerous. We can't leave things to one man."

"So, you've been plotting?"

"No." Blake explained his approach to Dave Reed and, because he had total trust in Bill Charman, he took out a copy of his draft amendments to the Emergency Acts and passed it to him. "We've got to have this. It's the only solution and it's going to take the House to bring it in."

Bill Charman read it. "You want to make this law?" he asked. "The Prime Minister is right, it's total freedom for local people to take over anything they like. It would destroy all our normal economic arrangements. Have you thought about that?"

"No, I haven't, and I'm not going to. Start doing that, and you'll find it's impossible. These amendments come from absolute and compelling necessity, and we've got to go where it takes us. Bill, I want you to support it. Your endorsement would carry a lot of weight."

"You must be mad," said Bill. "Put this about and you'll get the pair of us thrown out of the government."

"I don't mean now," Blake insisted. "I mean to put it forward at the right time, if it becomes necessary."

Bill Charman changed the subject. "There's something you should know," he said, "I've had one report that the Campaign is back to issuing threats. Our names are high on their hit list. Dudney thinks of it as an accolade, he seems quite pleased. I've also had a phone call from Dr. Hollins. It seems she took a threatening call on your behalf."

Blake felt an upsurge of anger. The phone call to Rachel indicated that more ruthless elements were taking over the Campaign.

"You could both move into the security zone," Bill added. "You'll be safe here."

Blake declined. "Alright," said Bill, "I'm with you on the requisitions. I hope you're with me on the need to resist the Campaign with all the force necessary?"

Blake felt he had been softened up by Bill Charman giving him the news of the Campaign's threats. "Why do you doubt it?" he asked.

Bill Charman smiled. "I don't doubt it. We'll leave it at that, then. We'll let events take their course. If your move succeeds it will leave the Prime Minister stranded."

"No," said Blake, "he'll survive. In this whole bloody mess, that's the one certain thing."

His car took him home and, as he tried to relax, he felt oppressed by the sheer complexity of events. The simple need to carry through the work on deep shelters should be enough to make it happen. Why must they return again and again to conflict? In this depressed state he found Rachel listening to the news.

"Are we really back to where we started?" she asked. "It seems all your work has come to nothing."

"Not exactly," he said. "There are one or two hopeful moves."

"I telephoned Bill Charman. I hope you don't mind. You've had a threatening call from the Campaign."

"Yes, he told me."

"Did he tell you about the policeman in your City?"

"Fraser?"

"They burned his house down, as a punishment, they said. They've set up their own courts. Now they're looking for him. He's had to go into hiding."

"How did you know about the fire?" he asked.

"It was on the news."

"Broadcasting that wasn't very bright. It's just what the Campaign wanted. It will intimidate a lot of people. Perhaps one of their supporters worked it into the news."

"But if they're burning down houses, what about us? I feel like doing something. I could speak to Sandra Dale. She wouldn't approve of these threats."

"I doubt if she has any influence now," said Blake. "The people of violence have taken over and they can justify anything. Anyway, they'd be delighted to know we were worried. We shouldn't give them the satisfaction."

"You're bloody hopeless, Blake. I don't know which is worse, their threats or your complacency."

"Well, we've been invited to move into the security zone. On the other hand, I could throw in the damned job. That would please the Campaign, and you've always wanted it."

Rachel looked at the dejected figure beside her. "Well, I've changed my mind. I think you should stick with it."

Blake was surprised. "Any particular reason?"

"I can't think of one good reason, except that you seem to upset everyone – your local party, your trade union friends, the Campaign and god knows who else." At last she smiled. "Anyone who can upset so many different people at the same time must be doing some good."

30

After some hours of fitful sleep, and at the first light of dawn, Blake set out for Westminster. His bodyguards avoided the crowd of demonstrators which had assembled overnight in Trafalgar Square. Instead, his car entered the security zone from the Embankment, where the way through was clearer. On arriving at the Command Bunker, he passed security checks and made his descent underground. The central operations room was again alive with signals personnel monitoring batteries of screens against a background of ringing telephones. The network of communications which radiated from Whitehall to each of the regional control bunkers was fully operational. Intelligence was being processed and printed out in a constant stream of reports. Responding to these, the Command Bunker was sending instructions to all units of the security forces.

Blake had expected to go through to the conference room for the early meeting of the Civil Contingencies Unit. Instead, he found Bill Charman in conversation with Dudney at the centre of operations. They explained that the meeting would have to go ahead without the Prime Minister. Having been up for most of the night, he was exhausted and wished to take some rest before the meeting of the National Consultative Council, which was scheduled for 10 o'clock. Blake was sceptical, suspecting other reasons for the Prime Minister's absence.

Throughout the country police and army chiefs were insisting on an immediate decision on the permitted scale of force to be used against the Campaigners. Even with the mass of intelligence which had been pouring into the bunker, it was still difficult to know precisely how the Campaign would move. Security chiefs suspected the Campaign of feeding misinformation into the intelligence system. Therefore, a range of adaptable responses had to be prepared.

The five members of the Civil Contingencies Unit moved into the conference room, where Bill Charman took the chair. Brigadier Culverton began by setting out the options.

The main objective of the Campaign was clear. It was to seize construction materials and transport them to the sites of deep shelters. The Brigadier referred to the maps spread across the table, which indicated the distribution of materials at production plants. In addition, there were many suppliers who held smaller stocks. The problem for the army commanders was how best to deploy their forces at every point where the Campaign could strike.

Culverton pointed out the Campaign's advantages. It could put vastly superior numbers into the field; it was a disciplined organisation with high morale; it had penetrated the government's communications systems; it had the support of the population; it could harass the security forces by disrupting services. It had been partly successful in undermining the morale of the troops and police. In combination, these advantages meant that the Campaign was a formidable opposition.

Against this, the government could now deploy the highly trained army units which had been held in reserve. These were reliable but their numbers were relatively small.

The Campaign was now engaged in violent reprisals. Overnight, the unprotected homes of some senior police officers had been burned down. Other police, named as being guilty of violent acts against the population, had been abducted and savagely beaten. The practice of publishing the names of guilty persons continued and was an effective part of the Campaign's tactic of intimidation. Despite this, it was certain that in the renewed confrontation, the Campaign would not rely on violent methods. Intelligence had revealed that a proposal to seize police officers and hold them as hostages against casualties amongst campaigners, had been rejected. Using their superior numbers with minimum violence, the Campaign would attempt to overrun and occupy places where materials were stockpiled.

He went on to explain that the deployment of troops and police had to be related to the permitted severity of the security response. Fewer forces using severe methods were equal to greater forces using softer methods. Three or four troops using automatic weapons with the licence to fire-at-will could easily protect a stockpile of materials. To do the same job using only batons would require troops and police in large numbers. Knowing this, the Campaign would attempt to keep the violence to a minimum because this would be to the advantage of their superior numbers.

Time would be the critical factor. The outcome of the conflict would also depend on how long the action continued. At a low level of violence the Campaign could sustain continuous pressure by rotating fresh numbers in the field. Prolonged attrition would wear down the troops and police. Without rest and recovery they would soon become exhausted and demoralised.

Culverton spoke with an air of calm detachment, and as Blake listened intently to the Brigadier's long and detailed analysis, it became apparent where the Brigadier was heading and he at last arrived at his conclusion. For the security forces to succeed, there must be a swift and decisive outcome. To achieve this, he wanted political clearance for the unconditional use of firearms. "The principle to be applied," he said, "is that army commanders must make the decision that will bring a quick end to the conflict, using the lowest level of force necessary."

Bill Charman was alarmed. "Surely, Brigadier, we won't use firearms straightaway? You've mentioned a decisive outcome. Can you explain what you mean by that?"

"It's very clear in my mind, Home Secretary," he said. "First, it would mean failure by the Campaign to seize the stocks. Second, their withdrawal and third, a position where they were no longer a threat. To achieve this, we must impose a swift and punishing defeat, compelling them to abandon any thoughts of further action. As I've said, it requires your clearance for an unconditional use of firearms and, I would add, without it we cannot win."

"Yes, I see," said Bill, "but it's going to be very difficult to justify, especially if the Campaign doesn't use that sort of violence first."

"But not because they're against it," said the Brigadier, "but only because it gives them the tactical advantage."

"Yes, I understand that, but it doesn't make our decision any easier."

The Brigadier was unequivocal. "Home Secretary, I can only give you the Services' view. Considering all the important factors, it is an inescapable fact that without the freedom to use firepower we will not succeed in the job we've been given."

Bill Charman was still reluctant. "It's very difficult without the Prime Minister."

"The Campaign is on the move," Culverton insisted. "We must have a decision now."

Blake was reminded that from the army view the way ahead was more straightforward than the politics of the conflict. Culverton was seeing the problem strictly in terms of his orders to stop the Campaign seizing materials, but in trying to anticipate the consequences of extreme violence, the political members of the Unit had to take a wider range of factors into account.

"One thing is also clear," said John Dudney. "If the Campaign's illegal methods succeed, there will be no ordered means of carrying out a proper political solution."

"I accept that," said Bill Charman. "There'd be chaos."

"Which won't even suit the Campaign," Dudney added. "Seen in this light, the use of firearms in upholding the law would be in the overall interest of the campaigners."

Blake was anxious to steer the Unit away from the course outlined by Culverton. "I agree with John about one thing," he said. "We've got to work for a political solution, and in fact we could be close to one. I'm very sceptical about the Brigadier's view of things. His arguments about what he calls 'a swift and decisive outcome' are based on the idea that the Campaign can be cowed into submission by the punishing example of killing its members in the field. But the risk here is that they could also take up firearms. Are we sure they haven't got them already? They would be able to argue that they used them in self-defence. Give them more martyrs and we could be looking at civil war. Has the Brigadier analysed the question of who would win a civil war? I don't think he has."

Culverton remained adamant and put further pressure on Bill Charman. "You've heard my assessment, Home Secretary, you've heard my advice. Without the use of firearms you will not be able to blame the army commanders for any failure." With this comment, it appeared that Culverton was preparing the ground for any failure to be firmly blamed on the politicians.

"Brigadier, no one has ruled out the use of firearms," replied Bill Charman. "I'm sure we agree. It must be an available option, but I was concerned because you gave the impression that we'd move straight in with firepower. I understand your position: you don't want things to drag out, but surely the army commanders can be given the discretion to act with restraint. Appreciate our position. We're going to have to justify it politically. You won't have to do it, we will, and it won't be easy. On your own admission, the Campaign has the support of the population." He turned to Blake. "It's clear, Blake. We've got to allow the use of firearms at least as a last resort."

"There's no way we can allow them to penetrate Westminster," said Dudney. "We must prevent that, regardless of the cost."

Blake realised that if the Campaign took over Westminster and seized the stocks of materials, it would destroy his initiative in the House. Any constitutional attempt to change the law in the Campaign's favour would become meaningless. "As you say, Bill, firepower as a last resort, but in my view we should not seek a swift and total victory. We should forget about that. I come back to what

I have said before. What we need from the Services is a holding operation which would give us time for a political solution."

After further argument, Dudney agreed, and Bill Charman turned back to Culverton. "You've got our clearance, Brigadier. We'll use firepower, but only as a last resort. For the time being we'll use methods which are consistent with a holding operation, with the minimum use of force. Let that be your instruction to the army commanders. Are you happy with what we've said?"

"You've shifted the objective, Home Secretary. You're saying now that we should merely protect the stocks, without forcing the Campaign to withdraw and abandon their action."

"Yes, precisely. Defend Westminster at all costs but prevent a seizure of stocks with a minimum use of force. In other words, buy us some time."

"That's going to be difficult," said Culverton. "Time is on the side of the Campaign."

At this, Bill Charman felt he should remind Culverton of the political realities. "What we often find, Brigadier," he said, "is that every option has got its problems. Then it becomes our job to work our way through them. We rarely get the result we expect but we can be certain of one thing. The indiscriminate use of firepower will cause immense problems. Your idea that it will produce a quick solution may be an illusion. That should guide your instructions to the army commanders."

For Culverton, Bill Charman's comments were little more than an evasion by the political members who were unable to face up to the real choices that were imminent. Instead, they had taken refuge behind vague phrases such as "the minimum use of force", which meant nothing. He knew that in the heat of conflict, combatants would be driven by their instinctive reactions without much thought for any wider questions of what was right. However, he also felt that he had said enough and that he should no longer persist. He would have to make the best of what he had been given.

Having made a decision, the five members of the Civil Contingencies Unit returned to the question of the deployment of the security forces. The reserve army units would be concentrated in the places where the main stocks of materials were held at production plants. Culverton moved quickly between the maps which covered the table and the communications centre from where he sent out a fresh stream of instructions.

With this in progress, Blake and Bill Charman moved to the operations room. With some time to go before the meeting of the National Consultative Council, they checked the reports coming into the Command Bunker. Roadblocks had been set up on motorways and key junctions, preventing the movement of campaigners. Helicopter cameras relayed pictures of campaigners filtering through minor roads and lanes. At some points they had overwhelmed the police, smashed the barriers and dumped them away from the roads. Some police vehicles had been taken over and were being used for the Campaign's own communications.

Bill Charman watched the scenes with growing anger. "It proves Culverton right," he said grimly. "With firepower they could easily be stopped."

"Don't be tempted," said Blake.

Anderson, the Police Commissioner, produced the Campaign's latest leaflet. "They're printing them by the thousand all over the country," he said. "It's pure sedition." Blake read it.

"To all members of the security forces. For the safety of you and your families, our Campaign is continuing the work on civil defence. Our sole aim is to transport materials to the sites of deep shelters. This task is in your interests so do not act against us. Protect your families by joining our Campaign. You have nothing to fear. We will protect you. Any criminal acting against our Campaign will be named and dealt with."

"A simple, direct message," said Blake. He was still suspicious of the reasons for the Prime Minister's absence from the meeting of the Civil Contingencies Unit. "You say he was tired, Bill?"

"Disappointed, I suppose, and apparently depressed. He's been enjoying his popularity. He could lose it now."

"There were no other reasons?" Blake asked.

"Possibly," Bill replied. "Knowing that we'd have to make a decision on the use of firepower, he stayed away. If things go badly, he can say the decision was made without him. If things go well, he can take the credit. Either way, he can't lose."

"Yes, that sounds like him," said Blake. "So, if things go badly, where will that leave us?"

"Where do you think? We'll get the blame. We'll be finished."

31

Leaving Brigadier Culverton in charge of the Command Bunker, the three Ministers left the operations room, took the lift to the surface and walked the short distance to the Home Office. Frank Bell and Ken Adams from the TUC had already arrived, having been brought through the security zone by official car. Also present was Sir Gordon Rowan from the Confederation of Industry. Members of the Campaign were conspicuously absent. The group waited for the Prime Minister in the room set aside for the meetings of the National Consultative Council.

Whether or not his earlier absence had been a ploy, the Prime Minister entered the room, again looking tired and grim-faced. With shoulders hunched, he took his seat and stared round the meeting. His voice was bitter. "We won't have the pleasure of the Campaign's company," he began. "I'm not surprised, nor am I concerned; in fact I'm relieved. We've got the government, we've got the trade unions and we've got management, so who else do we need? We are the ones who represent the country and, by working together, we can deal with any problem." His manner was remote, his remarks were unconvincing and left a feeling of unease around the table. "I think it would be useful," he continued, "if I were to summarise the economic situation."

Blake winced. With the campaigners on the move and the security forces being deployed, it was no time for such lectures. Despite this, the Prime Minister launched into a long and irrelevant review, the same well-rehearsed speech he inflicted on the Cabinet time and again.

He began with his slogan: it was costing the country far too much to produce much too little. He spoke of the state of employment, low production, poor productivity, high wage levels, the trade deficit and the excessive rate of public spending. Everyone must confront the basic problem: production should be more competitive. It had to be more than equal with the opposition. It had to forge ahead, producing high quality goods that people wanted, at prices they could afford. That was the challenge. The nation had to do all these things better than anyone else. That was the message to put out to everyone. Sublimely unaware of the realities that had brought the meeting together, he continued in what seemed gibberish. There was nothing in what he said that could connect sensibly with what was happening throughout the country.

As embarrassment spread through the meeting, and still distanced from immediate problems, the Prime Minister continued to speak over the heads of those present until, at last, his soliloquy came to an end.

"I began by saying that we have the government, the trade unions and management. What more do we need than cooperation between us now? In combination, we can set new wheels in motion and put this country right. That is our responsibility, that is our call to action and we must respond. From this moment we must go forward in a new spirit of cooperation, which will ensure our success. I want to ask each one of you. Is there anyone in this room who does not share the objective that I have set out?"

The Prime Minister seemed pathetic as he observed the silence of the meeting. After a lengthy pause, Blake offered a tentative response. "I'm sure we all agree Prime Minister, but at the moment we do have this particular crisis which does require our urgent attention."

With narrowed eyes and a suspicious glare, the Prime Minister turned on Blake. "Are you suggesting I don't know what is urgent? Are you denying that year in and year out I've been warning the country? But what has happened? My warnings have been ignored. Can anyone now expect to escape the consequences? Does anyone imagine that I could have done a better job?"

As the Prime Minister stared at the silent faces around the table, Blake tried to ease the meeting forward. "I'm sure you have everyone's confidence, Prime Minister. You were right to warn the country and no doubt our present problems could have been avoided, but going forward from where we are now, we do have to take immediate action."

The Prime Minister appeared to calm down. "Yes, well, that's all I'm saying. We've got to see a more constructive attitude. I've done my best so it's up to others now." As he continued, a fresh note of anger entered his voice. "The trade unions have been at fault. Management has been at fault. It's all been sectional greed and no one has thought of the country. If the trade unions had not been so short-sighted, so demanding and disruptive, we would be seeing a thriving economy, and we would have the resources to cope with present events. What we are seeing now are the consequences of their folly."

As the Prime Minister threatened to launch into a tirade against the trade unions, Blake glanced across the table at Frank Bell who was beginning to shift uneasily in his seat. If the Prime Minister continued, the burly secretary of the TUC would not contain himself for long. Yet again, Blake tried to divert the Prime Minister. "May I make a suggestion? It might be useful if..."

With raised voice the Prime Minister stopped him. "No, Blake, no. Why do you keep interrupting? I don't want to hear from you. I want to hear from the trade unions and from management. They are the ones who have got us into this mess." He confronted Frank Bell. "What is the TUC prepared to do? What have you come here for? Have you come to make more demands or have you got something to offer us for a change?"

Frank Bell sat rigid with anger. "One thing is for sure, we haven't come here to be insulted, so let's get that straight. Prime Minister, you're out of touch with reality. Our people have made all the sacrifices. Even the government will know that, when it comes to its senses."

"What do you mean by that?" the Prime Minister shouted. "I'm talking about the senseless actions of the TUC, the constant demands, the constant strikes and disruptions. You even shut the hospitals down. Did that make any sense? Sick people denied care. What sort of sense does that make?"

Ken Adams remained calm, placed a restraining hand in front of Frank Bell and answered the Prime Minister quietly. "I think what Frank is saying, Prime Minister, is that your accusations are unfair. You said to forget our past differences and cooperate. Well, that's precisely what we've done. We didn't like the credit scheme but we accepted it. We've done our best to make it work. We've worked with the local production boards and cooperated with this council. We know all the problems. The civil defence work has come to a halt because the materials are not being delivered on site. It comes down to whether the suppliers have done what they should. That's the question in front of us."

"I don't need you to tell me that," snapped the Prime Minister, "I was coming to it myself." He turned on Sir Gordon Rowan. "Why hasn't management done more? The credit scheme was voluntary because we assumed your people would play their part. Why are there still vast stockpiles of materials which your firms refuse to deliver?"

Like his colleagues on local production boards when the same question was asked, the President of the Confederation of Industry was embarrassed. He could only answer in the same way. "Surely, Prime Minister, it's been agreed all along that the scheme must not disrupt our normal economic arrangements. The trade unions insisted on it because they're anxious to protect real jobs. Well, equally, we have to ensure that business stays viable."

"I didn't ask for excuses," said the Prime Minister. "I asked you a question. I'll repeat it. Why are there still vast stockpiles of materials which your people refuse to deliver?"

"They may seem vast, but..."

"You're not answering, Sir Gordon. We know exactly what stocks are available because you've given us that information yourself. You did that because you expect the government to protect them. What you really want is our protection of your members' selfishness and greed. Is that the true answer?"

Unused to being hectored, Sir Gordon began to flounder. "Greed doesn't come into it, Prime Minister. It is solely a matter of what is viable. I could show you the figures."

"Figures? I don't want to see your figures. You could make them say anything. What we want from you is an assurance that the materials will be delivered."

"Well, I'm sorry, Prime Minister. I'm not in a position to give that assurance."

"You're sorry? Yes, we're all sorry. We've all got our excuses. The government is spending billions protecting your members' interests, but when I ask what you can offer us, you say you're sorry, you can offer us nothing. That's what it comes down to, isn't it, Sir Gordon?"

Unable to cope with the Prime Minister's overbearing manner, Rowan withdrew from the argument. "It's not as simple as that, Prime Minister."

"Oh, isn't it? There's nothing complicated about a little sacrifice and cooperation, if you've got the will to do it. Your members will never see that because they're blinded by their greed. Now you've got tens of thousands of people moving in on your plants, and you've brought it on yourselves. Your members have spawned this evil movement because of their greed."

"I don't think it's right for you to say that, Prime Minister. You can't hold my members responsible."

"Can't I? Have you come here to lay down what I can say? Let me tell you what you're here for. You're here to help this Council and you've failed. You've failed miserably."

Unwilling to accept the verbal onslaught, Rowan stood up and collected his papers. "I don't think we're serving any useful purpose," he said, as he turned his back on the meeting and walked from the room.

The Prime Minister shouted after him. "I never want to see you back in this building, Rowan. The Confederation can send someone else. I suppose you want protection through the crowds. Well you're not getting it. You can face them on your own. You can put your excuses to the mob. You created them."

As the door closed behind Rowan, the Prime Minister sat withdrawn and with hunched shoulders. He spoke to himself quietly, as if no one else was present. "They'd rather walk out than face the issues. Leave it to others. That's all we get when it comes to the test. Never mind what I can do, it's always a case of what others should do."

At last the Prime Minister looked up, raised his voice and banged his fist on the table. "Well there's one thing I'm not going to do. I'm not going to let the country slide into anarchy and chaos. We've been too tolerant, that's been our only mistake and if people won't cooperate, if they won't act on their own in a responsible manner, then all we can do is maintain order until they come to their senses. We won't shrink from it. We'll do whatever is necessary to maintain law and order and the authority of the government. We'll place no limits on the use of force. We'll do that no matter what the cost."

Unlike Rowan, Frank Bell was used to confrontation and he reacted sharply to the Prime Minister's threat. "You'll place no limits on the use of force? What does that mean exactly?" he asked.

The Prime Minister glared at him, "It doesn't need explaining. You understand plain English, don't you?"

"How far will you go?" Frank Bell demanded. "There's talk about the use of firearms. Is that what you've got in mind?"

"It's more than what I've got in mind. It's a total commitment. I repeat, there'll be no breakdown in the authority of this government, no matter what the cost. Is that clear enough for you?"

"But many of the campaigners are also our members. In coming to this Council, we've joined a government body, but we won't be party to extreme methods of crowd control."

"You seem to be having a lot of problems with the language, Frank. You've joined a consultative body and that means you're here to be consulted at the invitation of the government. It doesn't mean you're here to tell us what to do. Do you understand that?"

Frank Bell looked back to the Prime Minister. "We're here to make collective decisions, not to be used by the government."

"You mean you won't cooperate. No, you'd rather create chaos. Well, we're not going to allow it."

As the two members from the TUC stood up to leave, Frank Bell faced the Prime Minister squarely. "And we won't be associated with a bloody lunatic, either."

"That's right, walk out. You've proved my point. Well, you know where the door is. You don't need me to show you because that's one thing you do know; how to walk away from problems."

As Frank Bell left, he reversed the Prime Minister's final insult to Rowan. "Prime Minister, we never want to see you in any meeting again. You're finished. You've lost your senses and talked nothing but rubbish all morning. If there are any sane members of the government left, they'll realise that at this time they can't do without the TUC." He directed his last words towards the Prime Minister's colleagues. "And we won't be back until you've been removed."

Now completely possessed, the Prime Minister shouted at Frank Bell and Ken Adams as they left the room. "You won't be back because you only want to sabotage this Council. Don't worry, I'll make sure the whole country knows it. Get out then. It's no loss to us. You've never had two useful ideas to put together, neither of you, nor the TUC. Get out! Shut down some more hospitals. That's more in your line."

The Prime Minister turned to his colleagues. "You've seen it for yourselves. None of them cooperate. They don't know the meaning of the word. What has the TUC ever had to offer? Nothing. Even Rowan; you saw that too. When it came to the test, he walked out. I began this meeting by saying we should all work together. I outlined the causes of our problems. I put the question, how can you help? What did we get? Nothing. They ignore our warnings. They create this mess. Now we've got this campaign with its leaflets full of ultimatums, threats and seditious filth. We've got crowds on the streets. The media are hostile, trade unions, management and even our own government employees are unreliable. None of them can be trusted. They've all combined to produce chaos."

As the Prime Minister talked himself into a grim silence, Bill Charman, Blake and Dudney contemplated the wreckage of the National Consultative Council. At last, Dudney made a suggestion. "Prime Minister, I'm reminded that it's been some time since we held a full Cabinet meeting."

This immediately provoked the Prime Minister's suspicions. "Why do you say that?"

"I was going to suggest that perhaps a wider discussion might be useful."

"Have you no confidence in our arrangements?"

"Of course. I have every confidence."

"You're not making sense, Dudney. You clearly have no confidence. You want to change our arrangements." He turned to Blake and Bill Charman. "You see? I can't even trust my closest colleagues. Surely I've got a right to expect some loyalty. It's a minimum thing but even that's gone."

Dudney hastened to reassure him. "There's no question of my loyalty."

The Prime Minister stared through him. "If you've got any doubts you can do what the others have done. You can walk out. No one is stopping you."

Bill Charman became alarmed as he foresaw the disintegration of the Civil Contingencies Unit and stepped in quickly. "Prime Minister, John has assured you of his loyalty, what more can you ask? It's vital that the government stays intact. We've all got important work to do and I remind you, we should be getting on with it."

"All right, Home Secretary. I don't need reminding. Are all our plans for dealing with this Campaign in order?"

"They're well prepared."

"Have the reserve units been deployed? They are the least contaminated by the Campaign's seditious filth."

"We've pinpointed the areas where they'll be concentrated and they are ready for action." Bill Charman adopted a tone of special concern. "Prime Minister, I said that we've all got a vital job to do and none is more important than yours. You wouldn't suggest it for yourself because you're far too conscientious, but as our preparations are complete, may I suggest you take some further rest?"

The Prime Minister wavered on the edge of taking this to be a question mark against his competence. Risking another outburst, Bill persisted. "We all know you've been working harder than anyone and we don't want to see you exhausted. Particularly now, we need a fit and strong hand at the helm."

For a tense moment, the Prime Minister eyed Bill Charman suspiciously, then at last appeared to agree. "Maybe you're right, Bill. That could be sound advice. Yes, I'll need to keep on top of things."

"And in the meantime, we'll carry on."

"Alright, but take some advice from me. Don't trust the Services and the police too far. In a crisis like this they might get ideas about running the country, so keep them under close control. It helps if you sack the odd one or two."

Bill assured him. "We'll keep a close eye on all of them."

The Prime Minister stood up, and there were further moments of tension as his colleagues hoped that nothing would prevent him leaving the room. But now his rage had subsided and his manner was again remote. Having seen a brief period of national unity during which his popularity had soared, the Prime Minister was deeply disappointed. Now back in the grip of conflict, he had raged against his failure to control events. The meeting had been an outlet for his frustration. At last he spoke quietly. "Yes, I take the point, Bill. The next few days will be a strain. I'll get some rest and prepare for it. For the moment, I'll leave things with you."

As the Prime Minister left the room the tension drained from the three Ministers who were now left to direct the operations of the security forces. They closed in a group. "I expected a farce," said Bill Charman, "but not a disaster."

It's very difficult to know with him," replied Dudney. "You can never be sure if he's acting or not."

"He is tricky," Bill agreed.

It was true that Bill Charman had pressed him to take some further rest, but the Prime Minister only took advice that suited him, and in this case he had good reason for doing so. As at the earlier meeting where the use of firearms had been decided, by staying in the background now, the Prime Minister could dissociate himself from the worst consequences of impending violence. It was, therefore, possible that he wanted to distance himself from the events of the next twenty-four hours. If things went well, he could claim the credit. Otherwise, he could disclaim any responsibility. Being in the clear, his options would still be wide open. Bill Charman, Dudney and Blake were aware of the savage irony of their position. By being left in charge, they would be held to account for any worsening of the crisis. They could be removed with every justification, while the Prime Minister could re-emerge with a fresh initiative and a new team.

It was also likely that both Frank Bell and Sir Gordon Rowan had been manipulated. Knowing that the meeting of the National Consultative Council could produce nothing, and by causing them to walk out, the Prime Minister could now blame Frank Bell and Rowan for its collapse. Bill Charman agreed with Dudney that the truth about the Prime Minister was never to be found in what was apparent. He was a cunning survivor and not given to wilting under strain.

But whether or not the Prime Minister's actions had been deliberately manipulative, in his present mood it was a precaution that he should be kept out of the way for the next two critical days. In any emergency debate in the House, having him speak for the government was too great a risk. This placed the three remaining Ministers in a further dilemma. It was vital that the government was seen to be intact and strong. They were, therefore, bound to preserve the authority of a Prime Minister who had set the scene for their own possible downfall.

They came back to their immediate problems and decided that Bill Charman would stay in control of the Command Bunker in Whitehall while Blake would go north. John Dudney would go to the midlands, where the Campaign was moving to seize great stocks of materials held at major plants. Like Blake, he would liaise between the local army commander and Whitehall.

With time running against them, the three members of the Civil Contingencies Unit left the Home Office and dispersed.

32

Again, Blake flew north, assuming that Erica Field would be organising the Campaign's action. He imagined her plotting tactics and mobilising thousands of supporters against Champney's forces. It was unfortunate that the recent association between her and the Colonel would again be the first victim of the renewed conflict.

As Blake's helicopter neared its destination, Champney informed him by radio that, although troops and police had again enforced a security zone around the control bunker near the Town Hall, only diversionary action was expected at this point. The Campaign's main thrust would be aimed at the major stocks of materials held at plants outside the city. In view of this, the Colonel had set up new headquarters at a large plant that produced building materials.

The helicopter altered course and soon arrived at the plant, which was sited ten miles east of the City. It was in open country, a complex of buildings enclosed by a perimeter fence and bypassed by a main highway, with a service road giving access to the plant. Armoured cars blocked the way both at the junction with the main road and across the entrance to the brickworks.

Despite these barriers, on the common land surrounding the plant, campaigners were beginning to assemble, and were accompanied by trucks which had avoided the roadblocks. Throughout the plant stood the contentious stacks of bricks and concrete blocks. Police and troops were reinforcing the perimeter fence with the use of razor wire. To Blake, they seemed few in number. It was already clear that the security forces were hopelessly outnumbered.

On his arrival, Blake was met by an orderly who took him to an upstairs office in the administrative block. He found Champney studying a large map indicating the distribution of materials throughout the area.

The Colonel looked up. "Ah, Minister, have some army coffee. From the look of things, you'll have to get used to it."

Blake greeted the Colonel. "Does anyone get used to it?" he asked.

"Not really, but at least we're not in that damned bunker. We're in the open air with an all-round view, though you may not like what you see."

Blake took his mug of coffee and looked out over the surrounding common land. Keeping a distance, the campaigners were still building up their numbers and hoisting their messages to the security forces, urging them not to act against the Campaign.

Previously, the Colonel had been reluctant to discuss any political decisions, but now feeling at ease with Blake, he expressed his disappointment at the failure to impose compulsory requisitions. He spoke frankly about the problems of protecting the stocks of materials and referred to the map showing the many places that had to be covered and the ease with which the Campaign could divert the security forces in any number of different directions.

Blake listened to Champney's remarks, which were almost a repeat of the analysis presented by Brigadier Culverton earlier at the meeting of the Civil Contingencies Unit. Inevitably Champney arrived at the rules of engagement and the meaning of his instruction that firearms would be used only "as a last resort."

"I would have thought it clear enough," said Blake. "Where's the difficulty?"

"The difficulty," replied the Colonel, "which I'm not sure that Whitehall appreciates, is that we may have to use this last resort very early in the action. You've only got to look out of the window to see the reason yourself."

"I have looked out of the window, Colonel." Blake felt he should be more forthcoming. "I don't know what's in your mind, but if you're trying to tell me that it's madness to start killing people in an argument over a pile of bricks, then I wouldn't disagree."

"I suppose the government would say it's about more than that. It's about the authority of Parliament and our whole system of law and order."

"Yes, but anyone can justify anything." Blake returned to the window and stared at the crowd beyond the perimeter fence. "These campaigners haven't set out to break the law. They want to get on with some work. That's their sole aim. What we need is time, Colonel. Time to work out a political solution. Surely your instructions mention that?"

"There's reference to a holding operation," Champney replied, "but it's not very helpful." He repeated the point that time was on the side of the Campaign. He went back to his maps. "How long do you want?" he asked.

"That's impossible to say. The issues are complex, and people are unpredictable. I'm not even certain we'll get a political solution."

"Without the use of firearms," said the Colonel, "I can prevent a mass seizure of materials for possibly two or three days. That's the best I can do. After that, under continuous pressure from the Campaign's superior numbers, we'll need firepower."

"And looking further ahead," asked Blake, "what do you see as the final outcome?"

"To be frank, Minister, I think the Campaign will win. It's just not possible for the army to hold down the entire population using civilised methods. As for extreme methods, like the use of firepower, we have to look at it from the soldiers' point of view. I repeat what I said before. If they see their interests as being with the Campaign, why should they fight it? It's useless to make political decisions that can't be followed through at the point of action. I've said all along that the Campaign has won the argument. The argument was always our weakness."

Despite the seriousness of their situation, Blake could only smile. "Colonel, you'd make a good spokesman for the Campaign. You're almost preaching sedition."

"On the contrary, I'm being realistic. I think I know what is possible."

Now aware that Champney had a background in counter-insurgency, Blake could only accept his predicted outcome. However, a victory for the Campaign would be the result of force, and this could justify the violent actions of other power groups and lead to prolonged civil war. Backed by the authority of the House of Commons, the wide powers of requisition that were necessary would become law and would therefore be more widely accepted. However, he felt it was only with an escalation of the conflict that members would be compelled to vote them in. Blake explained his thinking to Champney. "What we need," he said, "is a build-up of tension that threatens civil war but doesn't actually go into civil war. I imagine that's a tall order."

Champney at once saw the possibility of blending his army skills with Blake's political experience, but he also had his reservations. "It assumes the kind of control that in practice we never enjoy," he said. "On the other hand, it helps to have an idea of what we're doing. So far, no one has had a clue."

"You said you could give us two days without the use of firearms," said Blake. "That should be something we could work with."

"We'll do our best," said the Colonel.

To Blake's surprise Champney called in a senior NCO, Sergeant Cummings, and instructed him to stop work on the perimeter fence. "But that fence is fragile, sir. It's worn out. It needs reinforcing," said the sergeant.

"Yes," said Champney, "but I've changed my mind. Take it down. You'll see the reasons later. Make sure the Company's transport is immobilised and well out of the way."

As the sergeant disappeared, Champney turned to Blake. "I want to look at things from the air. Care to join me?"

They left the office building and walked towards a waiting helicopter where Champney introduced Blake to Fraser's replacement, Police Commissioner Hume. All three climbed into the vehicle. It took off and circled the area. Talking loudly over the noise of the engine, Champney and Hume discussed the movements on the ground. Yet more campaigners were arriving, some on foot and others in vehicles which appeared to be having little difficulty getting through.

Hume was astonished to see troops removing the razor wire that had been strung in depth along the perimeter fence. He pressed Champney for an explanation, but the Colonel would only comment that the wire was unnecessary. Pointing to the main crowd of campaigners, Hume insisted they were within easy reach of the riot police, who were patrolling the perimeter fence, and should be dispersed with CS gas but Champney disagreed. Blake sensed that tension was already beginning to build up between the army commander and the new police chief.

Champney was more interested in a group of Land Rovers, and he instructed the pilot to get as close as possible. As the helicopter passed low over the vehicles, he strained to get a better view. The vehicles had been reinforced with iron plates at their front and rear ends. Having caught only a fleeting glimpse, Champney asked the pilot to repeat the manoeuvre. As they swooped and hovered, he stared again at the Land Rovers, intrigued by how they might be used.

Satisfied that there would be no immediate move against the plant, Champney ordered the pilot to head for the City. They followed the main highway, observing the roadblocks at the junctions of main roads. Long queues of vehicles were disrupting what was left of the normal life of the area, whilst the Campaign was still able to move its numbers across open countryside and through the network of lanes.

Champney noticed that a convoy of three lorries loaded with concrete blocks had been stopped against a barrier, and asked the pilot if he could land. The helicopter was eased down. The party clambered out and approached the police who were arguing with one of the drivers. "What's happening?" asked Hume.

One of the police explained. "We think these materials have been stolen, sir."

Champney thrust himself forward and spoke to the driver across the barrier. "Where did you get this stuff?"

"It's all legal," the driver replied. "We want to deliver it but the police won't let us through."

"If it's legal show us the invoices."

The driver produced his licence and various receipts. Champney took them. "We'll just check these papers," he said, and passed them to a police sergeant.

The driver became more aggressive. "We're going to deliver these goods." He pointed at the few police and troops. "It'll take more than this little lot to stop us. We can get thousands down here."

"Shut up," snapped Hume. "You've stolen these goods."

The driver turned to walk away. "If that's your attitude we'll go, but we'll be back."

"Stand where you are," shouted Hume. He barked orders to the police, who moved quickly through the barriers and surrounded the lorries. Four marksmen stood apart, with their weapons aimed at the driver. "Stand still and shut your mouth," Hume shouted again.

Champney, Blake and Hume walked a few yards to where they could talk amongst themselves. "If the papers are in order," said Champney, "we should let them through. Legality is the only argument we've got and we're bound to encourage it. In any case, I suspect we're being set up. They could use this to justify their own violence and I don't want it. We're too stretched already."

"I don't believe it," Hume insisted. "They could close in at any time but we've got more than enough firepower to keep them out."

The police sergeant returned, saying that the driver was a known campaign activist but that all his papers were in order. Champney walked through the barriers and spoke to the driver. "You're quite right, you're all legal. You can go through." He offered his hand. "Don't I remember you?" he said. "You've done a lot of good work at one of the deep shelters. No hard feelings, we're only doing our job. I'm sure you agree, we need to uphold the law."

The driver refused his hand and, as the barriers were moved aside, he climbed into the cab of his lorry. "Just shift that helicopter," he said. "It's in the way."

The party clambered back into the helicopter, which took them on to the control bunker. Champney checked its defences. With two squads of armed troops and riot police patrolling its high fence, he was satisfied. The party then passed through the steel doors of the bunker, entered the lift and made its descent to the operations room, where the officer in charge gave his up-to-the-minute report.

The Campaign was now engaged in widespread disruption. Power and water supplies had been disconnected from army units and security installations. The bunker was again having to operate on its emergency systems. Essential supplies, such as fuel and food intended for the troops, had been hijacked. Radio stations were under extra guard. This placed a greater strain on the already overstretched security forces. The Campaign had also stepped up its propaganda war, with the families of troops and police coming under increasing pressure. There had been more intimidation, the homes of more senior police officers having been firebombed.

On hearing the officer's report, Hume became angry at what appeared to be Champney's lax response to the situation. He appealed for a tougher line, insisting that the search and arrest programme should be carried out. "It makes no sense, Champney. Why are you allowing Erica Field and other campaign leaders to remain free?" he demanded.

Champney ignored him and made fresh contact with his junior officers, again checking the deployment of his reserve units. Convoys of lorries and helicopter transports were ready and waiting in positions from where they could move rapidly to the points where the major stocks of materials were held. As he made radio contact with each of his officers, he emphasised that the troops would come under severe provocation. They must be forceful and decisive, but, at the same time they must do everything possible to handle the campaigners with restraint and good humour. With a final check on communications between the bunker and his temporary headquarters at the plant, he appeared to relax. He suggested a hot drink and the party moved into the canteen.

Hume was unable to contain himself, again demanding a more aggressive initiative. Champney turned to him. "What do you think this operation is about, Commissioner?" he asked. "Do you think it's going to be settled by your mounted police bearing down on a few protestors with an old-fashioned cavalry charge?"

"No, I don't, and you shouldn't sneer at our experience."

"You don't seem to realise; this confrontation could escalate into civil war."

"That's precisely my argument, Champney, and it's not going to be helped by a soft response. That will only make things worse."

The Colonel persisted. "Try to understand, I haven't set out to be soft. It's a practical matter of using methods consistent with our object. We could very easily kill a few campaigners but where would that get us? It would only make our task more difficult."

Hume remained adamant. "I've never found that a soft approach gets you anywhere with criminals."

"But we're not dealing with criminals," said Champney. "We're dealing with decent people who think that what they're doing is right, and they happen to be a lot more formidable than your average law breaker, especially where they have the support of millions."

It was clear to Blake that Champney was running out of patience with Hume. Suddenly, Champney's voice took on a hard edge. "You do know, don't you, Hume, that we had some problems with your predecessor, the unfortunate Gavin Fraser? The Minister will tell you that during our last little set-to with the Campaign, things went reasonably well until his preference for acting tough got the better of him."

"Colonel, I know you got rid of Fraser. Are you now threatening to get rid of me?"

"I will do that if I have to, and I won't issue threats. I simply want you to know that this operation is not an outlet for your vindictiveness: neither yours nor anyone else's. Do we have that understanding?"
"All I understand, Colonel, is that you are in overall command."

"Good, then let's get out of this place. Let's get back."

They returned to the compound and re-entered the waiting helicopter. Speeding back to the plant, Champney again observed the congestion at the roadblocks. He decided to remove them and struggled into the forward compartment to issue his instructions. As he rejoined Blake and Hume, the police chief was still bewildered.

"You're going to allow the Campaign to move freely?" he protested. "Surely we should prevent it?"

"The roadblocks are doing more harm than good," said Champney. "They'll restrict our movements. They suit the Campaign more than us."

The steady build-up of campaigners outside the plant confirmed that the roadblocks were a waste of time and resources. The party landed. Champney sent for Sergeant Cummings, and invited Blake to join him on the flat roof of the office block. The roof commanded a panoramic view of the common land, surrounding the plant. The Colonel studied the crowd through binoculars. Joined by his Sergeant, Champney pointed out the reinforced Land Rovers that he had noticed from the air.

"As you say, sir, metal shields at front and rear. Their version of an armoured car, I suppose," said the sergeant.

"Do you think you could grab one?" Champney asked.

"We'll give it a try, sir."

"At least get a close look."

The front gate of the plant was opened and, with a squad of troops, Sergeant Cummings boarded one of the armoured cars which blocked the entrance. The vehicle moved forward, turned sharply then spurted across the common towards the group of Land Rovers. The move had been anticipated and, in turn, the Land Rovers moved off in different directions. The armoured car sped past campaigners, selecting one of the Land Rovers as its target. The pursued vehicle bumped and jolted its way across the open ground until it slewed to a halt in a deep rut.

Campaigners ran towards it in a race with the armoured car and, as they arrived together, fighting broke out. With the troops soon outnumbered, campaigners pushed the stricken Land Rover out of the rut, allowing it to speed off. As the fighting continued, the tyres of the armoured car were let down and, with this done, the campaigners backed off, leaving the troops roughed up and standing by their useless vehicle.

From his vantage point on the rooftop, Champney smiled behind his binoculars. He shouted orders and more troops took a second armoured car to the assistance of their comrades. Amongst the cheers and jeers of the campaigners, the troops pumped up the tyres of the first armoured car and eventually both vehicles returned to their positions across the entrance to the plant. Sergeant Cummings returned to the rooftop, looking dishevelled and embarrassed.

"You saw what happened, sir."

"Never mind. Did you get a good look?"
"It definitely has armoured plates, both front and rear."

"What about inside?"

"All I saw were some grappling hooks."

"Interesting. Any idea what they're for?"

"The steel plating means they want to get close," said Cummings. "The hooks suggest they want to pull or drag something."

"Like the perimeter fence?"

"They'd be ideal for that, sir. Especially now we've taken down the razor wire."

Champney smiled. "Good. Well done. That's all we wanted to know. Not too knocked about are you? Anyone hurt?"

"Not really." Cummings smiled back ruefully. "Though for a non-violent crowd they're pretty aggressive."

"Yes, well, so long as it's only fisticuffs. You'd better get sorted out."

As Cummings left the roof, Champney turned to Blake. "We're in for a long night, Minister. Nothing is going to happen for a while, so why don't you get some rest?"

"A good idea, but where?"

"You'll find the Board Room comfortable. As we're defending their damned plant, we may as well enjoy their comforts. You'll also find some whisky. We do have some powers of requisition and if I get a moment I'll join you."

The sky was now overcast and there was some slight rain. Blake pulled up the collar of his coat and stared at the bleak view, aware of the massed ranks of campaigners now on the move throughout the country. He was surprised that Champney seemed so unworried. "Colonel," he said, "I don't want to agree with Hume, but I can't see how you're going to stop that crowd overwhelming this plant."

"Maybe not."

"With this rain coming on, surely they'll soon make a move?"

"The rain will make a difference," said Champney. "My advice is to get some rest, Minister. I'll let you know if anything happens."

In the gathering gloom Blake left the rooftop and made his way through to the Board Room, where he found an armchair. He sat in the dark, but his attempt to relax was thwarted by the questions that crowded into his mind. What was happening in the rest of the country: should he make contact with Dudney? What progress had Dave Reed made in the House of Commons?

As he lay back he thought of the events which had led to the crisis. The strange interview with Sandra Dale when he was first warned of the approaching dangers. The arrest of Hurst and the growth of the Campaign. He and Bill Charman had presided over these happenings with no control over the growing conflict. Eventually, the pattern of events became blurred as his mind drifted from consciousness into shallow sleep.

He was woken up by an orderly. "Excuse me, sir. Colonel Champney says you might like to join him." Blake took some time to realise where he was. Only a shaft of light from the outer office penetrated the dark of the Board Room. "Yes," he said, "does he? Thank you. Where is the Colonel?"

"He's on the roof, sir."

"What's happening?"

"Nothing at the moment."

Blake stood up and in the half-light found his shoes. He groped his way from the Board Room, found his coat and made his way out, heading for the roof. The rain had increased, and a chill breeze passed over the office block. He found Champney, staring into the gloom.

"You'll need a cape, Minister," he said. "This rain is coming on fast."

"What's happening in this nightmare?" Blake asked.

Champney smiled. "We're seeing some action now, but they're taking their time. I've decided that we should put up some resistance."

Lights shone out from the plant, picking up movement in the crowd. Inside the perimeter fence stood ranks of riot police. Those in front formed a protective wall of shields. Behind them, rear ranks were ready to fire plastic bullets. These were reinforced by thin lines of troops. In the background were the stacks of materials, the object of the Campaign's attack. Overlooking the scene, Champney and Blake stood in the chill rain.

"I don't know what's keeping them," said Champney. "They've got the place surrounded. What more could they ask?" He looked sideways at Blake. "You'll find there's some hot tea, Minister."

Blake made his way down to ground level, collected an army cape and, after threading his way through the ranks of troops and police, found a field canteen. He took a mug of tea and began his return to the roof, but was stopped by Hume, who grabbed his shoulder.

"Do you see what's happening, Minister?" said Hume. "We're in a hopeless position, and it's all Champney's fault. I take no responsibility. We could have dispersed that crowd earlier in the day, but do you see their numbers now? We could have avoided this."

Blake looked at the agitated Hume whilst gripping his mug. "Careful, Commissioner," he said, "you're spilling my tea."

Hume stepped back. "You heard me advise the use of CS gas. You were a witness. I'm counting on you to support me."

"I think Champney knows what he's doing. Give him some credit, Commissioner. He's no novice."

"Don't you think I've had experience?"
Blake lost patience. "Look, not now Hume. I don't want to argue. I want to get back."

He left Hume standing in the rain and made his way back to the roof, where he rejoined the Colonel. "I don't know about the Campaign," he said, "but you've certainly upset Hume."

"Yes." Champney still stared at the crowd. "He'll get over it."

The Campaigners began addressing the security forces through a megaphone. Coming from the darkness, the message was hard and clear.

"We speak to all police and army personnel. We are here only to protect you and your families. We are here only to safeguard the community. Do not act against us. Your colleagues Brady, Davis, Simms and Rodgers, with many others, have joined our Campaign. They are now working to protect their families and the community..."

As the persuasive voice came out of the dark and echoed across the plant, Hume came hurrying up to the rooftop. "Champney, when are you going to put a stop to this inflammatory filth? It's outright sedition."

"I don't see what we can do," replied the Colonel. "Why are you worried? They won't influence you. Will they influence your men? I thought they were reliable."

"You know we've had absentees. We can't risk any more."

With his night vision glasses Champney stared more intently into the crowd. "You'd better get back to your men," he said. "Things are going to move at any moment."

Hume left in a rage, as the voice from the crowd continued with its blend of persuasion and intimidation.

"Our action is peaceful but we will be protected against criminal acts. We will win and no criminal will escape. For yourselves and your families, do not act against us. Join our Campaign..."

As the voice sent its message over the waiting lines of troops and police, the scene was still. Suddenly, and just discernible in the glare of lights, there was movement amongst the campaigners. Gaps appeared in the crowd, to reveal a line of Land Rovers. As one, they spurted in reverse towards the riot police, who opened fire with plastic bullets. The Land Rovers sped on to the perimeter fence and, on reaching it, stopped abruptly. From the backs of the vehicles grappling hooks were attached to the wire and in an instant the Land Rovers drove forward. The hooks engaged and a forty yard section of wire fence was ripped from its supports.

With the fence dragged clear, the hooks were cast free and the Land Rovers turned. With sirens screaming and powerful lights blinding the troops and police, they again advanced. For a moment, the police held firm, firing their useless volleys at the reinforced vehicles. The Land Rovers gathered speed, threatening to plough through the ordered lines of the security forces but with the vehicles still coming forward the nerves of the defenders broke. As one man, they turned to save themselves and scattered in confusion.

The Land Rovers came to a halt and, from behind them, streams of campaigners poured through the gap in the fence. More and more went through, overwhelming the troops and police and fanning out through the plant. At the same time, other campaigners cut away more sections of the fence, allowing yet more of their numbers to pour in.

Champney and Blake observed the scene from the rooftop. Within minutes the entire plant was occupied by the Campaign. Champney seemed unconcerned and spoke quietly. "We were right about those Land Rovers," he said. "We guessed how they'd be used."

Blake was still at a loss to understand the Colonel's tactics. "I thought we were in for a long night of violence."

"No, no," he said. "It's much too wet for that. I suggest we get out of this rain. What about some of that whisky, Minister? We should entertain our visitor."

He led the way off the roof and went into the office, where the orderly was staring from a window at the confusion. Taking a portable light, the Colonel went through to the Board Room and opened a cabinet, where he found whisky and glasses. He sat down at the table. "You will join me, won't you Minister?"

"I can't see much to celebrate." Champney poured their drinks and lit his pipe.

"You mentioned a visitor," said Blake. "Who are you expecting?"

"I would say Erica, wouldn't you?"

"I guess so, and we're bound to see Hume."

Champney grimaced. "We could do without him for a while."

They settled down to their drinks and waited. It wasn't long before Erica Field marched into the Board Room followed by her dutiful lieutenant, Stuart Coates. She stood with rain dripping from her jacket, obviously delighted.

Champney greeted her. "Erica, it's good to see you again. Not too wet, I hope. Come and share a whisky, we're all a bit damp."

"You can stuff your whisky, Colonel," she said. "This isn't a social call. We're here to do a job."

"Then you won't mind if we go ahead? It's subscribed by the Company and the Minister is leaving a credit note, so why not make it a social event?"

"Shut up, Colonel." Erica moved to the window and checked the scene outside.

Champney persisted. "Why be hasty? Surely you won't shift the materials tonight? It's late and the weather is foul."

Erica shouted instructions from the window. "Yes, use the company's transport. You'll find it's been immobilised, so check amongst our spares, and get this electricity back on."

"Any chance of reconnecting the water?" Champney asked her. "Our field canteen is running short."

Erica closed the window and turned to Coates. "Deal with the water. We'll need it ourselves."

Champney sat back and relit his pipe. "I still say we should all go home, Erica. I know there's a job to do but it's not one for us. Let the politicians sort it out."

"You do talk rubbish, Colonel," she said. "What politicians? We're in control."

"You mean you've replaced Parliament?"

"We're here to shift materials, that's all."

"But it puts you above the law, above Parliament. You realise that if you want to be the government you'll have to do all its work.

Who is going to be Prime Minister? Mr. Hurst? You'll have to collect the taxes and run the economy. It's not an easy job. You ask the Minister here. He'll tell you about the problems. He'll tell you about campaigns that suddenly spring up and take the law into their own hands. How are you going to say they are wrong? How are you going to deal with them? Do you imagine that I or any other officer would serve an illegal regime?"

"Just sit where you are, Colonel. Shut up and drink your whisky."

Lights came on throughout the plant. To keep her view, Erica switched them off in the Board Room. At last, satisfied that the Campaign's action was going according to plan, she switched the lights back on and turned to Champney.

"Who gave the order to fire plastic bullets?" she demanded.

"I did," said the Colonel. "Nothing happens here unless I order it. I'm in sole command."

"You mean you were in command. You've been occupied."

"Alright, but we didn't make it too difficult. You almost walked in. I don't believe anyone was hurt."

"That's just as well," she said. "There would have been reprisals."

Champney refilled his glass. "I didn't want to see anyone injured and no one has been, so let's be grateful for that. You know, Erica, I enjoyed working with you. I thought we got along just fine and I want to get back to it, but it's got to be done properly, within the law, through Parliament."

"You can work with us," she said. "You can join our Campaign."

Champney leaned forward. "There's a problem," he said. "My boss wouldn't approve of it. I wouldn't last long in the job. But as I've just said, I want to work with you, but not this way, Erica. I can't do it this way."

Suddenly an alarmed Stuart Coates returned to the room. He took Erica aside and spoke to her in a whisper. She switched off the lights, looked out of the window and then turned on Champney.

"You treacherous bastard," she said. "You sit here talking about working with us and at the same time you're bringing in more troops!"

She went quickly from window to window while Champney remained seated. Blake got up and looked out. All around the plant army transports were lumbering into position. Helicopter units were landing on the common land. Fresh squads of troops from the special reserves were assembling among the campaigners. Lorries, armoured cars and tanks continued to arrive until the plant was surrounded and more and more troops took up their positions.

Erica was enraged. "Champney, you're a treacherous bastard," she repeated, as she stormed from the room.

Blake returned to the table, sat down and topped up his whisky. He looked at Champney. "So, you let the campaigners trap themselves?"

Champney shrugged. "We can't chase them all over the countryside, and anyway, no one invited them. Nor are they trapped. They're quite free to go home. They won't do any good here."

An officer, a captain, came into the Board Room. "The place is secure, sir," he reported.

Champney's demeanour suddenly altered. His voice was crisp and authoritative. "Good. Leave enough men to stop the movement of materials and take the rest on. Stay in close touch with the bunker and keep me informed."

"Yes, sir."

"And remember, everyone must act with restraint. No force unless absolutely necessary. On no account must the men show their weapons unless I'm first consulted."

"That's understood, sir."

"And captain."

"Yes, sir?"

Champney glanced at the water dripping on to the Board Room floor from the officer's cape and smiled. "Fortunate weather, isn't it?"

The officer smiled back. "Yes, sir."

As the captain left, he passed Erica, who re-entered the Board Room, her eyes blazing. Champney raised his hands in mock self-defence. "Now that you've said what you think of me, can we carry on our conversation? This whisky isn't too bad." In an effort to reduce the tension he turned to Blake. "What do you think, Minister?"

"I've had worse," said Blake as he poured Erica a drink and pushed it across the table to where she stood fuming with anger and frustration. "I don't remember any conversation," she said. "You were doing all the talking."

"Yes, I do tend to go on," said Champney. "I just think that talking is better than fighting so why don't you say something? Let's have a convivial chat then go home and let Parliament sort it out."

"It's worse than useless," she said. "It's because of them that we're in this mess."

"Then we agree," said Champney. "You're right. The politicians haven't done a very good job but they can't all be bad. I know the Minister here has been working hard to get things right. I've said all along there must be a political solution and, although I'm strictly out of order, I'm reporting that to my own Commander and that may have an influence. We've got the Minister doing his best, you've made your own strong point tonight, so why don't we allow a bit of time for these pressures to work through the proper channels? There's no other way; legality and democracy go together." Whilst working with her, Champney had seen the way Erica rode roughshod over her comrades. It was with an ironic smile that he asked, "You do believe in democracy?"

"I believe in getting things done," she said, "but you're right about one thing, Colonel. You talk too much. It's action that counts and we can sit this situation out longer than you."

"Really? In all this rain?"

Blake decided to find out what was happening in Whitehall. He went through to the orderly in the outer office and was directed to a smaller room which had been set up as a communications unit. The signals officer routed him through to the Command Bunker in Whitehall. Eventually a harassed Bill Charman came on the line.

Blake was able to report on the stalemate that had been reached in his own area. In reply, Bill Charman said that the nationwide picture was confused, but it was clear that many pitched battles were taking place. Reporting on Westminster, he said the special units defending the security zone had kept control but only with the use of plastic bullets and stun grenades fired into the crowds. They were now ready to use lethal force. In the Midlands, Dudney was having a hard time. In response to the use of firepower by the forces, campaigners had produced an arsenal of shotguns and other weapons. This had created alarm, especially in the ranks of police, who were now deserting in increasing numbers. "There are many casualties," said Bill.

"Deaths?" Blake asked.

"Yes. We don't know how many."

"What about the House? Any progress with the debate?"

"It's going on now," said Bill. "Dave Reed has proposed your amendments to the emergency powers, but I can't get there. I can't move. I'm tied down in this bunker. You'll have to get back."

Although he had every confidence in Champney, Blake was reluctant to return to Whitehall. "Things are balanced here," he said. "I don't want to leave just yet."

Bill Charman began to sound desperate. "Well it's bloody embarrassing having none of us in the House. There's a lot of uncertainty. Members want to know where the Prime Minister is. I'm telling you, Blake, if you want your proposals voted in, you've got to get back."

"All right, Bill," he said. "I'll leave as soon as possible."

Blake put down his receiver and made his way to the outer office, where he almost bumped into Hume, heading for the Board Room. Hume's uniform was covered with mud, he had lost his cap and his face was bruised. He confronted Blake. "Do you see what those animals have done to me, Minister? They locked me up. I've only just been released by the troops. This is all Champney's fault and I'm going to have it out with him."

Blake gripped him by his collar and pushed him to one side of the office. "I understand how you feel, Comissioner, but I wouldn't go into that Board Room for the moment."
"What do you think you're doing?" Hume shouted. "Have you gone mad as well? Get your hands off me."

"Look, Hume, things are touch and go. Champney is making steady progress with Erica Field, but your presence won't help."

"They've occupied the plant. Do you call that progress?"

"Alright, but it's no good to them. They can't move the stocks."

"That woman should be under arrest."

Blake tightened his grip on the Commissioner. "I'm sorry you've been roughed up but we're not here to nurse your injured pride. There are thousands of campaigners down there and if anything happens to Erica Field, you'll turn them into a raging mob." Blake relaxed his grip and kept talking. "Leave it to Champney. He knows what he's doing. It's because of him that we've come this far. Left to you, we'd have had a bloodbath."

"I'm telling you, I'm going to put that woman under arrest." Hume appeared to calm down. "Maybe not now, but at the right time, I'll see she's arrested."

"We'll talk about it later," said Blake. "Why don't you have a hot drink and get yourself cleaned up?"

Blake steered Hume towards the door and watched with relief as he left the office. Blake arranged with an orderly to keep the Board Room out of bounds to everyone and to say it was on the instructions of the army commander. He then returned and took his seat as Erica was speaking. "You might think you've stopped us tonight, Colonel, but it's the last time you'll do it."

Champney was still trying to secure a withdrawal of the campaigners that would allow them some dignity. "How can I make you understand, Erica, I don't want to stop you. I do see the sense in what you're trying to do. You see how much we agree? Don't you think I'd like to go out into that plant and say to my men 'get those lorries loaded. Get them down to a deep shelter site'. That's what my men would rather be doing, but they can't do it. I can't tell them to do it, even though I want to. The reason is that I'm not a free agent and nor are you. It would be theft of property. It's a political mess and we can't sort it out on our own. It's got to be done by Parliament. Believe me, they'll have to take notice of the point you've made and I'll make sure they know it."

Erica looked dejected. She took up the drink that so far she had ignored, realising that for this night her action had failed. Champney sympathised with her dilemma but continued to press her. "Eventually, you'll be glad you didn't succeed tonight. If you'd got your way, the whole country would have slid into chaos."

"You do talk rubbish," she said. "It's already in chaos and only our Campaign can sort it out. I'll tell you something, Colonel. This is only the beginning of our action. We'll carry on and we'll win, because nothing can stop us."

"I know that in the end you can take over," Champney conceded, "but not without a lot of violence. Is that the sort of victory you want? One that may cost the lives of thousands of people? And even when you've won it, you'll only be another government in exactly the same position as this one, except that you'll have no legality."

At the risk of inflaming his previous bad feeling with Erica, Blake intervened. "We're already seeing deaths around the country, with many more injured, but an emergency debate has begun in the House of Commons, so at least we've come that far. You've got a lot of friends down there, Erica, but a threatened takeover will only antagonise them."

"If Westminster comes to its senses, it will only be because of our actions."

"Alright, but don't push it too far. If you threaten the authority of Parliament, it will turn against you with all its force, and you haven't even begun to see the full weight of that force yet. Your best move is to withdraw in an orderly manner and let me get back to Westminster, where I can press for a solution."

Erica remained silent as Champney moved to the window. He looked out into the teeming rain. With nothing happening, troops, police and campaigners were mixing freely under makeshift shelters. He made a further appeal. "Perhaps I do talk a lot of rubbish, Erica, but as an army man, I can give you some advice. It's obvious that your people won't stand in the rain all night. They'll want to go home, so if you have to retreat, do it in an orderly way. That way you maintain morale and keep your forces intact. I'll do a deal with you. If I lay on transport to get these people to their homes, will you help me organise it?"

Erica smiled bitterly. "You really want me to help organise a withdrawal? You call that a deal?"

"Well, they won't shift the materials. My orders are to prevent it and I'll carry them out. But I also respect your people and I want to get back to working with them. So, instead of seeing them drift away with their spirits crushed and their morale destroyed, I'll help you withdraw in a dignified manner. I'm offering you transport to where they live. What's wrong with that?"

Blake added his own plea. "You want compulsory requisitions. Well, we're working hard to get them, but don't make the job more difficult. Give us a decent chance of getting a good response from the House."

Erica sat down with a look of resignation but her voice was still determined. "If it fails," she said, "we'll be back with greater numbers and stronger reasons. As for your offer of transport, Colonel, you can organise it yourself. I won't approve, but I won't interfere."

Both Blake and Champney were relieved. "That's good enough for me, Erica," said Champney. "We'll do it that way."

As they left Erica in the Board Room, they were in no doubt that she was already planning her next move. They moved to the outer office, where Champney sent his orderly for a megaphone. "We've got to persuade these people to go home," he said to Blake. "It might be helpful if you joined me on the roof."

"I don't think so," said Blake. "I'm not popular with these people. I'll leave it to you, Colonel. You've been very persuasive so far."

Champney took up a position back on the rooftop, where his tall figure could be clearly seen in the glare of lights. He raised his megaphone. "This is Colonel Champney, the officer commanding the area. Can I have your attention?"

The crowd fell silent. Thousands of faces were exposed to the rain as they looked up towards him.

"Every policeman and every soldier respects the reasons why you are here. We share your concern, there is no argument between us. But your aims can only be achieved within the law and, in upholding it, our actions have been in line with what you all want. You have demonstrated the urgent need for the work on deep shelters to continue. As a result, an emergency debate has begun in Parliament and, to follow up your success, we have amongst us a Government Minister, Blake Evans, who is anxious to press your demands in the House of Commons."

Blake looked around at the mass of faces surrounding him but saw no distinction between police, troops and campaigners. Champney continued explaining, cajoling, setting out a new way ahead and speaking as if all those present, including himself, were joined in a common cause.

"Now, we must allow the Minister to leave. We must allow him to convert our demands into the means of securing our aims. We all want to carry on working together, and we have done more than enough to tell Parliament it has a duty to join with us and to enact new measures for the completion of our great project. We have achieved this and we are now able to leave. There is no reason for us to stand in the rain all night, so this is what I've arranged. I'm providing transport so that we can all get back to our families and our homes. In the meantime, we'll provide as many hot drinks as possible. It's a big job so I want some of you to come forward and help in our field canteens."

As Champney rejoined him, Blake's smile was one of admiration. "You should have gone into politics, Colonel."

"No thanks," he said, "I prefer the army. We don't get the arguments."

At last they were confronted by Hume, who by now had recovered his cap and cleaned up his uniform.

"Champney," he demanded, "are you seriously thinking of taking these people home?"

"Can you think of a better way of getting rid of them?"

"And you're giving them drinks?"

"Why not help, Commissioner? It would improve your image."

"Do you want to turn this thing into farce?"

"Yes," said Champney. "That is precisely what I'm trying to do. I prefer farce to tragedy, don't you?"

"You realise I've been criminally assaulted?"

"You seem alright. In the army we take that as an occupational risk. We don't make an issue of it."

"Well I'm not in the bloody army. I'm a senior police officer, and we do make an issue of it."

"Yes, but I don't see what we can do. Who are the guilty parties? We can't question every campaigner. We'd be here for weeks."

"That woman, Erica Field, she's one of the people responsible."

"That can't be right, Hume," said Champney. "She's been with me all evening."

"She's guilty of a dozen offences."

"Only a dozen? I'm not a lawyer but I imagine she's guilty of hundreds."

"Then arrest her."

"On all those charges? Think of the paperwork. I can do without it."

"If we don't arrest her now she'll be back tomorrow with the same crowd."

"We'll see."

"You're creating more trouble. That's all we'll get if you leave that woman free."

"We'll face it when it comes. Look around, Hume. You're the only one who isn't calm. You won't be needed here tonight, so why not go home and get some sleep?"

"That's if I've got a home to go to. They've probably burned it down. I'm telling you, Champney, I'm submitting my own report on everything that's happened. You can't stop that."

"You're lucky to have the time, Commissioner."

Hume turned his back and stalked off. Champney watched him go and shook his head. "There goes a one man conspiracy to incite a riot," he said wearily. "Where do you find them, Minister? I get rid of one and you give me a carbon copy."

"He's not my Department," said Blake. "Maybe it's hard to find one that's different."

Champney caught the attention of a nearby soldier. "Get me Sergeant Cummings."

They walked amongst the campaigners in the direction of a field canteen. A sheet of canvas was stretched over several steaming urns and two soldiers were handing out mugs of tea.

"Is there plenty?" asked Champney. "Got a spare one?"

The soldier handed him a mug. "It's a bit like feeding the five thousand, sir."

"Yes, well, keep it up."

Cummings arrived. "You wanted me, sir?"

"Yes, what's the mood of the place?" Champney asked him. "Could there be more trouble? What's your impression?"

"I think we're in the clear, sir. Everyone is soaked to the skin. I'm sure they'd like to get away."

"Good, I want you to organise the transport. Select a few drop-off points, but be cautious. We've still got to watch them. Use a few lorries and, if it goes smoothly, then use a few more. The important thing is to get them involved with organising it. You know the sort of thing."

"I see no problem, sir."
"By the way, Sergeant, did you notice? The way they used those Land Rovers. We were right. We were spot on."

"Yes, I did notice that, sir."

Champney gave out mugs of tea and with cheery good-humour persuaded campaigners to join in. Blake glanced at his watch. "Much as I'm enjoying your tea party, Colonel, I've got to get back to Westminster."

"Before you go, perhaps we can meet in my office."

They left the field canteen. Blake looked for his bodyguards and found them looking dry and remarkably fresh. He took a final look around the plant. The materials were still stacked high, unmolested. Some campaigners had drifted away, others were chatting with the troops. He turned his back on the scene and went to the office, where Champney handed him an envelope. "I'd like you to pass this report to Brigadier Culverton," he said. "It's not sealed, so perhaps you'd like to read it."

They left the office and walked in the still teeming rain towards a waiting helicopter. "This is the second time we've managed a truce," said Champney, "but I don't think we'll get a third."

Blake was unable to resist a word of congratulation. "Once again, you did a good job, Colonel."

"Not really. The weather did them in, but at least you've got your two days." As they stopped, Champney turned to him. "Minister, I know you'll do your best. Everyone here is counting on you."

This reminded Blake that the action had passed to Westminster, and his thoughts now focussed on the crucial debate. "I'll be in contact," he said as he joined his bodyguards in the helicopter which took off and headed south.

33

Damp and desperate to catch some sleep, Blake found himself again struggling to find comfort in the upright seat of the helicopter. Aware of his difficulty, the co-pilot arranged a stretcher and found some blankets. Blake lay down but, against the unremitting noise of the engine, failed to relax. He propped himself up, reached into his briefcase and took out Champney's report.

He glanced through the logistics of the security operation: the numbers of campaigners compared with those of the security forces, the success of the Campaign's arguments, its popular support, and the range of options open to the army commander in a scale of escalating violence. He then came to Champney's final paragraph.

"We are therefore moving rapidly towards complete breakdown; a point of extreme crisis with an unlimited potential for violence. In these circumstances, unless a political solution is reached immediately, the security forces must be prepared for civil war."

Since the emergency powers were applied, the government's actions had been decided almost entirely by the Prime Minister. At first he had seemed adaptable, welcoming new steps which might divert or counter the pressures weighing in on him, but at the point where these were too radical, he had faltered. Within the limits of moderation his response had been flexible, but where necessity had brought threats to the basic state of things, his nerve had given way. What had first appeared as a brave outlook had soon disintegrated into a fit of angry and sterile recrimination. It was a question now of whether the House would shrink from what had to be done.

Blake went through to the pilot's compartment. "Can we get some news?" he asked. "I want the Command Bunker in Whitehall."

"We can only get our landing instructions," said the pilot. "There's a security ban on information over the air."

"Then how can I know what's going on? Can you tune into the media?"

"There's no broadcasting, sir. It's been shut down since early evening. We'll be landing shortly."

"Before you do, circle round Westminster. I want to have a look."

"I can't do that, sir, my orders are to fly straight in and land."

Blake was defeated. "Just get there as quickly as you can. Isn't there any heat in this damned thing?"

He returned to the rear of the helicopter, almost stumbling over his bodyguards, who sat against the side of the compartment. Their dry and fresh appearance annoyed him. "Where the hell were you two all night?" he asked. "Never mind. Don't tell me."

He lay back on the stretcher, desperate for a change of clothes and feeling hopelessly cut off from events. Time dragged until eventually they approached their destination and landed in the Whitehall security zone. He snatched open the door, jumped to the ground and hurried towards the Command Bunker. Further irritated by security checks, he went to the operations room, where he was confronted by a harassed Bill Charman. "You've left it late," said Bill Charman. "We've got pitched battles all over the country."

"Not in my area," said Blake. "When I left, people were going home. What's happening in the House?"

"I don't know how it's going. I'm fully stretched here. I can't move from this place, and there's not a single member of our Unit on the front bench."

"What about the Prime Minister?"

"I've put out the word that he's exhausted, but it's left a huge gap. Dudney is on his way back and that's given me even more to do, so get down to the House now."

Blake took out Champney's report. "I've got this from our area commander. I want you to read it."

"I can't read that now."

Blake thrust the envelope into Bill Charman's hands. "Just read his conclusion."

Bill Charman read the final paragraph and passed it back. "There's nothing new in this," he said. "You don't seem to realise the scale of what's happening. It may be calm in your area but everywhere else we've got civil war. I've got army commanders all over the country wanting clearance for the unconditional use of firearms. I can't keep pace with it, so get down to the House and get a grip on that debate. Dudney will join you as soon as he can."

Blake realised that events in his area had given him a false impression. "I tried to get news on the way down but it's been blacked out." He sealed Champney's report and passed it back to Bill. "Give that to Culverton."

"He knows all this," Bill said. "Just get out of here."

Blake hurried out of the Bunker but on emerging at the surface realised there was no car. Seeing some army trucks he turned to one of his bodyguards. "Take one of those," he said.

"Yes sir, but they're army transport."

"I can see that. Just take one. Get on with it man."

His bodyguards approached the vehicle and dragged a soldier from the front cab. Blake climbed in and, as they drove off, in a rear view mirror glimpsed a dazed soldier standing in the road. He looked sideways at his driver. "You could have asked," he said.

His bodyguards stared impassively through the windscreen as if to make such a request was not in their nature. "Yes sir," one of them said.

Driving along Whitehall Blake looked back towards Trafalgar Square, but was unable to get a view. Parliament Square was alive with the hurried movements of police and Services. The air reeked of CS gas. Approaching Parliament, the vehicle stopped at more security checks and, within minutes, Blake walked briskly into the House where he went into the Chamber to find it crowded.

He found Dave Reed on the back benches. Dave looked up. "Where the hell have you been?" he asked. "Where's the Home Secretary? Where's Dudney? Where's the government for Christ's sake and where's the Prime Minister?"

"He's exhausted. Haven't you heard?"

"No one believes that," said Dave. "Come clean, Blake. What's going on? Is the government intact?"

"Don't start that rumour. We've been running a security operation. We can't be everywhere at once. There's no lack of government direction, but what's happening here? What about our All Party Group? Can we rely on it? Have you tabled our amendment?"

"Not exactly what you gave me. I had to do some bargaining, so it's been modified."

Blake was suspicious. "What do you mean by modified?"

"Look," said Dave, "you wanted to get it through and you left it with me, but Members are nervous. Unlimited powers of requisition with no compensation. It was too open-ended. It could have led anywhere, so we've got this compromise."

Their conversation was stopped by members urging them to be quiet. Marjorie Tyler, a strong traditionalist, had been called to speak, and a silence had fallen on the back benches. They moved into an adjoining corridor, where Dave explained. "Your powers of requisition were just too wide. This wording limits them strictly to what's needed for civil defence. It allows firms to appeal to an independent legal body. The same procedure will arbitrate on the amounts of credit. These are safeguards against reckless local authorities but, at the same time, it allows the work to go ahead."

Blake studied the text. "You say we can get this through?" he asked.

"I've done a lot of hard talking and you can never know until people vote, but with all this conflict I don't think they'll change their minds."

Blake was satisfied. "Alright, Dave, this looks good enough. You've done well. Yes, I'm happy. If the House doesn't approve, it will have to face the consequences."

"You'd better get down to the front bench. Is the Prime Minister really going to stay away?"

"Why, are you feeling lost without him? Forget the Prime Minister. It's time for this House to act."

Blake returned to the Chamber just as John Dudney arrived. Together, they slumped onto the front bench. Members listened intently as the firm, clear voice of Marjorie Tyler rang through the House.

"... The truth is, Mr. Speaker, this proposal does not come from the government. It has not even been discussed in Cabinet. It has been introduced over the head of the government. It is a panic measure and what is the justification for its reckless haste? Why should we take it on board with all its uncertainties and all its unforeseen consequences? There is no reason.

Be assured that our security forces will deal with the present disruptions. The chaos we are now seeing has been caused by people who seek to exploit our difficulties for their own political ends. They are a direct threat to the historic authority of this House. Even at this moment, at the doorstep of the House, this so-called Campaign is attempting, illegally and with brute force, to seize power. Can any member doubt that we must stand firm against it? Are we to be browbeaten into a hasty action which will not have the effect being hoped for? The results of this amendment will concede victory to mob action. Worse than that, it will create chaos and disruption far more serious than we are seeing at present."

Dudney looked at Blake. "I don't even know what we're talking about," he said. "What is the proposal?"

Blake produced a copy of the amendment to the Emergency Acts and passed it to him. "Essentially, it gives local councils powers to requisition stocks of materials and production facilities. It will last for the duration of the emergency."

Dudney glanced through the text.

"What's happened in the Midlands?" Blake asked.

"Disaster," said Dudney.

"Casualties?"

"Lots."

"Deaths?"

"We don't know how many. Casualties were unavoidable."

"How come we in the north avoided them?"

"You tell me."

The voice of Marjorie Tyler continued to dominate the Chamber.

"Surely, Mr. Speaker, it is our duty to set an example of calm, of measured response, of firm action and of faith in ourselves. A vote against this panic measure is a vote of confidence in our people. The challenge facing this House is one of leadership at a time of confusion; of resolve at a time of uncertainty; of determination at a time when doubt threatens to destroy the stability of our country. If we fail now..."

Blake turned back to Dudney. "The country is tearing itself to pieces and she stands here dishing out clichés. I hope you support this amendment, John?"

"I'm too tired to study it. Tell me one thing. Will it stop the violence?"

"Yes."

"Well, it's only a temporary measure, isn't it? I'm not going to argue over words. You'd better get on your feet."

Blake was relieved when, at last, it was suggested that a speaker for the Civil Contingencies Unit should be heard. Marjorie Tyler agreed to wind up.

"... Indeed, Mr. Speaker, I was drawing to a conclusion, so let me say this. The one fatal element that has caused our present situation has been our weakness. Perhaps this has been well-intentioned but nevertheless it has been misplaced, counter-productive and irresponsible. The circumstances in which we have been pressed into an emergency debate have been created by alien elements. They have coerced us into deciding on a measure which would have disastrous consequences. It would, therefore, be wrong to yield to the pressures of violence, blackmail and intimidation they have brought to bear. Are we to surrender to such pressures? No! I'm sure that every member of this House will repudiate them with utter contempt. I urge members to vote down this amendment but not with a view to doing nothing. Our priority is to remove the threat which stands against us. We must not, and we will not, capitulate to the mob. Then we shall take the proper time to consider more carefully prepared steps. I speak positively. I say we can resolve our difficulties, but not by being rushed into ill-fated measures which inevitably, will only make our problems worse."

To a murmur of approval, Marjorie Tyler sat down. Unaware of his dishevelled appearance, Blake jumped to his feet and the Speaker indicated that he had the floor.

"Mr. Speaker, I should explain the unusual absence of the Prime Minister and other members of the government Unit that has been operating with special responsibilities under the authority of this House. We have been detained at the head of the security forces, attempting to restore some order, and attempting to prevent our slide into irrecoverable chaos. I can tell you that the Prime Minister has carried a special burden. He has given everything of himself, day and night, and even now, his duties and those of the Home Secretary are preventing them from reporting to you from the front bench. We are now at a point when the responsibility for decisive action rests with you, the representatives of all our people. You are aware that as we debate this crucial amendment to our emergency powers, thousands of our security forces, police and troops, and thousands of our fellow citizens are suffering injury and even death. We do not know the numbers. All we know is that the list is not yet complete, and whether that final list will be numbered in many more thousands is being decided now by this House.

I heard it said that the many people who are taking action on the streets and in other places are alien elements. Mr. Speaker, these are our fellow countrymen and women and we stand in great danger of being alienated from them. We are not here to serve ourselves. I know of no other reason for the existence of this House but to serve the interests of all our people.

We have been urged not to rush into hasty measures, and to consider our actions carefully. Mr. Speaker, I have read the carefully considered reports of our army commanders. I have participated in the long discussions of our Civil Contingencies Unit, and I must tell the House, calmly and gravely, that all those reports and all our discussions point to the imminence of civil war.

I say that civil war is imminent. I do not say it is inevitable, but whether or not we now lapse into civil war depends on your vote here, tonight. If we fail to avert this act of self-destruction, will it really be with the use of our strengths? Surely if we now choose to destroy ourselves in bloody conflict, we shall only do it from weakness. We are not being intimidated by any alien elements. If we fail now we shall only do so because we are intimidated by the challenge of a new necessity: the necessity of constructive action and change.

We have been told that the consequences of the proposal before you are uncertain. Yes, this is so, but do we then stand helpless? Do we resign ourselves to the certainty of civil war because every outcome of our attempts to avoid it cannot be known in advance? Sometimes we need to take a brave leap in the dark. Faith has also been mentioned. Are we so lacking in faith that we cannot respond to the urgent demands which have arisen throughout the country? I do not accept that we are that kind of timorous people. The guarantees that are being demanded are another name for fear, a feeble excuse for not asserting the authority of this House in achieving what must be done for all our fellow citizens. We must act now with speed and decision and if this means some uncertainty, we shall accept it and we will resolve any difficulties as we go forward.

The amendment which is now in front of us will release the creative energies, the skills and talents which abound in our country. We cannot say 'no' to this vital need. There is only one threat facing this House, the threat that we might destroy ourselves in fear and indecision. Those who vote 'no' will vote to destroy our future in conflict and I, for one, will have none of it. Those who vote 'yes' will act in support of the millions who are waiting to use their boundless powers of action for themselves, their families and our country. Mr. Speaker, they must not be kept waiting any longer. I implore the House to vote immediately and in favour of this amendment. We must dispatch the good news at the earliest moment so that the injuries and deaths, and the continuing slide into greater tragedy, is stopped. I assure the House: every Minister with responsibilities in this crisis supports this amendment. We most urgently require it. It is the only immediate and practical means of ending the conflict and of uniting the country for the work that has to be done. In giving its assent to this proposal, the House will be saying to the people, 'we are with you, here are the means of doing the job. We will do it together, and we will do it now.' "

Throughout the debate, forceful speakers such as Marjorie Tyler, had emphasised the uncertainties surrounding the proposal. In the hands of local authorities, the new emergency powers were unpredictable. Set against this, Members also had to respond to the violence raging across the country. Some had witnessed at first-hand the pitched battles in Trafalgar Square and throughout the approaches to Westminster. They had seen clouds of CS gas rising from side streets, heard the thud of plastic bullets and, at times, the sinister crackle of firearms. The repeated charges of mounted police and the baton- wielding advances of riot squads had beaten back the campaigners. The many injured, police, troops and protestors, some with bloodied faces or carried on stretchers, had been hurried to waiting ambulances.

Members of the House were also aware that, at hundreds of production plants across the country the same battles were being fought. Now they had heard Blake Evans as he had described the imminence of civil war. It was clear to the majority that the uncertainties of the proposed motion were preferable to the terrible risks of escalating violence. As Blake sat down there was a moment of silent tension before the House erupted with cheers. A majority had made a decision and was concerned now only to get the vote through.

Blake relaxed on the front bench and caught a glimpse of Marjorie Tyler who sat rigid and grim-faced, one of a few who refused to join the cheering. With order restored, there was a speedy move to a division and soon members were filing through the lobbies. Blake went through with John Dudney, and the overwhelming majority who voted in favour. The mood was one of relief. He met Dave Reed and shook his hand. Their combined work with the All Party Group had finally come to success. Other members of the Group were engaged in self-congratulation.

Blake came back to Dudney. "We'd better get back to the bunker," he said. "We've still got a war on our hands."

Dudney was relieved. "But, hopefully, we can now end it."

"Yes," said Blake. "Even this place comes to its senses, eventually."

34

With the House of Commons having cleared the way for the requisition of production plants and materials, there was no reason for continued violence. However, it would take time to get this message through to the campaigners who were still engaged with the security forces throughout the country. Blake and Dudney returned to the Command Bunker in Whitehall, where they discussed with Bill Charman how to make contact with campaign organisers who had the authority to bring their action to an end. Bill told them that contact with Hurst had been lost. It was assumed he was in the area of Trafalgar Square, inflaming the crowds. Erica Field came irresistibly to Blake's thoughts, but she was active in the north and not on the Campaign's National Committee. In any case, she was incapable of taking a reasoned view.

As Bill Charman had previously negotiated with Betty Stevens and Patrick Laurie, he brought in Special Branch officers to locate the two activists. Since they had been under close surveillance this took very little time and a line of contact was soon established. At the same time, Culverton reported that the conflict at the edge of the Westminster zone was reaching a critical phase. Attrition was exhausting the security forces and, as it was impossible to bring in replacement troops, the use of firepower was quickly becoming the only means of resisting the campaigners. John Dudney instructed the Brigadier to continue to hold back on the use of lethal force.

It was decided that Bill Charman should speak with Laurie, making it clear that the Campaign must accept the authority of the House and comply with its decisions. The government unit was now on much stronger ground. With the enactment of the new powers, it had at last regained the initiative. Surrounded by the noise of telephones and images of violence on batteries of television screens, the Home Secretary waited as signals personnel arranged for an outside officer to get a radio receiver to Laurie. The campaign organiser was soon on the line and, as expected, was fully aware of everything that had happened. "In that case why haven't you stopped your action?" Bill Charman asked. "Why the continuing battle for Westminster? You must be mad to think you can take over the government."

"That's not our object," replied Laurie.

"It must be your object," Bill insisted, "but, if you deny it, then you can prove it by ceasing your action immediately. There is no sensible reason for what you are doing, and we will not tolerate a threat to Westminster. Up to now you have enjoyed the benefits of our restraint, but that's over. A decision has been made here that unless you stop your action now, special units of the security forces will advance using automatic weapons. Your people will either disperse or be shot dead where they stand."

"I don't see any point in this conversation," said Laurie. "We'll make our own decisions."

Bill Charman decided to step up the pressure. "Then let me add something else. You will be held responsible for the deaths and you will have to answer for them. Up to now you have enjoyed immunity from arrest but if you fail to withdraw, you and the entire Campaign committee will be arrested, tried and convicted by a Services court, which under the emergency has the power to carry out a death sentence. I will personally see that you are dealt with," he added.

Laurie put on a brave face. "Your threats leave me quite unconcerned," he said.

Bill Charman decided to leave Laurie in a state of anxiety by ending the exchange. "I have only one thing to say to you. Stop your action now, or face the consequences." With this he switched off his receiver.

For the first time Laurie felt inadequate. His background in ecology pressure groups had not equipped him for the high drama of confronting the state. He had just happened to attend the meeting organised by Hurst and Janice Fearn which gave birth to the

Campaign, and had joined its Committee. He had been as surprised as anyone to see it grow in a manner so rapid and ramshackle that it could hardly keep pace with good organisation. He had been one person who had urged the Campaign to act always with restraint, and he felt that, where there had been injuries and deaths the government should examine its own conscience.

Laurie also knew that the majority of campaigners would now only be concerned to continue the work on deep shelters and, having been given the means of doing so, would lose interest in any arguments with the government. In fact, he had already decided that the action should be stopped, but the Home Secretary's aggressive manner had made it difficult for him to say so.

There was some truth in the allegation that the Campaign included a disparate range of political groups, some of which were pursuing agendas that were more extreme than its official aims. It was likely to be these elements that were now continuing the violence under such slogans as "Smash the State."

To increase pressure on the campaigners, the political members of the Civil Contingencies Unit advised Brigadier Culverton that the moment was right to muster the special army units which had so far been held back. At the same time Patrick Laurie worked frantically to spread the word that all action against the government must cease. His actions were reported to the Command Bunker by undercover agents. Bill Charman was satisfied. He stared closely at a cluster of monitors showing the scenes in Trafalgar Square. Just inside the security zone, the special units had taken up positions with their ominous display of automatic weapons, but it hardly seemed necessary. In fact, Campaigners were already beginning to turn their backs on the Westminster fortress and melt away.

The three Ministers gave instructions that public broadcasting should be resumed. It was vital that the good news should go out to the country, and the best person to do that was the Prime Minister. "For all his faults," said Bill Charman, "he is still a key figure."

The Prime Minister had already moved from his accommodation in the Command Bunker and was back in residence in Downing Street. It was decided that John Dudney would remain in charge of the Bunker whilst Bill Charman and Blake should see the Prime Minister. This would be both to keep him in touch with events and to persuade him to broadcast, once again, to the country.

At this prospect, Blake wilted, but Bill Charman was more hopeful. Although he knew the meeting would be difficult, Bill was convinced that, as ever, the Prime Minister would seize an opportunity to renew his popularity.

35

The flow of information from around the country into the Command Bunker beneath Whitehall confirmed the steady withdrawal of the Campaign. Blake and Bill Charman set out for Downing Street. With army transports still moving troops throughout the security zone, they walked the short distance, hoping to freshen up. At Downing Street they were shown through to a lounge and, after some time, the Prime Minister joined them. Wrapped in a thick dressing gown, his manner was abrupt. "What do you two want?" he snapped. "I'm supposed to be resting."

Bill Charman knew from the outset that the meeting would be the usual round of gentle argument combined with flattery and persuasion. It was a ritual tribute that the Prime Minister demanded from his Ministers. "You heard the outcome of the debate, Prime Minister?" he began, tentatively.

"Yes, I did."

"A useful result, wouldn't you agree?"

"No, I wouldn't. You know what you've done? You've destroyed our entire system of government."

"But surely, Prime Minister, we've been vindicated. Parliament has asserted its authority and, as a result, the Campaign has withdrawn."

"Withdrawn? I'm not surprised. We've surrendered, so why shouldn't they withdraw? They'll be running the country from now on."

"I don't quite follow," said Bill.

With an angry expression and head bent, the Prime Minister walked up and down the lounge, giving not the least impression that he was exhausted. "Don't you see?" he said. "You've given all these powers to local authorities: local bodies controlled by renegades and god knows who else. They'll be a law unto themselves."

"But it will operate with the consent of Parliament. Parliament will remain the overriding authority."

"No," said the Prime Minister. "Parliament has consented to its own destruction. What sort of consent do you call that? You've handed control to hundreds of tinpot councils. From now on, they'll make the decisions, and where will that leave the government?"

Quietly and tactfully, Bill Charman continued to argue. "But it was carried by an overwhelming majority. It's what Parliament wants. Surely, Prime Minister, we're bound to accept the decisions of the House. It's now the law, and you've always said the authority of the law is paramount."

Blake added his own gentle pressure. "It's only an extension of the emergency powers, a temporary measure for the duration of the crisis. It's our quickest means of getting back to normal."
"How can we ever get back to normal?" The Prime Minister moved to the window and stared out into the gloom. "I won't go along with these arrangements. You can find someone else."

Whilst Bill Charman was anxious that the government should remain intact, he had no doubt that the Prime Minister would remain. "No one wants that," Bill said. "You're needed by the country, especially at this time. You're the one person to rebuild confidence and the unity which you always say is so important. Surely, unity must begin at the top and we should continue as a team. We respect your view that it's a bad decision but who is there better than this team to make it work in the best way possible? What we need now is a broadcast from you to the country. That always does a lot of good."

The Prime Minister weakened. "Yes, but I don't like what the House has done."

"We respect that…"

"Then again, I would never let pride come between me and my duty."

"What the country needs is reassurance, your reassurance that it can return to its strengths. A further broadcast at this critical moment could unite the country."

The Prime Minister relaxed. "Perhaps you're right." Aware that Blake had been one of the main activists in bringing in the new arrangements he turned to him. "You did a good job in the House last night," he said. "Unfortunately it was too good. You've landed us in a mess."

Blake continued Bill Charman's coaxing. "Well, if that's true Prime Minister, who better than you to get us out of it?"

After a long pause, the Prime Minister agreed. "Well," he said, "perhaps I've still got a job to do. I'm not like others. I'm not one to walk away from my responsibilities. Alright, I'll broadcast. Prepare a text then I'll add my own changes. I'll leave you alone and see what you come up with. Is everything else under control?"

"It's all been taken care of," Bill reassured him.

"Carry on then."

The Prime Minister left them in the lounge and, with relief, Blake turned to Bill Charman. "Was that touch and go, or not?"

"I didn't notice the devious bastard putting up much resistance," said Bill. "His way is now open. He'll return to popularity on the strength of what we've done."

"Yes, well," replied Blake, "one day, God willing, you'll be Prime Minister, and you'll do the same sort of thing."

The Prime Minister had faced a choice between relegation to the political wilderness or, once again, being seen as the architect of national unity. In choosing to broadcast, his vanity had thrust aside his objections to the new powers of local bodies. With little persuasion, it seemed that ego had displaced principle, but it was also possible that he had never seriously considered resignation.

The two Ministers drafted a text for the Prime Minister's broadcast. With scant reference to local production boards, they emphasised the need for order to be restored. Casting the Prime Minister in the role of strong leader, they concluded with an appeal for responsibility, sacrifice, cooperation and total commitment to the work on civil defence.

The Prime Minister returned and, as Blake and Bill Charman looked on anxiously, he read the text. His eyes narrowed in disapproval as he scanned the references to the National Consultative Council. "I'm not presiding over anything that includes Campaign activists," he said. "I won't sit down with them."

"Do you object to anyone in particular?" asked Bill, relieved that the Prime Minister had accepted the draft.

"Yes, I object to the whole bloody lot. And Sir Gordon Rowan, I don't want to see his face again."

"We'll arrange for his replacement."

"I don't mind Frank Bell. He said he wouldn't be back until I was removed. I want to see that loudmouth eat his words." The Prime Minister again glanced through the draft. "I see this solely as a means of getting back to normal. On that basis, I'll go along with it."

"We'll make the arrangements," said Bill, "and leave you to get some more rest."

Blake and Bill Charman left Downing Street and walked back to the Command Bunker. "All that's left," said Blake, "is to count the casualties."

"What's happened has been an outrage," said Bill. "In time, we should put a few people on trial."

"Why be vindictive?" said Blake. "Everyone was to blame. You can't single out individuals."

"Even if you're right, people need their scapegoats. A few trials will purge the country of its guilt."

"I find that disgusting," said Blake. "It's primitive. We don't need a ritual sacrifice."

"There's another reason." Bill said. "People need the assurance of strong authority. Ask yourself why they have been attacking us all night. It's because ultimately they depend on the government. If they didn't, they wouldn't be on the streets."

"You're wrong, Bill. We don't want reprisals. I'll have nothing to do with it."

"Suit yourself, but you won't be helping anyone."

At the Command Bunker, Dudney reported that suddenly, the entire country had gone quiet and he had advised that the security forces should be stood down. Blake was at last free to return home.

"By the way," said Bill, "we've had your house under close guard. You'll find it still intact."

Blake nodded and left. At the boundary of the security zone, the barriers were still in place. He got out of the car and looked around. The campaigners had gone, leaving troops and police standing by their stationary vehicles. Leaflets fluttered across the square. In the aftermath of violence, bricks, bottles and stones were strewn in every direction. Discarded and lying in heaps, the Campaign's placards still spoke their potent message. He returned to his car, which moved off at gathering speed. Slumped in the back, tension began to drain from his body. He looked forward now only to seeing Rachel.

On arriving home, he summoned up his last reserves of energy, eased himself out of his seat, walked across the pavement and let himself in. Rachel wasn't there. He picked up the telephone but it was dead. Then he saw her note.

"Blake – I'm at the hospital still treating casualties. What a waste! I just hope you've come through all right. See you as soon as I can. All my love, Rachel."

He went up to the bedroom, threw off his damp clothes, collapsed into bed and fell asleep.

He next found himself being woken up. Rachel stood over him, smiling at his outstretched body as he struggled back to consciousness. "I must have slept all day," he said. "Terrible dream, more like a nightmare."

"The nightmare happened," she said.

He pulled himself up. "I was afraid you'd been caught up in the violence."

She reassured him. "I'm all right, but where have you been? I tried to keep up with the news but it was shut down."

He tried to recall the past two days. "I've been everywhere. What's happening now? Did the Prime Minister broadcast?"

"It's gone out several times," she said. "Look, I'd love to join you but I must get back. We're still picking up the pieces and we can hardly cope."

Blake got out of bed. "I'll come with you. There might be something useful I can do."

She smiled. "It's about time."

36

After the conflict, a mood of depressed calm settled over the country. As the dead were buried and the injured cared for, the anger which had brought the population to the brink of civil war gave way to a numbed sense of tragedy. There had been shock and, in the days of mourning, people were withdrawn. But soon the compelling pressures to sustain life displaced the grieving for the dead and every community stirred itself into fresh action.

In his broadcast, the Prime Minister had spoken of the tragic waste of life brought about by unnecessary violence. The new powers of requisition had always been intended, he said, and were the best means of getting the country back to normal. With order restored, and with the government at the centre of national cooperation, he would personally ensure the success of the work ahead.

Local production boards sprang into fresh life, bringing together voluntary workers, the Services, trade unions and representatives of local firms. The materials which had been so savagely contested were released and work recommenced. With the barriers between need and supply at last swept aside, people were free to make their decisions and to follow them with immediate action.

This new activity was in sharp contrast to the deadlock of conflict in which the resources of communities had for so long been trapped. Strife and frustration were left behind. From the inertia of a divided community there was a shared sense of purpose and a surge of creative energy. Voices changed. Instead of the war of words, the endless rounds of sterile argument and mutual blame, there was a positive flow of ideas which advanced the work.

Despite the continuing threat from space, people drew strength from their combined efforts. Anxiety gave way to confidence and heightened morale. People found a new sense of purpose in the common cause.

Once again cooperating with Colonel Champney, Erica Field was active on the production board in Blake's area in the north. She enjoyed the satisfaction of seeing requisition orders issued against the materials which the Campaign had failed to seize, but these were soon used up. Under its new powers, the local authority requisitioned the plant. More materials were produced and distributed to the sites of deep shelters.

Again, Blake threw himself into the work of the Department. He was aware that beyond the work of basic construction, vast quantities of equipment would be required for heating, lighting, air filtration, sanitation, waste disposal, fresh water, canteen facilities and medical care. Adequate stores of food would require farms to increase production. Many families had begun work on small shelters in cellars and back gardens and, because these would relieve pressure on the communal projects, they were encouraged, but again, the materials and equipment had to be supplied. Plans were drawn up for converting the entire London underground railway system into one immense shelter for much of the city's population and this further increased the pressure of demand on industry and manufacture.

With its national overview, Blake's Department monitored the requirements of goods and materials and the lists of credit notes that flooded in daily from the local production boards. Before long, Chris Lawson took them up with Blake. "The scale is fantastic," he said. "Do you realise how far these requisitions will have to go? We need industrial plants, manufacture, raw materials, energy and transport."

"That's right," said Blake.

"We'll need agriculture. On my reckoning we'll need almost everything."

Blake agreed. "That's right," he said. "Things are produced throughout the whole economy. We'll have to go where necessity takes us."

"And what about all these credits? They're being issued with no control and we've hardly begun."

"That's what the Treasury said," Blake reminded him. "We'll create an impossible government debt."

"Impossible?"

"Of course. These credit notes are worthless bits of paper. If the totals were published any fool could see it."

"So, we're getting into a new round of argument?"

"Not necessarily," said Blake. "We could stop people finding out. I'll get Jack Brightwell. He's an expert on keeping information under wraps."

Blake called in the head of Department, who advised a meeting with Lindsay, the Chancellor. The Treasury was the only other Department monitoring the issue of credit notes. Any plan to conceal the national totals would require their cooperation.

Blake arranged the meeting and explained the problem. "You understand, Lindsay, it's not that I want secrecy. I'm apprehensive, worried about people's reactions if they find out. More trouble is the last thing we need."

"I do see the point," said Lindsay.

A conspiracy of silence was difficult. The credits were part of public accounts which the Treasury was bound to publish. It was agreed that the worst danger would come from publishing the credits as a single total. It was this figure that dramatised the amount outstanding and the alarming rate of its daily increase. At Brightwell's suggestion, the two Ministers agreed a formula. To make the total less accessible they would present the figures in a fragmented form, divided between hundreds of local authorities and under separate items such as labour, materials, machinery, equipment, etc. In this way, the single national total would be obscured by hundreds of documents listing thousands of items.

"If anyone wants the single total," said Lindsay, "they'll have to find it themselves within a vast mass of statistics. It won't be easy."

"This method also has the merit of publishing the figures in much greater detail," said Brightwell. "That justifies it."

"An amount of detail impossible to comprehend?" asked Blake.

"But, as an added safeguard, we can delay publication," replied Lindsay. "After all, this additional work means we're overstretched."

"I'm sure it's the right thing to do," said Brightwell. "We don't want anyone to become disillusioned."

"Exactly," said Blake.

Satisfied they had found a way of concealing information that could lead to more arguments, Lindsay leaned back in his chair. "You know, Blake," he said, "there's a paradox in all this. To be frank, my job is a lot easier. With all this credit note business, I don't have to juggle with government finance. I'm no longer trying to apportion meagre funds amongst competing claims while being told that hospitals will have to close if I don't find more money. It's not pleasant going to bed thinking I may have shortened someone's life because I've starved the health service of finance. All this civil defence work may be based on an illusion, but at least I don't have to worry. These local people want to get things done, they requisition what they need, they issue credits and I just sit here compiling the totals. Don't misunderstand me, I realise that it's a fool's paradise, and that the day of reckoning will come. In the end they'll all feel cheated."

"But, as you say," said Blake, "this isn't a good time for them to know it."

"According to the Prime Minister, it's our best and quickest means of getting back to normal. I've come to agree with that. We've avoided civil war and, once we're out of the crisis, we'll revert to our usual arrangements. All right, these credits are worthless, but at least we're preserving the basis of normality. In time, I'm sure everyone will appreciate it."

"In that case, local authorities can issue what credits they like."

"I don't see why not. In the long run it won't make any difference, but no one will ever see the cash."

"Just one more thing," said Blake, "there's no reason why anyone else in the government should know about this conversation, is there?"

"So far as I'm concerned we've had an informal chat," said Lindsay. He shrugged. "As you see, I've made no record."

Blake was interrupted by a call from Bill Charman, who wanted to see him urgently. As the meeting with the Treasury had come to a satisfactory end, he left for the Home Office wondering what new problem had arisen. On his arrival, Bill told him that Sandra Dale was about to report on the signals being transmitted by the space probe. She was able to present a clearer picture of the dangers from the approaching comet.

They waited only minutes before Sandra Dale entered the Home Secretary's office. As she sat down and took a bundle of papers from her briefcase, Bill Charman could hardly contain himself. "Well, Dr. Dale," he asked, "have you brought us good news, or bad?"

"A mixture of both," she said. "Observations from the space probe confirm that the comet is gigantic. However, the problems of knowing its exact size, and of fixing its orbit with precision, are still very difficult, but we do have a provisional view. When I say gigantic, I really do mean that it's far larger than anything previously recorded. In discussion with our American colleagues we've assessed the diameter of the comet's nucleus at about 50 miles and we think it might pass as close to Earth as 3 or 4 million miles. Inevitably a comet of this size, passing this close, will release vast quantities of debris into Earth's gravitational field. As we've always said, the smaller elements will burn up in the atmosphere. The larger masses will survive and fall to Earth's surface at cosmic velocity."

"At cosmic velocity?" Blake asked. "Does that mean we won't see them coming?"

"That's one way of putting it, but the fall of missiles is only one-half of the dangers. We also think that Earth will pass through a dense cloud of cosmic dust which might partially block the sun and produce a cold phase. If this happens, Earth's temperatures will fall."

There was a pause as the two Ministers considered Sandra Dale's grim report. "You mentioned some good news," said Bill Charman. "Can we have some of that?"

"Yes," she said. "We could have been heading for a cosmic collision. For humanity, that would have been the end. We can now say that a collision is unlikely."

"We'll try to take some comfort from that. What about Mr. Hurst's theory of a companion star to our sun? I believe he called it Nemesis. Does that still cause us concern?"

"No," she said. "It is possible that Nemesis exists and has wrenched our comet from its place in the cloud of comets that surround our solar system. No doubt, eventually, we shall know more about it."

"Well," said Bill, with a look of resignation, "I don't suppose it matters how our comet got here. We're grateful for the clearer picture, Dr. Dale. When will you have precise information on the movement of this thing?"

"Give us a few more weeks, Home Secretary," she said. "The space probe is doing a good job, but to give you a final answer is going to take a little more time. In the meantime, of course, it's vital that the civil defence work is completed."

"Yes, well, at least that's going ahead. We'll make sure it continues."

Throughout the meeting, Sandra Dale had spoken in her usual matter-of-fact, clinical manner, but Blake and Bill Charman could barely conceal their disappointment. Up to this point, given that the work of the scientific team was not complete, they had clung to the hope that the comet would pass by without delivering its cargo of missiles. A possible margin for error had given them grounds for optimism, but this had now been removed. On hearing Sandra Dale's dispassionate report, they accepted the certainty of mass destruction. It was real and it was approaching fast.

In line with cooperation between scientific teams across the Atlantic, it was agreed that the latest news of the comet should be released simultaneously in London and Washington.

37

The news of the comet was received with a mixture of fresh fears and relief. The dangers were frightening, but communities took courage from the work on their defences. Throughout Britain, every local authority moved with a new urgency, and to secure the means of completing the deep shelters, a fresh spate of requisition orders was issued. Manufacturing units were taken over and as these required their own materials, requisition orders were issued against the plants which supplied them. Throughout the network of industrial links, each requisition led inevitably to the next, until most production was under the control of local authorities.

Anticipating a period of reduced temperatures, food had to be stored against the time when its supply might be interrupted. Local production boards were expanded to include farming experts. A policy was implemented using pastures for the growth of cereals and storable vegetables, and producers who failed to comply had their farms requisitioned. Every spare scrap of land was searched out and brought into cultivation. Parks and some private gardens were taken over. Every person able to assist worked with whatever means were available.

Work began on converting the London underground railway system to a network of deep shelters. Tunnels were given extra lighting, and air filtration units were installed. Plans to cover the tracks with flat metal sections required more output from industry and manufacture. Throughout the country work on hundreds of deep shelters progressed rapidly. Some were cut into chalk downs. In one northern town, a labyrinth of tunnels which had been hewn out of sandstone for old wartime air-raid shelters was re-opened. Equipped with a hospital, it would protect 6,000 people. In addition to communal projects, the construction of small family shelters was aided by local production boards. Communications were expanded.

Radio stations aired suggestions from callers while pouring out information to assist with the work.

As more and more production facilities were requisitioned, the national work force had to accept a reduction in its cash incomes. The exchange of working time for credit notes provided no cash and, to ease problems, payments on rents and mortgages were suspended. Water, telephone and domestic fuel were supplied free and a system of free travel was introduced.

For the first time in years, shortages of labour appeared. In every area, army commanders mustered every available Service resource. Despite this and many other measures, the newly released powers of production were stretched to their full capacity. The difficulties were accepted, as morale remained high and a mood of optimistic resolve fired the population. Working frantically against the deadline of danger, every community was driven by a determination to survive.

Blake continued to work long hours at the Department. Through Chris Lawson, he was in touch with the work in his City and as part of the National Consultative Council, he was involved with national decisions. From his position in Whitehall he was able to monitor the information that flowed in from every locality. Monitoring the national effort from this commanding view, progress exceeded his expectations, but he was also aware of the steady collapse of normal economic arrangements. It appeared that the country was heading for a new crisis, and his fears were sharpened when he received a call from the Prime Minister's office saying that an urgent Cabinet meeting had been arranged.

The meeting came as no surprise. Though its role was diminished, from time to time the Prime Minister had recalled the Cabinet as a show of normal government. What worried Blake was its suddenness. His fears were further increased by a call from Lindsay, who insisted on seeing him prior to the meeting. Blake agreed, and within a few minutes the Chancellor arrived at his office.

"Do you know the reasons for this Cabinet meeting?" Lindsay asked him.

"No. I was hoping it was one of the Prime Minister's little charades."

"Well it isn't. First of all, Blake, I'm under pressure. People want to know the amount of credit owed by the government. I'm being pressed by the TUC, the Confederation and others, but I'm not worried about that, I can easily fob them off, but the Prime Minister has come under pressure from the House and MPs like Marjorie Tyler. He insists that I produce the figures in Cabinet and I'll have to comply. You realise, the total is quite fantastic."

"I don't see the problem," said Blake. "The Cabinet won't reveal the information. It's still governed by secrecy and there's no need to publish."

"These are public accounts. There's no legal basis for secrecy and, anyway, I'm not sure we can trust Marjorie Tyler. Have you never heard of leaks? She's still smarting from her defeat in the House and you've got to ask yourself, why she wants this information? I think she wants to make trouble."

Blake tried to reassure the Chancellor. "But what can she do? Alright, the credits are a fraud and she can make that public, but is anyone going to care? Lindsay, haven't you noticed? The whole country is concerned with survival. No one is interested in her backward attitudes."

For the moment, Lindsay was satisfied, but then continued. "There's something else," he said, "something much more serious. We're bankrupt. Normal business has been completely undermined. Our expenditure has increased, we're not collecting taxes and we've run out of cash. The government can't meet its cash commitments for more than six weeks. After that, the coffers are empty."

"You must have seen it coming."

"Of course I did. I said we were living in a fool's paradise, but the day of reckoning has come sooner than I thought."

"What do you want me to do about it?" Blake asked.

Lindsay shrugged. "I wanted you to be forewarned," he said. "I've got my own ideas, but you might come up with something. You've got two hours."

"I'll tell you one thing now," said Blake, "we can't stop the work. That's unthinkable. There's still a lot to do and we've got a shortage of labour."

Lindsay stood up to leave. "How would you like the Inland Revenue Department?" he asked. "With no taxes they're redundant. Can you use them?"

"What we need is extra food," said Blake. "Are there any gardeners amongst them? What about our Chancellor? Is he redundant?"

Lindsay remained grim-faced. "I grow delphiniums," he said. "Not much use at a time like this."

Lindsay left, and Blake considered the government's imminent bankruptcy. The Chancellor had said the Treasury had some ideas so he thought about it no further. He returned to his more straightforward work where simple necessity determined what had to be done. He carried on until it was time to leave for Downing Street.

On arrival he went through to the Cabinet Room, where he took his seat beside Bill Charman.

"Why the hurried meeting?" Bill asked him.

"We're bankrupt," said Blake.

"We've always been bankrupt."

"No Bill. I don't mean cash restraints, I mean no cash at all. No money to pay your policemen, the troops or anyone, in fact, no money to pay your salary."

"Oh. You mean that sort of bankrupt?"

"Yes. The desperate kind."

The Prime Minister swept into the room and took his seat. "We're here to deal with a new crisis," he began, "but first I want to remind you that I was never in favour of these new arrangements. I went along with them against my better judgment, but what the Chancellor has to tell us now justifies all my warnings. The local authorities have been reckless, and are now completely out of control. They've dished out credit notes to an impossible amount and, worse than that, they've reduced us to bankruptcy. We've got to sort it out, and I only hope that the people who wanted this have got some bright ideas. We'll begin with the Chancellor giving us the facts."

Lindsay looked up from his papers and Blake was surprised to see him unperturbed. "You're quite right, Prime Minister," he began. "We've built up an impossible debt and on top of that, we've run out of cash. There can be no blame attaching to the Treasury. We said it would happen and I am compelled to remind you, Prime Minister, you overruled our advice."

As the Prime Minister glared at Lindsay, Blake anticipated a stormy meeting. "I endorsed a voluntary scheme," he said. "I was always opposed to compulsory requisitions."

Lindsay continued. "What I was coming to is that the Treasury has changed its mind. I take the view now that it was right to adopt these measures, and incidentally, Prime Minister, you were absolutely right to go along with them."

Marjorie Tyler had been brought into the Cabinet as a restraining influence and to balance the views of those more easily given to change. She intervened. "I've been trying to get information out of the Chancellor about the level of credits, but I've had nothing but evasions. The figures issued by the Treasury are incomprehensible and this is deliberate. Why is the information being concealed?"

"That's an outrageous suggestion," said Lindsay. "The information is available in great detail."

Marjorie Tyler raised her voice. "No, it's deliberately confused."

"We're not getting into that argument," shouted the Prime Minister. "We all know where we stand. The point is where do we go from here?" He turned to Lindsay and softened his tone. "Chancellor, you surprise me. You don't seem to be concerned. You say you've changed your mind about these measures. What's your reason for that?"

Lindsay leaned back in his chair and stared into space. "We have to balance two sets of facts." he said. "On the one hand, we've come a long way with the construction of deep shelters. We've pulled back from civil war and throughout the country we have good order and high morale. Against this, our normal economic activity is in a state of collapse. The country is bankrupt. Our best projections tell us that as a government we'll be out of cash in six weeks. We won't be able to pay the police, the army or any government employee. There'll be no money for pensioners or the sick, and in fact we won't be able to pay the salaries of this Cabinet." He looked around the table with a wry smile. "You might find the last item the most worrying of all."

The Prime Minister was still perplexed by Lindsay's attitude. "Chancellor," he said, "I don't like sarcasm at any time, but especially not now. Surely, you've got something more constructive to say?"

"Prime Minister, you have always said that we should get our costs down. Well, in present circumstances, the best way of doing it is to get rid of them altogether. I'm proposing that for the duration of the crisis, we operate a cashless economy. In fact, there is no alternative. It would be the quickest way of getting back to normal. We in the Cabinet can take a lead by agreeing to forego our salaries until the civil defences are completed. If everyone in the country does the same, we can provide for all our needs as a free public service. In that way we will avert the crisis of bankruptcy. I propose that we suspend all money exchanges and freeze all bank accounts and cash holdings, including those held by the government."

There was a long pause as the Prime Minister realised that Lindsay was serious. "Is this your own idea, Chancellor?" he said eventually.

"It's been developed between myself and the Treasury," replied Lindsay, "but it's been dictated by the situation we are in. As I have said, there is no alternative."

"Yes, but I don't think it's practical," said the Prime Minister.

"It simply depends on everyone staying at their jobs," said Lindsay. "All they need do is continue working and I'm sure people will do it. We'll maintain industry, manufacture, agriculture, transport and every necessary service. Then, when the civil defences are complete, we'll revert to our normal economic arrangements. We've already suspended many payments so the logic now is to go the whole distance by suspending every use of money and providing for people's needs as a free public service. What matters most is our survival, and we've already seen that people are willing to cooperate."

The Prime Minister listened carefully as Lindsay pressed his arguments, and soon indicated that he was willing to accept them. "I must admit," he said, "that what you suggest could be a way out." He turned to Blake. "How far have we got with the civil defence work?" he asked.

"That's the point, Prime Minister," Blake replied, "there's still a long way to go and we dare not stop."

The Prime Minister turned next to Bill Charman. "What about you, Home Secretary, you haven't said much?"

"It's not just a matter of getting the work completed," said Bill. "As Lindsay has said, morale in the country is high but we should all be aware of how quickly this could change. We know from the space probe that we're up against a tight deadline of danger and we can't risk another break in the work. We've captured the initiative. The Campaign is falling away fast and we don't want it brought back to life. We've got to stay in control, and for that we've got to keep up the momentum of the work. I'm not an expert on economics but I'm happy to accept Lindsay's advice. A temporary, cashless economy would seem to be the answer and we should introduce it now."

John Dudney put a question. "If we provide for everyone's basic needs as a free public service, how do we prevent it being abused?"

"We shall have to rely on the social conscience of our citizens," replied Lindsay, "but seeing the present spirit of cooperation, why should we doubt it? Obviously, there will have to be food rationing. I believe the books are already printed. They've always been ready for an emergency and we can issue them within 24 hours."

"Yes," said the Prime Minister, "the idea is beginning to look more practical." He turned finally to Marjorie Tyler. "Can you think of any reason why this shouldn't go ahead?" he asked.

To the surprise of the Cabinet, she approved. "Like the Prime Minister," she said, "I warned everyone that we'd get into this mess but now that we're in it, what can we do? But it must only be a temporary arrangement. We must guarantee an early date for the resumption of normal trade and every production unit must be returned to the control of its owners."

The Prime Minister moved towards a conclusion. "In that case, all we need is to decide when we'll bring it in."

"The sooner, the better," said Lindsay. "I'm anxious to avoid another government pay-day. The more cash we have in hand the stronger will be our position when we revert to normal. My advice is to announce the cashless economy in a broadcast tonight and make it official from that moment. It should be immediate and with no advance warning."

"Alright," said the Prime Minister, "that seems to be settled. I'll broadcast tonight and make the new arrangements operative from 8 o'clock. It will speed up the work on civil defence. We'll push this damned Campaign further to the margins. We'll avoid the chaos of bankruptcy. We'll maintain the authority of a strong and stable government and we'll bring forward the time when we can get back to normal."

He gathered up his papers and this was a signal that the meeting was at an end. He joined Blake and Bill Charman. "Get some detail from Lindsay and draft a text for my broadcast. I'll then give it a final polish. You should emphasise getting back to normal," he said. "Concentrate on that."

Blake took up some points with Lindsay and retired with Bill to a private office where they worked on the draft. "I don't know why we bother," said Bill, "by the time he gave it his final polish, I didn't recognise our last draft."

"Yes, I noticed," said Blake, "but he does have one advantage. He never lets the facts get in the way of a good message."

"Even so," said Bill, "a moneyless economy isn't going to be easy. I'm impressed by what's happened but it's going to take a lot more cooperation."

Blake reassured him. "Don't worry, people are adaptable and they like a challenge, especially when they're working together for themselves. There's nothing new about cooperation, Bill. It's how we got here in the first place and it's still what we're best at."

Having completed the draft, Blake returned to his Department where he explained the new measures to Chris Lawson and Brightwell. The cashless economy would give new impetus to the work on civil defence and this would further stretch the Department.

38

On his way home Blake bought a selection of wines and Rachel was surprised to see case after case being stacked in the hallway. As his driver left, she turned to Blake. "Is this for the party before the Titanic goes down?"

He checked his list of select vintages of Bordeaux claret. "We may as well go out in a blaze of comfort," he said.

"But this is hoarding. You've said people shouldn't do it."

"So, you've discovered my weakness."

"Your drinking habit or your hypocrisy... and why the excess?"

He looked at his watch. "We should hear the Prime Minister. Then you'll know."

He took a bottle, went through to the lounge and poured their drinks. "Is this another one of your scripts?" she asked as they settled on the couch.

"It was, but this actor never keeps to his lines."

Again, the broadcast came direct from Downing Street. The head and shoulders of the Prime Minister filled the screen. His voice was calm and measured, his manner informal and reassuring.

"As I review the progress of our civil defences we can all feel pleased with ourselves. This is a time for self-congratulation. Working together at a great pace we've succeeded in carrying forward the work on civil defence. It's been a time of upheaval. We've all had to adapt, our resources have been stretched to their limits and we've had to do things in a new way. We've succeeded because we've all put the community before self-interest and I know we'll carry on doing so. There was never any doubt that we would respond to the challenge.

There are still many uncertainties. The dangers we face are still not fully known but this need cause us no alarm. We shall be prepared for any threat. Every member of the community will be protected. We can say this because we've overcome all our difficulties. There was a lack of government finance but we never allowed this to stand in our way. Adapting to the demands of the emergency, we did what was necessary, setting aside our financial problems and in doing so we've sustained our efforts.

Our progress has been so great that we can at last look forward to normal times, but we know the job is not complete. There is still a great deal to do and I gave you my assurance that the government is determined to see the work brought to a speedy conclusion. We will continue to sweep aside any further difficulties and therefore I want to tell you about the new emergency measures the government has decided are necessary.

We should all know that we as a government can do nothing on our own. We can take a lead, that's our job, but the country's success can only be achieved through the efforts and the cooperation of every person. Now, I must tell you that at an emergency Cabinet meeting today, I was advised by the Chancellor that the country's accounts have reached a final breaking point. Because our expenditure has vastly increased, and because as a nation our income has diminished, we will soon reach a point where we will be unable to meet our cash commitments. However, we will not allow this to stand in our way. We will not allow our great national project to come to a halt, but this means we must adapt to further emergency measures.

We intend that every essential service will be made freely available. For the duration of the crisis we will provide every necessity such as food, housing, lighting and heating as a free public service. Transport will be free. During the emergency all rents and mortgage payments will be suspended. Let me make it clear to you. No one will have to pay for any of these things.

But this will require that all payments are stopped. It means that wages, salaries and every other kind of income will be suspended. Therefore, as of now, every kind of cash holding will be frozen for the duration of the crisis. This will be a temporary cashless economy and we are compelled to introduce this for many reasons. We must avert the chaos of bankruptcy. We must allow the work on civil defence to go ahead. Above all, these emergency measures will provide us with the quickest means of getting back to normal life.

The success of these measures will depend on one simple action which every fit person in the country can take. There is no difficulty. Our success depends upon everyone staying at their jobs and continuing to work. That's all it needs, and I know that all of you will do it. Those who are producing our food, our people in transport and distribution, our people in mining, energy, industry and manufacture, those of us in the hospitals and in the country's administration; all we need do is stay at our posts and we will ensure that every person will be cared for. At the same time, of course, we must redouble our efforts to complete the civil defence projects.

We shall introduce a system of rationing. You'll find that ration books will be issued immediately, and this will not be new. In the past, a fair system of rationing helped to pull the country though times of trouble. You know, it's worth remembering, in those war years when the life of our country was last threatened, no one flinched from what had to be done. Everyone got together in a great national effort and thousands gave their lives. That's when we were at our best, when we were cooperating as a nation to protect the decencies of our way of life. Since then, we've found plenty to argue about. Sometimes we can be a quarrelsome people, but I know this, when it comes to it, at a time of dire threat, we can pull together as that generation did. Now, as then, we are the same people. We will follow their example of unity. We will stay at our jobs and we will redouble our efforts. I pledge to you the government's total commitment to the work which still lies ahead, and I know you will all respond in the part you each have to play. As never before, we all depend on each other. Putting away the quarrels of recent times, and organised as one great national team, we will take our country through any danger that the future may bring. Good night and safe times to you all."

As once again the image of the Prime Minister was faded from the screen, Blake switched off the television. He poured fresh drinks, returned to the couch and looked across to Rachel. She sat still, obviously moved by the Prime Minister's message. Her eyes were damp with emotion. Blake was also impressed. As ever, the Prime Minister had risen to the occasion. Whether his words had been sincere or had been conveyed with a cynical use of fine language was difficult to know and barely seemed to matter. He had spoken with warmth, said what was needed and what the country wanted to hear.

"And that was your draft?" asked Rachel.

"Bits of it were mine," he said. "The mention of war years was the Prime Minister's. He now sees himself as a great war leader."

"As for getting back to normal," she said, "some of us prefer things as they are. I see it in the hospital. We can also monitor the mood of the country. There's less stress and people are more confident."

"In spite of the dangers?" Blake asked.

"Yes. In spite of the dangers there's less anxiety. Even you've changed, so why would you want to get back to all that argument and frustration? Who in their right mind would want to get back to normal?"

"It's the reason for the cashless economy. Don't you mind not getting your salary?"

"Like a dutiful citizen, I'll do what the Prime Minister says. I won't desert my patients and so long as we get what we need, I can't see much difference. But I can see why you bought all that wine. You took advantage of privileged information. That was unethical."

"I notice you're drinking it," he said.

She smiled as she held up her glass up to the light. "I'm talking about your ethics, not mine."

"Perhaps the better question," he asked, "is where shall we store it? We might have to take cover in our cellar and there's not a lot of space."

"Really?" she said. "I imagined us occupying a luxury suite in your Command Bunker."

"With all those politicians, police chiefs and brigadiers? No thanks. I'm not going to oblivion with that lot."

"And who is going to oblivion?" she asked.

"All of us." he said. "When the bombardment begins, nowhere will be safe. It's Armageddon with a vengeance. Nemesis."

"Why the sudden pessimism?" she asked. "I know you think a lot of Sandra Dale, but she's not infallible. You speak of the Prime Minister acting out his performance, well, so do scientists, except they work in the theatre of the mind. Theorising is a creative thing, prone to error and all the vanities that afflict politicians."

"No," he said, "there's a world consensus. We're facing destruction and for all we've done there is no defence. Imagine the blast which caused the Great Meteor Crater in Arizona. One of the Henbury craters in Australia is 200 metres in diameter and 100 metres deep. Imagine our cities suffering that onslaught."

She shrugged and stood up. "Well, it won't happen tonight, so let's have a meal and go to bed. There's one thing, this wine is very good, so, for the moment let's enjoy it."
"And how long is a moment?" he asked

"As long as you want to make it," she said with a smile. "Eternity if you like."

"I'll settle for that."

39

Once the discovery of the comet was credited to Edward Hurst, it became universally known as "Comet Hurst". Astronomers, astrophysicists and other scientists, continued to work frantically to plot the orbit of the comet with precision. There were still fears that it might collide with Earth. Speculation intensified as to whether Uranus had been knocked on its side after colliding with a great comet similar to the one now approaching the inner planets. Even within memory, over a six-day period, the shattered pieces of Comet Shoemaker-Levy were seen to crash into Jupiter. Whilst nature was indifferent to the movement of its great forces, in people's minds such a collision with Earth could only be anticipated with fear and dread. It would bring an end to humanity.

It was therefore with great relief that communities were assured there would be no collision. Even so, the cratered surfaces of planets and moons were evidence of meteoric bombardment and there was no reason for thinking that this history of solar violence had ended. It was accepted as normal that every year thousands of meteorites entered the atmosphere. Most were heated to the point of incandescence but sometimes the mass of larger bodies survived. With the approach of the new comet, this normal attraction of meteorites would be increased. Only wishful thinking could dismiss a new and catastrophic rain of missiles.

Earth's geological record also revealed that meteorites falling at cosmic velocity had raised great clouds of dust. At these times, only weak light from the sun had filtered through, creating periods of freezing twilight. As Comet Hurst neared the sun and passed Earth, gas molecules would flow from its nucleus and if these emissions contained dust, a vast cloud would form its tail. Cosmic dust would form a barrier between the sun and Earth and during this period of cometary winter, the temperate zones of Earth would freeze. Even the tropics would become cold.

According to the theory of a dark companion star to the sun, as the star moved into a region of space closer to the solar system, it would disturb the equilibrium of millions of comets that surrounded the planets. In this view, the impending missile bombardment and climate change on Earth would result from a deadly sequence of disturbances beginning in the far depths of space. Moving unseen through these distant reaches was the death star – Nemesis. It was possible that it had wrenched the comet from its home in the Oort Cloud and dispatched it to the centre of the solar system. As it sped towards its rendezvous with Earth the comet would discharge rock debris. Earth would then drag this as missiles into its atmosphere whilst passing through an immense cloud of dust.

In this way, humanity's home in space would act as a final link in a chain of lethal attractions to become a hostile environment or even a place of human annihilation. At one time, dinosaurs had been lords of the planet. Successful and numerous, they had prospered over its surface but had then disappeared. They were destroyed by natural forces which in a more benign form had nurtured them. Similarly, the life of humanity was in balance with benign conditions and, in taking this for granted, it was difficult to imagine that such a blessing of nature could suddenly be withdrawn. Now there was a real and imminent prospect of oblivion.

Many continued to see the visit of the comet as a punishment from God. The prophecy of Armageddon had given a name to such divine retribution, and words from the Bible, previously quoted at the great demonstration in Trafalgar Square, promised a fate that was uttered with great foreboding. "I will show wonders in the heavens, and in the Earth, blood, fire and pillars of smoke. The Earth shall quake; the heavens shall tremble; the sun and moon shall be dark; the stars shall withdraw their shining and fall from the sky. Then shall be great tribulation, such as was not seen since the beginning of the world to this time." This text had been repeated many times but even in this prophecy there was some hope of redemption. For true believers, beyond the holocaust, there would be salvation and harmony.

And, from science, the lessons of astronomy, geology and the fossil record left little hope for survival. What hope there was depended on the human ability to adapt. This in turn rested on the will to cooperate and the ability to muster every resource for the preservation of life. At least now, the self-destructive conflicts which had crippled these powers of action had been swept aside. The road to unity had been agonized, but people could now look out at the dangers from a different kind of Earth where they all stood together. Having been trapped for so long in strife, and having endured its waste and suffering, they could only regret the self-tortured means through which they had at last discovered their strengths.

With the introduction of the moneyless economy a new efficiency emerged. As trade was suspended and incomes were set aside, the millions who had been involved with money transactions became available for useful work. This led to a reallocation of labour resources to immediate priorities. The national effort began with local initiatives and continued without central control or the overbearing dictates of Whitehall.

Production boards in all localities ordered their requirements of materials, equipment and machinery from the centres of distribution, and these were passed on to production plants. In their turn, factories and workshops ordered components from their own suppliers and this practice extended throughout the network of productive links. Without financial constraints, the system operated freely as a sequence of required goods, materials and services throughout production, distribution and energy supply. In this way, each individual with responsibilities at all points in the network was able to respond to the needs of the community without reference to an overall plan. It became an efficient, self-regulating system constrained only by some shortages of materials and work limitations of those involved.

Together with the Departments of the Environment, Industry, Agriculture and Energy, Blake's Department was again expanded with personnel brought in from redundant ministries such as the Treasury. The government's communications headquarters was switched from spying to the work of civil defence. Its powerful computers were adapted to processing the information which flooded into Whitehall from local production boards. Its statistical summaries clarified the required allocations of resources and provided a pool of information which monitored the progress of the work. The Services were integrated with civilian authorities. Television stations joined with radio, keeping up morale and broadcasting news of the progress of the great national project.

Around the world, under pressure from their populations, governments learned quickly from events in Britain. At first, with the work constrained by the limits on finance, the country had stumbled into a voluntary credit scheme, but this had failed. Then, introduced under the threat of civil war, compulsory powers of requisition had brought the nation to the point of bankruptcy. Finally, the cashless economy served as a model for worldwide action. Seeing himself as an international statesman, the Prime Minister addressed the United Nations and was acclaimed as the architect of world survival.

The United Nations organised aid between the most advanced and less developed countries. Anticipating a cometary winter when perhaps no food would be produced, the Food and Agricultural Organisation moved quickly into action, coordinating a rapid increase in world food production.

With equal urgency, cooperation developed swiftly amongst the world's scientific communities. In Britain, Sandra Dale and her colleagues had already worked closely with space agencies in America. With national barriers swept aside, a programme of international space observation was organised.

The Astronomical Laboratory in America became a centre of world information. As data was processed, an accurate profile of the comet's orbit was at last established. The first projections suggested by Sandra Dale and her team were proved correct. The size of the comet's nucleus dwarfed those of all other known comets. Where the nucleus of Halley's Comet was a mere 7.5 miles in diameter, the new comet's nucleus was a massive 50 miles. Its orbit would bring it as close as 3½ million miles to Earth.

Soon, Comet Hurst, could be observed through a small telescope or binoculars. On each successive night, with good visibility in the northern hemisphere, it became more distinct. It first appeared as an elongated dot and then as a sharp streak of light. It seemed innocuous. Its approach was compared with the long record of observed comets. In 467 BC, Greeks had recorded a fall of missiles while a brilliant comet had passed. In the year 66 a long, sword-shaped comet had threatened the people of Jerusalem and in 218, astronomers in China had witnessed the bright rays of Halley's Comet which became ever more fierce, causing panic in the population. The Bayeaux Tapestry depicted the same comet's visit in 1066 with courtiers gazing upwards in awe, while in Baghdad, astronomers described its great beam of light which left people stricken with fear. A comet of 1456 appeared in the form of a scimitar which advanced from the west. Its head was the colour of blood and round, like the eye of an ox, its tail fan-shaped like that of a peacock. It was feared as an agent of the devil and little more than a hundred years later, a comet was seen over Paris which caused such anxiety that some fell sick and died.

On clear nights and away from the glare of city lights, Comet Hurst became visible to the naked eye. On its final approach it was fantastic, terrifying and beautiful. Exposed to the sun, its nucleus rotated and ejected gas which was seen as a series of brilliant circles enveloping the solid core. Symmetrical, fan-shaped rays streamed from its rounded head. From horizon to horizon it lit the sky with a vast, elongated flame. As it came to its closest point to Earth its light became more intense. Its emissions of gas carried away dust particles with increasing velocity, which then trailed into space for hundreds of millions of miles. Its halo expanded, obscuring its nucleus with surrounding fire.

In cosmic terms, the passing of Comet Hurst was a near collision with Earth. Having been steered in a slight curve by Earth's gravitational pull, the comet went on its way round the sun. Solar forces bent its emissions of gas and as the angle of view altered, its tail of following flame changed into a huge bulge of light, even brighter than the sun.

In observing its spectacular passage, people remained calm, reassured by the constant stream of information put out by the Astronomical Laboratory, and broadcast to the world through radio and television. Frightening though it may have seemed, there was at first no threat to populations. The greatest dangers would follow in the wake of its departure. As the comet sped away, then would be the time of missile bombardment and, as Earth entered its cloud of spatial dust, the onset of a possible, cometary winter.

The final fixing of the comet's orbit suggested its periodical return but there was no evidence that it had ever passed so close. Its previous visits could have coincided with a safe position of Earth on the opposite side of the sun. Perhaps the comet was entirely new, making its first voyage to the centre of the solar system. It mattered little. As populations saw it receding, they held themselves in a state of readiness. At the first fall of any missile they would disappear from the surface and take cover underground. Across the planet people listened anxiously to the news. A time of tense waiting had begun.

40

Throughout the country the network of communications was in operation between every control bunker. Though the Command Bunker in Whitehall remained at the centre of the system, the links were adaptable with each part able to contact any other part. In addition, each regional control centre was linked by satellite to a World Information Service. Some technicians and key administrators had already moved underground. Blake continued to work in his office.

Bill Charman arrived and threw a file onto his desk. "That's it, Blake," he said, "the final distribution of Ministers, administrators, police and army commanders to every regional control bunker. You'll be back in the north. You know the area and all the people."

Blake ignored the file. "Have some coffee," he said.

"Coffee? Where did you get that?"

"We look after ourselves in this Department. It's the last you'll be offered, so make the most of it." Blake pushed the file away to the front of his desk. "As for your plans," he said, "I'm not interested. I'm staying in London, with Rachel."

"But she's been allocated a place with you," Bill insisted. "I took care of it personally. You'll both have comfortable accommodation."

Blake smiled at the petty privileges enjoyed by those in control. "That was thoughtful of you," he said. "Thanks, but no thanks."

"You're lucky. I'm stuck in the Command Bunker with the Prime Minister."

Blake was reminded that the Prime Minister's refuge had been excavated deep under the old War Cabinet Rooms and linked with the Command Bunker in Whitehall. "He always said there was nothing to worry about," he said. "Now, he's got his private bolthole."

Bill Charman continued to argue. "This isn't a matter of personal preference, it's about security. Whatever happens, we've got to keep the government intact and we've got to be spread across the country. That means you going north."

"Yes, but Rachel won't leave her hospital. She'll be part of an emergency medical team and I'm joining it. There'll be things I can do. She always said I should get a proper job."

Bill paced the office, trying to find more words of persuasion. "The heroics are admirable," he said, "but we've prepared a top government presence in every area and you're going against our plans. It should be obvious, we might have to use the security forces to control any disorder. I'm the first to admit that morale is high. Throughout the country there's a marvellous spirit, but if things go badly it may not continue. We may need strong government action, so your presence in the north is vital. The Prime Minister insists on it." He pushed the file back towards Blake. "I think you should look at our plans."

At last Blake picked up the file. Every page of its contents was stamped 'Top Secret'. He noted the updated list of ministers, civil servants, army and police personnel allocated to key positions throughout the network of control bunkers. Further pages outlined contingency plans for dealing with any renewed disorder. Reports from Special Branch listed the organisations, together with their main activists that should be treated as subversive. It set out guidelines for their arrest, and the powers of lethal force that could be used in case of resistance.

"I should tell you," Bill Charman continued, "things are not looking good. Some missiles have landed."

Blake was startled. "Where?" he asked.

"Somewhere in Eastern Russia. I'm not sure."

It was immediately clear that the release of information was under close government control. "Why are you keeping it secret?" Blake demanded.

Bill Charman evaded the question. "The point is," he said, "it makes the whole problem of security more urgent. I'm still optimistic that at some time we can get back to normal, but we know from Special Branch that some people have got different plans. They've got ideas about taking advantage and seizing control. Well, we've got to stop them."

"So, you've got new powers for the arrest and elimination of subversives?" Blake closed the file and threw it back on his desk. He remained adamant. "I'm staying in London with Rachel. Anyway, I've lost the stomach for more violence, and it's depressing that you've been planning for it."

"We're not looking for trouble. We're just keeping our options open." Gently, Bill Charman stepped up his pressure. "It's not what I think," he said, "the Prime Minister insists on it, and he's in a very strong position. He may not deserve his popularity, but it's a fact. Anyway, you're the best person to go. Do you want someone else up there?"

Blake thought of the credit the Prime Minister now enjoyed for the completion of the civil defences. It had all been due to the efforts of his colleagues, but that would make little difference if he wished to remove them. Blake also thought of the consequences of deserting the centre stage, and was anxious that no one with extreme views should replace him. He tried to satisfy Bill Charman. "All I'm asking," he said, "is that I'm in London while Rachel is on duty with her medical team. I'll stay in touch with the area. Remember, we've got a good man in the north, Colonel Champney. We can rely on him."

"But he's an army commander," said Bill Charman. "The Prime Minister insists on a senior political presence and he's right. We're not handing over to the Services, no matter how competent they are."

Blake gave more ground. "Alright. I'll maintain political responsibility but I'll do it from London. If there's any problem I'll go up there. With our communications, surely that's good enough?"

Despite coming from different political backgrounds Bill Charman had come to value their partnership and because Blake was determined to stay in London, he wavered. He was also aware that together, they were able to exert strong pressure on the Prime Minister. "I'll put it to him," he said. "Let's hope he accepts it."

The security file would be held in a strong room in the northern control bunker and Bill Charman insisted that sight of it should be restricted to Blake and the army commander. Blake probed him for more information. "I don't understand your fears," he said, "but perhaps you know more than you're telling me. In view of high public morale, you must have good grounds for preparing the extreme measures spelled out in that file?"

"Just precautions," said Bill Charman. "Whatever happens, we've got to keep control." He glanced at his watch. "We've a meeting of the Civil Contingencies Unit in half-an-hour. I'll see you in the Command Bunker."

As Bill Charman left, Janet came into Blake's office. The radio was now conducting a 24-hour news service, and together they listened.

"It has now been confirmed that meteorites have fallen in Scandinavia, Eastern Europe, Russia and North America. So far, falls have taken place in sparsely populated areas, with no reported injuries and no damage to buildings. There are unconfirmed reports of missiles falling into the sea off the south coast. These reports are a signal to all non-essential persons to take their places in shelter accommodation. Instructions for an orderly evacuation are now being given out on local radio. The World Information Service reports that the few recorded missiles have been small and that shelter accommodation will provide safe cover. Comet Hurst is now ten days past its nearest point to Earth. Analysis of data indicates that dust emissions from the comet's nucleus are light. Within four days Earth will enter the comet's tail, and it is now thought that the density of the dust cloud will be thin. Reports from around the world say that populations are calm. Speculation continues as to whether the comet is entirely new or is a return visitor."

Blake noted carefully the tone of the announcements which seemed frank, yet too soothing. It was possible that a policy of selective reporting was being operated. He turned down the volume and looked at Janet. "I want you to get out of here," he said. "I want us to carry on working together, so promise me you'll look after yourself."

She smiled. "I could ask the same of you."

As she left, Jack Brightwell came in. "You've heard the news," Blake said. "I want the building cleared immediately."

"It's already in hand, Minister."

"And what's happening with you?" Blake asked. "No doubt you'll enjoy the comforts of the Command Bunker?"

"Yes, but I'll keep an eye on the Department: our records are vital. I'm not convinced the end of the world has arrived," said Brightwell. "Things will have to carry on. We had the blitz in the war. I don't imagine this will be worse."

Blake could only smile at the calm assurance of his head of Department and his concern for continuity. "Yes, of course," said Blake, "you have it your way. Nothing ever changes but even so, be careful."

As Brightwell left, Blake turned up the volume of his radio.

"The Astronomical Laboratory continues to monitor the world pattern of missile falls, which remain few and show no sign of increase."

The bland voice of the news reader left him with a feeling of unease. He switched the radio off and left the Department. As he walked towards the Command Bunker the glare from the receding comet still lit the sky. Groups of workers were emerging from government buildings to begin their descent underground.

Blake was recognised by the armed troops guarding the Command Bunker. He made his way through its rambling network of lifts, stairways and passages. At the deepest level it was alive with activity. In the conference room, he joined Bill Charman and other members of the Civil Contingencies Unit - Dudney, Brigadier Culverton and Police Commissioner Anderson.

Blake took his seat and turned to Bill. "You've obviously had a hand in broadcasting policy," he said. "It's just too reassuring. Is it the truth?"

This irritated the Home Secretary. "What do you want them to say, that it's the end of the world or there'll only be a five percent survival rate? Alright," he admitted, "it's a bit worse than we're saying but we want an orderly move into the shelters."

John Dudney turned up the volume of his radio.

"... spectacular displays of shooting stars in the southern hemisphere. According to witnesses these showers are comparable with the brightest view of the comet itself."

"They make it sounds like a friendly fireworks show," said Blake.

"You've missed the important item," said Dudney. "The first missile has landed in the Home Counties, in Surrey."

"Isn't that where you live?"

"Yes."

The Prime Minister entered, accompanied by Lindsay. He stared at Dudney's radio, not wanting to hear reports of any missiles. "Shut that thing off," he snapped.

Dudney switched it off. "The news from the Home Counties is very disturbing," he said. "The last reported missile was in Surrey, the closest yet to London."

"Why are you surprised?" asked the Prime Minister. "Did you think Surrey would be immune?"

"No, of course not."

The Prime Minister's popularity had only sharpened his abrasive manner when dealing with his colleagues. He sat down and turned to Bill Charman. "We should begin with a report from the Home Secretary."

Bill Charman set out to be optimistic. "Everything is going according to plan," he said. "Under instructions from local radio, people are moving to their allotted places in the shelters. They are doing it in stages with no sign of any panic. What we're seeing is the success of all our plans."

The Prime Minister stopped him. "Yes, alright Bill, you can spare us the bromides." He hesitated. Unwilling to confront the reality of the missile attack he began to talk of the future. "I do take your point," he said. "We've done everything possible, but now we've got to think ahead. We've got to finalise our plans for getting back to normal. That's why the Chancellor is here, to set out a timetable. I think we should hear him."

Lindsay was embarrassed. The matter was inappropriate but having been instructed to attend, he began to introduce his programme for the unfreezing of cash holdings and the return of all production units to their owners. As he spoke, he was aware that no one but the Prime Minister was interested. Nevertheless, he continued. Beyond the crisis, he anticipated a renewed demand for all kinds of goods denied to people during the emergency. This demand would be the basis on which a reinstated exchange economy would expand. With the resumption of trade, the government would again collect taxes, and every Department would return to its normal work.

The meeting dragged on with other members of the Unit becoming restive. Eventually, Lindsay was interrupted. An official came into the room and spoke quietly to the Prime Minister, who remained impassive. As the official left, he looked around the table. "You may as well all know, there's been a sharp increase in the number of missile falls in the United Kingdom." He turned back to Lindsay. "Carry on, Chancellor."

This news heightened the atmosphere of embarrassment in the conference room and at last Dudney intervened. "In the circumstances, wouldn't it be right to adjourn?" he asked. "There's no great urgency about this matter."

The Prime Minister was unmoved. "There's nothing more urgent than our future plans. Why should we adjourn?"

"We should get to our stations," said Dudney.

"But we're fully prepared," said the Prime Minister. "We've just been told there's no panic in the country so why should we see panic down here?" Again he turned to Lindsay. "You were anticipating a period of reconstruction, Chancellor?"

Blake cut across Lindsay. "Prime Minister, these plans will need a lot more discussion and the issues are not yet clear."

"Why not?"

"This is not the time to go into it."

"You've obviously got a view," the Prime Minister insisted. "What's wrong with what Lindsay has said?"

Blake began to explain. "For example, he says that all production facilities will be returned to their owners, but under the emergency these have been greatly expanded with the use of voluntary, unpaid labour, so it's not clear who they belong to. The TUC will question their ownership, and that's only one point."

The Prime Minister frowned. "Has the TUC mentioned this to you?" he asked.

"No," replied Blake, "but I know how their minds work."

"Well, I just hope you keep this dangerous idea to yourself."
"They don't need any encouragement from me, but I don't want to go into it. I agree with Dudney, we should adjourn."

The Prime Minister raised his voice, became angry and glared at Blake. "We're going to deal with it now," he said. "The emergency measures have made a mockery of government control. I want them ended as soon as possible."

Bill Charman stepped in, trying to rescue the meeting from its absurdity. "Prime Minister, we've gone as far as we can in this matter. I'm sure the Chancellor could do with a little more time before he presents us with anything final. In the meantime, we should assess the damage in the country."

Lindsay picked up the cue. "Yes, I'll consult further with the Treasury. You said it yourself, Prime Minister. We've no means of anticipating the extent of any damage."

Seeing his colleagues ranged against him, the Prime Minister retreated. "All right, if you don't want to face up to it we'll adjourn, but I insist this matter stays at the top of our agenda." He turned back to Blake. "I see you've refused to take up your position in the north. It's caused a weak link in our control. I don't like it."

"I've already explained," said Blake wearily. "I have compelling reasons for staying in London, but I'll keep in close touch with my area and if necessary I'll go up there."

"Why should you pick and choose to the detriment of our plans?" asked the Prime Minister. "If it weren't for the good work you've done up there, we might have to think about your position."

"You won't mind if I take that as a compliment," said Blake.

"I just don't want any political control passing to army commanders." The Prime Minister took out the contingency plans for dealing with any threat to the government and faced Brigadier Culverton.

"Brigadier, I've been informed that various officers have agreed that if there is any danger of an illegal seizure of power, they themselves would take over the government to prevent it happening. What do you know about this?"

Culverton seemed surprised. "I know nothing about it," he said.

"Are you telling me that I know more about what's happening in the army than you? Perhaps you're turning a blind eye to these very unpleasant facts."

"But I'm not aware of any facts, Prime Minister. Such rumours always exist."

"So, what have you done about these rumours?"

"Nothing."

"Why?"

"Because we don't take them seriously," said Culverton.

The Prime Minister pressed him. "Brigadier, I don't like your complacency. The idea of a military takeover is as deeply repugnant to the people of this country as any other illegal seizure of power."

"And the army shares that repugnance." Culverton collected himself. "Prime Minister, let me give you my absolute assurance. If at command level we got wind of any such move, we would bring the matter straight to you."

"Good, now you're speaking a civilised language."

"It's the only language we know."

"Yes, I'm glad to hear it." The Prime Minister stared around the meeting. "As for any other kind of threat, I'm reminded, there's a great advantage in having the population underground. It gives us more control. Any unauthorised person at the surface must be treated as suspect, and dealt with summarily."

As the government Unit sat wasting time indulging the Prime Minister's obsessions, Blake became more desperate to know what was happening in the country.

"Prime Minister, you said I should keep a close check on my area. If you don't mind, I'll do it now."

Without waiting for a reply, he got up and left. He made his way through to the communications centre, where the signals officer put him in touch with Colonel Champney, who assured him that the move into the deep shelters was going smoothly.

"When will we see you?" Champney asked.

"Not immediately."

"You disappoint me, but it's all working well. Pity you're not here to see it. Even Hume has simmered down. Erica Field is leading an emergency rescue team. As you know, she's a pretty good organiser."

"What about missiles?" asked Blake.

"A few, but mainly small. We've just had something bigger at the edge of the City. I'm an army man but I still find them frightening and of course, we get no warning."

Blake recalled the data he had read on meteorites and Sandra Dale's descriptions of the speed of their approach and impact. "Yes, I can imagine," he said. "I'll keep in touch and maybe see you soon."

"We'll look forward to it," said Champney.

Blake put down the receiver, disturbed by Champney's remark that a larger missile had fallen on the outskirts of the City. It reinforced his impression that the missile attack was more severe than was being indicated by the news.

He went through to the equipment store, where he was issued with a personal radio which would connect him through the Command Bunker to all parts of the communications network. He checked his special pass which identified him as one of a select group with powers of absolute authority over any section of the security forces and civil defence volunteers. He was offered a pistol, which he declined.

Satisfied that he was fully prepared, he entered the passage that linked the Command Bunker with the underground station beneath Trafalgar Square. If the surface entrance to the bunker became blocked this outlet would be an escape route into the network of tunnels of the underground railway system. He walked along the well-lit passage and came to a massive sealing door, manned by armed guards. After one more connecting door and a further security check, he emerged onto the platform of the station.

41

People were streaming into the underground station. From the platforms they filed into the tunnels. They had already taken down bedding, together with a few personal items, and were now allowed one suitcase. Uniformed stewards gave directions, answered queries and used mobile carriers to ferry people to their allotted places.

Blake walked along the central gangway, while on each side the thousands who were escaping from the surface were arranging their temporary homes. Every fifty yards, side sections had been opened up to be used as recreation rooms. These would be available for watching films or borrowing books from small libraries. In addition, there were canteens, shower units and toilets. In some areas, carpets had been laid and stark walls had been painted with bright colours.

Having been immersed in the work of the Department, Blake had found few opportunities to see the progress of the civil defences. Now he saw at first hand what had finally been achieved. Against the deadline of danger and despite the chaotic manner in which they had blundered into the full use of resources, it seemed a miracle.

He passed families with youngsters running up and down the gangway, revelling in what to them was a strange adventure. An elderly couple were setting up folding seats beside their bedding. The allocation of spaces had taken no account of differences in social background. It had been decided alphabetically by the first letter of surnames in each area. The result was a mix that strengthened the feeling of solidarity that had been so apparent during the final stages of the work. A common threat had brought people together in a common cause.

Looking over the scene, Blake was reminded of the Prime Minister's mention of the war years when communities had been united in their efforts. Then, as now, the underground system had been used as a shelter against a similar threat from space when explosive rockets had landed without warning. He could only hope that the new bombardment would not be worse. He puzzled over the question of why people found it so easy to unite in time of danger when they seemed to find it difficult in times of peace. Finding no answer he moved on.

With vacant places on each side of the gangway, the move into the shelters was still far from complete. Eventually he arrived at the next station, where more crowds were descending from the surface. As he reached the platform he was approached by a steward who had noticed that Blake was moving against the flow of bodies. She advised him that he was going in the wrong direction and that he was not allowed to return to the surface. He showed her his pass and she apologised. Together they surveyed the crowds filing into the tunnels.

"It seems to be going well," said Blake.

"Not quite," she said. "There's a bottleneck at the entrance. It's causing delays."

"How long do you think they'll cope with being confined underground?" he asked.

"Boredom will be the enemy," she said, "but at the moment everyone is cheerful."

Blake moved on through a further tunnel. Young and old alike were behaving with extraordinary politeness, but how long would it last? The spaces were cramped and if the confinement underground were prolonged, tensions would inevitably appear.

At the next station he again showed his pass which brought immediate compliance. It was clear from the steward's response that all members of the emergency teams were aware of its authority. He made his way up to the surface where for the first time, he noticed some impatience amongst people who were queuing at the entrance to the station.

"What's the hold-up?" he asked a steward.

"There's a rumour that a missile has landed in the area and some people are arriving at the shelter before their time."

"Has this missile been announced over the radio?"

"It's only a rumour, sir, but the crowds are nervous. They believe it. They're not waiting for their turn, so we've got this congestion."

"In that case, stop checking their documents. It'll speed things up."

"Yes, but some of them may have come to the wrong place."

"Never mind. Let them down without any checks. It can all be sorted underground."

The stewards stopped their work, and the flow of people into the shelter increased. Blake looked up. With evening closing in, the light from the comet's tail was more intense. As it sped away, a bright halo still obscured its nucleus. The thought was irresistible: what damage would be left in the wake of this beautiful, but deadly, visitor from space?

He turned away, moved into the road and waved down a police car. Again showing his pass, he climbed into the back seat and spoke to the driver. "This story of a missile in the area. Any truth in it?"

"Yes sir. We've just come from where it landed. It seems to have been a fragment with only slight damage. There's a civil defence team on the spot."

Blake made contact with Bill Charman at the Command Bunker, telling him that with missiles falling people were getting to the shelters ahead of their allotted time. "The entrance checks are slowing things down," he said. "If we don't get rid of them there could be a stampede. I've stopped them here and you should stop them every where else."

Bill Charman agreed. Blake put away his radio and turned back to the driver and his colleague. "What are you two doing?" he asked.

"A routine tour of the area, sir."

"In that case you can take me home." He got into the back of the car. "It's going to be dangerous," he said, "driving around up here."

"These missiles are diabolical," the driver said, "but at least people have got the shelters."

"Is that thanks to the Campaign?" asked Blake.

"I suppose it is."

"No doubt you two were battling with them."

"One night in Westminster was very bad."

"So, what do you think of those battles now?"

"They should never have happened."

The words stuck in Blake's mind. It seemed that the driver had passed judgment on every past conflict. With the streets now cleared of all private cars, the police car drove without hindrance. The few other vehicles were those of the emergency rescue teams moving into position. Outside underground stations the queues of people were moving more quickly into the shelters. Blake was hopeful that within a short time the descent would be complete.

He arrived home having left the two policemen with a useless remark about being careful. As he let himself in, the neighbourhood seemed deathly quiet. He switched on the hall lights and went down to the cellar. To provide space for the storage of valuable items of furniture, he began moving cases of wine into a more orderly stack. He cursed himself for having left the task to such a ridiculously late hour. At the same time, he imagined the comforts being provided for members of the government, senior Services personnel and bureaucrats throughout the network of control bunkers. Having declined these privileges, he and Rachel had been given space at the headquarters of their emergency rescue team.

He brought a radio into the cellar, switched to the local station and listened for any news of the missile mentioned by the two policemen. Last minute instructions for the descent underground were still being issued. He turned to the national news.

"The pattern of missile falls in Europe continues on a much smaller scale than in other parts of the world. There is no indication that the number of missiles is increasing. In the United Kingdom, some minor damage has been caused in sparsely populated areas."

Blake switched off the radio. There was a wide difference between what the radio was saying and his own information. He made contact with the Command Bunker and was routed through to Champney in the north. "Just keeping in touch, Colonel. You mentioned a large missile on the outskirts of the city.   Can you tell me more?"

"Yes, as I said, it was nasty. It left a crater and devastated some houses."

"And you said there were injuries?"

"Yes and some fatalities amongst people who had taken cover in their own shelters. Erica's rescue team has been getting them out."

"Has it been mentioned on the news?"

"No, not yet, but they've had all the information."
"Thanks, Colonel, that's all. I'll stay in touch."

Blake was now convinced that the broadcasts were closely censored. Such a policy had never been discussed by the Civil Contingencies Unit, and he recalled Bill Charman's annoyance when asked if the news was broadcasting the truth. Perhaps it could be justified, but even so it was now clear the news was not to be trusted.

He carried on moving fragile items of furniture into the cellar until he heard the front door open. It was Rachel. She called down to him. He climbed up to the hallway and joined her outside the front door where she was looking up at the receding comet with its brilliant display of shooting stars.

"Awesome, isn't it?" she said.

"Yes," he said, "but if you look long and hard enough, you'll notice that some of those streaks don't fizzle out. Those are landing as missiles."

"So, if I see one coming, I'll shout a warning."

"Very amusing. Let's get inside. You may have a death wish but I haven't."

She followed him down to the cellar, where she saw clocks, china and glass. "According to the news, things are not too bad," she said.

"Forget what they're saying. It's meant to soothe our fears."

"That's not a good idea," she said. "If people can't trust the news, they'll believe every rumour. Without the honest facts there'll be more anxiety. I hope it's not one of your ideas."

"Not at all. I've had to discover it for myself."

They talked for a while about what they would need at their place in the civil defence headquarters. "Just think," said Blake. "You could have been dining with the Prime Minister in his suite."

"Pity you didn't arrange it," she said, "I've got to quite like him."

"You don't even know the man," he said. "What you like is a television image with a good script."

The telephone rang, and Rachel went up to the hall to answer it. Blake strained to hear her brief replies, then she replaced the receiver and called down. "You're right, Blake, things don't look good. A missile has landed near the hospital and I'm on call. We'll be picked up in a few minutes."

Blake put on his coat and checked his personal radio. He joined Rachel on the pavement where they waited under the glare of Comet Hurst and the frenzied streaks of shooting stars.

"I must admit," she said, "for the first time, I feel a little bit scared."

"Yes, well, I'm not the stuff heroes are made of," he said. "I don't even know why we're doing this."

"I think you know perfectly well," she said.

42

An ambulance appeared and stopped. As its rear doors swung open, Blake and Rachel stepped inside to join the medical team. Rachel made some hurried introductions. "Welcome aboard," said one of her colleagues. "I imagined the government holed up in some deep shelter."

"I should have been," said Blake.

The ambulance turned into the narrow street and sped towards the scene of the missile fall. With no traffic lights, it hurtled round a corner and almost collided with a civil defence truck. The truck went ahead with the ambulance close behind and within minutes they arrived. The missile had landed in the middle of a road, leaving a crater. On each side, houses had been obliterated and fires had broken out.

The team piled out of the ambulance. In some confusion, another ambulance and a second fire engine arrived. These were followed by a police car and an army truck with more rescue workers. The civil defence Chief studied a file of papers in the glare of the headlights. It was a list of local people who had taken cover in converted cellars or small backyard shelters.

The area was soon lit by arc-lights and Blake noticed a solitary figure staggering from a half-demolished house. The person stood, silhouetted against the glare of fires, pointing behind him and shouting for help. He turned and stumbled back into the smoking remains of his home. Two firemen in protective suits ran to the spot where he had disappeared and dragged him from the smoke. After passing him to the medical team, they moved into the collapsed masonry to seek out his wife.

The Chief confirmed that three adults had taken cover in the cellar of another house taken out by the blast. Some of the rescue team converged on the gap in the terrace and searched for survivors. Working with their hands, they threw the brick rubble aside, while firemen played their hoses, trying to damp out the smoke.

Blake joined others in searching for two more adults who were listed as having taken refuge in a backyard shelter on the opposite side of the road. Using his map, the Chief pointed out where they should be looking, an area strewn with bricks, slates and timber. Shouts went up for more light and a generator roared into life as a fire engine hoisted a ladder with arc-lights attached. With smoke seeping from the debris, Blake put a mask over his mouth. Across the road, where the man had emerged from the ruins of his home, he saw firemen carrying a woman to safety. Rachel was moving in quickly with members of the medical team, anxious to get the injured woman to an ambulance. The fires were being brought quickly under control.

Blake carried on searching, moving bricks and struggling with a beam of timber. He levered it out, removed more rubble, and heard a distinct sound of knocking. He called for help, renewed his efforts and, with a policeman pointing a torch, he found a step. Debris was passed from hand to hand and working on, he cleared his way down more steps to a door. Suddenly, the door opened inwards and Blake found himself face-to-face with a middle-aged man.

"Are you all right?" Blake asked the face in front of him. "There are two of you, aren't there?"
"Yes."

"You were near to a direct hit. You'd better get out and come with us."

To Blake's surprise the man began to argue. "We may not get another one. We've got everything we need. Thanks for clearing the door. Is it true these missiles never land in the same spot twice?"

The policeman became impatient. "How the bloody hell would we know that?"

"I mean, like lightning," the man persisted. "If it's the same with these missiles, we should be in the clear now."

"Are you coming with us or not?" said the policeman.

"No. Thanks again, but we'll stay." With this, he closed the door.

Blake shrugged at his companion. "Let's get back," he said.

They rejoined the rescue team, where Blake reported the incident to the Chief. The fires were out and the injured were being taken to the medical centre at the area civil defence headquarters. As arclights were being dismantled, Blake looked for Rachel and found her sitting in the back of their ambulance.

"We think there was another missile," she said, "some distance away. Did you see it?"

"No." He sat beside her. "About the wounded? Anything serious?"

"The smoke was the worst thing. They were all badly shocked and that lady has a broken leg. Part of the cellar collapsed."

Without warning, a blinding flash lit the entire district and for a moment, Blake saw Rachel's startled face in its light. The air was rent by a massive explosion, followed by a prolonged roar and a succession of crashes like thunder claps, which tailed off in a high-pitched scream. Flying debris battered the ambulance and the rear door slammed shut. Blake clutched at Rachel as they were both thrown to the floor. For a few shocked moments they lay together in a tangle.

Blake became aware of shouts outside the ambulance and, still holding Rachel, he asked if she was alright.

"I think I'm OK," she said, "apart from my legs. What about you?"

He knelt up and untwisted her legs as she slowly raised herself up and knelt beside him. "Let's get out," he said.

He pushed hard at the door, but it was jammed. A partition prevented their escape through the forward cab. He lay on his back and, as Rachel held down the handle of the rear door, he kicked out until finally it burst open. They emerged into the street, which was strewn with bricks, roof slates, glass and other debris. Blake grabbed a fireman whose face was streaming with blood and steered him back to the ambulance where Rachel was preparing dressings. He then approached the Chief, who was sitting dazed on the front of a truck.

"I've been hit," he was saying.
"We need help ourselves," said Blake.

The Chief shook his head. "No," he said. "Give me a minute. I'm beginning to realise, this is bloody dangerous."

"We need help," Blake repeated.

The Chief pulled a radio from his inside pocket and flicked a switch, but the radio was dead. "See that?" he said. "It took a hit. Probably saved me."

"Lucky, but how do we make contact?"

"The ambulance, trucks and police cars, they've all got radios. I'll soon feel better."

The Chief stood up and walked unsteadily back to the ambulance where injured members of the team were being treated. He spoke to Rachel. "What's the damage, doctor? Can we carry on?"

She glanced at him. "You don't look too good for a start."

"I'm alright. What about the others?"

"A few cuts and bruises." Rachel pointed to a rescue worker lying on a stretcher. "That man is badly injured."

"So, apart from him, you think we can carry on?"

"It's not for me to say, Chief. You'd better ask the team."

The Chief moved amongst the rescue workers, who agreed to carry on, then went to the cab of the ambulance, cleared the broken glass from the driver's seat and climbed inside. The radio had survived the battering and he made contact with headquarters. Using a torch, the Chief studied his map and received instructions on where to go next. He stepped down from the cab.

"There's been a massive fall," he said. He smiled at Blake. "We didn't need to be told that. They can't say about damage. We'll have to find out for ourselves. All I've got is a map reference. Other teams are on their way."

The injured rescue worker was placed in the back of a police car and taken to the medical centre at headquarters. The rest of the team gathered round the Chief. "We're about a mile from the centre of the damage," he said. "We're all a bit shocked, so we'll have hot drinks while we check out the vehicles. Other teams are moving in but no one knows what we'll find. Let's try to be on our way in fifteen minutes."

Rachel was checking medical supplies as Blake approached her. "That last fall could have been near our place," he said.

"Really?" She turned to him and although shaken, she was at last able to smile. "Then it's just as well we weren't at home."

Hot drinks were hurriedly prepared. The remaining glass was broken away from shattered windscreens and the engines of vehicles were started back to life. With equipment packed away, the ambulances, fire engines and trucks began to jolt their way over rubble. The convoy moved forward steadily into more damaged areas, its progress slowed by the build-up of debris littering the streets. It was brought to a halt near its destination, but bulldozers were already at the scene. The work of clearing a path was swift and soon the rescue team was able to move into the centre of the damage.

Other teams had arrived from the opposite direction and were already attacking the fires. Arc-lights had been hoisted to reveal a perfectly formed crater thirty yards across and a few yards deep. Blake looked around. In every direction buildings had been flattened. The entrance to an underground station had been demolished, cutting off access to a deep shelter.

The Chiefs divided the area into sections and allocated the work of rescue to each team. More lights were brought in to reveal a scene of frantic activity as rescuers burrowed into the rubble, searching for survivors. Contact was made with the section of deep shelter beneath the station where shock waves had been felt, but no structural damage was apparent at the lower levels.

Blake met up with the Chief. "Now that we're in the thick of it," he asked, "what do you think?"

"If the fires increase and begin to link up, we'll be in desperate trouble," the Chief replied, "and we're being too diverted by the rescue of people."

"You're saying it was a mistake to allow them to stay in their own shelters?"

"Yes, a big mistake."

Blake agreed. "There is something else," he said. "I hesitate to ask, but our home is nearby. Can I take a look to see if it's still standing?"

"With the pass you're carrying you can do what you like," said the Chief.

"No, Chief. It's for you to say. You're in charge."

"Then no. It's too risky. We've got enough problems without you going missing."

Blake rejoined the work of bringing out casualties from cellars and small shelters to points where they were examined by the medical staff. Some of the shelters had been dug deep to give good cover; others were shallow, leaving their occupants vulnerable. Drifts of dust and smoke were aggravating injuries.

He was signalled on his radio by the Command Bunker. It was Bill Charman. "We need a meeting, urgently," he said. "You'll have to come in. Take a police car."

"I told you, Bill, I'm staying with the rescue team."

"There are plenty of people for that work," Bill insisted. "We don't need heroics, what we need are decisions and with Dudney in the Midlands, we're short-handed. I don't have to tell you, things are getting desperate."

Blake relented. "Alright, I'll come in."

He found Rachel strapping up a young man's broken arm. "I've just heard from Bill Charman," he said. "He wants me in Whitehall."

"Your friend was always a nuisance."

"Yes. I'll tell him. I'll be back as soon as I can."

They embraced. "This turn of duty will end in an hour or so," she said. "I'll return to Headquarters and wait for you."

He concealed his reluctance to leave her. "I'll see you there," he said.

43

Blake commandeered a police car which drove cautiously from the scene. After twisting its way past piles of debris it picked up speed but then was forced to brake where a building had collapsed into the road. The driver reversed, turned and threaded his way through side streets. As the car sped through a further clear area, Blake noticed the distant flash and roar of a missile. As if in a maze, the car made faltering progress. After more obstructions and more filtering through side streets the car eventually found its way to Whitehall.

At the entrance to the Command Bunker, Blake thanked the driver and hurried through security checks. He made his way down to the conference room where he found Anderson and Culverton seated with the Prime Minister, who looked nervous. He welcomed Blake in an unusually friendly manner and noted his dishevelled appearance. "You've obviously been in the thick of it. Let me get you a drink," he said. As if to compensate for his earlier hostile attitude, the Prime Minister poured a drink from a cabinet on one side of the conference room. "We're just waiting for the Home Secretary."

Blake had been given no reason for the meeting, but suddenly realised that he had left his briefcase in the cellar of his house. It contained the highly secret contingency plans for dealing with any civil disorder or political threat. If it fell into the wrong hands, his position would be badly compromised.

Bill Charman arrived and took his seat. "Let's get started," said the Prime Minister. "I know Blake wants to get back to his team." He looked around the table. "No one can accuse this government of not being in the front line." He turned to Bill Charman. "I understand we're getting into some problems, Home Secretary. You'd better put us in the picture."

Bill Charman spoke with weary resignation. "We have to face it, we planned for the worst, but even so the ferocity of the missile attack has taken us by surprise. It began with a suddenness we never expected and it's given us problems we didn't anticipate. In the main we've done well. Most people have got good protection. They've moved into the shelters calmly and quickly but at the same time we've made one enormous mistake. We should never have allowed so many people to remain at the surface in their own cellars and makeshift shelters. The work of fighting fires and keeping a clear passage through the streets is being held up by the rescue of these people. As a result, there is a danger of uncontrolled fires joining up. There's a danger of a firestorm."

"We can't abandon these people," said Blake.

"I didn't suggest it," snapped Bill Charman, who was tired and tense. "I'm simply repeating what has been put to me by the civil defence Chiefs."

"I've seen it for myself," said Blake. "Our rescue teams are taking huge risks. Time is being spent on looking for people who are perfectly safe, whilst others are being injured or even killed. These people are a menace to themselves. They're diverting our resources and exposing our teams to unnecessary dangers. As for streets becoming blocked, I had trouble getting here myself."

"We know the effects of a firestorm," said Culverton. "If the fires link up, the entire city could be incinerated. It could even spread into the underground system and if that happened, no one would survive. Prime Minister, we have no options here. We don't want to abandon anyone but the control of fires must be our absolute priority."

Culverton's remarks sharpened Blake's fears. From the risks being taken by the rescue teams he knew the chances of Rachel's survival were slim. "We've got to get everyone underground," he said. "Tonight, even with the bombardment only just begun, our rescue team came close to being wiped out."

"I don't see any difficulty," said the Prime Minister. "I was chatting with people in the shelter beneath Trafalgar Square and what struck me was the amount of space they enjoyed. It seemed to me that there was room for a lot more. They could almost be doubled up." He turned back to Bill Charman. "Home Secretary, how was the space allocated?"

Bill Charman explained that it was not only a question of space. There was pressure on all facilities, including the supply of food and water. The number of people in each shelter had been decided with everything in balance for a lengthy stay. "If we crowd more in," he said, "the supplies won't last. It's one of the reasons why we allowed some people to stay at the surface."

"Yes, but you've said it yourself," replied the Prime Minister, "that was a mistake. We've had the advice of the civil defence chiefs and we've got to take Culverton's point. We must avoid a firestorm, and that means giving every priority to keeping the streets clear and to fighting fires. Either we get the people still on the surface into the deep shelters or we abandon them. Well, I've no doubt what they would want. They'd prefer the overcrowded conditions. Wouldn't you?"

Bill Charman was compelled to agree. "We'll clear the surface shelters and get everyone underground, but that gives us other problems," he insisted. "With the extra numbers, the deep shelters won't be able to cope with people's needs for very long. If the missile attack continues, conditions will become intolerable, and I'm not sure how we'll control that situation."

"But in any case," the Prime Minister continued, "we've got no control over the people on the surface. They're free to do what they like. What are their motives in wanting to remain at large? Have we checked them out? I don't think so. Were they simply relieving pressure on the deep shelters? I don't see why we should assume that. There could be looting. We're all aware of the political risks. No, we'll have more control if they are all underground."

The Prime Minister had at last revealed his strongest reason for wanting every person to be contained in a deep shelter, but the decision also suited Blake. It would reduce the risks being taken by Rachel and the rescue teams.

"That's settled, then," concluded the Prime Minister, "we'll put out instructions over every radio service. We want all non-essential persons in the deep shelters. Let's get on with it. Inform Dudney in the midlands, and you, Blake, inform your people in the north. We want this carried out immediately."

Coffee was brought into the conference room but Blake was anxious to get back to his team. He swallowed a few hurried mouthfuls and went out to the communications centre where a signals officer put him in touch with Champney. Immediately, he noticed the Colonel's serious tone.

"Things have got very difficult, Minister. There's a lot of damage and many fires. I've ordered everyone on the surface into the deep shelters."

"You're ahead of us, Colonel, I was about to advise that. How are people taking it?"

"Morale is still good. Everything now depends on how long the bombardment lasts. We've had injuries and our first death about an hour ago and more since then. I'm sorry to say that Erica Field has been injured, a crushed pelvis. Naturally, she was in the middle of it, ignoring all the risks, I suppose. You know what she's like."

"That's very bad news."

"It's one reason why I ordered a total evacuation. The danger to our rescue teams was unacceptable."

"I'll leave you to get on, Colonel. If you see Erica, give her my best wishes."

"I'll do that, Minister."

Blake put down the receiver. Any thought of the bitter disputes and past bad feeling between himself and Erica were swept aside by the news that she had been injured. Having done so much to ensure protection for the population, she was now one of the first victims of the missile attack. He was saddened, and felt a fresh anxiety for Rachel.

He needed a police car and looked for Anderson who was still in the conference room. Before he could speak, the Prime Minister turned to him. "Everything satisfactory in the north?" he asked.

"They're ahead of us, Prime Minister. The army commander is already moving everyone underground."

"You mean he acted on his own?"

"Surely it's what we wanted."

"We can't have army commanders acting on their own." A look of alarm spread across the face of the Prime Minister as he looked across to Culverton. "Brigadier, is this man reliable?"

"Champney? Of course. Perhaps a little unorthodox."

"Unorthodox? My reports tell me that he associates freely with leading Campaign activists."

Blake intervened. "Prime Minister, the woman you're talking about has just been injured trying to rescue people."

"That doesn't alter the fact that she's a leading Campaigner. Do you think she's changed?" Again, a deep suspicion overcame the Prime Minister. "These fanatics never change. They may seem quiet at the moment, that's part of their tactics. Do you imagine they're going to broadcast their intentions; going to let you in on their conspiracies? Are you really that naïve?"

"I'm not naïve, Prime Minister. I'm like everyone else, too busy trying to save the country."

"But this is the time of greatest danger, don't you see? We're diverted, we're off guard. This is when they'll seize their opportunity. They're all over the place, disaffected members of the Campaign. They haven't disappeared, and now we've got an army commander acting on his own with one of their activists. Are you telling me you find that reassuring? Have you already forgotten that these people tried to take over the government?"

As the Prime Minister continued to express his fears, both Anderson and Culverton muttered their excuses and left the room. Blake spoke gently, urging the Prime Minister to keep a sense of proportion.

"Get some rest," he said, "I really do have to go."

The Prime Minister remained adamant. "It's vigilance we need, not rest."

Blake left the dejected figure sitting alone in the conference room, found Anderson, and arranged for a police car. He interrupted Bill Charman, who was in contact with Dudney. "You'll have to get a grip on the Prime Minister, Bill, he's lost it. I think he's finally cracking up."

"Really?" said Bill. "I thought he seemed better."

"Well, he isn't, he's worse. And get a grip on Special Branch. God only knows what they've been telling him. I'm leaving."

"Be careful."

Blake hurried up to the surface. The sight of the comet and its surrounding dazzle of shooting stars brought his thoughts back to the dangers. As the police car arrived he greeted the driver and his companion. He looked at his watch. With luck, the rescue team should have returned to civil defence headquarters.

The car drove off but was soon obstructed by a bulldozer which was clearing a path for a fire engine. The car stopped, reversed, turned and began to explore a route through side streets. Again, they were forced to a halt in a blocked road where unattended fires were raging in buildings on each side. The car retreated, turned and again tried to filter through side streets. The driver stayed calm as yet again they were forced to a halt. Blake began to despair of getting through. After retracing some clear ground they tried another route and found themselves near the river, driving east. Behind them, the sudden flash of a missile lit up the car and Blake listened for the roar of its descent. Though miles away, its distinct sequence of thunder-like claps, tailing off into a scream, could be heard.

The outlook across the river gave them a wider view of the horizon and, in the far distance they saw missiles falling at regular intervals. Against the background of violence they turned north past stations where people were again descending underground. Brought to a further stop against the edge of a crater, the police car again turned back and searched for a new way forward. For a short distance they made better progress. With no clear direction and after running blindly into more dead ends, they at last neared their destination. The journey seemed to imitate the tortured route, through trial and error, taken by communities before they had at last arrived at a means of safeguarding their lives.

"The worst should soon be over," said the driver.

"You think so?" replied Blake.

"That's what the news is saying."

"Really?"

The deeper levels of the civil defence headquarters had been extended from the passages and cellars beneath the local Town Hall. The facilities now included a communications and medical centre, with living quarters for the rescue team. The entire unit was linked by tunnel to an underground car park and the wider network of deep shelters.

As the police car drove down to the car park, Blake expected to see the vehicles of the rescue team, but there was no sign of them. He hurried to the communications centre and was told that the team was on its way back but was having difficulty getting through the blocked streets. He could only wait and listen to the national news.

"... a definite pattern of missile falls is now emerging. Intense bombardments in Australia, North Africa and eastern Russia appear to have stabilised. If the same pattern is followed in Europe, it is likely that the United Kingdom is now undergoing its most intense period of missile bombardment. Having reached a peak, it is anticipated that the number of falls will soon begin to reduce. Against the background of this more encouraging news, it has been decided that every non-essential person should take advantage of deep shelter protection. Although this further evacuation will increase pressure on facilities, reports from around the world indicate that this will be necessary for only a short period."

Blake walked away from the announcements. The idea that the missile attack had reached a peak was pure invention. Nor had the news given the true reason for the final descent into the deep shelters: the threat of a firestorm.

He was at last told that the rescue team was about to arrive, and he returned to the car park, where he waited at the entrance. Within minutes, a convoy of vehicles rolled in and as he picked out Rachel's ambulance, he felt a stab of anxiety, wondering if she was safe. The ambulance stopped and he opened the back door to find her chatting with colleagues. Her clothes were in disarray and her hair and face were covered in dust.

"You look terrible," he said, as he helped her out. She smiled as they linked arms and walked with the rest of the team towards the austere comforts of the civil defence headquarters. In the canteen, Blake found the Chief who commented on the removal of all people from the surface. "It's bound to save lives," he said, "and if they stay underground long enough we might breed a new race of troglodytes."

Blake asked about his and Rachel's accommodation. "It's not much," said the Chief, "it's a small room but it's as deep and safe as you'll get."

He led the way down to a storeroom which was about ten feet square. Against its concrete walls, a single electric bulb hung from the ceiling giving a harsh light. The room was piled with boxes containing food supplies and Blake began moving them into the passage. In its bare state the room was grim but at least it was dry, warm, private and well protected.

The Chief returned with helpers, who brought camp beds, bedding and some items of furniture: a small carpet, a cupboard, a table and two chairs. Blake moved them into position, but they did little to relieve the stark atmosphere of the concrete store room.

Having cleaned herself up, Rachel joined him and looked round. "Is this our new home?" she asked.

Blake shrugged. "What did you expect?"

"I didn't expect a prison cell."

"Hopefully, it won't be a long sentence."

44

The ferocity of the bombardment increased. Blake kept in constant touch with Bill Charman at the Command Bunker and with Colonel Champney in the north. Each day there was more damage to buildings, roads, railways and power lines. In one place a reserve of oil was set on fire, in another, a store of food received a direct hit. Somewhere else, a power station was put out of action and an entrance to a deep shelter was blocked.

With the removal of all non-essential persons from the surface, emergency services were able to concentrate on clearing the streets. Day and night, every available bulldozer was at work, with each fresh driver taking over as the previous shift ended. With more freedom to move, the fire services were able to attack the numerous fires which had threatened to link up as one great firestorm. Fractured water mains were repaired and emergency systems which pumped water from rivers were brought into use. Damaged communications were hastily restored. Volunteers risked being killed in the explosions or by the rain of debris swept up in the blasts. Damaged buildings collapsed into the streets and in Blake's area, a team clearing a route through a blocked junction was almost wiped out by a further missile which landed nearby.

The medical rescue teams were at last able to devote themselves entirely to looking after the men and women of the emergency services. Blake always accompanied Rachel's team, which was on call for eight hours every day, but mostly worked for longer. Dreading the return of each tour of duty he carried on with mounting anxiety. Facing dangers, the group was drawn closely together, and with every call they responded quickly, each person fitting in smoothly with the work of the rest of the team.

Casualties were brought back to the medical unit at civil defence headquarters, sometimes an injured fireman, sometimes the driver of a bulldozer, or a member of a repair team. The badly injured were moved on to the hospitals in the deep shelters. Sometimes the team returned with dead bodies and for a time a gloom would settle over the team, but in the fast-moving action of further calls, as more casualties needed rescue, downcast feelings were quickly set aside. Inevitably, there were injuries amongst the team. Some were severe and Blake knew that soon, the luck that he and Rachel had so far enjoyed would run out. Despite the risks, the team carried on with good-humoured determination. The smashed windscreen and battered sides of their ambulance became the proud symbols of their resolve.

Blake was appalled by the mounting destruction. Some areas had become desolate landscapes, a chaos of broken walls and strewn rubble. Unless the bombardment stopped soon there would be no homes left so that even after the missile attack, people would continue to live underground.

Between explosions and the terrifying screams which marked the descent of each missile, the atmosphere was strangely still. With no wind or rain, a pall of dust and smoke hung over towns and cities. Temperatures seemed abnormally low, which appeared to confirm the onset of the cometary winter.

Held deep underground, the great mass of people listened intently to the news, which was a carefully crafted blend of apparent honesty and optimism. Some bad news was released but always accompanied by a greater emphasis on hopeful signs. It was admitted that the bombardment in Europe was intense, but this was balanced with the news that globally, the pattern of falls was reaching a peak. It was predicted that falls in the United Kingdom would soon diminish.

Operating from their own bases, the emergency teams had little direct contact with the people held in the shelters. Nevertheless, reports of devastation and the strange cold atmosphere began to find their way underground. Official assurances that the dust content of the comet's tail was low and would produce no problems were in sharp contrast with the personal accounts of conditions which filtered down from the surface.

Every day, Blake discussed the number of missile falls with Bill Charman, who insisted that a peak would soon be reached. "Don't you see," he argued, "a definite pattern is emerging."

"I'm seeing it from out here. The falls are still increasing."

"Yes, but the rate of increase is slowing down. The upward curve is flattening out."

"You mean the city is being flattened."

"Damn you, Blake, we're trying to work up some better news."

The graph being plotted in the Command Bunker, showing the trend in the pattern of missile falls, was the most accurate source of information but it was kept secret. Blake trusted that Bill Charman was telling him the truth but this did little to relieve his anxieties. The apparent reduction in the rate of increase had to be set against the falls of some massive missiles, one of which took place in the north but was never mentioned on the news. According to Colonel Champney, it had landed in open countryside, leaving a crater over 300 metres across and 20 metres deep. The blast had devastated the surrounding area, almost destroying a nearby village. If it had fallen on a city, this one missile would have killed thousands of people.

As time passed the mood of people crammed into the deep shelters became more and more tense. The final evacuation had disrupted the carefully prepared balance of allotted space, provisions, leisure areas and facilities. Conflicting reports on what was happening at the surface caused distrust and rumour. Artificial light caused the natural sequence of day and night to become blurred. Sleep patterns were disrupted, people became listless and prone to rapid shifts between apathy, anxiety and boredom. With the risks of a firestorm a secret and the true extent of the devastation concealed, the extra people who had been moved into the deep shelters during the first hours of the missile attack were blamed for the crowded conditions. Factions developed, tempers became short and minor disagreements became bitter disputes.

With people's lives suspended in a world of timeless uncertainty, rumour threatened panic and order became fragile. Irrationality took over the minds of some groups, who became convinced there was no reason for their confinement. They demanded to be allowed up to the surface, and as reports of the deteriorating situation were sent to the Command Bunker, Bill Charman and Brigadier Culverton brought forward their plans to keep people contained, using special units of the security forces. Prepared to use the utmost force, squads of armed guards were posted to every section of the deep shelters. Stewards made every effort to improve morale, hoping that good news would soon replace the bland assurances of the government's information.

At last there was some hope. Throughout the control system there was optimism as the rate of increase in the number of missiles continued to slow down. Eventually, the upward curve of the Command Bunker's graph reached a plateau. With the numbers stable for some days, the Astronomical Laboratory confirmed that for the first time since the bombardment began, fewer missiles had been reported by the global monitoring service. It seemed that the tide of the onslaught had turned.

Slowly the pressures on the emergency services relaxed. There was less damage to vital installations. The fleets of bulldozers found it easier to keep the streets clear of rubble. Fire fighters were less stretched and Blake was relieved that there were fewer calls on the medical rescue teams.

With a declining number of missile falls being recorded from hour to hour, projections of when the last missile would survive its deadly passage through Earth's atmosphere were constantly revised. As this information was broadcast, the millions of people crammed into the deep shelters could at last anticipate a time when they could return to the surface.

Throughout the bombardment, there had been no opportunity for Blake or Rachel to check on their home and with fewer missiles falling and more time on his hands, Blake mentioned it to the Chief.

"If you're determined to take a look, I'll come with you," he said. "We'll make it official, a tour of inspection."

They went up to the car park, climbed into a Land Rover and moved off. The Chief looked up at the gloom which hung over the city. "The atmosphere is abnormally calm," he said, "so cold and still."

Blake was exhausted from prolonged anxiety and working long hours with the team. "What's normal?" he asked. "I've forgotten."

"I'm sure it's the beginning of the cometary winter."

"The news says different."

The Chief drove on. "I don't see how they can know that."

"Nor do I."

Blake viewed the smashed landscape and thought forward to the task of reconstruction. In some areas the pattern of streets could hardly be recognised. With a single lane cleared, the Land Rover drove at speed and soon arrived at its destination. There were gaps where some houses had been taken out by blast and some still standing had been gutted by fire. He feared the worst. The Chief checked his map, drove a short further distance and came to a stop. Blake got out and viewed his battered house. A chimney was gone, every window was broken and the roof had been stripped of its slates.

He reached through the broken glass of his front door and released the latch from inside. The hall was piled with fallen plaster which he pushed aside with his foot. He made his way cautiously upstairs. In the bedroom, he looked up at the sky through the collapsed ceiling and open roof. The missing chimney pot had fallen onto their bed. He eased it to the floor and was surprised that the room seemed dry. After collecting clothes for Rachel, he returned downstairs. The lounge was also covered with debris of fallen plaster and broken glass, but looking around, he could see no structural damage. In the cellar, he was relieved to find his briefcase with its top secret documents.

The cases of wine were still intact, and satisfied that he had seen enough, he returned to the Land Rover.

"You've been lucky," said the Chief.
"You call that luck?"

The Chief glanced down the road towards a gap in the terrace where some houses had been blown away. "It could have been worse," he said.

Blake looked again over the battered Georgian house he shared with Rachel. Since being built, it had seen many changes and even survived previous bombings. "Look, Chief," he said, "I don't want any special favours, but if I could get the roof covered it would keep things dry."

The Chief smiled. He admired the way Blake had worked tirelessly with the team after refusing the privileged comforts of a control bunker. His request seemed modest. "We'll find you a tarpaulin," he said, "but don't get too previous, we may not be in the clear."

They considered taking a wider tour, but decided against it. "You've just said it," said Blake. "It could still be dangerous, so let's get back. After all we've come through, it would be stupid to get killed at this stage."

As they drove back to Headquarters, they talked about the priorities of reconstruction. The Chief said he would compile a list of houses that were habitable; this would allow some people back to their homes. Those remaining in the shelters would be able to work by day at the surface. "They'll want to get on with the job," the Chief said, "so we'll need to start planning."

In fact, Blake had already anticipated the work ahead and on arriving back at Headquarters, continued making notes on the further work of the Department during the time of reconstruction. With the government bankrupt and the suspension of normal trade, it was clear that use of voluntary labour was the only way forward.

He was joined by Rachel, who noticed the clothes he had brought back. "So you've been to the house?" she said. "Why didn't you say? I would have come."

"It's still dangerous out there."

"So, what's the damage?"

"Well, if you don't count the windows and the roof, we've still got a home. All the ceilings have collapsed and a chimney crashed onto our bed. The Chief says we've been lucky."

"What about our wine cellar?" she asked. "I imagine you looked there first."

"It's intact."

"You could have brought some back."

"It's a bit early to celebrate."

He looked at her. Throughout the bombardment, her spirits had never faltered. Always of slender build, she was now thin and pale. Her clothes hung on her worn body, and he wondered how much longer she would be able to carry on. The good thing was that their last shift of duty had passed with no call-out. In their cell-like refuge, he sat at the small table and worked on his notes.

She stretched out on a camp bed. "Don't you ever stop?"

"If this is the end," he said, "it's also a new beginning."

She looked across to him. "I'm glad we've been together through it all, that's been the good part."

He smiled as he carried on writing. "I don't remember having a choice."

"There was a choice, you know there was."

45

Unchanged for perhaps billions of years, Comet Hurst sped past the sun to continue its journey into the outer reaches of the solar system. As it faded from view, the fire of its coma diminished and its vapour trail was reduced to a sharp streak of light. With its departure, the number of missiles went into sharp decline. The media gave out the good news: the bombardment would soon be ended. This prediction was calculated from data gathered by the Global Monitoring Service. Though he was still doubtful, Blake had no reason to question the enthusiasm of Bill Charman in their daily contacts. For some days, no missile had landed in the area covered by his rescue team. A new mood of optimism lifted the spirits of the emergency services.

It was further confirmed by the Astronomical Laboratory that the comet's emissions of dust had been light and much less than had been feared. There would be no cometary winter, only the risk of slightly reduced world temperatures. The comet's nucleus was clean: a massive conglomerate of ice and frozen gases carrying solid stony material. The predictions of the scientific community were proved correct. As the comet neared the sun, and as its rotating nucleus was subject to partial melt-down, many thousands of rocks had been released. Under the pressure of erupting gases and freed from their icy prison, these rocks had spun into space to become the main source of the missiles which had bombarded the planet.

Blake was summoned to the Command Bunker for a meeting of the Civil Contingencies Unit, and as he entered the conference room he noticed that Lindsay, the Chancellor, was present. Only the Prime Minister was missing but within a minute he followed Blake into the room. His step was jaunty and he smiled as he placed his papers on the table and sat down.

"No doubt you've all heard," he began, "for over twelve hours no missile has landed in Europe and the United Kingdom has been clear for two days. We won't yet say it in public, but it's likely that the bombardment is over. We can assume it, and we've got to plan for it." The Prime Minister glanced through his reports. "Coming to the bad news, you're also aware of the destruction. Housing, buildings of every kind, roads, railways, bridges, power stations, factories, even Parliament; they've all suffered damage; some of it severe."

"What do we know about injuries and deaths?" asked Dudney.

"We don't have up-to-the-minute figures, but I can tell you one thing. Without the emergency services, the numbers would have been horrendous." He looked towards Blake. "The medical rescue teams have saved thousands of lives and Blake, you stuck with it all the way through. You set a marvellous example. I might even say, inspirational."

Blake distrusted the Prime Minister's show of goodwill. "I did some lifting and carrying, that's all."

"No, you did a lot more. You were part of a government team that showed leadership." The Prime Minister leaned back in his chair and looked around the table. "You know, I make no apology for saying it; we can all take a lot of credit for the way we've handled this crisis. It's been appreciated throughout the country. It's been appreciated throughout the world. Don't forget, we led the way. We didn't just set an example at home, but abroad as well." He paused as he stared again at his reports. "However, we all know that in this life, solving one problem only gives rise to the next. I'm told that conditions in the deep shelters are unbearable. We're being pressed hard for an indication of when people can return to the surface." He turned to Bill Charman. "Home Secretary, you've discussed this with the Civil Defence Chiefs and no doubt you've made plans."

Bill Charman had stayed in close contact with Sandra Dale and the scientific team. He had at last been advised that the continuing danger of stray missiles did not justify holding the population underground. "What I propose is this," he said. "If we stay clear of missiles over the next forty-eight hours, we should begin a phased evacuation from the shelters. First to leave will be people with their homes intact and with them, people with special skills. They may still have to sleep in the shelters but if we remain free of missiles, we could increase their numbers until we've mobilised a work force. The speediest and most efficient way is to leave the organisation to the local authorities. They will know their own problems best, and we can issue guidelines. Blake's Department can coordinate their efforts and indicate where resources are most urgently needed."

"Yes," said the Prime Minister, "the release of a few people will improve morale and encourage everyone. However things are not quite as straightforward as you seem to suggest. I don't want to introduce a sour note. I realise this is a time for celebration, but what about looting, Bill? If we release these people, what's to stop them raiding derelict houses and taking what they want?"

"I don't think we should anticipate looting," Bill replied. "The power of shame is a strong disincentive, and when people cooperated to complete the civil defences we saw that crime almost disappeared."

"I accept that," said the Prime Minister, "but we can't expect it to last. We can't relax on security."

"That presents no problem. The security forces will be the first into position. With the routes clear through every town and city, and with all our communications restored, there'll be no difficulty in keeping control."

"I think we should go further," said the Prime Minister. "We know from the past, from war years, there was a good public spirit, but even then, posters gave warning of the penalties for looting. They said that looters would be shot, and we should do the same."

"Prime Minister, that would be excessive."

"I think you're missing the point, Bill," the Prime Minister insisted. "Such posters would demonstrate the authority of the government. It's not just a matter of looting. We face a testing time in bringing things back to normal. Many people may resent giving back control to the owners of production plants. Others won't want to give up the powers they've enjoyed in their local communities. Inevitably, there'll be a great deal of argument, so I want the security forces to maintain a high profile. I want posters on display where every person will see them. The posters should give a clear warning that looters will be shot, and this will be a forceful reminder to any troublemakers that they won't be tolerated."

As he paused, there was silence around the meeting. By now, all the members of the Civil Contingencies Unit were aware of the Prime Minister's obsessive fears. Whilst he could give the impression of strength, his remarks could also suggest weakness and anxiety. Whatever the case, his insistence on extreme security measures cast an air of gloom over a meeting that should have been a celebration.

The Prime Minister looked down at his notes. "This brings us directly to the main question." He looked at Lindsay. "Chancellor, can you now suggest a date for getting back to our normal economic arrangements?"

Having attended the meeting against his better judgment, Lindsay was still reluctant to reply. "The last time we discussed this matter, we agreed to wait and see the extent of the damage. Prime Minister, you mentioned the massive task of reconstruction. Well, the question still remains, who is going to pay for it? The government hasn't got the money. We could, I suppose, work out the cost of reconstruction at the prices when we suspended incomes and trading, but the amount would be so great that I see no point in trying to calculate it. There's no alternative but to continue the emergency measures. We should carry out the work of reconstruction in the same way that we dealt with civil defence, that is, through voluntary cooperation and a cashless economy."

The Prime Minister frowned. "You haven't answered my question, Chancellor. I'll repeat it. Can you suggest a date for our return to normal?"

"I don't see how I can reply," said Lindsay. "I can only repeat that we should carry out the main work of reconstruction with voluntary labour whilst providing for people's needs as a free public service. Then, we should monitor the progress and fix a date for our return to normal as the work nears completion."

The Prime Minister continued to press him. "So you do have some kind of programme?"

"What I have said is that eventually, there should be no practical difficulty in getting back to normal."

"Well, I don't like it," snapped the Prime Minister. "It's all too vague. In any case, the emergency powers only give us the right of requisition for the work of civil defence. We can't say that the work of reconstruction is civil defence, so what you're proposing, Chancellor, is illegal."

Blake was startled by this last remark. "Prime Minister," he said, "I've seen the damage at first hand. Many thousands are homeless. There's not the slightest doubt that people will want to rebuild their communities using voluntary labour. Lindsay has said that there is no other practical way, and we've no need to worry about legal quibbles. Parliament can make all the necessary adjustments to the emergency powers."

This reminded the Prime Minister of Blake's previous influence in the House through the All Party Group, and his attitude changed abruptly. "You've built up a handy little power base, haven't you, Blake?"

"I'm not interested in power. I want the work to go ahead as smoothly as possible."

"I haven't forgotten your disloyalty in appealing to the House over my head. Don't worry, I know exactly how you planned it."

"I'm not worried, Prime Minister. You can think what you like, and no doubt you will, but don't become a victim of your imagination."

As the Prime Minister began to tremble with anger, Bill Charman stepped in. Like Blake, he was bored with the Prime Minister's obsessions and rapid changes of mood, but he also wanted unity. "Prime Minister, if what Lindsay says is true, that there's no hope of financing the work of rebuilding, any premature return to our normal arrangements would only cause frustration. Fresh conflicts could arise and that could be a threat to security. On the other hand, if we carry on with voluntary labour, we'll get efficiency, high morale and we'll make rapid progress with the work. We'll be a popular government, and that will give us a stronger base from which we'll be able to deal with any hostile elements."

"As I understand it," said Dudney, "we begin with some advantages. Using voluntary labour, we've got an efficient way of producing building materials and we can apply this to anything else we need. We've got reserves of basic foods and for future supplies we're told that farming won't be disrupted by severe cold. So, with these advantages and by continuing the cashless economy, we'll complete the reconstruction much sooner. That will mean an earlier return to normal. Prime Minister, I agree with the others, there's no point in trying to set a date now."

Whereas Dudney, Bill Charman and Blake were arguing from necessity and practicality, the Prime Minister was driven by his fears. At the same time, his instinct for survival made him aware of his isolation and, as he had done in the past, he soon backed down. "Alright then," he said, "we'll continue the emergency measures. Once we're definitely clear of missiles, I'll announce the decision in a broadcast. We'll monitor the progress of the work and prepare a programme for getting back to our normal way of life." He looked again round the meeting. "That is what we all want, isn't it?"

"Of course," Bill Charman assured him.

"Good, so where's the argument? There isn't one." The Prime Minister paused as if to reflect on events. "What we should realise," he said, "is that people gave up their incomes and worked voluntarily because of the threat to their lives. It was a matter of survival. Their cooperation was prompted by pure self-interest. But now, with the threat gone, you'll find that attitudes will change. You won't see the same cooperation. You'll find that people will want a return to ways that express their normal self-interested outlook."

As the Prime Minister continued, the purpose of his remarks became clear. "These may not be pleasant facts," he said, "but then we're not here to flatter human nature, we're here to be realistic. I'm not saying that natural self-interest is a bad thing. In fact, it's been a driving force, bringing benefits for all, but it can be misdirected. It must sometimes be restrained. For this reason, in the time ahead, I want the security forces to maintain a high public profile. This will assert the government's continuing authority and instill a required sense of order and discipline in the minds of the public. Is there anything else?"

Having seen the dedication and self-sacrifice of the emergency teams, Blake felt there was a great deal he could say in denying the Prime Minister's cynical view of the public, but there was no point. Having learned to take events one stage at a time and to avoid, if possible, confrontations with the Prime Minister, he was happy that the work of reconstruction would be commenced under the cashless economy.

"If we're getting back to normal," said Dudney, "shouldn't we get back to regular Cabinet meetings? And we should also think about a general election."

"All in good time, John," said the Prime Minister as he swept up his papers and brought the meeting to a close.

Blake went out to the communications centre, where he made contact with Colonel Champney and briefed him on the decision to evacuate the deep shelters in stages.

"When are we going to see you?" asked Champney. "Sooner rather than later, I hope."

"Yes. What about Erica?"

"She's recovering fine. She'll soon be up and about, tormenting our lives, no doubt."

"Then we really are getting back to normal?"

"I'm afraid so."

Blake returned to the civil defence headquarters, where he found Rachel. With much less to do, she suggested a visit to their battered home. They approached the Chief. "You promised me something to cover my roof," said Blake.

"Leave it with me," said the Chief. "I'll see it gets done."

"No," Blake insisted, "I said, no special favours. I'll do it myself."

From the stores they took two large squares of tarpaulin, carried them to the car park and loaded them onto a truck. After finding a ladder, the Chief tied it on. "I'm not sure you should be doing this on your own," he said, "I really don't think this is a good idea."

Rachel smiled. "But the Minister is versatile," she said.

"Yes, I noticed," said the Chief. "I'll be touring the area. I'll look in on you."

They got into the cab of the truck and their arrival at their house was the first time that Rachel had seen it since the onset of the bombardment. From the street, she stared at the stripped roof and broken windows. Throughout the ordeal her spirits had never sagged, but now, on seeing their shell of a home, she gave way to a look of despair. "How can we move back into this?" she asked.

Blake tried to cheer her up. "Don't worry, it's basically sound. Just like the government."

"I don't find that a bit reassuring," she said. "We should take advantage of your privileged pass and move into something luxurious. I'm sick of all this equality. You democrats always come off second best."

He ignored her, placed the ladder against the house and after collecting tools from the cellar, carried a tarpaulin up to the roof. Scrambling over the rafters, he spread it out and nailed it into position. From the pavement Rachel observed his efforts. "Normally you could pay someone to do it," she shouted. "See what you've done with your cashless economy? You've lost your power over people to get things done and given yourself a lot of problems. You didn't think of that, did you?"

He yelled back. "Find some more nails."

He fixed the tarpaulin and came down from the roof to join Rachel in clearing glass and fallen plaster from the house. Gripping the chimney pot which had crashed through the roof onto their bed, he eased it downstairs. Anticipating the time when it would be replaced, he stood it outside. They removed dust from books which had been strewn over the lounge floor and checked the clocks and porcelain which had been stored in the cellar. They were undamaged. As they made steady progress, clearing the passage and downstairs rooms and dumping bucketfuls of debris into the back garden, Rachel's spirits began to revive. She could at last glimpse the prospect of returning home.

The district was deserted and they worked alone in an atmosphere that was silent, still and cold. Hazy light gave an impression of the sun trying to break through. Standing in the street, Blake surveyed the surrounding damage and tried to picture the return of the population to the ruins of the city. The bombardment had been unsparing and in its aftermath cellars and derelict buildings would provide only crude shelter. Until the reconstruction was well under way, life would be mere survival, providing for little more than basic needs.

The outlook seemed bleak but as he stared at the desolate scene, he was also aware of the many ways in which the population had changed. Mindful of this, he began to see the destruction in a more hopeful light. Throughout the ages, cities had been reduced by fire and bombardment, but survivors had always returned to confront disaster with fresh hope. Perhaps this time a different people would emerge from a subterranean existence. This time, perhaps, people would rebuild their communities using their new powers of unity and cooperation to bring about a final end to conflict. Surely this was possible?

He returned to the back garden, where he rescued timber from the smashed fences. After using it to board up broken windows, he found Rachel struggling to bring up a case of wine from the cellar.

"We'll take it back to Headquarters," she said.

He frowned in disapproval. "I don't think that's fair," he said. "We shouldn't flaunt it."

"We won't flaunt it, we'll share it."

A look of pain spread across his face. "A whole case?"

"You've got loads of the stuff."

"But it's like gold dust and with a colder climate there won't be any more."

"The government says it's not going to freeze."

"I am the bloody government," he said, "and we don't believe our own propaganda!"

"Well, I don't care."

Seeing that she had made up her mind, he gave in. "Alright, stop struggling."

He took the case of wine, carried it out to the truck and satisfied that the house was now sealed, packed away tools and loaded the ladder. As he drove back to Headquarters, past heaps of rubble and the shells of burnt out buildings, through streets and squares he could barely recognise, he looked across to Rachel. "These days you're always covered in dust," he said, "but you seem to be feeling better. Any particular reason?"

She laughed as she brushed herself down. She moved close to him, took his arm and smiled. "Maybe I am. Who's asking?"

On their return they found the Chief working on plans for the phased evacuation from the shelters. He apologised for not looking in on their work. "You managed?" he asked.

"Of course," replied Rachel, "I told you, the Minister is versatile."

"I suppose that's how we all survive," said the Chief.

"Yes, and he's one of the great survivors."

After cleaning up, they joined the rest of the Medical Rescue Team in the canteen. Rachel produced the case of wine and the meal became a celebration. They were joined by other members of the emergency services, more bottles appeared and, with Rachel moving amongst the tables filling up glasses, every remaining tension disappeared. In this unlikely underground setting, the party carried on into the night.

46

As the country waited, Blake continued to plan the future work of the Department. After two further days, he woke early and tuned in to the national news. No more missiles had fallen. Not only the United Kingdom but the entire area of Europe had been clear for over three days. He got up, collected hot drinks from the canteen and returned to the small room where Rachel lay in bed. He placed a gentle hand on her shoulder.

Bleary-eyed she raised her head. "What is it?" she asked.

"Overnight there were no more missiles."

She sipped her drink. "This so-called coffee is disgusting. What's it made from?"

He thought for a moment. "I've no idea. Look, this is what we've been waiting for. The bombardment has ended."

"That's why I'm sleeping," she said as she pulled the blankets over her head.

Blake gathered up his notes, packed them into his briefcase and found the Chief, who was already at work in his office. "This is it," he said. "I need to get to Whitehall. I want a vehicle."

The Chief advised him that with tighter security he had been allocated an official car with bodyguards.

"I don't need them," said Blake. "Give me a Land Rover. I'll drive it myself."

The Chief shrugged. "You're the Minister. What do I tell your driver?"

"Tell him to take a month off."

Blake took the keys to a Land Rover, went to the car park and drove to Whitehall, where he was surprised to find Jack Brightwell moving through the Department, checking for damage. Blake greeted him. "Don't tell me you've stayed here throughout the missile attack?" he said.

"Not exactly," said Brightwell, "but I have kept my eye on things. We've come through very well but then of course the building has a history of being bombed so I'm not surprised. The windows have gone and there are minor problems on the roof, but there's no reason why we can't begin work."

"In this cold?"

They went through to Blake's office. The floor was littered with broken glass, documents and scattered correspondence. "The remains of your interrupted work," said Brightwell.

Blake gathered up the papers, placed them in a bin and dumped it outside his door. "This might hurt you, Jack, but I don't want to see that lot again. Create a permanent pending file and store it in the basement. We've now got other priorities."
Brightwell frowned. "There must be continuity," he said.

"Then again," replied Blake, "perhaps not."

They moved into Janet's office. "I've checked on the staff," said Brightwell, "we've had some casualties but your assistant is well. She'll be back as soon as she can get here."

"That is good news," said Blake, "but she can't work in these conditions. Surely you agree, Jack, the temperature is unusually low?"

"I don't think so. Not for the time of year."

After selecting a small office, they found some plastic sheeting and fixed it over the broken windows. Blake brought in a gas burner and fresh water from the Land Rover and as he made hot drinks, the heat from the burner began to warm the room. Brightwell produced a radio, arranged seats around a table and in this makeshift setting they began the work of bringing the Department back to life. From his notes, Blake suggested the priorities of action. The most urgent need was the restoration of telephone links. With all communications restored, the reconstruction would begin and streams of information would again flood into Whitehall from the local production boards.

"In the past," said Brightwell, "the damage was not so bad, but we can still learn a lot from those years."

This was a reminder to Blake of the ravages of World War II. "When that war ended," he said, "I believe it was a time of great optimism. What happened to all those great hopes?"

"Yes, it's true, said Brightwell. "Expectations were high, but these events come and go and nothing really changes."

"Is that all we learned?" Blake asked.

"Naturally, Minister, after great traumas, people expect things to be different, but the main features of our lives are constant. I often think we'd be happier if we accepted that."

Blake could only smile at Brightwell's view of an unchanging world that underpinned his bureaucratic complacency. "No, Jack," he said, "it's change that's constant. The trick is to change things for the better."

He was signalled by the Command Bunker. It was Bill Charman, who was indignant that Blake had dismissed his bodyguards and commandeered a Land Rover. "Once again, you're compromising our security arrangements," he said.

"You're only speaking for the Prime Minister, Bill. If I'm in an official car, he knows exactly where I am. Do try to resist his paranoia."

"It's you who's paranoid. We're concerned for your safety."

"That's rubbish, and you know it."

"Alright, there's something else. The Prime Minister is just beginning a broadcast. Listen in and let me know what you think."
"What about the Land Rover?"

"Forget it."

Blake smiled, tuned into the broadcast and invited Brightwell to join him in listening to the reassuring tones of the Prime Minister.

"... I want to congratulate the whole country. The spirit in which we've endured the ordeal has been magnificent. I'm sure that none of you will object if I single out those who have carried out the work of the emergency services. In due time the record will be known. It will speak of individual acts of bravery and heroism. It will be a record of courage equal to anything in our country's past. These are men and women who risked everything to save others. They had only one thought and one concern, to save their families, their neighbours and their communities. We will remember their example and we shall mourn the loss of those who died. Their actions bear witness to the finest qualities of humanity and they will never be forgotten.

But I have to tell you that we have lost a great deal. We face a massive task of reconstruction. I have been advised that the work of rebuilding will be no less than was the work of civil defence. I'm told it could be a bigger job. Therefore, it must be clear to all of us that we cannot attempt a premature return to our normal way of life. There is no possible means of financing this great task. Therefore we shall continue to work under the same emergency measures that have already been so successful. I know that all of you will carry on in the same spirit of cooperation.

Praying that the last deadly missile has fallen on our islands, we shall now begin the work of recovery. We will rebuild our means of life, our factories, industrial plants, our vital communications. We will restore the fabric of our communities, our homes, our schools, our hospitals. Nothing will stand in our way..."

Blake switched off the broadcast. "You don't mind, do you Jack? You've got the message."

"He speaks well, Minister."

"Then you approve of him?"

Brightwell was noncommittal. "I'm sure most people would say he's a good leader."

"Yes, so I gather."

The Prime Minister's remarks were in contrast with the cynical view of human nature he had expressed earlier in the privacy of the Civil Contingencies Unit. Blake thought yet again about the strange duality which divided the Prime Minister between his public persona and his private behaviour. Like a political chameleon, his personality could adapt rapidly to any changed condition.

As the days passed without missiles, it was accepted that the bombardment had finally ended. Local production boards sprang back to life and worked with civil defence teams, which began a nationwide assessment of the damage. Skilled people were the first to emerge from the shelters to add their numbers to the emergency repair teams. Others with their homes intact were able to return to life on the surface. Having been confined underground in their cramped spaces, they were relieved to be involved with the work of reconstruction. Neighbourhood groups were formed for the task of salvaging bricks, timber and other materials. Field canteens were soon distributing food in every town and city, whilst fractured water mains were repaired and standpipes were set up in every street.

The staff returned to the Department and as Janet arrived, Blake embraced her. She was well and delighted to be back. Within minutes her cheerful presence was relieving the chill atmosphere of the office. Communications with local production boards were given priority and soon, as information on local needs began to flow into the Department, Blake and his colleagues were able to say which facilities should first be restored.

With reserves of coal stocks and basic foods in place, the greatest demand was again for building materials. Energy came back on stream through an improvised grid, production boards gave priority to the supply of sand, cement, building blocks, bricks, tiles and glass. As the materials became available they were distributed throughout every region. With a shortage of skills, trained workers took charge of volunteers, who learned quickly, and whose enthusiasm made up for their lack of experience.

Although born of necessity, the cashless economy was now accepted on its own merits as an efficient way of getting things done. It had released the powers of the community and in doing so, it had fired the actions of every individual with a common purpose. Conflict had been replaced by a cooperation which enabled problems to be solved without disruption. Cooperation seemed to come naturally and with every person taking on real powers of responsibility, decision-making and action, the work of reconstruction quickly gained momentum.

At last there was an explanation for the low temperatures. During the bombardment, fires had raged in temperate and tropical regions, spreading across prairies, forests and open heaths. Fires had been started in buildings, industrial plants, fuel depots and other places where combustible materials had been stored. The news that the light dust content of the comet's tail would give no problems was true but no one had anticipated the vast smoke cloud which had been carried up to high altitudes and which was now circling the planet. Filtering through the barrier, sunlight had been reduced. Despite assurances that the smoke would soon disperse, the effects on world agriculture were yet to be seen. For a time, reduced temperatures would limit farming in some areas, and this cast doubt on the assumed abundance of food stocks. Once again, food production became a priority.

Blake and Rachel continued to stay in their tiny room at their civil defence headquarters. By day Rachel returned to her duties at the hospital. Each morning, Blake took her there in the Land Rover he had commandeered. He then drove on to his Department to work long hours processing the flood of statistics which monitored the progress of the nationwide task. Throughout the return journey he was also able to observe at first hand the work of reconstruction which began every day at first light.

To justify the presence of armed police and troops, and under instructions from the Prime Minister's office, a campaign was begun against looting. Posters warned that looters would be shot, but these were resented as an affront to the spirit in which people were again cooperating. Many were torn down as soon as they were put up.

Seeing the speed of the repairs to Rachel's hospital, Blake sometimes thought back to the strike of the maintenance workers and the violent confrontations between pickets and police. There was no sign of that conflict now. Keen to visit his constituency, he eventually found the time to fly north. His past visits had been mostly in response to crises, and included his desperate attempts to save his position in his local party. Recalling the time when his journey had been diverted to the plant where campaigners had gathered to seize building materials, he asked the pilot to fly over it. The helicopter passed over the roof of the office block where, during the night of siege, he and Colonel Champney had stood in the rain overlooking the crowds. He could almost feel the presence of Police Commissioner Hume urging that canisters of CS gas be fired into the crowd. The perimeter fence was still lying stretched across the common where it had been dragged by the campaigners before they overran the plant. Open on every side, the plant was now in full production and, as he saw materials being taken to the City, the past confrontation seemed absurd.

The helicopter flew on towards the City centre, soon touching down in the compound of the control bunker. Champney was waiting and as he stepped down, Blake greeted him. "I see you're still in the bunker, Colonel."

"I'm trying to get out of it. It's the government that's still in the bunker. Why are you so worried about security?"

Unwilling, or possibly unable, to explain the Prime Minister's fears, Blake parried the question. "Habit, I suppose. You've got no problems?"

"No, but I've got men tied down when they could be doing better things."

Champney had arranged for Blake to visit Erica Field, who was still recovering in the medical unit of the shelter which had been excavated near the Town Hall. They decided to walk and passed through the gates of the compound, which were still guarded by armed troops. Again, Blake was reminded of the night of violence, when the occupation of the car park site had been so savagely contested. On reaching the shelter, a lift took them down to one of the lowest of its many tiers. In the bright light of the medical unit, its concrete walls seemed brutally harsh. Erica smiled as they approached her bed and Champney passed her some books.

The unlikely friendship between the army commander and the campaign activist was again apparent as Champney spoke warmly. "I've brought you some good news, Erica. There's a hospital ready at last. We can move you out of here."

"I'll be glad to see some daylight," she said. She looked towards Blake. "The Colonel told me about your work with the medical rescue team. I'm glad you came through all right. As you can see, I wasn't so lucky."

Blake thought back to their bitter arguments, but also to the success of the civil defences and the work of reconstruction. These were happy sequels to the night when he last faced her in open conflict. "Chris Lawson tells me you're badly missed," he said.

This was a reminder of her absence from the local production board. "He comes to see me," she said. "He and the Colonel keep cluttering the place with bits of greenery."

Blake looked at the arrangement of leaves and the few flowers that did little to relieve the concrete surrounds of the ward. "We're all looking forward to seeing you back in circulation," he said.

She smiled at his embarrassment. "You always were a rotten liar, Blake Evans. You know very well it's the last thing you want. I'm a bloody nuisance."

He shuffled awkwardly on his feet. "Yes, well," he said, "we'd never make progress without the odd nuisance. There's still a lot to do."

"Really?" she said, "for people like us? I don't think so. I'm told that all the arguments have gone and if it's true, there's no place for you, me or the Colonel. When the drama ends, the players lose their parts. We should accept that and retire."

"I like the sound of that," he said.

Despite her comments, Erica showed a keen interest in everything that was happening. They chatted on until it was time for Blake and Champney to attend the local production board. They left the deep shelter and walked to the Town Hall, which was still only partially usable. After joining Clive Poole and Chris Lawson, Blake sat in on the meeting of the board, which began with a long and tedious discussion on the problem of glass supplies. The increased production to meet the City's needs was taking time. From the information which had come to the Department, Blake was aware of the difficulties, but with more than enough to do at his own end, he was unwilling to be involved in the details of the local work. He observed the friendly and efficient working of the board and after a time, he left.

Flying back to London, he thought about Erica's apparent wish to fade from the scene. Perhaps she was right to say that the personalities who had been in the forefront of confrontation no longer had a role. With the power struggles ended and the arguments and deep divisions gone, the protagonists could disappear into anonymity. Erica's own base, the Campaign, had melted away. The name of Hurst was being forgotten as quickly as it had first come to dominate the news. The role of government had diminished. Although the Prime Minister still presided over meetings of the National Consultative Council, it was little more than a showpiece, giving him a public presence. Frank Bell stayed with the Council for the same reason. The work of the TUC in defending the interests of trade unionists against employers was suspended.

The initiatives in the work of reconstruction had passed to local production boards, with useful government Departments acting in support. Without central control, the work depended on a combination of millions of decisions and actions being taken every day by people at work.

Nevertheless, at the same time, the Prime Minister, Lindsay and the Treasury were carefully monitoring the progress of the work and preparing the way for an early end to the cashless economy. Discreetly, the Confederation of Industries was looking towards the return of all production units to their owners. With many new facilities having been brought into production by voluntary labour, the TUC and others were preparing their arguments about who exactly owned them. These background moves carried the prospect of a renewed clash of interests and a return to conflict.

Blake shut them from his mind and carried on the work of the Department, which soon settled into a routine. His personal concern was to see his and Rachel's home repaired, but anxious not to assert any pressure from his position of influence, he waited patiently. At last, a team of builders moved into the street where their house had stood derelict. With the help of local residents, bricklayers, carpenters, roofers and electricians worked their way through the buildings, completing the basic repairs and replacing houses that had been blasted away. With electricity and water reconnected, and with the roof, windows and ceilings restored, they at last returned to their home. In time, they would put their own finish to the basic repairs.

Despite the long hours that Blake and Rachel spent at their places of work, they also got to know all their neighbours. Each evening, Blake walked along the street, seeing the progress of the work and chatting with residents, who talked about their experiences during the missile attack. The long ordeal of waiting in the cramped shelters could at last be recalled with humour.

No trace of Comet Hurst could now be seen. Out of sight, it sped on its way. The continuing streaks of shooting stars were mere reminders of the dazzling displays which had lit the sky during the bombardment.

The dismantling of the metal sections which had covered the tracks in the underground railway system, marked its end as a network of shelters. It also signalled a final end to the crisis. Rachel invited neighbours for a celebratory drink, which became a party as more people from the street joined in. Blake added a case of wine and dishes were contrived from the plain, rationed food.

Over the din of music and loud conversation, Blake thought he heard the telephone. From the crowded lounge, he struggled out to the hall and answered it. On the line was Bill Charman.

"You'll have to speak up," Blake shouted. "There's a party going on."

"Yes, I can hear it."

"It's a pity you're not with us."

"Listen, Blake. There's a full Cabinet meeting tomorrow. The Prime Minister and Lindsay are setting a date for our return to normal."

Blake had been expecting it. "What sort of date?"

"They're saying nothing 'till tomorrow."

"Bill, that's not good news in the middle of this party."

"I'm sorry. I didn't mean to spoil it."

"No, of course you didn't." Blake made a sudden decision. "Look Bill, I won't go along with it. What you call a return to normal, I can't see any reason for it."

Bill Charman was surprised. "Oh. I see."

"But I can see a lot of reasons against it."

There was a long pause. "Well, why not come in early," Bill said. "We'll talk it over. Who knows, I may even agree."

"I'll see you in the morning." Blake put down the phone. Looking for his drink he pushed his way back into the lounge where he bumped into Rachel.

"Cheer up," she said, "this is a celebration. Why the serious face?"

"I've just had a call from Bill Charman. There's a Cabinet meeting tomorrow. They're setting a date for returning to normal."

"I don't know what you mean."

"You know what I mean by normal?"

"No, I don't. I prefer what we've got now. We have returned to normal."

493416

Made in the USA